The Fortunes of Casanova
and Other Stories

The Fortunes of Casanova

and Other Stories

RAFAEL SABATINI

Selected and Introduced by
JACK ADRIAN
Foreword by
GEORGE MACDONALD FRASER

Oxford   New York
OXFORD UNIVERSITY PRESS
1994

Oxford University Press, Walton Street, Oxford OX2 6DP
Oxford New York Toronto
Delhi Bombay Calcutta Madras Karachi
Kuala Lumpur Singapore Hong Kong Tokyo
Nairobi Dar es Salaam Cape Town
Melbourne Auckland Madrid
and associated companies in
Berlin Ibadan

Oxford is a trade mark of Oxford University Press

First published 1994

British Library Cataloguing in Publication Data
Data available

Library of Congress Cataloging in Publication Data
Sabatini, Rafael, 1875–1950.
The fortunes of Casanova, and other stories / Rafael Sabatini ;
selected and introduced by Jack Adrian ; foreword by George
MacDonald Fraser.
p. cm.
Includes bibliographical references
1. Casanova, Giacomo, 1725–1798—Fiction. 2. Europe—
History—18th century—Fiction.
3. Historical fiction, English.
I. Adrian, Jack. II. Title.
PR6037.A2F67 1994
823'.912—dc20 92–44506
ISBN 0–19–212319–X

1 3 5 7 9 10 8 6 4 2

Typeset by Best-set Typesetter Ltd., Hong Kong
Printed in Great Britain
on acid-free paper by
Bookcraft (Bath) Ltd.
Midsomer Norton, Avon

Foreword

George MacDonald Fraser

He was born with a gift of language, and a sense that history was alive. Thus, adapting his own description of Scaramouche, one may fairly describe Rafael Sabatini himself, with one qualification, that while Scaramouche had no patrimony but laughter and scepticism, his creator had a wealth of literary talents besides: an elegant style which, if elaborate, was a model of clarity, scholarship without ostentation, strong narrative force, a gently caustic humour, and, above all, a mastery of plot which gave his work the precision of a well-balanced watch.

You have the measure of the man in a random choice of those meticulous opening sentences which grace his novels:

'King James, fully recovered from the terrible fright occasioned him by the Gunpowder Plot, had returned to his norm of pusillanimity.'

'Charles Stuart-Dene, Marquess of Alverley, looked at humanity, and wondered why it was.'

'"Speak of the devil," whispered La Fosse in my ear.'

I defy anyone not to want to read on. It is like being addressed by an urbane, erudite uncle who, we quickly discover, is at heart a buccaneer, for Sabatini's stories abound with drama and melodrama, action and excitement and brilliant colour, as well as minute period detail. No writer, not Scott nor Dumas nor Stevenson, has brought the past to life more vividly or accurately, or persuaded more millions that history, far from being dry, is one great true adventure story. If he was a romantic, he was also a realist: his scholarship, aided by his fluency in several languages, was deep, and his portraits, factual and fictional, of the Borgias, James I, Frederick the Great, Fouché, Wellington, Casanova, Elizabeth, Torquemada, and a great gallery of others, are almost without exception fair and faithful miniatures in print.

History-telling was his gift, in an assured worldly manner which invited the reader into intellectual fellowship: he assumes we have read Saint-Simon and Petrarch, Horace and Esquemelin, Burck-hardt and Dante, and of course we are familiar with Anne of Cleves' portrait (no mere picture to Sabatini, but 'the document from the brush of Holbein'). And if we are not, then, to paraphrase Captain Blood, it's the fine scholars we'll be by the time he's done with us.

He was, alas for his literary reputation, a prodigious best-seller guilty of the cardinal sin of entertaining the masses in films as well as in books. But if Sabatini is not 'taught', thank heaven, he is to be learned from by any who seek instruction in the craft of writing or the matter of history. This century has seen no greater expert in the two combined.

The stories collected here are from his early days (what he called his nonage), and in them are the germs at least of that skill which was to invest his novels. To those who know him, they will be of much interest; to others, they may serve as an introduction to that historical world which he so splendidly illuminated.

Acknowledgements

I should like to express my gratitude, as always, to the staff of the Bodleian Library, Oxford—those in the Old Library Reading Rooms, the Copying Department, the Stack, the out-station at Nuneham Courtney, and in particular to Richard Bell, Head of Reader Services—for all their varied and indispensable assistance in the preparation of this volume. I should also like to acknowledge the help and advice given to me at one time or another by Bob Adey, Mike Ashley, Peter Berresford Ellis, Professor Douglas Greene, Bill Lofts, David Rowlands, and Robert Sampson; Janice Healey, of the British Film Institute; Philip Knightley, Dr Christopher Andrew, Dr Nicholas Hiley, Major R. Shaw of the Intelligence Corps Museum, and, especially, the clearly indefatigable Julian Putkowski; as well as George MacDonald Fraser for his enthusiasm, and my editors Michael Cox and Angus Phillips for their, at times, quite extraordinary patience. Finally, I am indebted to my colleague and friend Jesse Knight, of Santa Clara, California, who is currently at work on a biography of Rafael Sabatini, but who has very generously provided me with much fascinating information, and numerous valuable insights into Sabatini's character.

Contents

Introduction

Jack Adrian

'Rafael Sabatini', wrote the critic Lewis Melville in 1924, 'is our outstanding "costume" novelist. He is also an historian of repute.'

This dual role, of popular novelist and historian, was not one with which Sabatini himself was comfortable. His novels reflected a profound grasp of historical detail (particularly of the Italian Renaissance) but were at the same time, bewilderingly, roaring bestsellers. His popularity brought him wealth; yet with wealth, it seemed to him, came a marked falling-off of the academic acclaim he had enjoyed before sudden, and immense, sales transformed him from a middle-aged and only moderately successful writer into a world-famous novelist.

In the early part of his career he wrote two historical biographies—of Cesare Borgia (1911) and Tomas de Torquemada (1913)—both of which gained favourable critical and academic attention, as did his first series of 'Historical Nights' Entertainment' (an ingenious blend of fact and fiction used to explicate crucial events in European history). This latter was issued in bookform in 1917 by Martin Secker, a highly reputable house which also published the 'Uniform' Henry James, the early 'new realism' novels of Compton Mackenzie, a strong series of analytical studies of Pater, Dostoevsky, Gissing, Hardy, Tolstoy, Yeats, and Ibsen by such young literary lions as Middleton Murry, Edward Thomas, Forrest Reid, Lascelles Abercrombie, and Ford Madox Ford, as well as, in the same season as *The Historical Nights' Entertainment*, Norman Douglas's classic *South Wind* and Frank Swinnerton's *Nocturne*.

By the time of Melville's comment the position had changed dramatically. His publisher was now Hutchinson, his stable-mates included H. de Vere Stacpoole, Marie Corelli, Rider Haggard, and Ethel M. Dell, and Sabatini himself was, in sales terms, a star of the first magnitude. His three most recent novels, *Scaramouche* (1921), *Captain Blood* (1922), and *Fortune's Fool* (1923), were selling in their tens of thousands in Great Britain, their scores of thousands in America; his previous works, once dowdy backlist material that might sell a few hundred copies a year before lapsing through lack of interest, were all now being rushed back into print, to the immense profit of his publishers. Only a few months later he was to be the startled recipient of a cheque for $10,000, as an honorarium from a grateful Metro Pictures whose film of *Scaramouche*, a vehicle for the sultry talents of Ramon Novarro, had been (in 1990s parlance) the biggest grosser of the age, though it was soon to be outstripped by the Vitagraph version of *Captain Blood*.

Yet even then Sabatini was about to embark upon the writing of one of his longest and most thoroughly researched novels, the history of Bellarione Fortunato, *Bellarion the Fortunate*, prince (in all but name), scholar and master-of-war of the *quatrocento*, in which his meticulous scholarship, though lightly applied, invigorates every chapter, bringing a turbulent era glowingly to life. The dichotomy between painstaking scholarship and mass popularity— the serious historian praised by the critics and the writer of swashbuckling bestsellers shunned by them—was never resolved during Sabatini's lifetime and has done much to diminish, even destroy, his reputation since his death.

Rafael Sabatini was born in 1875 in Italy—in Jesi, a small town some 25 km inland from the Adriatic port of Ancona—and had a long and productive life, though one not untouched by tragedy.

His father was Italian, his mother came from Lancashire. Vincenzo Sabatini was a celebrated tenor who specialized in Italian opera and performed in most of the world's leading opera houses. Sabatini's mother, Anna Trafford, had been sent from England at an early age to study piano at the Milan Conservatoire, but had then been advised to change careers when it was discovered she possessed a fine soprano. She too toured the world incessantly, meeting Vincenzo in 1874 in Manila, where they married. In the early 1880s, wearying of this strenuous existence, they retired to Portugal, opening a voice-training academy in Porto; Vincenzo was later knighted by Don Luis I, King of Portugal, assuming the title *Maestro-Cavalieri*. Some years afterwards they moved back to Italy, settling in Milan where, amongst others, Vincenzo taught the young John McCormack.

Sabatini did not follow in his parents' peripatetic footsteps. On the contrary, he was, in the words of his friend Reginald Pound (a former editor of the *Strand Magazine*), 'a man of the study and the library'. For most of his career his chief pleasures, apart from reading, were skiing in Switzerland and fishing in England, preferably in Herefordshire: for the last two decades of his life his home was the Wye Valley, in a house he rebuilt for himself near Hay.

This disinclination to venture much abroad (other than the occasional lecture tour) was perhaps due to the enforced wanderings of his early life. At the age of only $2\frac{1}{2}$ he was summarily dispatched to England, to the home of his grandfather in Liverpool, where he stayed for nearly five years while his parents continued their touring. When they moved to Porto, Sabatini, then aged 7, was recalled to their side, beginning his education at a school attached to a Trappist monastery; in the late 1880s he was shuffled off to the cantonal school in Zoug, Switzerland, where he first experienced the heady joys of skiing; then at 17, he was shipped off back to England, again to his grandfather's in Liverpool, where work was found for him as a translator for an import firm dealing mainly in Brazilian coffee.

This was by no means a dead-end. To Sabatini, a natural linguist (he was even then fluent in Italian, French, German, Spanish, Portuguese, and English), the work was not arduous and allowed him plenty of time in which to indulge his chief passion of reading. His interests lay not with such chauvinistic concoctors of Victorian boys' fiction as Henty or Ballantyne, but in far more cosmopolitan fare: Dumas *père*, Scott, Shakespeare ('for the stories'), Schiller, Cervantes, Alessandro Manzoni, and particularly Stanley J. Weyman. Much later, to Esther Forbes, a publicist with his American publishers Houghton Mifflin, he wrote: 'Before I first left England at seven I read—but if I were to tell you what I had read, you would not believe me.' As well as using his spare time to read he also wrote, at first for Liverpool newspapers. Then in the late 1890s he began to make contact with sympathetic editors of national periodicals.

His earliest traced story, the Weymanesque 'The Vicompte's Wager', appeared in *Harmsworth's Magazine* in September 1899. There were almost certainly others prior to this, possibly written for the numerous weeklies that existed at the time, all of which featured a short-story slot. *Harmsworth's* later became the *London Magazine*, flagship for a generation of the middle-brow end of what was to become Lord Northcliffe's vast Amalgamated Press. Sabatini was to write frequently for the *London* in later years, though even more prolifically for its all-fiction stable-mate, the *Premier Magazine*.

Meanwhile he veered away from Alfred Harmsworth's fledgling empire to the rival Pearson group, where he found an agreeable niche for the next five years. Ironically, the story that gained him entry, written in a style and a genre entirely removed from the historical, was 'The Curate and the Actress', a light modern comedy which the *Royal Magazine* published in November 1899. With his next story, however, 'Sword and Mitre', which appeared in the following issue, he turned back to the past.

Years later, at the height of his fame, he tended to look back on the period of his apprenticeship through to the First World War as one of almost unrelieved drudgery—'twenty lean years of arduous toil', as he wrote in an autobiographical sketch for *The Liverpolitan* in 1935—although hindsight was to a certain extent, perhaps, influenced by more recent events outside his writing life (the tragic death of his only child, his failed first marriage). He also felt that his enormous success was due not so much to skill as to blind chance. Fame was not achieved overnight, and when it did come, in 1921, it was so stupendous, and so startlingly sudden, that it seemed to him that for twenty years he had been somehow cheated.

Where it had formerly taken half a decade for one of his novels to sell perhaps 5,000 copies (and then only through rare US sales—out of the seventeen books he wrote prior to 1920, only seven were taken up by American publishers), now, almost literally at a stroke, his new novels were achieving sales of 50,000 or 60,000 copies in a single year. And yet his work, he felt, was not so very different now to then. There was also the lurking suspicion that publishers' judgements were not to be trusted. After all, the book that had become such an extravagant bestseller in America, and thus throughout the world, within the space of less than twelve months, *Scaramouche*, had been turned down flat as unpublishable, not only by his previous American publishers Lippincott but by five or six other houses as well, and had only been accepted by his new American publishers, Houghton Mifflin, on the urging of a single director who, almost by a fluke, had happened to pick up the by now dog-eared manuscript.

Yet those two decades, from 1900 through to 1920, were hardly lean, and the toil was perhaps not quite so taxing as Sabatini liked to recall. Indeed, almost at the very outset of his career he was rewarded by entirely unlooked-for success. A series of short stories about a band of outlaws in Germany (set during the Thirty Years War) he wrote for *Pearson's Magazine* in the early 1900s attracted the attention of Pearson's controlling editor, Peter Keary, who summoned the 26-year-old author to London and, during a half-hour interview, commissioned a full-length novel. This was *The Lovers of Yvonne* (1902), a tale of Mazarin and the Fronde insurrection which Sabatini later disowned—'a very bad [book] . . . I blush . . . at any chance mention of it.' Nevertheless, at the time, he not unnaturally regarded its publication as the most important event in his career, giving him the creative boost he needed to spread his wings.

As a result he began cautiously to move away from the Pearson group into other markets, including the *English Illustrated Magazine*, *The Bystander* and *Chambers' Journal*. At the same time he wrote a second novel, *The Tavern Knight* (1904: the Battle of Worcester and the escape of Charles II), the serial rights to which he managed to sell to the high-paying glossy weekly, the *Sphere*. This finally persuaded him to leave Brazilian coffee and '[fling] myself more or less recklessly into . . . living by my pen'.

However, despite the dispirited picture he painted thirty years later, over the next fifteen years Sabatini prospered, publishing at least one book a year, his two monumental studies of Cesare Borgia and Torquemada, well over a dozen novellas, as well as a few score short stories. He married Ruth Dixon, daughter of a prosperous paper-merchant (their only son, Rafael-Angelo, was born in 1909), and progressed, fairly smoothly, up the social scale, from a village near Chester, on the banks of the Dee, to Battersea Park, London, then Hampstead Heath, and finally to a Thames-side cottage in Laleham, downriver from Staines. His earnings, too, while nowhere near the astronomical sums he was to achieve during the interwar years, were far from negligible. Most, if not all, of his novels were serialized prior to publication in book form, at anything between thirty and fifty shillings per thousand words for a story that might run to 120,000 words, or more. Few of Sabatini's novels were less than 100,000 words in length; some, such as *The Strolling Player* (1913) and *The Sea-Hawk* (1915), ran to a massive 150,000 words.

He was also an imaginative short-story writer at a time when fiction magazines flourished on the bookstalls. Not all editors appreciated his brand of historical fiction, but a useful minority were wholly supportive. One of these was David Whitelaw of the Amalgamated Press, who before and during the First World War ran the *London Magazine* (only just behind the prestigious *Strand* in sales and popularity; rather ahead in production values). Whitelaw was later to become controlling editor of the AP's fiction and general-interest monthlies, and in 1914 launched the all-fiction *Premier Magazine*. Casting around for new writing talent, he invited Sabatini, then producing crime and romance stories in a desultory way for the *London*, to contribute purely historical material.

For Sabatini this offer was to have momentous consequences. Whitelaw was one of the great British magazine editors, a man of sharp intelligence and perception, whose grasp, even then, of what constituted mass-appeal was celebrated. Furthermore, although he knew precisely what the reading public wanted, and duly gave it to them, he was never afraid to nurture an author or champion a genre he felt they *ought* to want. Sabatini was a case in point, for he was writing historical fiction when the genre was passing through one of its drearier phases.

Since the retirement of Stanley J. Weyman in 1908, and despite the annual effusions of the Baroness Orczy (now, in any case, so jaded by her hero the Scarlet Pimpernel that she was forced to attribute ancestors to him and write about them instead) or the Arcadian froth of Jeffrey Farnol and tireless *feuilletonists* such as Agnes and Egerton Castle (the 'Ecod!' school of costume romance), no single author had been boosted into any kind of prominence by either critics or the vast, and at the time infinitely more influential, circulating library readership. Sabatini himself wrote novels that were distinctly superior to the usual library fodder—in his work the explication of the social background, the manners and mores of the times, was quite as crucial as the cannon's roar or the clash of cutlass on glaive—and Whitelaw let him have his head, at the same time (doubtless prompted by an earlier short series of stories by him featuring the low-life exploits of Bernouin, valet to, and spy of, Cardinal Mazarin) suggesting an emphasis on rogues and scally-wags rather than the pomp and grandeur of great events.

This suited Sabatini, who had a fondness for the breed and whose sardonic humour and ingenious imagination perfectly matched the subject. Although he wrote for other magazines—*Cassell's*, *Pall Mall*, the *Storyteller* and (later) the *Grand Maga-zine*—by far the bulk of his work was now done for Whitelaw: well over fifty short stories and novellas during the next eight years.

There were tales of innocents caught up in the toils of the Spanish Inquisition and the French Revolution, tales of clever revenges (Sabatini was a great believer in, and in his plots a skilful utiliser of, the principle of an eye for an eye), tales of down-at-heel highwaymen, cozening sharpsters, drastically unsuccessful thieves. By no means 'all history' (as his publishers Hutchinson boasted in their promotional material during the interwar years) was his backcloth, but he was fully at ease in the Italian Renaissance, Carolean and Georgian England, France during the Terror (pluck-ing heroes from, unusually, both the aristocrats and the *sans-culottes*), and could certainly adapt his research techniques, at any rate for the short narrative form, to just about any event of sig-nificance in European history from the thirteenth to the early nineteenth centuries. This last was triumphantly demonstrated in the 'factional essays' he wrote at Whitelaw's urging for the *Premier* from 1916 to 1919—his first two series of 'Historical Nights' Enter-tainments'—in which he shrewdly analysed critical historical turning-points, tragedies and desperate events, dressing up his narratives in fictional form yet at the same time adhering scrupu-lously to recorded facts and keeping speculation to the minimum.

A particular penchant in his stories for spies and undercover agents during this period may have reflected real life, since Sabatini worked for the Intelligence Service during the Great War, although precisely in what capacity seems impossible now to ascer-tain. Many writers of the period were co-opted into a loose con-federation of propagandists for the Allied cause under the direction of Charles Masterman (the Wellington House group), and it is likely that Sabatini (who took out naturalization papers in 1917) was one of them. A reference in one of the official registers indicates that his linguistic talents may have been utilized by the Foreign Office for the purposes of keeping a covert eye on its Italian allies. Whatever the case his liking for rogue-heroes in the end led to success quite beyond his wildest imaginings.

In 1919 he wrote a vivid psychological drama of the French Revolution concerning one André-Louis Moreau, scion (although unknown to him) of the nobility. In dangerous times Moreau takes as his pseudonym—almost a *nom de guerre*—'Scaramouche', after the braggadocic buffoon of the Italian *commedia dell'arte*, and deviously plots the destruction of an aristocrat who has murdered his best friend, only to discover that the murderer is his own father. During the course of the novel, *Scaramouche*, Moreau joins a band of strolling players; boundlessly energetic, he writes their plays, stars in them, and shamelessly pursues bookings, at the same time composing anti-monarchist tracts, becoming an expert swordsman and orator and, in the end, a Revolutionary hero who, at the moment of his triumph, when the position of Representative of the People is about to be conferred on him, renounces the Revolution to protect the woman he loves. (In the splendid sequel *Scaramouche the Kingmaker*, written a decade later, Moreau busies himself with restoring the monarchy and is on the verge of success in his plan to destroy the Jacobin leaders when, in a typically mordant Sabatiniesque twist, he discovers that the Royalist faction is as treacherous as the anti-Royalist, whereupon he sabotages his own labyrinthine scheme, thus ensuring the triumph of the Revolution.)

Despite the croakings of his publishers that 'no one is reading historical fiction these days', *Scaramouche*, dramatic, highly coloured, swift-paced yet densely plotted, was a phenomenal bestseller on both sides of the Atlantic. In Britain, particularly, it was precisely the kind of involved, and involving, tale readers craved after nearly half a decade of the most brutal and debilitating conflict in history and, of more immediate relevance, a lingering coal-strike that seemed to offer ominous parallels with recent events in Russia. From a threatening present *Scaramouche* was an exhilarating escape into a past where dangers were entirely vicarious. And even while *Scaramouche* was enjoying immense sales Sabatini was already transforming a series of piratical tales he had written for David Whitelaw into a seamless novel, *Captain Blood*, which, in 1922, not only set the seal on his own success but ensured that all at once *everyone* was reading historical fiction.

Although now, quite suddenly, a wealthy man and a courted writer of repute Sabatini's life-style did not alter much. His outlook on life, often translated into his novels, was profoundly sceptical: it seemed to him that a capricious Fate had dropped riches in his lap and could easily pluck them out again; and perhaps deal him some other, and far more devastating, blow. The death of his much-loved son in 1927, in an avoidable car accident, merely served to strengthen this view. It was followed inevitably by the break-up of his marriage, since Rafael-Angelo had become over the years the only link between Sabatini and his wife. Never a clubbable man, he now increasingly isolated himself on the Herefordshire-Welsh border, in his cottage near Hay, and when writing friends came to stay, as the naturalist and novelist John Moore discovered when he dropped in one afternoon in 1932, the conversation more often than not was 'Not of our common trade of words, but of flies and rods and rivers, and the queer habits of fish.'

In 1935 Sabatini married again, this time to Christine Dixon, the ex-wife of his former brother-in-law, Hugh. Though twenty years younger, Christine was everything that Ruth had never been: artistic, a sculptress, a lover of the countryside; an ideal companion. She brought with her a 19-year-old son, Lancelot, who was in temperament almost a twin of Rafael-Angelo.

What seemed at last an idyllic existence—writing, fishing and an annual pilgrimage to Switzerland—was all at once shattered by the American IRS, who determined that high-earning British authors were not paying enough tax. Bestsellers such as Sabatini, Sax Rohmer, and P. G. Wodehouse were abruptly presented with ferocious retrospective tax demands (in Wodehouse's case a staggering £50,000). On behalf of his brother-writers Sabatini fought the case through the American courts, and lost. Though not crippling to one who lived quietly, the bill was still enormous. A far more appalling shock was to follow. In 1940 Lancelot joined the RAF, gained his wings, and in celebration flew over Hay in his Hurricane, saluting both Sabatini and Christine as they waved in the grounds of their house below. Seconds later, and for no apparent reason, the plane plunged into a field across the Wye from them, bursting into flames. Lancelot died instantly. In a dreadful irony the crash occurred thirteen years almost to the day after Rafael-Angelo's death.

The remarkable thing is that through all of these crushing personal blows, Sabatini not only continued writing but produced some of his finest work. *The Romantic Prince*, a stirring novel of the Burgundian court, appeared in 1929, though written in 1927, shortly after the tragic and futile death of his son. In the miserable period after leaving Ruth in 1930 he wrote *Scaramouche the Kingmaker*; while awaiting the divorce in 1931 he was busy with *The Black Swan*, in many ways his greatest novel of piracy. During the 1930s he was able convincingly to re-create the swashbuckling world of Captain Blood in two further volumes of short stories. A swift-paced 'thriller' of Bonapartist intrigue, *Venetian Masque*, published in 1934, was followed by *Chivalry*, his magnificent tale of the *condottieri* of the *quatrocento*. During the interminable tax trial he wrote the bulk of *The Sword of Islam*, his epic tale of the Barbary corsairs, and after the harrowing experience of Lancelot's death he researched and finished his life of Columbus, a superb novel of suspense and discovery which, at the same time, richly evokes its period and has all the merits of a great biography. Writing, for Rafael Sabatini, was surely a mighty bulwark against an unkind world.

He died in 1950 at the age of 75, still writing and just twelve months after his last novel *The Gamester*, the riveting story of John Law, the extraordinary Scottish banker and gambler who nearly bankrupted France, was published.

In his reminiscent article for *The Liverpolitan* in 1935 Sabatini remarked that he chose the historical novel as his 'line of work for the sole but very proper reason that it was a form that interested me'. His models were surprisingly few.

Though he admired Scott, he felt the author's effects were at times too contrived; Dumas *père* was a master of the broad brush-stroke, the hectic (at times reckless) narrative sweep, though he was not overscrupulous in the matter of first-hand research, which was for Sabatini something of a hobby-horse; S. R. Crockett, the Scottish romancer, was perhaps too parochial, and stylistically somewhat laboured; the dreamy feyness of Maurice Hewlett, at least in his early *Forest Lovers* phase, did not appeal much to Sabatini, the man of action as well as romance (Hewlett's over-idealized version of the *quatrocento* bears little resemblance to that of the younger writer). He did, however, give fulsome praise to the American novelist Mary Johnston, who burned like a comet in the early years of the century, at precisely the time Sabatini himself, at the outset of his career, was most vulnerable to influence.

Johnston's first novel *The Old Dominion* (1899), rich in Old South lore and imagery, follows the dashing career of Sir William Berkeley, who, transported to the Colonies and enslaved for treason, leads a revolt of his fellow-prisoners before escaping into the wilderness—a plot Sabatini later utilized when he came to write *Captain Blood*. Her second book, *By Order of the Company* (1900), a wild success on both sides of the Atlantic (in America it had been titled *To Have and to Hold*), was set against the 1622 Indian massacre at Jamestown, and though she wrote of other lands and periods her best novels are those which depict her native country in Colonial times.

An early, and ardent, suffragette, Johnston wrote a number of incisive polemical pamphlets during the 1900s (including one for the Equal Suffrage League of Virginia entitled 'The Status of Women'), although in her novels she had a weakness for melodrama over drama and characters out of stock (the seducing villain in *By Order of the Company* is called Lord Carnal). Nevertheless, her stories galloped along and in Sabatini's eyes she had the enviable talent of seeming to write 'not of things studied, but of things remembered, of things personally witnessed'. Even so, despite his early enthusiasm, Johnston paled into insignificance before Sabatini's main influence, indeed his idol: the British writer Stanley J. Weyman who, almost single-handedly, rescued the historical novel from its late-Victorian doldrums.

Weyman (1855–1928) signally deviated from the norm of the British historical novelist of his day in a number of important ways, not least in his offering to the public a new kind of hero: the villain—or at any rate the arrogant and bullying bravo redeemed by his own reckless and, in the end, selfless courage (Gil de Berault in *Under the Red Robe*, Raoul de Mar in *The House of the*

Wolf). This 'often unacknowledged power' (in the words of the critic Margery Fisher)—the individualizing rather than the stereotyping of his chief characters—marked Weyman out at once as a writer of some depth and subtlety, and one who was at the same time willing to take a risk with the fixed opinions of his readers (that the hero should invariably be 'noble'), and thus their loyalties.

Fascinated by history but put off from writing about it by publishers' indifference, Weyman, a failed barrister, began his career as an author in the 1880s (to bolster up his wretched legal earnings) by writing stories of domestic life in the Trollopean manner. He only turned fully to costume drama when a contemporary clerical novel, *The New Rector* (1891), flopped badly. *A Gentleman of France* (1893: court-life, conspiracy, and adventure in the reign of Henry III of France) was an immense success, gaining extravagant praise from Stevenson ('it is the most exquisite pleasure'). Weyman's career took off in spectacular fashion and he became the most popular historical writer of his day, deftly combining action and adventure with skilful construction and a firm sense of period.

His method was to set a vigorous and swift-paced story-line against a deeply researched historical background (he read widely, and travelled extensively in Europe), and he was arguably the first writer to treat the genre as a serious art-form rather than merely a vehicle for swashbuckling action, though he never stinted in that direction either. His later novels, such as *The Great House* (1919) and *Ovington's Bank* (1922), written in a glorious Indian summer of creativity when he returned to the Trollopean mode after a twelve-year absence from writing, are his most assured, depicting in extraordinary and fascinating detail English social life in the post-Regency period.

However, although it was Weyman's swashbuckling qualities that so influenced his peers—his genius for describing ambushes, chases, and pell-mell escapes—it was his capacity for hard research, together with his immaculate structuring of a story and a radical use of distinctly unheroic heroes, that attracted the young Sabatini, whose early novels quite outpace those of the older writer, especially in the matter of the ruffian-as-hero. In *The Tavern Knight* the hero is Sir Crispin Galliard, a 'bawdy rakehelly godless sottish ruffler'; in a drunken debauch at the start of *Bardelys the Magnificent* (1906), Marcel de St Pol, Marquis de

Bardelys, an 'impudent, boasting coxcomb', makes an infamous wager (that he will woo and win Roxalanne de Lavedan) with the even more scoundrelly Compte de Chatellerault. During the course of each novel both men are realistically transformed from 'loutish, blood-hungry rogue(s)' into heroes seared by danger and bitter experience.

At times Sabatini rang the changes on the villain-as-hero theme by upending it and presenting the hero-as-villain (what Margery Fisher has termed 'the Hero in Eclipse'): that is, the hero who is treacherously used and, to escape his plight, must become a villain. Peter Blood, a good man, is condemned by the infamous Judge Jeffreys to slavery in the West Indies (for healing a wounded fugitive from the bloodbath at Sedgemoor), but escapes by turning buccaneer. In *The Sea Hawk* (one of Sabatini's most popular and successful novels, twice filmed), Sir Oliver Tressilian, betrayed by his venomous half-brother and shanghaied into the Spanish galleys, escapes and becomes Sakr-el-Bahr (the 'sea hawk'), most feared of the Barbary corsairs and commander-in-chief to the Basha of Algiers, Asad-ed-Din. Yet another twist is the villain who renounces his past but then must return to it in order to become a hero, as in *The Black Swan* (1932), in which ex-pirate Charles de Bernis once more takes on the mantle of his old profession in order to destroy the ogreish Tom Leach.

In this, Sabatini was a distinctly modern writer. In his novels and stories his main characters often, and realistically, take the rogue's path to get what they want; they are pragmatists rather than idealists, even when their motives are pure—and on occasion their motives are by no means entirely pure. Sabatini admired craft, cunning and guile quite as much as he admired straightforward smartness.

This is most strikingly demonstrated in his championship, in book after book, of the arch-villain of the *cinquecento*, that 'most vicious and depraved prince of rogues, the devil incarnate', Cesare Borgia. In much the same way as those present-day Ricardians who are bent on establishing that Richard III was not the monster of popular legend, Sabatini dug deep into primary, rather than secondary or tertiary, sources, and took the view that because much of the original anti-Borgia literature and sentiment had been directly inspired by enemies of the clan its reliability was, at the very least, suspect. His Borgia *œuvre*—*The Justice of the Duke* (1912: seven short stories), *The Banner of the Bull* (1915: three novellas), the play *The Tyrant* (1925), as well as his principal brief for the defence, the massive and massively researched *Life of Cesare Borgia* (1911)—convincingly portrays a ruthless and pragmatic politician in an age of arbitrary violence and ever-shifting loyalties.

It is perhaps less surprising that Sabatini was attracted to the adventurer, philanderer, and con-man Giacomo di Casanova, who in many ways embodied all the qualities he found fascinating (even, perhaps, mildly admirable). For most the fact that Casanova was a scholar and a wit, and a writer of some grace, compensates for his various misdemeanours; for Sabatini the reverse was the case. Casanova's redeeming features were undoubtedly that he was an outright rogue and rascal who gulled his way across Europe, through court and nunnery, in the end gaining more kicks than ha'pence. But then Sabatini also had a fondness for that other brassy swindler, Guiseppe Balsamo, who preferred to be addressed by the wholly spurious title Count Cagliostro.

Sabatini revitalized—even revolutionized—historical fiction with his guileful and swashbuckling rogue-heroes. The 1920s saw a dramatic proliferation in the number of historical novels written, as a glance through old publishers' catalogues shows. He also had the good fortune to score a sensational success at a time when another story-telling medium was growing in popularity and sophistication. His novels translated well to the screen, gaining him an audience far in excess of any of his predecessors. His influence was thus wide ranging. Captain Blood alone, during the interwar years and after, spawned a host of imitations, in books and on film, many of which not only crossed genres but media. If Sabatini had not existed it is doubtful that Leslie Charteris' 'brighter buccaneer' Simon Templar, the Saint, would have been quite the dashing hero he became, and although the American pulp-writer Johnston McCulley created his famous masked avenger Zorro in 1919, his later Zorro stories owe much to Blood, just as the Zorro movies— indeed many others—are indebted in one way or another to that first Vitagraph Blood film. The single image of an actor swinging through the air, clinging to a rope with one hand, a sword in the other, whether clad in Lincoln green or Ruritanian jodphurs and boots, is pure Captain Blood.

Even today, over forty years after his death, Sabatini's spell is potent. The historical novelist Dorothy Dunnett moves in much the same richly textured and sardonic world, and George Mac-Donald Fraser's Harry Flashman is the rogue-hero taken to its inevitable extreme, while *The Pyrates* (1983) is his pixilated homage to all things piratical, and to the Sabatini canon in particular. More recently the American writer Tim Powers has further refertilized the Sabatini swashbuckler, in *On Stranger Tides* (1987), skilfully blending high-seas adventure with sorcery and black magic.

During his lifetime Sabatini produced six volumes of short stories as well as three series of his 'factional essays', the *Historical Nights' Entertainment*. Though possessing great dexterity in being able to match a complex plotline to a flowing narrative drive in the long (sometimes the very long) novel, he was also a master of the shorter form. Out of the twenty tales in this present collection only three have appeared in book form before. All are as vivid and picaresque as those Sabatini collected in his final volume, *Turbulent Tales* (1946), and feature a parade of assorted low-lives, from rakehells and roaring beaus to swindlers and secret agents, scoundrels and police spies and scapegrace scallywags who get the better of pompous pillars of society.

Full of pace, colour, incident and plot, the stories range, in period, from the sixteenth to the eighteenth centuries; in real, compositional, time from 1907 to 1937. Six of the tales in the Casanova section were originally published in the *Grand Magazine* as a series in 1918, the remaining three in the *Premier*: all are drawn from Casanova's own *Memoirs*, for which Sabatini had a particular fondness, and are fine examples of his 'factional essay' method. Two of the earlier stories, 'The Risen Dead' and 'Brancaleone's Terms', were later expanded into full-length novels, the latter from 6,000 words in 1914 to the 140,000-word *Sword of Islam* a quarter of a century later. Sabatini had a gift for being able successfully to fatten out acorns into oak trees, and a positive genius for reworking an adroit narrative twist again and again, though each time suitably re-apparelled. 'Duroc' (included here) is a 4,000-word tale of the Terror, originally published in Isabel Thorne's excellent little short-story magazine the *Weekly Tale-Teller* in 1915; three years later Sabatini used the same basic plot-twist, though expanded to 6,000 words and updated to a First World War espionage setting, in a story called 'Intelligence'; over two decades later 'The Recoil' appeared in the *Strand* (probably the very last short story he wrote): precisely the same twist-ending but now in a story of 8,000 words set at the time of the First Empire. Yet each version is able to stand on its own.

An anonymous critic in the 1930s dubbed Sabatini 'the Prince of Storytellers'. This of course is reviewers' shorthand, a neat way of epitomizing talent in limited column-inches, though not a title— with its pulp-fiction resonances—Sabatini himself especially relished. His work was never deliberately aimed at a mass audience, although ironically he achieved spectacular popular success. But then Rafael Sabatini's life was full of ironies, both light and dark. Still, the reviewer's cap fits: and no more so than in this present collection.

Rogues' Gallery

The Risen Dead

S IR GEOFFREY SWAYNE was hanged at Tyburn.

A merry, reckless, roaring soul had been Sir Geoffrey, and if it was said of him that in ten years he had never gone sober to bed, yet was it confessed that he was a pleasant, humorous gentleman in his cups, just as he was a pleasant, humorous gentleman in all the other traffics that made up his rascally life. If he lost his money at the tables, he did so with an amiable smile in his handsome eyes and a jest on his lips. If at intervals, more or less regular, he would beat his wife, periodically kick his servants down stairs, and systematically grind the faces of his tenants, yet all these things he did, at least, with an engaging joviality of demeanour.

In short, he was a very affable, charming scoundrel, and all England was agreed that he richly deserved his end. And yet, the humour of the thing—and it was just such a jest as Sir Geoffrey would have relished had it been less against himself—lay in the fact that although none of the rascally things he had done could be considered by the law of England reason enough for hanging him, the crime for which he was hanged—that of highway robbery—was the one crime it had never occurred to him to commit.

The thing had fallen out in this wise:

Sir Geoffrey, riding Londonwards, from his home near Guildford, one evening in late March, had been held up on Wandsworth Common by a cloaked figure on a huge grey mare. The failing light had gleamed from the barrel of a pistol, and the highwayman's tone had been one that asked no arguments, admitted of no compromise. But Sir Geoffrey in the course of his blustering career had become a useful man of his hands. One blow of his heavy riding-crop had knocked aside the highwayman's pistol, another had knocked in the highwayman's head and tumbled him headlong from his saddle.

Sir Geoffrey was master of the situation, and, mightily pleased by it, he bethought him of the spoils of war, which were his by right of conquest. Without a qualm—nay, with a laugh and the lilt of a song on his lips—Sir Geoffrey had dragged the stricken toby-man into the shelter of a clump of trees, and exchanged his own spavined horse for the fellow's splendid mare, on which he had blithely pursued his road.

But before he had gone a couple of miles he had caught the sounds of a numerous party galloping behind and rapidly gaining on him. Now Sir Geoffrey's conscience—if so be he owned one—was at rest. He had done no wrong, leastways no wrong that should make him fear the law, and so he rode easily, never thinking of attempting to outdistance the party which came on behind—a thing he might easily have done had he been so inclined, bravely mounted as he was.

So the others came on, hailed him, and when he paused to ask them what they craved, came up with and surrounded him.

'We have you this time, "Scudding Tom,"' they cried, and fell to ill-using him, pulling him down from his horse, and bestowing upon him epithets for which he was utterly at a loss to account. But he was not a patient man. He had been assaulted, and it was a thing he would not suffer, although, as he plainly saw, they were sheriff's men that had set upon him. So he blithely laid about him, and contrived to crack a couple of heads before they had bound him and flung him, helpless, down upon the road, livid, blasphemant, and vastly furious.

A stout rubicund gentleman, in black with silver lace, who had stood well apart whilst the fighting had been in train, came forward now, swelling to bursting point with his own importance, and denounced Sir Geoffrey for the tobyman who had robbed him an hour ago. He was, he said, Sir Henry Talbury of Hurlingston, in the County of Kent, one of his Majesty's Justices of the Peace. He had been to collect certain sums of money in London, and was returning with a leather bag containing a hundred guineas, of which this ruffian had relieved him.

Sir Geoffrey heard him, and having heard him realized the situation, spat from his mouth the filthy rags with which he had been gagged, and spoke—

'You pot-bodied fool,' said he, for he had a rare virulence of tongue upon occasion. 'You gross, beer-fattened hodman, let me

free of these bonds, and get you back to your pigs at Hurlingston
ere I have you flayed for this business. I am Sir Geoffrey Swayne,
of Guildford, as you shall learn more fully to your bitter sorrow.'

The little man's fat face lost some of its plethoric colour, but it
was in rage that he paled, and not in any fear that Sir Geoffrey—
being tightly bound and helpless—might inspire him.

'Are ye so, indeed,' he snapped, and his little eyes looked evil as
a rat's. 'I have heard of ye, for a gaming, dissolute scoundrel.'

'Oh 'sblood!' panted Sir Geoffrey, writhing in his bonds. 'You
shall be spitted for this, like the Christmas goose you are.'

'And so, 'tis to highway robbery that your debaucheries have
brought ye?' The little man sniffed contemptuously. 'I'm nowise
surprised, and ye shall hang as a warning to other scapegraces.'

And hang he did as Sir Henry promised him. Under the flap of
his saddle they had found a bag with Sir Henry Talbury's name
upon it and the hundred guineas he had mentioned contained in
it. It was in vain that Sir Geoffrey told the true story of his meeting
with the tobyman, thus explaining how he had come by the grey
mare—which had proved his undoing, for it was the mare, not the
man, that had been recognized. The fellow who rode that great,
grey beast was known to the countryside as 'Scudding Tom', and
nothing more, his identity never having been revealed. The court,
whilst praising his ingenuity, laughed at his tale. They realized
that he was Sir Geoffrey Swayne—he had brought a regiment of
witnesses to swear it—but they were no less satisfied that Sir
Geoffrey and 'Scudding Tom' were one and the same person. It
sorted well with his general reputation, and besides Sir Henry
swore to him as being the man who had robbed him, and whether
he swore in good faith or out of revenge for the things Sir Geoffrey
had said to him when he was overpowered, it might be difficult
to say.

But Sir Geoffrey was hanged, and the world was done with him,
although Sir Geoffrey was nowise done with the world, as you shall
hear. His lands—or what was left of them out of all that he had
gamed away—were forfeit to the Crown, and his widow stood thus
in peril of destitution. Not even his handsome body did they leave.
For when it was cut down, still warm, from the gallows, it was sold
to Dr Blizzard, a ready purchaser of such commodities for dissect-
ing purposes.

But the old doctor had bought more than he knew of this time, for upon the insertion of the knife into one of Sir Geoffrey's legs—the point at which the doctor had elected to start his work— Sir Geoffrey had suddenly sat upright on the slate table, stretching his limbs, and letting forth a volley of blood-curdling imprecations, which all but slew the doctor by the fright they gave him.

Then, memory of past events returning to his wakening mind, the rake had checked himself, blenched a little and looked awesomely about him. The doctor, quivering in every nerve, his teeth rattling in his head, vainly sought to crush himself behind a tallboy, to protect himself from the material, and pattered long-forgotten prayers to heaven for protection against the immaterial—for, scientist though Dr Blizzard was, he could not here discriminate with which he might have to do.

'Rat me!' spluttered Sir Geoffrey, still looking about him, 'and is this hades?' He shivered, for he was naked. 'It is colder than I would have credited from what they told me,' said he. He caught sight of the doctor's scared, grey face, horn-rimmed spectacles, and wig gone rakishly awry in the efforts the man made to conceal himself.

'Faith!' he pursued with a chuckle, 'but it's a place of surprises. You've a monstrous mild look, sir, for Satan—neither tail, nor cloven hoof, nor pitchfork? Gad's my life! but you're a disappointment.'

He swung himself down from the table, and found his limbs so cramped that he howled a second in pain.

At last, perceiving what manner of resurrection was this, the doctor took heart and came forward. 'God 'a mercy!' said he, 'I've heard of such things, but I'd never have believed it.'

'You've an odd turn of speech, old Lucifer. Are you a devil, or are you not?'

'I'm no devil,' the doctor answered testily.

'Then who the devil are you?'

'Man, you were hanged at Tyburn this morning,' quoth the doctor a trifle irrelevantly.

'Was I so? Egad! I was coming to think that I had dreamed it.'

'Oh, it was no dream. You were hanged. You are Sir Geoffrey Swayne.'

'Then I'm in hades, after all. But of your pity lend me a cloak, for it seems I'm more in danger of being frozen here than burned.'

The doctor gave him the garment he craved, and explained the situation. Sir Geoffrey was incredulous. The doctor heaped up arguments, cited precedents.

'It is recorded,' he said, 'of a woman, in the reign of Edward III, regaining consciousness after having hanged for four-and-twenty hours, and of another woman at Oxford a hundred years ago who came to life again after having hanged for half-an-hour, besides other instances I've read of, yet discredited until now.'

The doctor was waxing excited, and Sir Geoffrey had much ado to restrain him from running out to tell all London of this resurrection.

'I'm dead,' he told the doctor, with a grin, 'and dead you'll leave me, or, by heaven, it's dead you'll be yourself. I was hanged, and there's an end to it—leastways until I've had a talk with that Kentish lout they call Sir Henry Talbury.'

He told the doctor the true circumstances of his case, and he so succeeded in convincing him of the truth of it that the old man was won over to befriend him, and put him in the way of having justice done him after all. But that night Sir Geoffrey sickened of a fever, and was forced to keep his bed some days, so that a week had passed before he was able to leave the doctor's house, and make his way to Hurlingston.

Blizzard lent him ten guineas and made him a present of a suit of black Camlett, a hat, and a brown *roquelaure*, his own clothes having been reduced to rags by the violence that had attended his arrest. Thus equipped, Sir Geoffrey arrived at Maidstone at six o'clock in the evening of the first Monday in April. From Maidstone to Hurlingston was a distance of some four miles, which Sir Geoffrey covered afoot, reaching Hurlingston Manor as dusk was falling.

He stepped briskly up the long white drive that wound its way between regiments of trees, to the clearing that fronted the grey, severely architectured house. From long French windows to the left a shaft of light, emerging through half-drawn curtains, fell with a golden glow upon the lawn. One half of the window itself stood open, for it had been warm as a day of summer. Sir Geoffrey paused, and his eyes roved towards that glowing aperture. He hesitated in his original intention of boldly asking for Sir Henry. He turned aside, and still pondering, he drifted rather than walked, until he was in line with the opening, and able to look into the room. A second he stared with dilated eyes, then with a sharp indrawing of breath he sped forward, nor stopped until he was crouching at the window, peering into the room.

Within sat the Justice of the Peace, like a toad with his legs wide, and his wig on his knee. He was sucking contentedly at a long-stemmed pipe, and at his elbow was a decanter and a half-filled glass of sparkling yellow wine. His huge dome-like head shone in the light of a pair of candles that stood in their massive silver sticks on either side of the papers spread out in front of him.

Before him stood a woman all in black—a tall, nobly-proportioned woman, with a high nose and a handsome, high-bred face. She was speaking, and her fine eyes were full of supplication. Sir Geoffrey drew nigh and listened as he deemed he had the right to, for the woman was Lady Swayne.

'Sir,' she was saying, 'of your charity I do implore you again that you investigate this matter, and as sure as you're sitting there you shall discover that Sir Geoffrey was no robber, whatever may have been his sins. Sir Henry, you have made a widow of me. Do not make me a beggar also. I ask for justice—tardy justice—that my husband's estates be not confiscated from me.'

Sir Henry withdrew his pipe from his gross lips.

'Madam,' said he, 'your husband was found guilty by judge and jury. He was "Scudding Tom," the highwayman—there's never a doubt of it.'

The curtain rings rang harshly on the ensuing silence. The woman turned her head and screamed; the man looked up and gasped for breath. His face blenched, the pipe dropped from his nerveless fingers and broke into a dozen fragments on the floor; for there, between the dark green curtains, the lamplight falling full upon his face, which gleamed a ghostly white against the black background of the night, stood the wraith of Sir Geoffrey Swayne.

He stood there, enjoying the sensation his advent had created, a sardonic grin on his white face, a glitter mighty evil in his bold, black eyes.

The woman was the first to gather sufficient courage to address the apparition. Sir Henry had a desire to crawl under the table, and if he did not indulge it, it was because his limbs, palsied with fright, refused their office.

'Is that you, Geoffrey?' the woman whispered hoarsely, craning forward, her face white to the lips. 'Speak!'

And then a cunning notion shot through Sir Geoffrey's subtle mind. Of what avail to protest his innocence? What proofs had he? A judge and jury had found him guilty; the thing was done with. He must play a subtle game if he would retrieve his lands from confiscation, and the nature of it was at once apparent to him.

He stepped airily forward a pace or two, and the curtains fell together behind him with a shudder.

'My name, madam, is not Geoffrey. It is Jack—Jack Haynes, better known to the vulgar as "Scudding Tom," gentleman of the road. Your servant, madam, and yours, sir.' He made a leg first to the lady, and then to the knight.

Sir Henry's colour was returning. It came back in a flood until it seemed as if he were doomed to apoplexy. A grunt escaped him. He sought words in which to utter his amazement, his perplexity and his dawning dismay. But the woman was beforehand with him. She had stared a moment at her husband in unbelief. Then, as if convinced—and well she might be, knowing Sir Geoffrey hanged—she swung round upon Sir Henry, her arm dramatically outstretched.

'You have heard him, Sir Henry,' she cried. 'You have heard what he says. Will you believe me now, when I tell you again that you were mistaken? Here is the proof I needed. Will you do me justice now?'

'Wait, madam,' growled the knight. Then to the man: 'What brings you here?' he demanded.

'I am tardily come, sir,' answered the other, 'but I could not come before. I—I was detained. Yet am I here now, and, it seems, still in time to do some good. I am come to tell you that it was I who robbed you of your hundred guineas, and not Sir Geoffrey Swayne, whom you have hanged for the deed. 'Tis said that I resemble him, and indeed it must be so since you swore to him as being the man who robbed you. 'Twas an unlucky thing for him that when I held him up he should have knocked me from my mare and bestridden her himself, for the mare was well known—and belike 'twas the mare convinced men so easily that he was "Scudding Tom". So much for the ways of justice!'

Sir Henry stared at him with fallen jaw, and his thoughts were far from pleasant. This fellow was indeed the very image of Sir Geoffrey, so like in figure, feature and in voice, that neither he nor the man's own wife could have sworn that he was not Sir Geoffrey himself, but for the unquestionable fact that Sir Geoffrey was hanged a week ago. The sight of that incredible likeness convinced him of the error there had been. The man he had hanged was the very counterpart of this one. Small blame to him, then, for having sworn away the other's life. Yet a sudden choler stirred the fat old knight, as much against himself for the life he had sworn away, as against this fellow for having been the cause of it.

He heaved himself to his feet, acting upon a sudden impulse. His neglected wig tumbled from his knee and lay on the ground beside the pieces of his shattered pipe, whilst its owner lurched across the room in the direction of the bell-rope.

'Whither away, Sir Henry?' came Sir Geoffrey's voice suavely; and, moved to look over his shoulder, the knight's progress was arrested, and his heavy underlip shuddered in affright against his teeth, for he was staring into a levelled pistol. 'I have not walked into the lion's maw without precautions, sir,' said he. 'I'll trouble you to sit.'

But the woman, who had been considering him with scrutinizing eyes, raised a hand and waved it imperiously to Sir Henry.

'Ring the bell, sir,' she bade him briskly.

'Madam,' smiled Sir Geoffrey, 'be not harsh with me. Besides, upon what charge would you have me taken?'

'Upon the charge of highway robbery,' thundered the knight. Nevertheless he sat down, as he was bidden. 'By your own confession, it was you who robbed me on Streatham Hill.'

'Bloodthirsty tyke,' returned the other. 'Have you not hanged one man already for that deed? Gads, my life, sir, you may not hang two men in England for one man's offence.'

Sir Henry considered him a moment, writhing under the insolence of the fellow's tone. 'Your resemblance to the late Sir Geoffrey is very thorough,' said he drily. 'It is little blame to me for my mistake. But if we have hanged one man for your robbery of me, yet there are counts enough besides, against you on which to hang you as well.'

'Maybe; but you'll drop the subject, or there'll be one count more—the death of Sir Henry Talbury.'

His lips smiled, but his tone was resolute, his eyes alert. Sir Henry, finding the subject as little to his own taste as it was objectionable to his visitor, dropped it there and then. Sir Geoffrey crossed to the door and turned the key.

'Sir,' said he, 'and you, madam—for Sir Geoffrey I am sorry, though the world has it he was a nasty rogue. But I am here to prove that, at least, he was not the thing for which they hanged him. He was no robber. Restitution must be made to his widow. I have his death upon my conscience. I'll not have more.'

'Why, there we are at one,' Sir Henry agreed. 'Since I have seen and heard you, it is my wish, no less than yours, that Lady Swayne should not suffer more than already she has done. Will you depose?'

'Let me have pen, ink and paper, and it shall be done at once.'

Sir Henry supplied his needs, and Sir Geoffrey sat down to write.

'You'll be so good as to sit there—as far from the bell as the width of the room will allow,' he bade the knight. 'Make an attempt to have me apprehended, and I shall take a look at the colour of your brains—if so be you have any.'

'Damme, you knave—'

'Peace, sir. Do you not see that I write?'

They left him to it, Sir Henry and Lady Swayne sitting silently in his presence, whilst his quill scratched its way across a sheet of paper, his pistol beside him on the table ready to his hand.

At last the confession that should save Sir Geoffrey's lands, now that it could no longer save his life, was accomplished. When it was done, he rose and went to ring the bell, then admitted the servant who answered the summons, and relocked the door when he was inside. In the presence of the magistrate, the lady, and the lackey, he swore to and signed his depositions, and they appended their signatures as witnesses. He emptied the sand-box over it, and, bowing to them, his bearing grave, his lips mocking, he strode off in the direction of the window by which he had entered. He paused, his hand upon the curtains, and looked back over his shoulder.

'Lady Swayne,' said he, 'I have done you some service this

night. Let your gratitude see to it that I may go my ways without fear of pursuit.'

She nodded her assurance. His roving eye smiled a moment on the knight.

'Good-night, old beer-barrel,' said he, and so leapt out into the darkness, and was gone.

Lady Swayne shivered a little, and, moving to the table, took up the paper he had written and studied it a while. The bewildered lackey unlocked the door and departed at a curt nod from his master. A thin smile parted the lips of the woman, it was almost as a faint reflection of the smile that had haunted Sir Geoffrey's face.

'Madam,' said Sir Henry, with a rough attempt either at seeking or at giving consolation, 'you'll bear me no deep ill-will for my error. I deplore it grievously. I shall ne'er forgive myself. And yet, madam, the estates shall remain yours—have no doubt of that; and if all they say be true, belike you'll enjoy them better alone than in Sir Geoffrey's company. He was no over-pleasant mate for any woman; a bullying, drunken, wife-beating scoundrel, who——'

'Sir,' she broke in, 'he was my husband. Will you be so good as to ring? I'll be departing now.'

It was a week before Sir Geoffrey found his way home to Guildford. He had tarried by the way until the last of Dr Blizzard's guineas was exhausted. One night, at last, he strode, as bold and debonair as ever, across the threshold of his home and bade a servant, who was new to him, to conduct him at once to Lady Swayne.

He stood in his wife's presence, the door closed; they two alone.

'Helen, my girl,' he cried—for on occasions he could be a very lover to the wife he had so often beaten—'you played your part bravely at Hurlingston. It is as much to you, sweetheart, as to myself that I owe this re-unition. I'm with you again, my girl; and if I may not safely live in England, we'll sell the old home and begin life anew in a new world.'

She let him say no more. She had risen, and was regarding him from under knitted brows, her lips compressed, her bosom heaving under its black satin bodice.

'Mr. Haynes,' said she, at last, 'have your wits deserted you?'

His jaw fell, the boldness left his air and glance. 'God 'a mercy!'

he gasped. 'Were you deluded too, then? Did you not recognize me? Helen, I am Geoffrey Swayne.'

'Go tell it to fools, man,' said she. 'Geoffrey Swayne was hanged at Tyburn, as all the world knows.'

'Aye, hanged was I, and yet I came to life again.'

'A likely story—such things are common happenings,' she smiled ironically.

He took a step forward, his brow black as thunder now. 'Madam,' he snarled, 'you are fooling me. You know me, yet will not own to me. Saw you not the writing of my depositions? Knew you not the hand? And if that were not enough to convince you, look you on this.' He thrust back the hair from his brow, revealing a long livid scar above the temple. But the sight of that identifying mark left her unmoved.

'Sir Geoffrey had just such another scar,' said she quietly. 'He came by it in this very room, one night when he was drunk. He had raised his whip to strike me, but lost his balance and fell, cracking his head against that hand-iron. Aye, your likeness to Sir Geoffrey is very amazing, yet are you not Sir Geoffrey,' she continued. 'You are Mr Haynes, known to the vulgar as "Scudding Tom", gentleman of the road, against whom there remains sufficient to hang you. Bear you that in mind,' she added impressively, 'nor push me too far, lest I forget my gratitude.'

He was upon her like a panther. He caught her wrist until it seemed he must snap it, all the blackguard in him risen like scum to the surface of his vile nature.

'Madam, you shall be whipped,' he promised her through his teeth. But the bell-rope was within her reach. Too late he sought to drag her from it. She had caught it in her free hand, and his dragging her sent a clanging peal reverberating through the house.

He let her go, and fell back quivering with rage, his face ashen. She recovered, and spoke coldly to him.

'Mr Haynes,' said she, 'I will forgive you this out of consideration for the service you have rendered me. I will even do more. You spoke just now of seeking your fortune in the New World. I counsel you to follow so excellent an intention. In England you go hourly in danger of capture, and "Scudding Tom" will unquestionably hang if he be taken.'

The door opened, and a servant stood before her. She bade him wait outside until she summoned him again. Then, to her husband, she continued:

'So follow my advice, and get you to America, as you proposed. In return for the service you did me by your depositions, I'll pay you half-yearly the sum of fifty pounds for life, so long as you remain out of England; and here you have your first six months' pension, which will enable you to get you beyond seas. Go now, and God be with you, and lead you into better ways of life. You have widowed me by your evil courses, and a widow I'm like to remain.' Her tone was full of a meaning he did not miss. He stared a moment, then his eyes moved to the roll of notes on the table before him, where she had placed them.

Fury had failed him; he sought to cajole.

'Helen, my girl,' he began. But the heart of the too-often beaten wife had been broken overlong ago to be still sensible to prayers of his.

'Robert!' she called, raising her voice, and instantly the servant reappeared. 'You will re-conduct this gentleman, and lend him a horse to ride to Bristol. Give you good-night, sir.'

With distorted features, Geoffrey Swayne turned to fling out of the room. But she called him back. 'You've forgotten something,' said she, and she pointed to the notes upon the table. A moment he looked at her almost furtively, a suggestion of crouching in his attitude, something akin to that of a hound that had been whipped. Then he took the notes and thrust them into his pocket.

In silence he went out of the room, and so out of her life.

The Bargain

MR HAWKESBY stirred in his great chair and, half awake, opened his eyes to blink at the fiery reflection of the evening sun, which glared at him from the glass of his tall, well-furnished bookcase. Incuriously he looked round to see what had disturbed his slumbers, then he leapt wideawake to his feet, so violently that a little shower of powder rained from his carefully dressed hair to settle upon the neck and shoulders of his velvet coat.

Leaning against the solid mahogany table, midway between the open window and the chair in which Mr Hawkesby had rested, stood a man, a stranger, in a suit of homespun the worse for wear, ragged stockings, and a pair of silver-buckled shoes all spattered with mud and dirt. Hawkesby's face paled, for nature had not made him overvaliant. His first thought was that he had to do with a thief—and a thief who knew what he was about, for in the handsome, inlaid secretaire yonder reposed a bag containing three hundred guineas—rents collected that morning by Mr Hawkesby's bailiff.

The stranger raised a hand in a mild gesture of supplication.

'I beg that you'll not be alarmed,' said he, his manner that of a gentleman. 'I'm no robber. You'll be Mr Hawkesby?'

'I am,' answered the man of the house, his voice sharp. 'How came you here?'

The stranger waved a white, slender hand, a hand at odd variance with his clothes, in the direction of the open window and the blossom-laden trees of the orchard beyond. 'That way,' he said.

'Oh, that way?' Mr Hawkesby mimicked him; for, seeing him so tame, his own courage was returning fast. 'And what may you be wanting with me, my man?'

The other left his position by the table, and took a step towards the young squire. Mr Hawkesby retreated towards the bell-rope.

'Keep your distance, my man,' said he, his tone less arrogant.

'Don't ring, Mr Hawkesby!' cried the other in a tone of such sudden alarm that Hawkesby paused, his fingers on the rope. 'I've come to ye for shelter. 'Tis a hunted man I am this day.'

'You're glib enough with my name,' said Hawkesby. 'What may yours be?'

'Look me in the face, sor, an' ye'll never need to ask,' answered the other with a smile that was between sorrow and jauntiness. Hawkesby looked as he was bidden, and he saw that the man wore his own hair, black as coal and tied in a queue, from which a few escaping strands had matted themselves about his brow. It was a fine, distinguished countenance, but Hawkesby was not aware that his eyes had ever encountered it before. He said so, and a whimsical smile lifted the corners of the intruder's close-lipped mouth.

'Black hair, black eyes,' he recited, 'arched eyebrows, hooked nose, thin lips, sallow complexion, a mole on the right of the chin, and a scar over the right temple'—he pushed back his matted hair, and showed a milk-white line—'stands five foot ten, and is of a slender shape. Have ye read that description nowhere of late, Mr Hawkesby?'

Hawkesby fell back a pace.

'Egad!' he exclaimed, and then again, 'Egad!'

'Just so,' said the Irishman, with a shrug.

'Then you're——'

'Miles O'Neill, your most obadient, Mr Hawkesby,' said the Irishman, making a leg.

In a quiver of apprehension, not of the man but of the things that might result from the man's presence, Hawkesby now approached his visitor.

'In Heaven's name, why are you here, Mr O'Neill?' quoth he, and his face was pale, his blue eyes wide with horror.

'I lay at Appleby last night—at Mr Robertson's,' said the fugitive. 'He tould me that should I need shelter farther south, I'd find it at your hands. I was for rachin' Lancashire, and I'd niver have throubled ye, but that from Orton hither I have been followed.'

'Followed?' cried Hawkesby in alarm. 'Followed hither? And by whom?'

'By a dhirty rogue who caught a glimpse of me as I was lavin' Orton. Shure, an' he dodged me footsteps ivery moile of the foive.

Half a moile from here I led him through a confusion of lanes, and
lost him. Glory be to God! There's a thousand guineas on my head,
but the earning of them'll not be his, the dhirty shpy.'

'How knew you this to be my house? How knew you me?'

'More by luck than controivance, faith! I was hidin' in the
orchard there, and seein' a window convaniently open, I bethought
me that beloike I'd find closer hiding-room within doors. By your
coat-of-arms over the fireplace yonder I saw that I'd found luck for
the first toime since I joined the Prince's banner.'

Hawkesby looked at him out of eyes that did not exactly beam
with welcome. He had contrived to keep the Tories in ignorance of
his connection with the Cause, for all that it might be a matter of
common knowledge in the ranks of Charlie Stuart's followers. His
had been but a half-hearted devotion, for he was by no means
a man of rash impulse. His head governed his heart always; it
governed it now, and he misliked the risk he might be running in
harbouring this notorious rebel.

Still, the man before him looked in sore need of aid. His face
was pale, and there were black lines beneath his eyes that lent
them a haggard look. In what sorry condition were his garments
we have already seen. Yet he bore himself with a certain jauntiness;
when he spoke of being hunted he did so with a devil-may-care
manner that should have earned him sympathy from a stone image.
Hawkesby was not altogether insensible to this, and he felt, too,
that he would be for ever shamed did he turn this fugitive out of
doors without more ado. So, however reluctant he may have been
at heart, outwardly at least he made a decent show of befriending
O'Neill. He invited him to rest in the great easy-chair, whilst he
went in quest of food and wine.

'For, I take it, you'll welcome refreshment, Mr O'Neill,' said he.

'It's little enough of it I've had since the shlaughter at Culloden,'
laughed the Irishman as he dropped into the great chair and
stretched his dusty legs luxuriously.

Hawkesby fetched him some cold pigeon-pie, a loaf, and a flask
of French wine, and, setting the things before him on a small
table, he bade his visitor fall to. O'Neill did so with a will, and
when he had eaten he turned a scornful eye upon the slender, lily-
shaped glass his host had set before him.

'Have ye no such thing as a bumper, now, about the house, Mr

Hawkesby?' quoth he. 'There's a health I'd be after dhrinkin' with all me heart.'

Hawkesby rose with a shrug of impatience to fetch the thing his guest craved. O'Neill filled it to the brim, and emptied it twice in brisk succession—thereby exhausting the flask. He drank first to Mr Hawkesby's long life, and next to the Duke of Cumberland's short shrift. Hawkesby fetched more wine—a brace of flasks this time. The rebel's eyes sparkled at sight of them.

''Tis a power of dust gets in your throat a-walkin',' said he. 'Aye, an' the weather's hot an' all. Here's long loife to ye agin, Mr Hawkesby.' And again was a bumper poured down that amazing gullet. 'Ye're not drinkin' yerself,' he expostulated, making himself mightily at home.

'If you'll pardon me,' said the other stiffly, 'it is not my habit of an afternoon.'

'By me sowl, ye should acquire it, thin,' was the laughing answer, and O'Neill emptied the second flagon into his tall glass. 'Ye're missin' a power of loife!'

Hawkesby sat himself on the arm of a chair, and craved news of the Prince.

'Where left you his Highness?' quoth he. 'Is he still in the heather, know you, or has he contrived to ship for France?'

But the question did no more than suggest a fresh toast to the rebel. He raised his glass to the light, and eyed the blood-red colour of the wine with a fond glance.

'Here's a health to his Hoighness, where'er he may be!' He drained his bumper. '*Super naculum!*', he laughed, as he turned it up, and made a bead on his thumbnail.

'You've a fine thirst, sir,' said Hawkesby a trifle tartly.

'An' it's yourself would have the same, bedad, if ye'd run with the Scots from Culloden. But it's an iligant wine,' he added politely as a further reason.

'The battle should never have been delivered as it was,' said Hawkesby, who, like many another, could criticize what he could never have had a hand in doing. 'The Prince should have fallen back behind Nairn Water.'

'Maybe,' quoth the Irishman pensively. 'But ye'll allow it's an ill thing to fall back on water or behind it.' And he reached for the wine, to add point to his meaning. 'I'll give ye the sow's tail to Geordie!' said he, and with that the flagon was emptied.

Hawkesby affected not to notice that again the wine was done, lest hospitality should force him to fetch more. A gallon of good French claret should be, he thought, enough for any man; and Hawkesby was careful by nature to the point of stinginess. Once more he sought to draw his guest into talking of the Cause, and he did so with moderate success for a little while. But presently O'Neill sank back in his chair and fetched a sigh.

'Shure, talkin's dhry work,' said he, and he held a flask to the light to make certain it was empty.

The hint was over-broad to be ignored. Hawkesby fetched another brace of bottles from his cellar, swearing to himself, however, that they should be the last. He was beginning to dislike his guest exceedingly. There were more toasts when he returned. If O'Neill had been half the fighter that he was the drinker, surely the side he fought for should have been victorious at Culloden. He pledged all manner of men and all manner of events; it was 'long loife' to this, and 'bad cess' to that, until his last bumper stood before him and he appeared at a loss for a subject. Indeed, there was by then an ominous flush on his cheek and a sparkle in his eye that had not been there when first he had clambered into Mr Hawkesby's room.

Hawkesby began mightily to fear for him now—and more for himself. Here was a plight! The man was a rebel with a thousand guineas on his head; he had been recognized and followed from Orton to this neighbourhood. What if he were to become too drunk to move, and so were to be found in Mr Hawkesby's house? He began to expostulate with his guest. He spoke of caution, and as politely as he could he suggested to O'Neill that there was danger for him in drinking as he was doing. He went so far even as to seek to remove the last bumper. But O'Neill's hands shot out at that sign of danger, and his fingers encircled the glass in a resolute clutch.

'Bedad!' he hiccoughed. 'The man was hanged that left his dhrink behind him.'

'I'm thinking, sir, that should the same fate overtake you it will not be from the same cause,' was Hawkesby's irritable answer. But the Irishman was not to be offended. He emptied his glass, and got unsteadily to his feet. His wits were surely all soaked in wine

by now, for he waved his hand in the air and broke suddenly
into song.

> It's Geordie he came up to town,
> Wi' a bunch o' turnips in his crown;
> Aha, quo' she, I'll pull them down,
> And turn my tail to Geordie!

'For Heaven's sake, sir!' gasped Hawkesby, in very real affright;
'You'll have the house about my ears. Silence, man, if you value
your life at a farthing! Are you not afraid?'

'Afraid?' roared O'Neill; and it almost seemed for a moment that
he was offended. Then he laughed aloud and long, and for answer
broke into another Jacobite ditty—

> O that's the thing that ne'er can be,
> For the man's unborn that'll daunton me!
> O set me once——

Abruptly his song ceased. His mouth remained opened—nay,
fell wider—and his eyes stared with a sudden look of horror past
his host at the window to which Hawkesby had his back. With a
premonition of what was afoot, Hawkesby swung round, then
stood, his face livid, scarce breathing in his affright.

Leaning on the sill of the open window was a man of swarthy
complexion, whose face was rendered villainous now by the leering grin with which he surveyed the room's occupants.

A three-cornered hat was set rakishly upon his loose, untidy
hair, and he wore a scarlet riding-coat of velvet, very soiled and
frayed, with tarnished gold lace and dirty, torn ruffles. Seeing
himself observed, he waited for no invitation to enter, but set his
hands upon the sill and vaulted lightly into the room. He was a
tall, powerfully built man, and he flourished a long, gleaming
pistol.

'Mr Hawkesby, your servant, sir,' he leered, with an ironical
bow. 'Mr O'Neill, your very humble servant.' And coolly stepping
aside he locked the door.

Hawkesby looked askance at O'Neill. The Irishman's knees had
been loosened, either from drink or from fright, and he had sunk
limply to a chair, where he sat staring foolishly at the intruder.

'Bedad!' he muttered at last in a thick voice. 'Ye're as persevering as a shpider. I t'ought I'd losht ye, me friend.' And as he spoke his hand went fumbling towards the breast of his coat. The bully's weapon came level with his brows.

'I'll trouble you to put that pistol on the table,' said he, with a snarl; and O'Neill sheepishly relinquished the weapon he was slyly drawing.

Hawkesby stepped to the bell. His was the courage of despair. He braced himself, and—

'What do you want, my man?' he demanded, with pretended firmness.

'Just your friend, Mr O'Neill, yonder,' said the fellow, with a grin. 'He's worth a thousand guineas to me.' Hawkesby laid a hand on the bell-rope. 'Oh, ring away, Mr Hawkesby; ring away!' the ruffian airily encouraged him. 'Fetch in your servants; fetch in the whole town to see how you shelter and befriend a rebel.'

Hawkesby's hand fell back to his side. The affair looked ugly. He turned to O'Neill to see how the rebel took matters, hoping in his heart that the fellow would surrender before more harm was done. But O'Neill made no shift to move. Instead, he was settling himself more comfortably in his chair. He eyed the spy with a from-head-to-foot glance of contempt.

'An' who the dickens may you be, me man?' quoth he.

'I'm a loyal subject of King George's.'

'Bedad, ye look it, sor,' answered O'Neill, as bold as brass; 'ye look it; and ye look, too—if one may judge by externals—as if there moight be a price on your own dhirty head.'

Hawkesby, watching the bully, saw the shot strike home. The fellow's eyes dropped uneasily, he shuffled where he stood, and there was a pause before he answered, still truculent, but with half the assurance gone out of him:

'You'll be leaving my affairs alone, and you'll be treating me respectfully. The constable'll be none too inquisitive if I hand over to him the notorious Mr O'Neill.'

'Maybe; but Mr O'Neill'll be after arousin' the conshtable's inquisitiveness,' said the rebel, with an ugly look. It was plain he saw the weak spot in his opponent's hide. Hawkesby was thinking briskly. An idea had come to him—an inspiration. He had ac-counted himself lost, for the sheriff would want to know where O'Neill had been captured, and the bully, not a doubt of it, would

inform him. He was cursing the hospitality he had extended to this
drunken fugitive; he had begrudged it when he saw how dear it
was like to cost him in wine; how much more, then, did miserly
Mr Hawkesby not begrudge it now that he saw how dear it was
like to cost him in good gold guineas?—for clearly this fellow must
be bought off. His voice, cold and precise, cut into the momentary
silence.

'It is quite clear,' said he to the spy, 'that you are in no condition
yourself to approach the constable. You'll need to go before the
sheriff, and there'll be awkward questions asked.'

'I'm no fool,' snapped the spy, 'and you'll not make me one.
They'll welcome me very cordially when I take them Mr O'Neill.
They'll not ask many questions—saving, perhaps, as to whereabouts I came upon him. Why, if they had a grievance against
me—which I'm not saying that they have—this day's work should
earn me a pardon.'

'That's as it may be,' sneered O'Neill.

'Just so; but you'll not alter it with talking.'

'I might alter it with something else,' interpolated Hawkesby, in
a tone that drew the brisk attention of the others. 'Listen to me,
now. If you yield up Mr O'Neill, and even if no questions are
asked concerning yourself, the Government's a mighty slow pay-
master. You may wait a long time for your thousand guineas.'

'True,' the man confessed.

'Will you strike a bargain with me, now? What'll you take,
money down?'

The fellow looked up, licking his lips—it was a lick of
anticipation.

'You speak me very fair,' said he, his head on one side, his
glance shifting from one to the other of the men. 'I'll take five
hundred guineas for my bargain.'

'Don't listen to the thafe!' said O'Neill contemptuously.

'You shall have a hundred,' was Hawkesby's answer.

The man laughed scornfully. 'You're jesting,' said he. 'Come,
now; say four hundred, and Mr O'Neill may go his ways for me.'

'One hundred,' repeated Hawkesby doggedly. It was in all conscience money enough to pay for having entertained O'Neill. More
he would not give, betide what might. But neither would the other
abate further. Seeing Hawkesby resolute:

'Come, Mr O'Neill,' said he at last, his pistol raised to enjoin obedience, 'we had best be moving.'

'Aye,' said O'Neill gloomily, 'I'm thinkin' we had. I'm much obliged to you, sor——' he began, turning to Hawkesby. But Hawkesby broke in excitedly:

'No, no! You must not go.'

'Well, well,' said the bully, 'you shall have him for three hundred guineas. Now that's reasonable. He's worth a thousand to any man. Three hundred guineas, money down, and he's yours.'

Hawkesby stood with his shoulders to the mantelshelf, his face very white, his lips very tight. He must clear himself from this position. His neck would certainly be stretched if O'Neill were taken in his house. Yet, three hundred guineas was a deal of money! And then the devil—or else something that the spy had said—breathed a wicked suggestion into his miserly soul.

'Three hundred guineas is all that I have by me,' said he, in a hard voice. 'Yet you shall have the money.' And thus the bargain was concluded, and Hawkesby took a heavy bag from the secretaire, where it was locked, and banged it on the table. The spy peered at the yellow contents, weighed it appreciatively in his hands.

'I'll take your word for the amount,' said he, and with a flourish of compliments he took his leave, and departed by the way he had come. Hawkesby, meanwhile, turned a deaf ear to O'Neill's warnings. At last, when the man had disappeared, the rebel leapt to his feet. In his excitement he seemed completely sobered.

'Mr Hawkesby,' said he, 'I'm eternally your debtor. Yet forgive me if I tell ye ye've done a mad thing.'

'How?' asked Hawkesby, his eyebrows going up and his hand toying idly with the pistol O'Neill had placed on the table when the spy had bidden him.

'In allowing that ruffian to depart with the money. You should have kept him here till I was gone. It is odds he'll go fetch the constable, and still seek to earn his thousand guineas.'

'Aye,' said Hawkesby, with a singular smile. 'It is odds he will.'

'Then, bedad, give me the pishtol, and let me after him before he's clear of the orchard.' And, making shift to go, O'Neill held out his hand for the weapon. Instead, the muzzle was presented at his head.

'Stand where you are, Mr O'Neill,' said Hawkesby, in a voice of steel. There was no timidity about him now. He was safe and brave behind his pistol. He backed across the room, the weapon levelled at the rebel, who eyed him with fallen jaw. For the third time in that afternoon Hawkesby's hand went to the bell-rope. This time his fingers closed upon it, and peal after peal went reverberating through the house.

'What are ye doin'?' gasped O'Neill.

Hawkesby showed his teeth in a ghastly smile, his face livid.

'Mr O'Neill,' said he, and his voice was crisp and cold, 'if that ruffian fetches the constable, he'll be too late. You heard what he said. You are worth a thousand guineas to any man. You are worth that sum to me. I've bought you, and I'm—going to sell you again. I've driven a shrewd bargain in you.'

The rebel stared at him a moment, unbelief in his face. Then he drew himself up, the last vestige of his drunkenness departed, and a singular smile—a mocking, cynical, yet exultant, smile—upon his hawk face.

'So that is your loyalty to the Cause; that your devotion to the Prince?' said he. 'Bedad! If ever Charlie comes to his own he shall hear of this. But since it's so—why I'm glad it's so. You are mighty well served, Mr Judas Iscariot Hawkesby; three hundred guineas is a mort of money to lose over any man.'

'It's hardly lost,' sneered Hawkesby. Then, as O'Neill moved to the window, 'Stand, or I fire!' he shouted.

'Foire, and be hanged,' said O'Neill. And Hawkesby, angered and desperately afraid of losing his prey, fired one barrel after the other. But the only sound that broke the stillness of the room was the click of the hammer on the empty pan and O'Neill's soft contemptuous laugh. The pistol was not loaded.

There came a sound of feet, and a knocking at the door.

With a last laugh O'Neill dropped from the sill and sped through the orchard like a hare, to vanish in the twilight. Hawkesby, shaking in every limb with the fear that had come upon him born of an awful thought that had arisen in his mind, sprang to open. In flowed a stream of servants, and after them, walking briskly, stained with dust, came Mr Robertson of Appleby. At sight of him, Hawkesby checked the words that were on his lips. He caught his visitor by the lapel of his coat and drew him aside. His habit of caution was with him now, excited though he was.

'Did Miles O'Neill lie at your house last night?' he whispered.

Robertson stared at him a moment. 'No,' said he at last; 'but it is odd you should ask, for I came to tell you that Miles O'Neill was taken last night at Penrith. I heard of it this morning.'

'I have been robbed!' screamed Hawkesby. 'Robbed of three hundred guineas.'

They saw the disorder of the room, with its strewn flagons, and they opined him drunk. By the time he had convinced them he was sober it must have been too late, for his ingenious visitors were never taken.

The Opportunist

TO follow the early career of Capoulade down its easy descent of the slopes of turpitude were depressing and unprofitable. He had reached the stage at which he pocketed his pride and—like the adaptable opportunist that he was—passed from the artistic plane of swindling to the clumsier methods of purse-cutting and housebreaking. The pursuit of the latter brought him one night into the domicile of Monsieur Louvel.

Old Louvel was a man of fortune and the owner of an unique collection of old Italian jewels, and this was the lure that attracted Capoulade. Did rumour prove well founded he hoped to derive enough profit from this night's work to enable him to lead, here-after, a life of ease and honesty in some foreign land; for Capoulade was disposed enough to be honest once it should cease to be worth his while to be dishonest.

He stood in Louvel's room at dead midnight, facing the press which he had been at considerable preliminary pains to ascertain was the repository of the treasure that was to make him honest—a treasure useless to Louvel, a mere hoard of artistic miserliness. Six steps across the room; twenty seconds to cut a panel; five minutes to secure the booty and make good his retreat—that was all that he now asked of Fortune to the end that his salvation might be wrought. Yet niggardly Fortune denied him even that little.

For even as he took his first steps towards the press a loud knock fell upon the street door. It reverberated through the silent house, it found an echo in Capoulade's heart, and sent an icy chill through the marrow of his spine.

The knocking was repeated, vigorous and insistently; and Capoulade groaned to reflect how soundly they must sleep, how fine and rare the opportunity that was being ruined for him.

Then came other sounds—shuffling steps of slippered feet de-scended the stairs; the street door was opened. Voices sounded awhile, then the slippered feet reascended, accompanied now by a heavy, booted tread.

Physically Capoulade was a coward, but morally he possessed the courage of ten men. So averse was he from going empty-handed from that treasure-chamber that he decided at all costs—despite his thudding heart and chattering teeth—to remain until this newcomer should have gone either to bed or back to the streets from which he had been so inopportunely admitted.

A moment later he repented this decision in a passion of alarm. The steps were approaching the very room in which he stood. A shaft of light entered under the closed doors and thrust out along the gleaming parquet to Capoulade's feet. Swift and silent as a shadow, he crossed to where a curtain masked an alcove, and there he hid himself, prayers on his lips and a knife in his hand, desperate and vicious as a cornered rat.

The door opened, and old Louvel, in nightcap and white quilted dressing-gown, advanced, candle in hand. He was followed by a tall, showily dressed young gentleman, Theodore Louvel, his son, who filled in Lyons the high office of agent to M. Turgot, the Comptroller-General.

In silence the old man crossed to the press, unlocked the double doors and threw them wide.

'There,' he exclaimed, anger quivering in his voice, 'let the evidence of your own eyes satisfy you.'

He held the candle aloft, so that its light shone upon rows of shelves—all empty.

His son took a step forward, staring. From behind his curtain Capoulade stared, too, in amazement and chagrin.

'But what does it mean?' cried Theodore at last. 'What, then, has become of the treasure?'

There was a dry, contemptuous laugh from his father.

'Ask yourself rather than me,' he croaked. 'You have not by any chance kept an account of the sums of which you have drained me in the last two years? When I remonstrated with you, you laughed. When I sought to restrain you by refusing you the money which you demanded, then, like a dutiful son, you threatened my life. Thus, you said, you should inherit that which I withheld.'

He turned his vulture face upon his son, and a smile of mockery, ineffably bitter, twisted his lipless mouth.

'I have given you the rope you needed, and you have hanged yourself. In two years you have had from me five hundred thousand livres—and all is gone. I sold my treasures little by little, and there is nothing left.'

'I'll not believe it!' cried Theodore.

Louvel shrugged his narrow shoulders.

'Believe it or not, it is true. There is nothing for you. You may kill me now, if you will. I have seen to it that my death, at least, shall not profit you.'

With black, scowling brows Theodore faced his father, pondering him as if he would read the mind behind that cynical old mask.

'It is a lie!' he said at last, between his teeth. 'How do you live if you have nothing—eh? Answer me that.'

The old man leisurely closed the press and placed the candle on the table.

'You would, perhaps, deprive me of the little I have retained to ensure me from perishing of hunger?'

'Ah! You confess, then, that all is not as you represent it?' was the quick retort. 'You can save me from this ruin that impends— and save me you shall—you must! Do you hear? You must!'

'You had better kill me, and take what you can find,' the old man mocked him. 'I would as soon perish by your hand as starve. The deed, too, would set a fitting climax to our relations.'

'Will you not understand that it is but a loan that I require?'

'It has always been a loan.'

'This time I will repay—I swear it.'

'You swear it? *Farceur!* Out of your beggarly salary from the Comptroller-General?'

Theodore took a turn in the room, his face as white as his powdered hair, his eyes anxious. At length he paused.

'It is but ten thousand livres I need, and it is the price of my salvation from ruin and shame.'

'So has it always been,' sneered his father.

'But I will repay you, I say!' was the vehement, almost frenzied answer. He plucked a paper from his pocket. 'Listen!' he insisted. 'You are acquainted with Madame Lobreau?'

There was nobody in Lyons to whom that lady's name was not familiar. Under years of her capable management the Grand

Theatre of Lyons had been raised from a mere puppet-show until it might have rivalled the most brilliant playhouses of the capital, not excepting the famous Comédie Française.

'Do you propose to murder her in her bed and steal her jewels?' Theodore swore furiously under the spur of this sarcasm.

'Will you listen to me seriously?' he demanded. 'This lady holds her managerial privilege from the Comptroller-General, in whose power it lies to deprive her of her theatre. I am the Comptroller's agent in Lyons, and it lies within my power to dispossess her. Now, it has occurred to a certain Monsieur de Noirmont that, considering the handsome yields of the Grand Theatre, it should be worth his while to deal liberally with me to the end that I might enable him to step into Madame Lobreau's shoes. I trust I have made myself clear?'

'Yes, yes.'

Old Louvel was always ready to be interested in schemes that promised profit. The proposal to dispossess Madame Lobreau of the fruits of her labour and talent was a rascally one. But at heart old Louvel himself was a rascal, worthy father of his worthless son.

'Then listen to this,' rejoined Theodore. He unfolded his paper and read aloud:

In consideration of the Grand Theatre of Lyons being placed under my control and management, I hereby agree to pay the Sieur Theodore Louvel the sum of 10,000 livres, and further to allow him an annuity of 8,000 livres for as long as the said Grand Theatre shall continue under my management.   HENRI DE NOIRMONT

Old Louvel, who had stood hand on ear while his son read the agreement, pursed his lips like one in thought.

'Let me see it,' he requested. His son delivered him the paper, and the old man examined it, assuring himself of its genuineness. Then he pondered again.

'Very well,' he said slowly at last. 'You shall have the ten thousand livres by tomorrow evening as a loan, but this agreement remains in my hands as security until I am repaid.'

Theodore protested blusteringly. But his father held so stubbornly to the condition that the Comptroller's agent was forced in the end to submit.

'But I must have the money early in the morning. Monsieur—er—the man in whose debt I stand has given me until noon tomorrow to find the money.'

'If by noon tomorrow Madame Lobreau is no longer manager of the Grand Theatre the money will be at your disposal. Tell me,' he added, 'how soon may I expect to be repaid?'

'I shall place M. de Noirmont in possession of the theatre in a fortnight. I dare not do it sooner, for the sake of appearances.'

'Very well.'

The old man locked away the document in a secretaire, took up the candle, and re-conducted his son.

After Capoulade had heard the street door close upon the departing Theodore and the old man mount the stairs on his way back to bed, he crept out of his alcove.

His feelings were those of a man who has been swindled. He had come there at the peril of life and limb to possess himself of old Louvel's collection of Italian gems, only to learn that these had already been sold to pay the gaming debts of that villain Theodore. He was naturally indignant.

He advanced moodily towards the window and opened it with caution. He paused in the act of bestriding the sill, and chuckled softly at his own inspiration. He took the night into his confidence.

'To make opportunity your slave is the whole philosophy of life,' he said.

Next morning he waited upon Madame Lobreau at her residence, representing himself as an actor fallen upon evil days.

'You are come,' she greeted him, offering him a chair, 'to seek my help. Hélas, monsieur, you come too late!'

'Madame,' loftily answered that tatterdemalion, 'you are entirely at fault.' He sat down with the air of one who has the right to do so. 'I do not come to seek your aid, but to offer you mine.'

He stemmed her questions with a gesture which—were he the actor he had announced himself—might have made his fortune as *Sganarelle*. No man was ever more sensitive to his surroundings than Capoulade, and already he was saturated by the theatrical atmosphere in which he found himself.

'Madame,' he announced dramatically, 'you have been dispossessed of your theatre.'

'Is it known already?' she exclaimed.

'Not to the world at large. But to me—Capoulade—even the very reason of it is known.'

'Monsieur,' she protested, bridling, 'I have heard enough and more of these trumped-up reasons. A cruel, an infamous swindle has been perpetrated to rob me of my rights—the rights earned by years of labour.'

'Adversity, madame, is blunting the edge of your judgement.'

And in lordly gesture he waved the dirty ruffles that hung like weeping willows over his dirtier hands.

'The reasons known to me are not the lying, trumped-up reasons expressed to you and to be laid before the Comptroller-General by your enemies. The reasons that I bring you are the real ones.'

And he proceeded to disclose to her the infamous compact existing between Louvel and a certain M. de Noirmont.

Madame Lobreau went white and red by turns as she listened.

'But yes,' she cried. 'It is no more than I might have suspected. You convince me that it is the truth. If we could but lay proof of it before the Comptroller-General, how I should trample upon those that would ruin me!'

Capoulade launched his thunderbolt.

'Madame,' said he, pulling a paper from his pocket, 'the proof is here. Listen to the agreement signed by Monsieur de Noirmont.'

She heard it in amazement, and, what time he was reading the terms of that scandalous contract, subconsciously she was taking stock of him, and neither his shabby raiment nor his keen, wolfish face was of a quality to inspire her with confidence.

'Monsieur,' she asked him, when he had finished reading, 'how does it happen that you are in possession of this document?'

He looked at her out of his keen black eyes, scenting the suspicion that was awake in her. He wisely deemed it a time for frankness.

'Madame,' said he, 'I am here to serve you—that is my guarantee that you will not betray me. I am not exactly an actor. Such parts as in my time I have played have been played upon that broad stage we call the world. In short, madame'—and he dropped his eyes in a delicate assumption of shame—'I am just a thief.'

'And you stole this paper from M. Louvel?' she asked.

He bowed.

'It occurred to me that by appropriating it I might at once perform a worthy action and compensate myself for my trouble.'

'But how compensate yourself?' she enquired, knitting her brows.

Capoulade explained that such a document should not be without its marketable value. She agreed, and offered to purchase it for a *louis d'or*. Capoulade gasped.

'Twenty francs, madame?' Then he laughed. 'Perhaps it has not occurred to you that I might easily get a thousand times that sum from M. Louvel.'

'Then in your own interests you had best take it to M. Louvel,' was the uncompromising answer.

Capoulade rose with great dignity.

'I am an honourable man, madame,' he informed her, 'and I prefer to be on the side of honour. Therefore I come to you, for I should prefer to deal with you.'

'But if you find me unreasonable you would no longer scruple to go to M. Louvel?'

'I should scruple, madame, but I should go,' said Capoulade.

Thereafter they bargained for the best part of an hour, the negotiations being protracted by madame's mistrust of Capoulade. It was not until he rose to leave her that she made up her mind.

'Very well, sir,' she said. 'You shall have a thousand livres; five hundred now in exchange for that document, and my note of hand for the other five hundred, payable when I am once again in possession of the theatre.'

Capoulade considered.

'If I agree, madame,' he asked, 'how do you propose to act?'

'Why, I shall go straight to Paris and place the matter before the Comptroller-General.'

'You might bungle the affair,' he objected, 'in which case I should lose five hundred livres. I insist, madame, upon accompanying you, and you must consent to be guided by my advice.'

She made some demur at first, but ended by agreeing, reflecting that his advice might, after all, be useful.

Madame Lobreau took a post-chaise that very evening, and, accompanied by Capoulade, now in a suit of black and looking almost respectable, she set out for Paris.

She possessed some little influence, and by exerting it she

obtained, three days later, an interview with M. Turgot, the Comptroller-General. Accompanied ever by Capoulade, she was ushered into the great man's room in the Tuileries.

There, for once in his life, the little rogue was rather out of countenance. He was overawed by the splendour of his surroundings, and not a little scared by the elegant man with the weary face and wide-set eyes who sat at the ormolu-encrusted writing-table.

'I am come to tell you, monsieur, that your agent in Lyons is a rogue,' was madame's uncompromising opening. 'He abuses the authority which you have vested in him by selling appointments for his own profit.'

Now, it happened that Monsieur Turgot placed the utmost confidence in Louvel. He flashed his searching glance upon the pair, and Capoulade shivered.

'You allude, madame, to the revocation of your licence for the Lyons theatre,' said the Comptroller in a voice that was as weary as his countenance. 'My agent gives the soundest reason for the step, which I approve whilst deploring its necessity.'

Madame breathed gustily.

'May one enquire your agent's reason, monsieur?'

Monsieur took up a paper.

'Amongst others, madame, he finds that a class of play is being encouraged in which the new and unhealthy doctrines of the rights of man, and the like, are being exploited.'

'But, monsieur, that is utterly false.'

'I must prefer my agent's judgement,' said that composed and weary gentleman.

Madame gasped as if for breath. Then:

'If I can lay proof before you, monsieur, that Louvel has dispossessed me so that he may earn a bribe, what then, monsieur?'

'Such an abuse of authority shall be punished.'

'Good,' said madame, with satisfaction. 'Will you give yourself the trouble to read this?'

And she produced Capoulade's document.

Monsieur Turgot perused it with frowning eyes. He turned it about in his fingers.

'You pretend that this is genuine?' he said contemptuously.

'Certainly, monsieur,' snapped Capoulade.

The Comptroller's eyes were levelled upon him for a moment.

'Who is this?' he enquired.

'My secretary, monsieur,' replied madame.

'Ah! And how does this document, if genuine, come to be in your hands?'

Again it was Capoulade who interposed.

'It—it was—procured, monsieur.'

'Procured, was it? Now listen to me, both of you. In view of your categorical accusation of Monsieur Louvel, I shall summon him to Paris. If he prove guilty he shall be fitly punished and your theatre shall be restored to you. But if, as I suspect, this document is a forgery, then the law shall deal with you both, and rigorously.'

Madame Lobreau was assailed by momentary panic, partly allayed, however, by Capoulade's show of confidence.

'Sir,' he said, 'may I, in the interests of justice, venture upon a suggestion?'

'In the interests of justice all suggestions are welcome,' replied M. Turgot sardonically.

Capoulade bowed.

'Then, monsieur, I would very respectfully submit to your consideration that not Monsieur Louvel's word but only the subsequent events themselves can prove whether this document is true or false, and I would suggest, again very respectfully, that you allow the events to speak.'

M. Turgot frowned thoughtfully.

'And how long do you suggest that the matter should lie in this suspense?' he asked.

'A fortnight, monsieur, should prove long enough,' said Capoulade.

The Comptroller pondered the matter yet a moment.

'Be it so,' he said, and upon that dismissed them.

The fortnight that ensued was for Madame Lobreau a period of considerable anxiety, which not all Capoulade's assurances sufficed to allay. When, at the end of it, there came a summons from Monsieur Turgot, that anxiety was converted into positive alarm. She obeyed it, nevertheless, and Capoulade went with her to the Tuileries once more.

Monsieur Turgot was very grave, and his manner less weary and sardonic than when last they had seen him.

'Madame,' he announced, 'I have here a letter from my Lyons agent, Theodore Louvel—a letter received five days ago—in which

he announces to me that he has found in a certain Monsieur
Noirmont your successor at the Grand Theatre.'

'Ah!' said Capoulade.

'Immediately upon receiving it I desired Monsieur Louvel to
wait upon me. I judge no man unheard. He has just arrived, and is
awaiting audience. I deemed it well that you should be present at
the interview.'

Nervously madame expressed her gratitude. Capoulade trembled
a little.

Theodore Louvel was introduced—raffishly elegant and impud-
ently at ease, no whit discouraged by the presence of Madame
Lobreau, though guessing she was there as a plaintiff.

'A complaint has been lodged against you, monsieur,' said the
Comptroller, when Louvel had made his bow and his compliments. 'It is alleged by Madame Lobreau that the reasons you
urged for dispossessing her of the theatre are ill-founded.'

Theodore smiled deprecatingly.

'Of course, monsieur, but I can affirm that I had no interests to
serve other than those of his Majesty.'

'Naturally,' said Monsieur Turgot. 'And yet madame goes so far
as to say that you were bribed by M. Noirmont.'

'That,' replied Theodore, 'is an obvious calumny.'

'True,' said Monsieur Turgot. 'And yet madame's story is oddly
circumstantial. She can even tell me the sum paid by this Noirmont. It was, she says, ten thousand livres.'

Louvel's aplomb fell from him for a moment. He stood chap-
fallen, and his colour changed. But his recovery was swift. He
repudiated the charge with all the heat of offended virtue.

'Look at this, monsieur,' said the Comptroller, 'and tell me if
you have ever seen it before.'

He held out the document which Capoulade had sold to Madame
Lobreau.

Louvel took it nervously, but as he scanned it he recovered his
composure. He almost laughed when he placed it on the Comptroller's writing-table.

'An impudent and an obvious forgery, monsieur. Noirmont's
very name is misspelt.'

'Yet,' was the slow answer, 'this document, if forged, as you say,
is oddly prophetic. It has been in my hands a fortnight—a fortnight, do you understand? Can you explain how it came to foretell

so accurately the name of the man to whom the control of the Lyons theatre has since been granted by you?'

'Why—why——' faltered Louvel; and there he paused, staring in dismay at the smiling Comptroller. He was utterly bewildered—utterly without answer to so incredible a statement. 'But that is not possible, monsieur,' he cried out at last.

'I tell you that it is so, monsieur. You cannot explain the circumstances, eh? It is at once mysterious and convincing—a remarkable combination. Be good enough to wait in the ante-room, Louvel. We shall talk of this again.'

The dumbfoundered agent stumbled blindly out of the room in the wake of the servant summoned by M. Turgot. Then for some moments the Comptroller wrote rapidly, watched in silence by Madame Lobreau and Capoulade.

'There, madame,' he said at last, 'is an order to my new agent in Lyons to restore you possession of your theatre. In all the circumstances I will ask no questions about this document you brought me. I confess that I am curious, but if I knew all perhaps my duty would not permit me to deal with you as generously as I desire to deal.'

Bewildered, but clear, at least, upon the all-important fact that she was once more in possession of her theatre, Madame Lobreau expressed her thanks and took her leave.

'What did he mean?' she asked Capoulade when they were outside the palace.

Capoulade grinned. In his immense relief he was proud of his exploit.

'Why, you see, Louvel was right,' he confessed. 'You see, that document—*enfin*, I wrote it as well as I could from memory, after hearing Monsieur Theodore read it to his father. I am afraid my spelling——'

'You wrote it?' Her voice became shrill. At last she understood. 'Then it was a forgery. Why, you have swindled me.'

'Ah, no, madame. I undertook that your theatre should be restored to you, and I have your note of hand for five hundred livres payable when that shall be accomplished. It is accomplished, madame. But,' he added, as an afterthought, 'I must improve my spelling.'

The Plague of Ghosts

CAPOULADE had made the discovery that honesty is the best policy. He was in hiding in an alley near the Carousel at the time, and in hourly expectation of capture and harsh treatment as an anti-climax to his three years' career of ingenious and successful crime.

He was persuaded that from this Paris, to which an evil hour had brought him, there could be no escape, for he was well-informed that M. de Sartines' ubiquitous agents were diligently seeking him. So he set his wits to work, and resolved upon a course whose boldness would have appalled a stouter but less ingenious spirit. If he would find safety he must look for it under the very wing of the Minister of Police. Such was the resolve he took. Dishonesty, he realized, was stale, it was failing him in his adversity, and he would mark his scorn of that fair-weather friend by abandoning its pursuit, and ranging himself hereafter on the side of law and order—always provided that M. de Sartines should prove the astute opportunist he was reputed.

The brilliant notion once conceived, he was not the man to delay its execution. The same spring day, whose waking hours had been devoted to its conception, saw him, towards noon, in the ante-chamber of the famous Minister. Thus far he had penetrated without hindrance, and he now sent M. de Sartines a message to the effect that a certain M. Quélaure, whose acquaintance with criminal methods was vast, sought to place his services at the Lieutenant-General's disposal.

From the ante-chamber to the chamber is but a step; yet it was the one step in his journey from the Carousel to the presence of M. de Sartines which Capoulade had expected to find fraught with difficulty. Instead, he found it astonishingly, discomposingly, easy. He had not been waiting more than a few moments when an usher approached him with the message that M. de Sartines would see him at once.

He took a deep breath, like a man about to plunge into deep waters, and he might have been observed to pale a little. Here was the situation he had boldly sought: yet, despite his unparalleled effrontery, he did not relish it now that it had arrived. The notion which had seemed a finely daring one two hours ago, seemed now incalculably rash, and he found himself wishing that he had given it longer consideration before so recklessly proceeding to act upon it.

Thus, feeling very much as the fly may have felt after it had accepted the spider's invitation to walk into its parlour, he stepped into the famous policeman's office. At a littered writing-table he beheld a richly apparelled gentleman, in the prime of life, with a hooked nose and a pair of eyes grey and wide-set that were submitting him to an undisguised and searching scrutiny.

'Monsieur Capoulade,' said that gentleman, in the most affable voice in the world, 'I have been expecting you for some days, although I had not presumed to hope that you would do me the honour of a spontaneous visit.'

Capoulade felt his knees sinking under him, as many another criminal had done in the presence of that dread man from whom nothing seemed concealed. 'Monsieur—' he gasped, and there he stopped, his cheeks blanched and his ferrety eyes as wide as he could make them. What, indeed, remained for him to say? Sartines laughed musically.

'You are surprised that I should know you?' murmured the Minister, with a lift of the eyebrows, and it flashed through the little rascal's mind that if ever he had need of effrontery, he had need of it now.

His aplomb returned. 'Immensely flattered,' he answered, with a bow.

Sartines' smile broadened. He liked self-possession, accounting it one of the qualities that make for worldly success.

'I understand from your message—although you sent it under a *nom de guerre*—that you are seeking service with me, and that you suggest that your acquaintance with criminal methods should render you a valuable agent?'

'Yes, monsieur,' answered Capoulade, a world of mingled hope and despair in his mind. 'I am sick of crime, and I have a mind not only to be honest, but to make war upon the dishonesty of others.'

Sartines settled himself comfortably in his chair, and for ten minutes Capoulade could make nothing of the conversation that ensued, which was now serious, now rallying on the Minister's part. Suddenly the Lieutenant-General asked a question.

'Monsieur Capoulade, are you interested in ghosts?'

Capoulade's eyes dilated slightly.

'Monsieur, I have never met one.'

'I can afford you the opportunity,' was the Minister's calm reply. 'If you care to avail yourself of it, I have employment for you, if not—there is always the Châtelet.'

Capoulade shuddered, and moistened his lips.

'I should have preferred, monsieur, that you could have entrusted me with some affair in which I should have to deal with ordinary mortals; but if you give me to choose between the Châtelet and the ghost, why, then, I must take the ghost.'

'Then it is settled. My information is that the Château de la Blanchette, in Maine, is infested by a plague of ghosts. You should be acquainted with the place, for I understand that you burgled it six months ago.'

'I knew nothing of the ghosts, or I should have hesitated,' rejoined Capoulade, with an effrontery that provoked a smile from Sartines.

'You know now,' said the Minister, 'and if you are anxious for an affair with ordinary mortals, you shall have that as well. A deal of spurious silver is circulating in Maine at present, and my agents trace its source to the town of La Blanchette. Since you are going there to rid the Château of its plague of ghosts, I will further entrust it to you to rid me the town of this plague of coiners. I should not be surprised if the elucidation of one mystery affords the explanation of the other. Former agents of mine have failed over this same task. To you shall belong the honour of succeeding. I may take it that you accept?'

Sartines was justified of his assumption, for poor Capoulade was between the sword and the wall, and must be content with any terms that were offered him. And so, entrusted with this double mission, he left Paris for Maine that very afternoon.

He travelled by post without incident as far as Chartres; and here his luck came signally to his assistance, thrusting him into conversation with a neighbour who had joined the coach at the post-house of that city. In itself this was a trivial matter, a daily happening among travellers; but in Capoulade's case it had this much of interest that ere they had been acquainted an hour the conversation between them had turned upon the supernatural. It was this new travelling-companion—a healthy, hearty, rubicund fellow, of some forty summers—who had introduced the subject. And Capoulade had not allowed it to be lightly thrust aside by other topics. Ghosts were concerning him very closely just then, and he was of a mind to discover all that he could concerning their habits. His companion seemed no less anxious to pursue the subject, with the consequence that Capoulade had presently mastered the facts—surprising by virtue of the coincidence they covered— that his name was Coupri, that he was the intendant of the Sieur de la Blanchette, and that he was on his way to the Château de La Blanchette to investigate a matter of supernatural apparitions with which the place was said to be plagued.

'Nobody has resided at the Château for the past five years with the exception of a Monsieur Flaumel and his son, who are acting as stewards. They are honest fellows both, and the estate has thriven under their rule, of which they render my master a six-monthly account. Of the ghosts they know nothing, and refuse to believe in their existence. But six months ago M. de la Blanchette's two children went down there with a nurse, intending to remain for the vintage. Three nights was all they could endure, and they were obliged to return to Paris lest the children's minds should suffer from the terrors to which they were nightly submitted. A month ago Madame de la Blanchette, herself, accompanied by a maid, went to Maine in consequence of her doctor having ordered her a few weeks in the country. She slept at La Blanchette one single night, and returned to Paris next morning, vowing that nothing would ever cause her to set foot again across that accursed threshold. It is in consequence of this that my master is sending me down to see what I can discover.'

Capoulade looked at his stolid, merry face, and envied the man his courage. 'You are not—not afraid?' he suggested.

'Afraid?' roared the other. 'Fichtre! I am taking a brace of pistols to bed with me. I promise you I shall solve this mystery.'

Capoulade sidled closer to him. Here, indeed, was the very comrade he needed. He put on a sober, mysterious air.

'I perceive that you are sceptical,' said he, a note of reproof in his voice 'It is a dangerous attitude in which to approach the supernatural. Your patience, monsieur,' he cried, waving aside the other's threatened interruption. 'You are referring to matters of which my knowledge may be more extensive than your own. I am an investigator of the supernatural.'

'A what?' exclaimed Coupri, making of his companion a closer scrutiny than hitherto. There was about Capoulade, with his unpowdered black hair tied in a stiff queue, and his keen, sallow, almost wolfish face, an air that lent colour to his amazing statement.

'I am an investigator of the supernatural,' he repeated. 'I have made it the subject of some profound researches, which have taught me, at least, that it is an ill thing to approach such a task as yours in the spirit of mockery by which I deplore to see you actuated.'

Some of the high colour left Coupri's healthy cheeks.

'But, name of a name, monsieur!' he gasped, 'am I to understand that you believe—that your studies have made you a believer in such things?'

'A staunch believer,' said the rogue impressively, 'convinced against my will, converted by mortal terror from such unbelief as is inspiring you to make a jest of the matter. Your pistols are very well, my friend, if there is chicanery at work—and, indeed, I do not say that there is not. But such weapons will prove of little avail if it should be a question of—of the impalpable.'

In Coupri's eyes the matter of the ghosts of La Blanchette began to assume formidable proportions. He sat glum and silent for a moment; then he laughed, to convince himself that it was a laughing matter.

'Bah!' he scorned. 'All may be as you say; but at La Blanchette I am convinced that there is nothing but trickery, and I shall deal with it with powder and lead. They will prove great exorcizers.'

But despite this outward fanfaronade his mind was grown uneasy, and of this Capoulade was quick to detect the signs on the fellow's honest countenance.

'Monsieur,' said he, speaking very seriously, 'if I were not afraid of presuming upon our slight but interesting acquaintance'—here he bowed to his companion—'I would suggest that you take me with you to La Blanchette. You might find the fruits of my studies of service.'

He had timed his proposal excellently, and it was pounced upon with flattering eagerness by his fellow-traveller. 'Together,' ended the honest Coupri, 'we cannot fail to solve the mystery, I with my natural weapons if the ghosts be flesh, you with your supernatural ones if they be spirits.'

Thus was the matter arranged between them, and Capoulade concluded from the adroitness with which he had worked to the end he desired, that M. de Sartines might congratulate himself upon his new agent.

They arrived at La Blanchette on the morrow, and Coupri made no secret of the business that had brought him, presenting Capoulade to the elder Flaumel as a fellow-servant who had been chosen to accompany him.

Flaumel frankly laughed at them.

'Come now,' said he, with scornful amusement, 'to what old wives' tale has the sieur been listening? There are no ghosts at La Blanchette. Jacques and I have dwelt here these ten years, and never sound or sight of them has disturbed our slumbers. A night, a couple of nights at the most, will convince you, mon cher.'

'Madame de la Blanchette has ordered us not to stir from the château until I can present her with some explanation of these disturbances. I hope the ghosts will take an early opportunity of manifesting themselves, or my stay may be protracted. The sieur wishes to make holiday here with madame. He considers that it is time he occupied this château of his. But madame refuses to accompany him until the mystery has been cleared up.'

Flaumel shrugged his narrow shoulders.

'My explanation—the only explanation,' said he, 'is that madame had the *migraine* when she was here.'

'But what of the nurse and the children?' cried Coupri.

'Pish!' he sneered. 'The nurse was no doubt frightening them with some ghost stories, and succeeded in frightening herself as well. The sleeping apartments are gloomy enough for the rest.'

And with fresh expressions of his scorn, the old steward passed on to other matters and asked for news of the sieur. Capoulade had been scrutinizing him closely, but had seen in his demeanour nothing to excite suspicion. Besides, why should the fellow have set himself wantonly to frighten women and children—assuming that he had a hand in the apparitions?

He was a slender man, whose countenance had been mellowed by age into a set of benignity, oddly contrasting with the villainous countenance of his son Jacques. Capoulade looked at the younger Flaumel's low forehead, flat nose, and eyebrows between which there was no division, and mentally pronounced him a knave to be watched.

He spent the remainder of the day roaming the grounds, where all was green with the fresh, pale green of spring, and Coupri went with him, but talked little. They supped with the two Flaumels—there was no woman at La Blanchette—and when they had supped, it was the elder Flaumel who lighted them to their rooms.

Coupri had insisted that he should lie in the chamber occupied by madame during her recent visit, and he further insisted Capoulade should have a room in its immediate neighbourhood. To this Flaumel made no difficulty, and Coupri was conducted to the bedroom known as the sieur's chamber. It was a lofty apartment, panelled in oak to a man's height, and half-filled by the great canopied bed. Facing the bed, above the wainscot, stood a life-sized portrait of the present Sieur de la Blanchette's great-grandfather—a rakish gentleman of the time of the fourteenth Louis. Seen in the yellow, flickering light of their tapers, the apartment wore a sombre, gloomy air—in itself almost enough to complete the rout of Coupri's courage. Nevertheless, it was with a brave display of being at his ease that he drew the pistols from his bosom and laid them on a chair at his bedside.

'If any ghost disturbs me, my good Flaumel, I will see how it takes a charge of lead.'

Wishing him good-night, and still laughing over that last pleasantry, Flaumel withdrew, and escorted Capoulade to his room across the corridor. That done, he stepped back and rapped on Coupri's door. The intendant opened it at once.

'Monsieur Coupri,' said the steward, between seriousness and mockery, 'I must confess that, after all, I am not quite easy concerning you. You are sleeping so far from our apartments, my son's and mine. I am satisfied that you will not be troubled, and yet, perhaps it is best to be prepared for anything. If you will step down the corridor with me I will show you where Jacques and I are lodged, so that you may call us should you require anything.'

Troubled by this half-descent from his lofty scepticism on the

part of Flaumel, Coupri went willingly with the steward, to be
shown the whereabouts of the latter's quarters. That done, he
returned to his chamber, closed and securely locked the door; then
taking a copy of Monsieur Le Sage's droll story of 'Le Diable
Boiteux' from his pocket, he flung himself, fully dressed as he was,
upon his bed, his pistols within easy reach, and disposed himself
for his vigil.

For best part of an hour he read undisturbed, and reassured by
the peace of the room, his late qualms might have been dissipated
but that whenever he looked about him, peering into the shadows
that lay thick about the chamber, the gloom of the place chilled his
courage anew.

Suddenly the stillness was broken. Reclining on his elbows he
lay and listened, and he felt his flesh creeping as he did so. There
was a sound as of someone faintly scratching on the wainscot
opposite; and for all that his eyes were on the spot, he saw
nothing.

'A mouse,' he sneered aloud, as if seeking to encourage himself
with the sound of his own voice. 'What a poltroon I become!'

The next instant he had fallen back with a stifled scream. A rush
of cold air had swept past him, extinguishing the candle in its
passage. Again he strove to master himself, and for all that his
pulses thundered fearfully, he put forth his hand and groped for
his pistols. Clutching one of them, he sat up and waited, his teeth
chattering in his head. He wished in a subconscious sort of way
that Capoulade was nearer than across the corridor, and that there
were no locked doors between them. Then he ceased to wish
anything, ceased to think anything, as a grim horror took him and
held him spellbound. Fronting the bed at a man's height from the
floor, a white, luminous patch was spreading, like a phosphorescent
cloud, and out of it boomed a horrid groaning sound followed by a
shriek of hellish laughter.

The sweat stood in icy beads on Coupri's brow. He bethought
him of prayers learnt in childhood, and he pattered them in a
frenzy. Then from out of the luminous cloud a form began to shape
itself, a figure immensely tall, swathed in a winding sheet, and—
horror of horrors—surmounted by a hideously grinning skull with
eyeballs of glowing fire. And the shrieks of it filled the chamber
and froze the very marrow in Coupri's bones.

Then in a flash his late scepticism recurred to him, and with it his resolve to test the ghost with lead. Mechanically almost he raised his pistol, and blazed with both barrels at the apparition. A burst of laughter answered him; next a glowing skeleton hand slipped from the cerecloth and held out two bullets which it let fall on to the parquet floor. Coupri heard the double thud of their fall, then, with a scream, he swooned.

When he recovered there were lights in his room, and Capoulade and the two Flaumels were at his bedside. Their questions as to what had happened he could but answer with entreaties that they should let him depart at once from that hideous chamber, and so in the end it was arranged that he should spend the remainder of the night in Capoulade's room and Capoulade's company.

But it was not until next morning, not until the comforting light of day had dispelled the horror of the night, that Coupri could be induced to tell his companion what had chanced. Capoulade listened attentively and very gravely, but when the end of the story came his glance brightened a little. After they had broken their fast, he took Coupri for a ramble through the grounds, and then it was that he communicated an idea that had occurred to him.

'Does it not seem somewhat strange that a spirit being a thing impalpable, a thing of no substance to be affected by bullets, should yet have the wherewithal to grasp those same bullets and fling them back?'

'Ask me not,' groaned the intendant. 'Who am I that I should explain these marvels? Never again will I doubt; never again will I mock.'

'My good Coupri, you go too fast. To doubt unreasonably is assuredly an ill thing, but in this case I will make bold to say that nothing has happened yet to warrant any change from your late scepticism.'

'Nothing?' gasped Coupri. 'Do you say nothing has happened?'

'I will add, Coupri, that, with your permission, it is I who will sleep in the sieur's bedchamber tonight—I hope to some purpose.'

Coupri, like the good soul that he was, sought to dissuade the young man; but Capoulade would not be dissuaded; he insisted that in the Sieur de la Blanchette's interests, it was Coupri's duty to further him in this last attempt to solve the mystery of this plague of ghosts; and Coupri let him have his way.

He had yet to contend with the opposition of the two Flaumels, when they met at supper. After last night's happening, following as it did upon the two former scares, they seemed, themselves, to have abandoned their scornful attitude, and they entreated Capoulade not to expose himself. But he was firm in his determination.

'I cannot believe Coupri's preposterous story,' was his astonishing declaration. 'The poor fellow has been the victim of a morbid imagination. The proof lies in the fact that we could find no bullets when we searched the chamber, although he swears he saw them cast there.'

Flaumel shrugged his shoulders, and Capoulade drawing a brace of pistols from his pocket proceeded to load them under the eyes of the company. He placed them on the table, and the talk proceeded desultorily until Flaumel rose to make fast the doors.

From the hall they heard him calling, agitation quivering in his voice, and Coupri and Capoulade started up and ran out to him. He was standing on the steps outside the door, and when they came up he told them of a white, shrouded figure that had passed round the corner of the house. They started in pursuit, but though they made the tour of the château they saw no indication of Flaumel's vision.

'Mon Dieu!' groaned the old man, as they were re-entering the hall. 'Am I too become a visionary, or is the place really accursed?'

Capoulade's answer was one of contemptuous incredulity.

'Monsieur Flaumel, for shame! I had thought better of you. You are becoming the victim of these old wives and their fancies. I am for bed.'

He re-entered the dining-room, passing the younger Flaumel, who was coming forth in quest of his father, and taking up his pistols, Capoulade accompanied the others to the floor above. At parting with Coupri, he exacted a promise that should he hear a shot he would at once repair to him.

'But,' he added, 'do not keep awake to listen for it; for the odds are greatly against your hearing it. I shall laugh at you in the morning.'

With that they parted, and Capoulade entered his bedroom and closed the door. He set the pistols he had carried on a chair, as Coupri had done the night before, and his candle beside them. Then he lay on the bed and waited.

Two hours went by, and Capoulade was beginning to fear disappointment, when, suddenly, there came, as on the previous night, the scratching on the wainscot to attract his attention. But instead of looking in the direction of the sound, he furtively peered behind him. He saw what he had expected. One of the panels of the wainscot at the head of the bed slid silently aside, leaving an open gap. Then came the rush of cold air which had so frightened Coupri, and Capoulade was in darkness.

He lay quite still and watched the luminous cloud appear, and as he watched his thoughts were very busy, but no thrill of fear unnerved him. The gibbering, howling skeleton grew clearer. Capoulade smiled grimly in the dark, and left the pistols on the chair untouched. From his breast-pocket he drew a fresh one, levelled it with a steady hand, and fired one barrel at the apparition.

A frightful scream rang through the chamber—no shriek of laughter this—and the ghost tumbled forward and down a height of some six feet, striking the floor with a thud.

In an instant Capoulade had his candle alight again, and he was leaning over the prostrate form, which had ceased to glow now that the candle's yellow light was upon it. He stooped and pulled aside the sheet, then rolled the figure over on its back and plucked away the cardboard death's head.

Beneath that mask the ashen face of the younger Flaumel was revealed, and in one of his clenched hands Capoulade found two bullets. Above the wainscot, where the Sieur de la Blanchette's portrait usually stood, a black gap now yawned.

In that moment the door opened, and Coupri, looking very white, stood on the threshold.

'*Voilà!*' said Capoulade, pointing to the figure. 'I've laid the ghost. But he'll recover to answer M. de Sartines' questions yet.' Then, suddenly, his hand went up, levelling his pistol once more and covering the elder Flaumel, who entered. 'Throw down that pistol, or you're a dead man,' he commanded savagely, and the old man obeyed him.

When father and son were fast under lock and key, Capoulade

added one or two words of explanation to make things clear to Coupri's slow mind.

'Last night, after you had laid your pistols down, Flaumel called you from the room on pretext of showing you where they lodged. Whilst he was doing this, his son was drawing the bullets from the charges of your pistols. They did the same by me tonight, when the old man led us round the château to hunt a spectre. But I had a third pistol in reserve to exorcize the ghost with.'

'But', stammered Coupri, still bewildered, 'to what end should they have sought to frighten all who came to the château?'

'Who shall say? There are men whose minds never rise above childishness.'

But Coupri shook his great head. 'No, no,' said he, 'that is no explanation. It must be that, for some purpose, they wanted to have the château to themselves, as during the past five years.'

Capoulade looked at him, then he smote his thigh with his hand, and swore a great oath. 'You have said it,' he cried, for he had suddenly remembered his second task—the discovery of the coiners who were pouring spurious silver into Maine. He now recalled Sartines' words, that the elucidation of one mystery would probably afford the explanation of the other.

They made search in the château, and at last, in a secret chamber, to which they found access through the passage opened by the Sieur de la Blanchette's picture, discovered crucible and moulds and other implements of that nefarious craft, beside a quantity of base coin in bags. All this, together with their two prisoners, they conveyed to Paris.

M. de Sartines complimented Capoulade upon his address and definitely enrolled him in his army of secret agents. And if Capoulade kept back one of those bags of Flaumel's coins, to the end that he might obtain good value for bad money, it must be remembered that the transition from dishonesty to honesty is not accomplished all at once.

Brancaleone's Terms

ORDINARILY Dragut Reis—who was dubbed by the Faithful 'The Drawn Sword of Islam'—loved Christians as the fox loves geese. But in that summer of 1550 his feelings acquired a far deeper malignancy; they developed into a direct and personal hatred that for intensity was second only to the hatred which the Christians bore Dragut.

The allied Christian forces, under the direction of their emperor, had smoked him out of his stronghold of Mehedia; they had seized that splendid city, and were in the act of razing it to the ground as the neighbouring Carthage had been razed of old.

Dragut reckoned up his losses with a gloomy, vengeful mind. He had lost his city; and from the eminence of a budding Basha in the act of founding a kingdom he had been cast down once more to be a wanderer upon the seas.

He had lost three thousand men, and amongst them the very flower of his fiery corsairs. He had lost some twelve thousand Christian slaves—the fruit of many a desperate raid by land and water. He had lost his lieutenant and nephew, Hisar, who was even now a captive in the hands of his inveterate enemy, Andrea Doria. It is little wonder that he lost his temper, too. But he recovered it quickly, that he might set about recovering the rest. He was not the man to waste his days in brooding over what was done. Yesterday and today are but as pledges in the hands of destiny.

So he returned thanks to Allah, the Compassionate, the Merciful, that he was still alive and free upon the seas, with three galeasses, twelve galleys, and five brigantines; and bent his energetic, resourceful, knavish mind to the matter of making good his losses.

Meanwhile, he had been warned by the Sultan of Constantinople, the Exalted of Allah, that the Emperor Charles, not content with the mischief he had already wrought, had, in letters to the Grand Signior, avowed his intent to pursue to the death 'the

pirate Dragut, a corsair odious to both God and man'. He knew,
moreover, that the emperor had entrusted the task to the greatest
seaman of the day—to the terrible Admiral of Genoa, Andrea
Doria, and that the Genoese was already at sea upon his quest.

Now, once already had Dragut been captured by the navy of
Genoa, and for four years, which it afforded him little satisfaction
to remember, he had toiled at an oar aboard the galley of the
admiral's nephew, Gianettino Doria. He had known exposure to
heat and cold; naked had he been broiled by the sun, and frozen
by the rain; he had known aching muscles, hunger, and thirst;
filthy, crawling things, and the festering sores begotten of the
oarsman's bench; and his shoulders were still a criss-cross of scars
where the bo'suns' whips had lashed him to revive his flagging
energies.

All this had Dragut known, and he was not minded to renew the
knowledge. It behoved him, therefore, to make ready fittingly to
receive the admiral.

And by way at once of replenishing his coffers, venting a little of
his vengeful heat, and marking his contempt for his Christian
pursuers, he had made a sudden swoop upon' the south-western
littoral of Sicily. Beginning at Gergenti, he carried his raid as far
north as Marsala, leaving ruin and desolation behind him. At the
end of a week he stood off to sea again with the spoils of six
townships and some three thousand picked captives of both
sexes.

He would teach the infidel Christian dog to allude to him as 'the
pirate Dragut, a corsair odious to both God and man'. He would
so, by the beard of Mahomet!

He put the captives aboard a couple of his galleys, in charge of
his lieutenant, Othmani, and despatched them straight to Algiers,
to be sold there in the slave market. With the proceeds Othmani
was to lay down fresh keels. Until these should be ready to rein-
force his little fleet, Dragut judged it well to avoid encounters with
the Genoese admiral, and with this intent he kept a southward
course along the coast towards Tripoli.

Towards sunset of the day on which Othmani's galleys set out
alone for Algiers, a fresh breeze sprang up from the north and
blew into the corsair's range of vision a tiny brown-sailed felucca,
as it might have blown a leaf in autumn. It was hawk-eyed Dragut

himself who, lounging in the poop of his galley, first sighted this tiny craft.

He pointed it out to Biretta, the renegade Calabrian gunner, who was near him.

'In the name of Allah,' quoth he, 'what walnut-shell is this that comes so furiously after us?'

Biretta, a massive, sallow fellow, laughed.

'The fury is not hers, but of the wind,' said he. 'She goes wherever it blows her. She'll be an Italian craft.'

'Then the wind that blows her is the wind of Destiny. Haply she'll have news of Italy.'

He turned on his heel and gave an order to a turbaned officer below. Instantly the brazen note of a trumpet rang out, clear above the creak and dip of oars. As instantly the rowers came to rest, and from the side of each galley six-and-twenty massive yellow oars stood out, their wet blades glistening in the evening sunlight.

Thus the Moslem fleet waited, rocking gently on the little swell that had arisen, and its quality was blazoned by the red and white ensign charged with a blue crescent, which floated from the mast-head of Dragut's own galley.

On came the little brown-sailed felucca, hopelessly driven by what Dragut accounted the breeze of Destiny. At last, when she was in danger of being blown past them, Dragut crossed to meet her. As the galley's long prow ran alongside of her, grappling-hooks were deftly flung to seize her at mast and gunwale, and but for these she must have been swept over by those gigantic oars.

From the prow, Dragut himself, a tall and handsome figure in gold-broidered scarlet surcoat that descended to his knees, his snowy turban heightening the swarthiness of his hawk face, with its square-cut black beard, stood to challenge the crew of that ill-starred felucca.

There were aboard of her six scared knaves, something betwixt seamen and lackeys, whom the corsair's black eyes passed contemptuously over. He addressed himself to a couple who were seated in the stern-sheets—a tall and very elegant young gentleman, obviously Italian, and a girl, upon whose white, golden-headed loveliness the corsair's bold eyes glowed pleasurably.

'Who are you?' he demanded shortly, in Italian.

The willowy young man answered for the twain, very com-

posedly, as though it were a matter of everyday life with him to be
held in the grappling-hooks of a Barbary pirate.

'My name is Ottavio Brancaleone. I am from Genoa on my way
to Spain.'

'To Spain!' quoth Dragut, and he laughed. 'You steer an odd
course for Spain, or do you look to find it in Egypt?'

'We have lost our rudder,' the gentleman explained, 'and we
were at the mercy of the wind.'

'I trust you have found it as merciful as you hoped,' said Dragut.
He leered at the girl, who, in affright, shrank nearer her companion. 'And the girl, sir? Who is she?'

'My—my sister.'

'Had you told me different you had been the first Christian I
ever knew to speak the truth,' said Dragut, quite amiably. 'Well,
well, 'tis plain you're not to be trusted to sail a boat of your own.
Best come aboard, and see if you can do better at an oar.'

'I'll not be trespassing on your hospitality,' said Brancaleone,
with that amazing coolness of his.

Dragut wasted no time in argument. It was not his way. Of the
grinning, turbaned corsairs who swarmed like ants upon the prow
he flung a half-score down into the felucca. Brancaleone had time
to stab but one of them before they overpowered him.

The prize proved far less insignificant than at first Dragut had
imagined. For, in addition to the eight slaves acquired—and the
girl was fit to grace a sultan's harem—they found a great chest of
newly minted ducats, which it took six men to heave aboard the
galley, and a beautifully chiselled gold coffer full of gems of price.
They found something more. On the inside of the coffer's lid was
engraved the owner's name—Amelia Francesca Doria.

Dragut snapped down the lid with a prayer of thanks to Allah
the One, and strode into the poop cabin, where the girl was
confined.

'Madonna Amelia,' he called softly, to test her identity. She
looked up at once. 'Will you tell me what is your kinship with the
Admiral of Genoa?'

'I am his granddaughter, sir,' she answered, with something
fierce behind her outward softness, 'and be sure that he will
terribly avenge upon you any wrong that is done to me.'

Dragut nodded and smiled.

'We are old friends, the admiral and I,' said he, and went out again.

A mighty Nubian bearing a torch—for night had now descended with African suddenness—lighted him to the galley's waist, where, about the mainmast, lay huddled the seven pinioned prisoners.

With the curved toe of his scarlet slipper the corsair touched Messer Brancaleone.

'Tell me, dog,' said he, 'all that you know of Messer Andrea Doria.'

'That is soon told,' answered Brancaleone. 'I know nothing, nor want to.'

'Therein, of course, you lie,' said Dragut. 'For one thing, you know his granddaughter.'

Brancaleone blinked, and recovered.

'True, and several others of his family. But I conceived your question to concern his movements. I know that he is upon the seas, that he is seeking you, and that he has sworn to take you alive, and that when they take you—as I pray God they will—they will so deal with you that you shall implore them of their Christian charity to hang you.'

'And is that all you know?' quoth Dragut, unruffled. 'You did not, peradventure, sight this fleet of his as you were sailing?'

'I did not.'

'Do you think that with a match between your fingers you might remember?'

'I might invent,' said the Italian. 'I have told you the truth, Messer Dragut. Torture could but gain you falsehood.'

The corsair looked searchingly into that comely young face, then he turned away as if satisfied. But as he was departing Messer Brancaleone called him back. The Italian's imperturbability had suddenly departed. Anxiety amounting almost to terror sounded in his voice.

'What fate do you reserve for Madonna Amelia?' he asked.

Dragut considered him, and smiled a little. He had no particular rancour against his prisoner; indeed, he was inclining to admiration for the cool courage which the man had shown. At the same time, there was no room for sentiment in the heart of the corsair. He was quite pitiless. He had been asked a question, and he answered it without malice.

'Our lord the Sublime Suleyman,' said he, 'is as keen a judge of beauty as any living man. I do the girl the honour of accounting her a gift worthy even of the Exalted of Allah. So I shall keep her safe against my next voyage to Constantinople.'

And then Brancaleone's little lingering self-possession left him utterly. From his writhing lips came a stream of vituperation, expressions of his impotent rage, which continued even after the Nubian had struck him upon the mouth and Dragut had taken his departure.

Next day a slave on Dragut's galley who had been taken ill at his oar was, in accordance with custom, unshackled and heaved over-board. Brancaleone, stripped to his delicate white skin, was chained in the fellow's empty place. There were seven men to each oar, and Brancaleone's six companions were all Christians and all white—or had been before exposure had tanned them to the colour of mahogany. Of these, three were Spaniards, two were Italian, and the other was a Frenchman. All were indescribably filthy and unkempt, and it was with a shudder that the delicately nurtured Italian gentleman wondered was he destined to become as they?

Up and down the gangway between the rowers' benches strode two Moslem bo'suns, armed with long whips of bullock-hide, and it was not long ere one of them, considering that Brancaleone was not putting his share of effort into his task, sent that cruel lash to raise a burning weal upon his tender flesh. He was sparingly fed with his half-brutalized companions upon dried figs and dates, and he was given a little tepid water to drink when he thirsted, which was often. He slept in his shackles on the rowers' bench, which was but some four feet wide, and, despite the sheepskins with which that bench was padded, it was not long ere the friction of his constant movement began to chafe and blister his flesh.

In the scorching noontide of the second day he collapsed fainting upon his oar. He was unshackled and dragged out upon the gang-way. There a bucket of sea-water was flung over him to revive him, and the too-swift healing action of the salt upon his seared flesh was a burning agony. He was put back to his oar again with the warning that did he permit himself a second time the luxury of swooning he would have the whole ocean in which to revive.

On the third day they sighted land, and towards evening the

galleys threaded their way one by one through the shoals of the
Boca de Cantara into the spacious lagoon on the north-east side of
the Island of Jerbah, and there came to rest.

It was Dragut's intent to lie snug in that remote retreat until
Othmani should be ready with the reinforcements that were to
enable the corsair to take the seas once more against the Admiral
of Genoa. But it would seem that already the admiral was closer
upon his heels than he had supposed, and that, trackless as are the
ocean ways, yet Andrea Doria had by some mysterious means
contrived to gather information as he came that had kept him upon
the invisible spoor of his quarry.

Not a doubt but that the folk on that ravaged Sicilian seaboard
would be eager to inform the redoubtable admiral of the direction
in which the Moslem galleys had faded out of sight. Perhaps even
that empty felucca left tossing upon the tideless sea had served as
an index to the way the corsairs had taken, and perhaps from the
mainland, from Monastir, or one of the other cities now in Christian
hands, a glimpse of Dragut's fleet had been caught, and Doria had
been warned. Be that as it may, not a week had Dragut been
anchored at Jerbah when one fine morning brought a group of
friendly islanders with the alarming news that a fleet of galleys was
descending upon the island from the north.

The news took Dragut ashore in a hurry with a group of officers.
From the narrow spur of land at the harbour's mouth he surveyed
the advancing ships. What already he had more than feared became
absolute certainty. Two-and-twenty royal galleys were steering
straight for the Boca de Cantara, and the foremost was flying the
admiral's ensign.

Back to his fleet went Dragut for cannon and slaves, and so
feverishly did these toil under the lash of his venomous tongue,
and of his bo'suns' whips, that within an hour he had erected a
battery at the mouth of the harbour and fired a salute straight into
the Genoese line as the galleys were in the very act of dropping
anchor. Thereupon the fleet of Doria stood off out of range, and
hung there, well content to wait, knowing that all that was now
required on their part was patience. The fox was trapped, and the
sword of Islam was like to be sheathed at last.

Forthwith the jubilant Doria sent word to the Emperor that he
held Dragut fast, and he despatched messengers to the Viceroys of

Sicily and Naples asking for reinforcements with which, if necessary, to force the issue. He meant this time to leave nothing to
chance.

Dragut, on his side, employed his time in fortifying the Boca de
Cantara. A fort arose there, growing visible under the eyes of the
Genoese, and provoking the amusement of that fierce veteran,
Doria. Sooner or later Dragut must decide him to come forth from
his bottle-necked refuge, and the longer he put off that evil day
the more overwhelming would be the numbers assembled to destroy him.

Never since Gianettino Doria had surprised him in the road of
Goialatta, off the coast of Corsica, on that famous occasion when he
was made prisoner, had Dragut found himself in so desperately
tight a corner. He sat under the awning of the poop of his galley,
and cursed the Genoese with that astounding and far-reaching
fluency in which the Moslem is without rival upon earth. He
pronounced authoritatively upon the evil reputation of Doria's
mother and the inevitably shameful destiny of his daughters and
their female offspring. He foretold how dogs would of a certainty
desecrate the admiral's grave, and he called perfervidly upon Allah
to rot the bones and destroy the house of his arch-enemy. Then,
observing that Allah remained disdainfully aloof, he rose up one
day in a mighty passion, and summoned his officers.

'This skulking here will not avail us,' he snarled at them, as if it
were by their contriving that he was trapped. 'By delay we but
increase our peril. What is written is written. Allah has bound the
fate of each man about his neck. Betide what may, tonight we take
the open sea.'

'And by morning you'll have found the bottom of it,' drawled a
voice from one of the oars.

Dragut, who was standing on the gangway between the rowers'
benches, whipped round with an oath upon the speaker. He encountered the languid eyes of Messer Brancaleone. The repose of
the last few days had restored the Italian's vigour, and certain
thoughts that lately he had been thinking had revived his courage.

'Are you weary of life?' quoth the infuriated corsair. 'Shall I have
you hanged ere we go out to meet your friends out yonder?'

'You're very plainly a fool, Messer Dragut,' was the weary
answer. 'Hang me, and you hang the only man in all your fleet

who can show you the way out of this trap in which you're taken.'

Dragut started between anger and amazement.

'You can show me a way out of this trap?' he cried. 'What way may that be?'

'Strike off my fetters, restore me my garments, and give me proper food, and I'll discuss it with you.'

Dragut glowered.

'We have a shorter way to make men speak,' said he.

Brancaleone smiled, and shook his head.

'You think so? I might prove you wrong.'

It was odd what a power of conviction dwelt in his languid tones. The corsair issued an order and turned away. A half-hour later Messer Brancaleone, nourished, washed, and clothed, once more the elegant, willowy Italian in his doublet of sapphire velvet and in pleasantly variegated hose of blue and white, stepped on to the poop-deck, where Dragut awaited him.

Seated cross-legged upon a gorgeous silken divan that was wrought in green and blue and gold, the handsome corsair combed his square black beard with fretful fingers. Behind him, stark naked save for his white loin-cloth, stood his gigantic Nubian, his body oiled until it shone like ebony, armed with a gleaming scimitar.

'Now, sir,' growled Dragut, 'what is this precious plan of yours—briefly?'

'You begin where we should end,' said the imperturbable Genoese. 'I owe you no favours, Messer Dragut, and I bear you no affection that I should make you a free gift of your life and liberty. My eyes have seen something to which yours are blind, and my wits have conceived something of which your own are quite incapable. These things, sir, are for sale. Ere I part with them we must agree the price.'

Dragut pondered him from under scowling brows savagely. He could scarce believe that the world held so much impudence.

'And what price do you suggest?' he snarled, half-derisively, by way of humouring the Genoese.

'Why, as to that, since I offer you life and liberty, it is but natural that I should claim my own life and liberty in return, and similarly the liberty of Madonna Amelia and of my servants whom you captured; also, it is but natural that I should require the restoration of the money and jewels you have taken from us, and since you have deprived us of our felucca, it is no more than proper that you should equip us with a vessel in which to pursue the journey that you interrupted. Considering the time we have lost in consequence of this interruption, it is but just that you should make this good as far as possible by presenting me with a craft that is capable of the utmost speed. I will accept a galley of six-and-twenty oars, manned by a proper complement of slaves.'

'And is that all?' roared Dragut.

'No,' said Branacaleone quietly. 'That is but the restitution due to me. We come now to the price of the service I am to render you. When you were Gianettino Doria's prisoner, Barbarossa paid for you, as all the world knows, a ransom of three thousand ducats. I will be more reasonable.'

'Will you so?' snorted Dragut. 'By the splendour of Allah, you'll need to be!'

'I will accept one thousand ducats.'

'May Allah blot thee out, thou impudent son of shame!' cried the corsair, and he heaved himself up in a fury.

'You compel me to raise the price to fifteen hundred ducats,' said Brancaleone smoothly. 'I must be compensated for abuse, since I cannot take satisfaction for it as between one honourable Christian gentleman and another.'

It was good for Dragut that his feelings suddenly soared to a pitch of intensity that defied expression, else might the price have been raised even beyond the figure of the famous ransom that Barbarossa had paid. Mutely he stood glowering, clenching and unclenching his sinewy hands. Then he half-turned to his Nubian swordsman.

'Ali——' he began, when Brancaleone once more cut in.

'Ah, wait,' said he. 'I pray you calm yourself. Remember how you stand, and that Andrea Doria holds you trapped. Do nothing that will destroy your only chance. Time enough to bid Ali hack off my head when I have failed.'

That speech arrested Dragut's anger in full flow. He wheeled upon the Genoese once more.

'You accept that alternative?'

Brancaleone met his gaze blandly.

'Why not? I have no slightest fear of failure. I have said that I

can show you how to win clear of this trap and make the admiral
the laughing-stock of the world.'

'Speak, then,' cried Dragut, his fierce eyes kindling.

'If I do so before you have agreed my terms then I shall have
nothing left to sell.'

Dragut turned aside and strode to the taffrail. He looked across
the shimmering blue water to the fortifications at the harbour's
mouth; with the eyes of his imagination he looked beyond, at the
fleet of Genoa riding out there in patient conviction that it held its
prey. The price that Brancaleone asked was outrageous. A galley
and some two hundred Christian slaves to row it, and fifteen
hundred ducats! In all it amounted to more than the ransom that
Kheyr-ed-Din Barbarossa had paid for him. Yet Dragut must pay it
or count his destiny fulfilled. He came to reflect that he would pay
it gladly enough to be out of this tight corner.

He came about again. He spoke of torture once more, but in a
half-hearted sort of way; for he did not himself believe that it
would be effective with a man of Brancaleone's mettle.

Brancaleone laughed at the threat and shrugged his shoulders.

'You may as profitably hang me, Messer Dragut. Your infidel
barbarities would quite as effectively seal my lips.'

'We might torture the woman,' said Dragut the ingenious.

On the words Brancaleone turned white to the lips; but it was
the pallor of bitter, heart-searing resolve, not the pallor of such
fear as Dragut had hoped to awaken. He advanced a step, his
imperturbability all gone, and he spat his words into the face of the
corsair with the fierceness of a cornered wildcat.

'Attempt it,' said he, 'and as God's my witness I leave you to
your fate at the hands of Genoa—ay, though my heart should burst
with the pain of my silence. I am a man, Messer Dragut—never
doubt it.'

'I do not,' said Dragut, convinced. 'I agree your terms. Show me
a way out of Doria's clutches, and you shall have all that you have
asked for.'

Trembling still from his recent emotion, Brancaleone hoarsely
bade the corsair call up his officers and repeat his words before
them.

'And you shall make oath upon this matter,' he added. 'Men say
of you that you are a faithful Moslem. I mean to put it to the test.'

Dragut, now all eagerness to know what plan was stirring in his prisoner's brain, unable to brook further suspense in this affair, called up his officers, and before them all, taking Allah to witness, he made oath upon the beard of the Prophet that if Brancaleone could show him deliverance, he, on his side, would recompense the Genoese to the extent demanded.

Thereafter Dragut and Brancaleone went ashore with no other attendant but the Nubian swordsman. It was the Genoese who led the way, not towards the fort, as Dragut had expected, but in the opposite direction. Arrived at the northernmost curve of that almost circular lagoon, where the ground was swampy, Brancaleone paused. He pointed across a strip of shallow land, that was no more than a half-mile or so in width, to the blue-green sea beyond. Part of this territory was swampy, and part was sand; vegetation there was of the scantiest; some clumps of reeds, an odd date palm, its crest rustling faintly in the breeze, and nothing else.

'It is really very simple,' said the Italian. 'Yonder lies your way.'

A red-legged stork rose from the edge of the marsh and went circling overhead. Dragut's face empurpled with rage. He deemed that this smooth fellow dared to mock him.

'Are my galleys winged like that stork, thou fool?' he demanded passionately. 'Or are they wheeled like chariots, that I can sail them over dry land?'

Brancaleone returned him a glance that was full of stupefaction.

'I protest,' said he, 'that for a man of your reputation you fill me with amazement. I said you were a dull fellow. I little dreamed how dull. Nay, now, suppress your rage. Truth is a very healing draught, and you have need of it.

'I compute, now, that aboard your ships there will be, including slaves, some three thousand men. I doubt not you could press another thousand from the island into your service. How long, do you think, would it take four thousand men to dig a channel deep enough to float your shallow galleys through that strip of land?'

Dragut's fierce eyes flickered as if he had been menaced with a blow.

'By Allah!' he ejaculated; and gripped his beard. 'By Allah!'

'In a week the thing were easily done, and meanwhile your fort there will hold the admiral in play. Then, one dark night, you slip through this canal and stand away to the south, so that by sunrise you shall have vanished beyond the skyline, leaving the admiral to guard an empty trap.'

Dragut laughed aloud now in almost childish glee, and otherwise signified his delight by the vehemence with which he testified to the unity of Allah. Suddenly he checked. His eyes narrowed as they rested upon Brancaleone.

' 'Tis a scurvy trick you play your lady's grandsire!' said he.

The Genoese shrugged.

'Every man for himself, Messer Dragut. We understand each other, I think. 'Tis not for love of you that I do this thing.'

'I would it were,' said the corsair, with an odd sincerity. And as they returned to the galleys it was observed that Dragut's arm was about the shoulders of the infidel, and that he spoke with him as with a brother.

The fact is that Dragut, fired with admiration of Brancaleone's resourcefulness, deplored that so fine a spirit should of necessity be destined to go down to the Pit. He spoke to him now of the glories of Islam, and of the future that must await a gentleman of Brancaleone's endowments in the ranks of the Faithful. But this was a matter in which Brancaleone proved politely obdurate, and Dragut had not the time to devote to his conversion, greatly as he desired it. There was the matter of that canal to engage him.

The Italian's instructions were diligently carried out. Daily the fort at the Boca de Cantara would belch forth shot at the Genoese navy, which stood well out of range. To the admiral this was but the barking of a dog that dared not come within biting distance; and the waste of ammunition roused his scorn of that pirate Dragut whom he held at his mercy.

There came a day, however, when the fort was silent; it was followed by another day of silence, in the evening of which one of the admiral's officers suggested that all might not be well. Doria agreed, laughing heartily in his long white beard.

'All is not at all well with that dog Dragut,' said he. 'He wants us within range of his guns. The ruse is childish.'

And so the Genoese fleet continued well out of range of the empty fort, what time Dragut himself was some scores of miles away, speeding for the Archipelago and the safety of the Dardanelles as fast as his slaves could row.

In the words of the Spanish historian Marmol, who has chronicled the event; Dragut had left Messer Andrea Doria 'with the dog to hold'.

Brancaleone accompanied the Moslem fleet at first, though now aboard the galley which Dragut had given him in accordance with their agreement. And with the Genoese sailed the lovely Amelia Francesca Doria, his chest of gold, the jewels, and the fifteen hundred ducats that Dragut—grimly stifling his reluctance—had paid him. On the second day after leaving Jerbah, Messer Brancaleone and the corsair captain parted company, with mutual expressions of goodwill, and the Genoese put about and steered a north-westerly course for the coast of Spain.

It was some months ere Dragut learnt the true inwardness of Messer Brancaleone's conduct. He had the story from a Genoese captive, the captain of a carack which the corsair scuttled in the Straits of Messina. This fellow's name, too, was Brancaleone, upon learning which Dragut asked him was he kin to one Ottavio Brancaleone, who had gone to Spain with the admiral's grand-daughter.

'He was my cousin,' the man answered.

And Dragut now learnt that in the teeth of the opposition of the entire Doria family, the irrepressible Brancaleone had carried off Madonna Amelia. The admiral had news of it as he was putting to sea, and it was in pursuit not only of Dragut, but also of the runaways, that he had gone south as far as Jerbah, having reason to more than suspect that they were aboard one of Dragut's galleys. The admiral had sworn to hang Brancaleone from his yardarm ere he returned to port, and his bitterness at the trick Dragut had played was increased by the circumstance that Brancaleone, too, had got clear away.

Dragut was very thoughtful when he heard that story.

'And to think,' said he afterwards to Othmani, 'that I paid that unconscionable dog fifteen hundred ducats, and gave him my best galley manned by two hundred Christian slaves that he might render himself as great a service as ever he rendered me!'

But he bore no malice. After all, the Genoese had behaved generously in that he had left Dragut—though not from motives of generosity—the entire glory of the exploit. Dragut's admiration for the impudent fellow was, if anything, increased. Was he not, after all, the only Christian who had ever bested Dragut in a bargain? If he had a regret it was that so shrewd a spirit should abide in the body of an infidel. But Allah is all-knowing.

The Poachers

THEY were a hangdog-looking pair as they rode into Liphook on that sunny morning of May. One was short and weedy, with bony shanks and a hungry countenance, the other was a little taller and a deal bulkier, but bloated of face and generally flabby. They were dressed in a soiled and tawdry imitation of their betters, and each looked every inch the gallows-bird that he was.

They drew rein on the little patch of ragged turf before the Lame Dog, and the portly Nathaniel, without dismounting, called for a nipperkin of ale, whilst the weedy Jake—who had received some elements of education, and was never weary of parading his scholarliness—became engrossed in the contents of a bill nailed to the post that bore the sign of the inn.

It had for title the arresting phrase, 'One Hundred Guineas Reward.' It began with WHEREAS, and ended with GOD SAVE THE KING, all in fat letters. In between there were some twenty lines of matter in smaller type, with the name of THOMAS EVANS boldly displayed amidst it.

Ominous as was this advertisement to the rogue who, under the style of Captain Evans, had now for some months been working the Portsmouth road, it nevertheless filled Master Jake with envy. It spoke of fame and success in his own line of industry, such as seemed far indeed beyond the reach of himself and his colleague.

They were a pair of London foists—to use the term of their own thieves' cant—a couple of sneaking pickpockets who never should have attempted to soar to higher things, and who were bitterly regretting their recourse to robbery in the grand manner. So far it had not proved profitable; at least, not commensurately with its perils. Yesterday evening, grown bold under the spur of necessity, they had attempted to demand toll from the London coach—thereby usurping the privileges of Captain Evans himself; but they had bungled the matter through inexperience, and had been ignominiously driven off by the guard's blunderbuss. Indeed, but that the guard himself was so scared that he could not keep his limbs from shaking, they might have brought away a charge of lead apiece for their pains.

You will now understand Jake's feelings of envy as he scanned that proclamation. He felt that it would be many a year before the justices honoured himself in like fashion, before his own unkempt head became worth a hundred pounds to any man who could come and fetch it.

In his nasal, sing-song, cockney tones, he proceeded labouredly to read the advertisement aloud for the benefit of his unlettered associate. He was interrupted by the advent of the ale. When they had paid for it, they had but fourpence left between them, and, unless fortune were singularly benign, they were very likely to starve. Sullen and downcast, they departed and rode on side by side with no word passing between them. For sixpence either would have cut the throat of the other that morning. They turned out of the highway into a pleasant, well-hedged by-road a little way beyond Liphook, and they ambled slowly forward in the dappled shade with the fragrance of hawthorn all about them. It was their unspoken hope that here they might chance upon some lonely wayfarer—preferably of the weaker sex, or at least someone who would give no trouble. And the very next turn in the road brought them face to face with one who, in the distance, looked a likely quarry. This was a slight gentleman astride of a tall, roan mare with a white blaze. He was dressed all in black, like a parson, yet with more worldliness and elegance than would have been proper in a parson. The three-cornered hat over his auburn bag-wig was pulled down to shade his eyes; for our gentleman was reading. The roan was proceeding at a walk, the reins loose upon her neck, whilst her rider, gripping her flanks easily with his knees, was deeply engrossed in the book he held, which was a translation of the diverting adventures of a Salamanca student named Gil Blas.

Our rascally twain sighted him from afar, and by common impulse drew rein, and looked at each other. Jake winked portentously. Nat nodded, and licked his lips. Then, again by common impulse, they quietly backed their screws round the corner they had just turned, and there, out of sight of that solitary and studious wayfarer, they waited. They had one pistol between them, and it was Jake—the gunner of the expedition—who had charge of this.

He drew it, looked to the priming, breathed on the barrel, and rubbed it on his threadbare sleeve to increase its lustre.

Round the corner plump into that ambush rode our student, and——

'Stand!' thundered Jake, levelling his weapon.

The rider looked up, checking instantly as he had been bidden, and displaying a keen, wolfish face that did not seem to tone quite well with his studious habits and demure apparel. Indeed, a certain raffishness hung about him despite his clothes. He seemed compounded of an odd blend of courtier and lackey.

He considered the rogues who challenged him, and they found his expression disconcerting.

He displayed none of the sudden terror they had hoped and expected to inspire. Instead, his glance was vaguely contemptuous in its nice mingling of amusement and surprise. Calmly he closed his book and slipped it into his pocket, whilst from under his left arm he took the heavy riding-crop that had been tucked there.

'What's this, you rabbit-suckers?' he demanded.

Jake thrust his pistol a couple of inches nearer, as if to insist upon its presence.

'It's this,' said he, 'and it's your purse we want. Come, sir, deliver!'

'Now, here's impudence, ecod!' was the amusedly scornful answer. 'Am I to be hunted on my own preserves by a couple of poaching tykes?'

He moved suddenly. Swift and abruptly as a flash of lightning his heavily loaded crop smashed down upon the dirty hand that held the barker, and knocked the weapon into the dust. Then he had plucked a pistol from his own holster, and thus in the twinkling of an eye made himself master of the situation.

Jake nursed his injured hand, grimacing with pain. Nathaniel snatched up his reins, stricken with sudden panic. But his flight was arrested as soon as conceived.

'Stand, hog!' our gentleman summoned him; 'or I'll turn you into bacon with a bullet.'

They stood at his mercy, and he surveyed them with that sardonic eye of his.

'On my life, you're a fine pair of tobymen!' he admonished them. He read their true natures as easily as he had read the diverting history of the Salamanca student. ' 'Twas an ill hour in which you left your town kennels, you rats, to turn gentlemen of the pad and take toll in the heroic manner! Turn out your pockets, you cony-catchers, and let us see how you have thriven! Turn 'em out, I say, and hand over your poachings!'

They obeyed him with a ludicrous alacrity, and revealed the miserable state of their affairs. Our gentleman in black surveyed with an eye of scorn the copper coins in Nathaniel's dirty palm.

'How long have ye been poaching upon my preserves?' he demanded. Receiving no answer: 'Speak out, you muckrakes!' he bade them. 'I am no sheriff's officer. I am Captain Evans, of whom you may have heard.'

Jake needed but this confirmation of what already he had suspected. He fell to fawning upon the notorious gentleman of the pad, and proceeded to relate a moving tale of misfortune. The Bow Street runners had been on their trail in town, and they had taken to the country for a change of air and of method. So far, however, they had not prospered as highwaymen. They had robbed a parson two days ago, but his purse had held but three poor shillings, of which all that remained was the fourpence Nathaniel had displayed. Finally came the admission that they were hungry; and thus a business begun with a fiercely bellowed 'Stand and deliver!' ended now in a piteous whine for alms.

Captain Evans considered them. At length he addressed Nathaniel.

'Get down, pig-face,' he commanded, 'and fetch me that barker!'

Obediently Nathaniel dismounted, picked up the fallen pistol, and delivered it to the captain. Evans dropped it into his pocket. Then, restoring his own weapon to its holster, he took the heavy crop, and, tucking it under his arm again, he finally addressed these rogues.

'Ye inspire me with little confidence,' said he. 'Still, I have a notion. If I were to toss you a guinea, you would be in no better case when that was eaten. I'll do better by you, and, meanwhile, I'll mend your emptiness. Follow me, but at a distance, for I'd not have it thought I keep such rat-bitten company!'

On that he wheeled his mare about, and rode off briskly along the road by which he had approached. The twain looked at each other. Nathaniel's prominent eyes asked an obvious question.

'Ay,' said Jake; and they set out to follow.

The captain led them a half-mile or so down that by-way, then for a short distance along a narrow, grassy lane to a cottage that stood back in a little patch of land—a little, white-washed house set in a miniature orchard, as innocent-looking a retreat as could have been conceived. Within the gate he waited for them to come up with him, and when the horses had been stabled in a lean-to, he conducted them within doors to what was at once the kitchen and the living-room. He bade them to table, and, having set meat and drink before them, took his own seat apart, and smoked thoughtfully whilst they noisily satisfied their hunger.

From time to time he would fling them a disdainful glance, and from time to time they would steal awed looks at him, noting his boots of fine leather and his silver spurs, the cut of his handsome black coat, and the extravagance of his ruffles—which, incidentally, were not as clean as they might have been, although that was too nice a point for our tatterdemalions.

Captain Evans was a man of ideas. It was not for nothing that he had been reading the adventures of Gil Blas that morning. He had been greatly taken with the description of the retreat of the robbers who captured the Salamanca student, and he was romantic enough to desire on a lesser scale to organize a somewhat similar band in the pleasant county of Hampshire—at least, the notion assailed him when he came to consider how he might turn these two starveling thieves to account. They were to form the nucleus of the band, which he would rule as captain absolute. Thus, you see, he was concerned with improving upon the heroic traditions of the high toby.

He unfolded his scheme to the twain, when at last they had fed. It was as yet a little vague and inchoate in its details, but the main lines it should follow were plainly indicated, and he expected it to be greeted with enthusiasm. At the conclusion he addressed himself more particularly to Nathaniel.

'Well, pig-face,' he questioned, 'how does it seem to you?'

'My name,' said the flabby rogue, 'is Nat.'

'Maybe, but pig-face becomes you better. Will ye work with me?'

And he looked from one to the other.

Jake agreed with alacrity to the plan, profoundly honoured to

serve under so illustrious a leader. Nathaniel, more reluctant because resentful of the lack of respect shown him by the captain,
required to be persuaded by his fellow. But in the end it was
settled; the twain were to be enrolled under the captain's banner.

The nature of the active service upon which they were to adventure had yet to be considered, and the captain promised to consider it forthwith. Meanwhile, since they showed signs of slumber
as a result of their gross overfeeding, he let them rest for today and
recuperate their energies.

'Ye'll be snug and safe here, so that ye lie close,' he assured
them, rising. Then he issued an order. 'Now that ye've eaten, clear
the table and wash the platters clean. 'Twill be some employment
for you while I'm gone. I shall be back tonight.'

With that he left them.

They heard the hoofs of the roan go padding down the lane,
then at last Nathaniel loosed his pent-up wrath.

'I'll be triply durned,' said he, 'if I turn scullion to any ruffling
cove of the pad! Wash the platters!' He snorted angrily. 'Skewer
my vitals, do I look like a scullery wench?' He rose in his rage at
the indignity. 'And he called me pig-face, the dirty thief! And—
and you, Jake, ye fool, let him beguile you with his smooth cant
into promising to serve with him! Fine service, i' faith! Us'll risk
our necks while his lordship takes the plunder. If ye've an ounce of
sense in your ugly head, ye'll come away with me this instant!'

Jake raised his weasel face, and looked at his fellow with shrewd,
narrowing eyes.

''Tis the way o' fools and drunkards,' he moralized, 'that they
must think all the world in their own case. Sit down, you cackling
Tom o' Bedlam, and listen! I know ye're an unscholarly, ignorant
cove that can't read for yourself. But didn't I read ye what it said
on a paper outside the Lame Dog at Liphook this morning? Didn't
ye hear that the Guvviment be offering a hundred guineas for the
capture o' this ruffling cove?' He paused a moment to give more
effect to what he was about to add. Then he closed one eye slowly.
'Us'll earn it,' he said softly.

Nathaniel stared, his mouth gaping, his eyes bulging. Then he
smacked his dusty breeches, and again invited someone to skewer
his vitals. Thereafter they discussed the matter.

Captain Evans returned towards evening, and he came at a

breakneck gallop, which in itself might have warned his newly
enrolled followers that something was wrong. He was breathing
heavily when he entered the kitchen, where the twain awaited
him, and his face gleamed white in the gathering dusk. He dropped
to a chair, and mopped his face with a handkerchief; raised a wig,
and mopped his cropped head as well.

''Od's life, my lads, a near thing!' he panted.

The sense of peril oozed from him like perspiration, and, catch-
ing the infection of it, they sat still, watching him, and awaiting his
explanation.

''Twas that sleuth from Bow Street, Baldock—the shrewdest
catchpoll in the country. He's been on my heels this month past
and more. I fooled him once out o' sheer wantonness, and it is an
unforgiving dog, without humour. But I'll fool him again ere all is
done. He has never seen my face save once, and then it was so
disguised that he'd never recognize it. Yet this evening he was
within an ace of laying me by the heels. There was a trap set for
me. I had taken a fat purse 'twixt this and Petersfield, and I was
returning, when I stopped for a pint of claret at a roadside inn. But
for a friendly ostler who gave me a hint, I'd have had more than
my pint of claret, and 'tis odds ye'd never again have seen Captain
Evans, unless ye went to his hanging.' He stretched his legs, and
breathed more easily. 'Give me to drink, one o' ye. There should
be ale in the cupboard there.'

It was Jake who did him the service he asked, and fetched a jar
from the cupboard. There was little left in it, no more than a
cupful, but the captain drained it gratefully. Then he fished out of
his pocket a green silk purse with a glint of gold showing through
the meshes—a purse which he had taken that afternoon.

'And now, my lads, we must part company,' he informed them.
'The sleuths are too hot upon the scent, and the moment were ill-
chosen for the association we had thought of. If we stick together
you will but increase my danger, whilst I shall bring danger upon
you, too. I am for the West Country for a season, until the
Portsmouth Road is clear of Baldock and his runners. 'Twas but to
warn you that I returned tonight. You must fend for yourselves,
my lads: and here's to help you on your way.'

On the word he flung the silk purse on to the table, where it fell
with a mellow chink.

His generosity, both in this and in having taken risks to return to warn them, must have touched hearts less vile. Them, however, it left unmoved, save by greed and the sense of the need for urgent action. Jake fastened a lean claw upon the purse, and his eyes were two glistening beads.

''Tis very generous of you, captain,' said he; and it almost seemed that he sneered.

Captain Evans rose.

'And now, fare you well,' he said.

As he spoke the pair of them leapt at him. Taking him utterly by surprise, they bore him struggling to the ground under their combined weight. He was strong and agile, and almost a match for the pair of them—almost, but not quite. The fight that ensued was fierce and long-drawn. The captain writhed and twisted, grappled, kicked, and smote at them, and before he was overpowered that savage, silent scrimmage had swept across the length of the kitchen floor, raising a cloud of dust, knocking over chairs and table in its furious course. But in the end they had him helpless, bound hand and foot; sweating and panting from his exertions, wigless, dusty, and with disordered garments, glaring at them with furious eyes.

Nathaniel righted one of the chairs that had been knocked over. They forced the captain into it, and bound him firmly to it with cords which they had prepared. Thus powerless, his white face writhing with anger and contempt, he cursed them fiercely for a moment.

'What are ye at all?' he asked them thereafter. 'Could I be mistook? Are ye a couple of dirty catchpolls who have tricked me into believing ye are upright men?'

The flabby Nathaniel, who, winded by his labours, had dropped wearily to a chair, had a miserable pretext ready.

'Ye called me pig-face!' he said, with a show of being offended.

'I see,' said the captain. 'And it was that led you to remember that I am worth a hundred guineas to any that can take me.'

He was on the point of adding something more, but it occurred to him that invective was not likely to help him here, that never had he been in more desperate plight since once when the constables had actually fastened their talons on him. What saved him then was his presence of mind, his ready wit. And that was the only weapon that remained him now. He took their measure accurately. He saw that they would no more be loyal to each other than they had been to him did they perceive a course of profitable disloyalty. His first aim must be to separate them so that he might deal with each in turn. He threw back his head, and laughed—a thing so unexpected that it set them staring at him in alarm.

'Faith,' he said, 'the situation has its humour! I've been a fool, and I'm no such curmudgeon, after all, as not to know that a fool must blame only himself, and pay the reckoning.'

' 'Tis the proper spirit,' said Jake. And he proceeded diligently to empty the captain's pockets.

They yielded him another purse, a gold snuff-box with a jewelled crest, a watch, a couple of valuable rings, and, finally, a brace of barkers. He piled the plunder on the table, and Nathaniel fell to inspecting it, chuckling.

The captain watched them, his wits busy.

'Perhaps ye've chosen wisely,' said he presently. 'Ye make better thief-takers than tobymen. Ye'll turn king's evidence against me, thus save your dirty necks, and pocket the reward that Baldock covets. Ay, 'twas shrewdly thought.' He coughed. 'Gad, the dust is thick in my throat. Give me a drink.'

'The ale is done,' said Jake, who had his suspicions of the captain's amiable philosophy.

'Ay, plague on't,' growled Nathaniel, lifting the jar.

'True,' said Evans. 'I had forgot. But there's a bottle of brandy upstairs in my bedroom—in one of the drawers of my chest.'

Nathaniel's eyes glowed sombrely.

'Go fetch it, if ye will. Ye'll need to break the lock, maybe; for I cannot mind me where I left the key.'

Nathaniel departed without further persuasion. They heard him at work overhead, and the smash of woodwork told of the ardour of his search. Since, as a matter of fact, there was no such bottle as the captain suggested, that search was likely to be protracted.

The captain looked at Jake.

'Seize this chance,' he said softly. 'Set me free, and I'll pay you twice the sum the Crown is offering for me. More, Jake, I'll make your fortune ere all this is done.'

Jake scowled, displaying not the slightest sign of compliance. But then the captain had not expected any.

'And who's to warrant me that?' sneered the rogue at last, when he had overcome his surprise at the impudence of the proposal.

The captain nodded his head in the direction of the table.

'Why, there,' he exclaimed, 'you have a good two hundred guineas' worth at the least. 'Tis twice as much as the reward, and more easily earned. Sweep it into your pocket, man, and let us begone while that drunken fool is busy above stairs. Make haste, man! Cut me these cords!'

He watched the slow kindling of Jake's eye, the gradual loosening of his mouth, and he was satisfied that the rascally idea he had released was biting deep into the scoundrel's brain. Then followed precisely what the captain had expected. Jake moved furtively towards the table, his lips twitching, his whole countenance alert and somewhat scared. He swept the two purses and the rest of the plunder into his pockets. Then he took up the pistols and examined them. One was his own weapon, of which the captain had dispossessed him on their first encounter. It was loaded and primed, and so he dropped it also into his pocket. The other one was a barker that the captain had emptied that afternoon to scare the postilion of the gentleman he had robbed. It had not since been reloaded, and it may have been due to this that Jake laid it down again.

Then, without another word or so much as another glance at the prisoner, he stepped quickly and softly to the door.

Seeing this, the captain raised his voice in protest.

'Ye'll never leave me, Jake!' he cried, in simulated horror.

Jake leered at him over his shoulder in silence. Then he pulled the door open, passed out, and closed it gently after him.

The captain smiled to himself and waited. He heard Jake leading a horse into the open, while the fool above stairs continued his quest for the phantom bottle. In another moment hoofs went thudding down the lane, gathering speed as they receded. The captain laughed outright. So far things had sped excellently, and he was rid of one of his enemies. True, the thing had been achieved at considerable cost. But our tobyman was no niggard with the fruits of his ventures.

Minutes passed, then down the stairs, breathing noisily and swearing fluently, came Nathaniel.

'Skewer my innards,' said he, as he entered, 'I can't find no

plaguey bottle.' Then he stopped short and looked about him.
'Jake!' he called. And then, 'Where's Jake?' he enquired.

'Gone,' said the captain.

'Gone!' echoed Nathaniel, uncomprehending. 'Gone where?' He
rolled forward into the room.

'Why, to some stuling-ken, belike, to dispose of the plunder. He
went off with it what time ye were rummaging for the brandy.' He
laughed at the other's blank face. 'Ye're a confiding soul—nay, a
durned confiding soul.'

Nathaniel rolled his eyes to the table, and saw its emptiness of
all save the pistol.

'Ye don't mean that he's bubbled me!' he cried, on a whimpering
note.

'What else?' wondered Captain Evans.

'That he's not coming back?' Nathaniel insisted, still disbelieving
his senses.

'Oh, he may be coming back. But if I were you, I should pray
that he may not, or at least I shouldn't stay for him.'

'What d'ye mean?'

'Gad!' said the captain. 'I vow ye're the flabbiest fool that ever
cut a purse. What do I mean? Why, isn't it plain? If he comes back
at all, he'll come back with Baldock, and take you together with
myself, turning king's evidence against the pair of us, and thus
making sure of the hundred guineas reward in addition to all the
rest.'

It was a blow that winded Nathaniel. His face turned first
purple, then pale. To express his amazement, his realization, and
his poisonous rage, he swore with a most disgusting fluency. Then
he paused.

'I'll not believe it!' he cried. 'He'll never be so dirty a tyke as
that.'

'You've but to stay if you desire to ascertain precisely how far his
villainy will go.'

'But, man——' Nathaniel checked. His eyes alighted on the
pistol lying on the table. 'Nay, now. He'd never have left his
barker if he meant such business as that.'

'The barker! Ha!' said the captain, with an odd inflection; and he
added sharply, 'Look at it!'

Nathaniel snatched it up.

'Unloaded!' said he; and with that his last, lingering, hopeful doubt was dissipated.

Utter consternation invaded his soul, and overspread his face. To linger here now was to await certain capture, as the captain so shrewdly had warned him.

'Odds rot the plaguey thief!' he snarled. 'If ever I meet him ag'in, I'll——'

He stopped. He had no words in which to express the horrors he would perpetrate upon the person of his treacherous associate. Then, abruptly, he snatched up his ragged hat, pressed it upon his no less ragged head, and made for the door.

Now, this was not at all as the captain desired it. He did not himself believe for a moment that Jake would undertake any such desperate adventure as to fetch Baldock. He was convinced, in fact, that Jake would be perfectly and wisely satisfied with the result of his treachery to his comrade as it stood, and would avoid a risk in which he might well lose all, and find his way to the gallows in addition.

Nevertheless, he had no desire to be left pinioned there as he was. He had rid himself of one of his captors, and was about to rid himself of the other, and he flattered himself that he had contrived the thing with a rare thoroughness; but, before Nathaniel abandoned him, he must see to it that he was set at liberty.

'Hold!' he shouted. 'Are ye going to leave me here to fall into his hands?'

Nathaniel shrugged, and lifted the latch.

'Is this how you repay me for warning you? For you'll admit that but for my warning you 'ld never ha' smoked his full intentions. You'd ha' lain in Petersfield Gaol with me this night. And would ye desert me now?'

'Each for himself,' said Nathaniel callously, and opened the door.

Then the captain played his trump-card.

'Are ye going to put another hundred guineas in that weasel's dirty pockets?' he cried.

Nathaniel checked at that. He turned, his face grimly resolute.

'No, by gad! No, sink me!' he declared.

'Come, now, that is better. Besides, my friend, I can show you how to overtake him yet, and turn the tables on him.'

'How?' quoth Nathaniel, with fresh eagerness.

'How?' said the captain; and he smiled. 'Gad! There's not a drawer or ostler in an inn on all the Portsmouth Road but is my friend. They'll set me on his track, and when we've got him——But bestir, man; we'll talk of that as we go!'

Nathaniel produced a knife, and slashed away at the prisoner's bonds. Evans rose, and stretched himself, a little numb from the pressure of the cords upon his arms and legs. He straightened his disordered garments, and bent down to dust his breeches.

'Give me my wig, Nat,' he said, pointing to it where it lay in a corner of the room.

Nathaniel, unsuspecting, stooped to do his bidding, nor rose again. For, swift as a cat, the captain leapt upon him from behind, and bore him to the ground, wielding in his right hand the empty pistol which he had snatched up from the table.

Pinned there, prone, with the captain's knee in the small of his back, Nathaniel squealed like a stricken rabbit, what time the captain mocked him.

'You pig-faced foist!' he said. 'You to play the tobyman! You to rob in the grand manner! You to ruffle it on the pad! Odds my life, you dirty thieving dawcock, I hope this will cure you of all such vanity. And you thought you could hold Captain Evans—you! Bah!'

The captain tapped him sharply over the head with the butt of the empty pistol, and rose, leaving him stunned where he lay. Then he adjusted his wig, took up his hat and riding-crop, and left the cottage.

But in the lean-to an unpleasant surprise awaited him. The horses stabled there were the two screws upon which Nat and Jake had ridden. His own roan mare with the white blaze was gone, and he realized that it was Jake who had taken her. In an exceeding ill-humour, and breathing redoubled vengeance now that his chances of overtaking Jake to effect it were considerably diminished, the captain rode off on the better of those two sorry nags.

He made straight for Liphook and the Lame Dog, hoping there to pick up news that should set him on the track of the renegade. The news he found was of another kind.

'It is well for you, captain, that ye didn't come a half-hour ago,' was the greeting he received from Tom, the drawer.

And thereupon the fellow told his tale:

'There was a gentleman here who swore he had been robbed this very afternoon twixt this and Petersfield. With him was Baldock, the thief-taker, who swore 'twas yourself had robbed the gentleman, and likewise swore to lay you by the heels. And then, whilst they were in the taproom, up rides a down-at-heel scarecrow of a fellow on your own roan mare, captain. The gentleman who had been robbed was sitting by the window, and no sooner does his eye light on this traveller than up he jumps in a great heat, swearing that this was the man who had robbed him.

'"Are ye sure?" cried Baldock, all of a shake in his eagerness.

'"Certain sure," says the gentleman. "I couldn't be mistook; though the rascal's face was masked there was no mask on the nag, and I 'ld recognize that white blaze anywhere."

'That was enough for Baldock. He whistled, and in the twinkling of an eye they had that scarecrow off the mare, and they was going through his pockets. And there, sure enough, it seems, they found some rings and other things of which the gentleman had been robbed this very day.

'The rogue swore that he was not Captain Evans. He told a wild tale of how he had come by those trinkets. He protested that he had himself captured Captain Evans, and that he had him bound fast in a place to which he offered to lead Baldock. But the Bow Street runner laughed at him.

'"Ye've bubbled me afore, Captain Evans," says he, "and I'll be blistered if ye bubble me again! I have ye safe this time." And they carried the poor devil off to London.'

The captain's laughter pealed forth.

'I was sorry for the poor rogue,' said the drawer, 'and I might ha' helped him. But, o' course, it weren't for me to be doing that at your expense, captain.'

'Small need for sorrow on his account, Tom,' the captain assured him. 'The rogue is well served for his impudence in setting up for a ruffler of the pad. The high toby is a place for gentlemen, egad, and he was no better than a poacher. What of the mare, Tom?'

'They took her along.'

The captain sighed.

'I've paid dear for my folly, Still, when all is said——Bah! Give me a pint of claret, Tom, and lace it well with brandy. I am somewhat shaken by this adventure.'

The Sentimentalist

CAPTAIN EVANS—to give him the rank he had assumed for decorative purposes and without having any real claim to it—rode out of Godalming alone and early one fragrant summer morning, leaving his younger brother, Will—in conjunction with whom he was in the habit of 'working', as the term was, the Portsmouth Road—snugly abed at the Black Boar Inn. He was bound for Petersfield, or, rather, for the Fox and Hounds, which invites custom a mile or so to the north of that prosperous little township, and he rode in answer to an urgent message from Tim, the ostler, whom he subsidized to keep him informed of such movements upon the road as it imported him to know in the way of business. Tim had bidden him to be at the Fox and Hounds not later than noon, intimating that he would then have an important communication for our captain. But the captain, having risen early, found himself breasting the slopes in the neighbourhood of Thursley by nine o'clock—as recorded by a watch which a week ago had been the property of the Bishop of Salisbury, and which could not, therefore, be suspected of inaccuracy.

It followed that the captain had an hour or so to spare over and above the necessary time in which to complete the journey without undue exertion, and no sooner had he realized this than he caught sight of a yellow chaise coming into view on the brow of the hill above him. A man of quick decision—which, after all, is the first essential of success in his difficult calling—the captain swung his mare to the right, and vanished down a narrow lane that opportunely offered itself. Fifty yards down this lane he halted, swung aside again, and, putting the roan at a low fence on his left, landed in a meadow. He rode gently back towards the road, took up a position behind a clump of trees, and waited, vigilant and invisible.

The carriage came lumbering down the hill, a two-horse post-chaise, yellow as a buttercup in the morning sun, betraying nothing of its contents. More pressed for time, the captain might have allowed the hired vehicle to go unmolested. It was not his way in these days to take risks where he was not sure of profit; but with an hour or so on his hands, and the very freshness of the morning stimulating his young blood to high adventure, he resolved to investigate at closer quarters.

Back he went by the way he had come, and along the lane out into the open road, there to turn and trot in the wake of the coach, which was heading for Godalming. At a pace that, without being hot enough to alarm the travellers, yet steadily lessened the distance between himself and the chaise, Captain Evans drew alongside. It was his intent—and in accordance with his usual practice—first to reconnoitre, and then, if satisfied, to ride ahead and turn to deliver the attack.

He was the last man to shirk a hazard, but he had long since realized that for success on the high-toby, as on the field of battle, prudence and the elimination of the unnecessary risk is as essential as courage. He had, you see, an orderly mind even in disorderliness, probably resulting from the fact—to be read in Mr Whitehead's 'Life' of him—that he had been bred up for the law by his father, a prosperous Welsh farmer. For the rest, he had found the law more amusing in the breach than in the practice, and the open road more attractive than a musty attorney's office.

He drew, then, alongside of the coach, and looked boldly in, as any other traveller might have done. Nor was there anything of the ruffian in his appearance to alarm those who might come under his inspection. He was dressed with sedate elegance in a riding-suit of grey, with silver lace, and the lustrous brown hair under his three-cornered hat was neatly clubbed.

To his vexation, he found that the curtains of the chaise were drawn, which would make his projected adventure more of a leap in the dark than ever. But even as he looked one of the curtains was whipped aside, and straining through the window came the head and shoulders of as delicious a piece of young womanhood as ever the captain—something of a dilettante in these matters—had contemplated with satisfaction. She seemed a part of that sweet, fragrant summer morning; at least, she found in it a very proper setting. Her complexion, now somewhat pale, was as delicate as a dog-rose; her eyes, which were very wide, were as blue as the flawless sky overhead; her hair was an aureole of sunbeams; and, to complete the lovely appeal of her, from parted lips came a cry for assistance. On her shoulder he observed, in his swift, comprehensive glance, a man's lean brown hand endeavouring to force her back into the chaise.

'Help!' she cried to him. 'Help! Oh, sir, deliver me!'

'Deliver you?' says the captain, taken aback. 'To be sure I will.' And then he added, 'I am the very angel of deliverance, so I am!' which was neat and quick of him, although the humour of it must of necessity escape her.

Another moment—time to pluck a barker from his holster—and he was roaring 'Stand!' in his grandest manner to the postboy.

The chaise rattled and creaked to a standstill, and the captain swung down from the saddle and threw open the door with an air. Here was romance, and it was for him to play his part in it. Out of the chaise came a fiery buck, in fine clothes and a mighty temper, using language that left no doubt that he must be either a great gentleman or a pickpocket. Considering a certain raffishness that hung about him, and the deep-bitten lines in his face, which advertised an age beyond the first seeming, the captain placed him without hesitation outside the former class, and came promptly to the conclusion that he could have no business on so fine a morning in a chaise with that gracious little lady.

The froth of foulness being blown off, we come to the ale of his opening interjection.

'Who the devil are you, sir, and what the devil d'ye mean interfering between a gentleman and his wife?'

'I'm not his wife, sir!' cried the lady. 'Don't believe him.'

'I shouldn't dream of doing so, indeed,' says Captain Evans. 'Be good enough to honour me with your commands, ma'am, and depend upon their instant execution. I take it you want to be rid of this gentleman's company?'

'I do, sir—I do!' she cried, hands pressed fervently together in appeal to this potential rescuer, and fear in her glance.

'You hear the lady and you see,' said the captain. 'I hope you'll not stop to argue.'

The buck swore most unbecomingly through his teeth, threatened to do horrible things to this intruder, but kept his fierce eyes on the gleaming barrel of the captain's pistol.

'Sink me now!' he ended. 'D'ye make yourself this lady's champion?'

'It's a fine morning for knight-errantry, whatever.'

'Knight-errantry, d'ye say? Faugh! Look now! I don't know who the devil you may be, but since you come so cursedly interfering——' He broke off and glared at the captain. 'Now, why the devil should I be taking you into our confidence?' he wondered savagely.

'To save the lady the trouble,' suggested the captain.

'Knight-errantry!' sneered the buck again; and then a gleam of inspiration came into his bold eyes. 'You play knight-errant with a pistol! Faugh!'

'I'll play it with anything you please.'

The morning sun and the little lady had between them got into the captain's blood, so that business was quite forgotten.

'Will you? Will you take a turn with me as one gentleman with another, so that we may settle this matter of your unwarranted intrusion in my affairs?'

'You mistake,' said the captain. 'It's the lady's affairs I'm intruding in, and not unwarranted, but by her invitation, whatever.'

The gentleman sneered.

'You are splitting straws.'

'Shall I be splitting your windpipe?' says Evans, without heat.

'Let us to it, then,' says the gentleman.

'With all my heart.'

Thereupon the gentleman peeled off his laced coat and put it across the window, so that it hung half on one side, half on the other, of the open chaise door. The captain observed that it was a mighty fine coat, and wondered from force of professional habit what the pockets might contain.

Then the buck lugged out his small sword and stood waiting. The captain's preparations were less elaborate. He restored his pistol to its holster and came forward sword in hand. The little lady, standing now in the door of the chaise, with fluttering bosom and eyes in which fear was deepening into terror, cried out at this.

'Oh, sir, oh, sir, why do you consent?'

'I am wondering myself, ma'am.'

'Get your pistol again, sir. He will surely kill you. He is a dreadful—dreadful man.'

'The last one I killed was much dreadfuller—yes, indeed,' said
the captain. He lied in this for the sheer humour of it, for in all his
wild career he had never yet made himself guilty of taking life.
With that he made a leg very prettily. 'Are you ready, sir? Then on
guard, if you please.'

The buck flashed the lady a malicious glance—a glance which
said as plainly as words, 'I'll deal with you presently, my girl, and
you shall pay for having brought this upon me'—and so fell on
guard.

In his readiness to fight, the captain found confirmation of his
first judgement of the fellow as an adventurer embarking upon a
shady enterprise. A gentleman sure of himself and his position
would have taken any way but this to settle such a matter as the
present one. Further, this same readiness to fight argued a confidence in himself based, no doubt, upon skill and experience.
Now, the captain was no less confident of his own powers, being
himself a considerable man of his hands; but he realized at once
that, unless this affair were to have in one way or the other an
issue more serious than he could desire, he must end it almost
before it were begun.

It was a trick that had done him good service aforetime, and it
did not fail him now. Scarcely had the blades touched each other
in the first engagement than the captain dropped his point, whirled
it under and round his opponent's hand, and then straightened his
arm. It was all done in one movement with the speed of lightning,
and at the end of it—almost before the fine gentleman realized
that a disengage had taken place—there was a foot or so of the
captain's blade well home in his sword-arm.

The fellow uttered a howl of pain and rage, and the sword
dropped from his nerveless hand. Captain Evans wiped his steel
with a dainty lace kerchief, then sheathed it, and tossed the handkerchief away with an air. Then he addressed his adversary, who
was swearing and groaning and clamouring for help to staunch his
wound, all in one.

'I think, sir, you're lusty enough to help yourself,' said he.

Thereupon our gallant, evidently in mortal terror lest he should
bleed to death, pulls a handkerchief from the breast of his shirt,
and, holding one corner of it in his teeth and the other in his left
hand, sets about putting a bandage about his arm, going down on

one knee by the side of the ditch for greater ease in doing so.

'Ma'am,' said the captain, 'there's a scoundrel disposed of, and you may continue your journey in peace. To ensure it I'll escort you some part of the way, if you'll suffer me.'

'Oh, sir!' said she consentingly, whereupon the captain slammed the door of the chaise, swung himself up into the saddle again, and ordered the post boy to proceed.

But at the first crack of the whip up jumped the wounded buck, suddenly realizing what was taking place. In expectation of this, the captain had pulled his mare squarely across the road to bar the other's way.

'My coat!' screams the other in a frenzy. 'My coat, sir, if you please!'

Now, it seemed to Captain Evans, as it must seem to you, more than ordinarily singular that a gentleman in the buck's position, a gentleman who apparently had lost so much that morning, should be so supremely concerned with the trifling loss of a coat. So impressed, indeed, was the captain that when miss would have thrown the gentleman his garment he interposed, and bade her retain it as a keepsake.

'You're a deal too hot,' he informed the buck. 'You'll be the better for a cooling.'

And with that rode off in the wake of the chaise, leaving our fine gentleman in shirt and breeches, the incarnation of dismay and rage.

A mile or so they may have ridden, miss ever and anon putting her head from the window to cast a remark at her escort, and her escort doing his best to answer her becomingly, when at last she gave the order to halt.

'Sir,' she said, 'could you not tether your horse behind and ride with me? I feel that I owe you explanations.'

'Madame,' quoth he, very gallantly, 'I could no more be guilty of forcing a lady's confidence than of refusing so charming an invitation.'

And he proceeded to do as she suggested.

'You'll think that I have behaved very oddly, sir, in claiming your assistance,' she began, as soon as he was settled at her side.

'Since dealing with the object of your trouble, ma'am, I think the behaviour very natural. What I don't understand is how you

came to be running off with that fellow—for that, I suppose, was
the situation.'

Round eyes looked at him in enquiry, and also in surprise at his
penetration.

'He called himself your husband, ma'am,' the captain explained,
'which I took to be an anticipation of his hopes.'

'Oh, sir, I must tell you everything, and cast myself upon your
mercy. Perhaps you will then direct me how to act.'

With that she told her story—told it with downcast eyes and
troubled countenance, her hands listlessly folded in her lap. The
gentleman's name was Lake—Mr Julian Lake he called himself—
and, met by chance at Ranelagh in the first instance, he had
followed her down into the country to Petersfield, where she dwelt
with her guardian, Sir Henry Woodbridge. He had come into her
life in a moment of crisis. A young gentleman—whose name she
left out of her story—to whom she was promised in marriage, and
to whom she was deeply attached, had run off with a lady whose
identity she also refrained from disclosing. And then Mr Lake had
swooped down upon her, an impetuous whirlwind of a lover, with
an air of the great world about him to dazzle her, and, as women
will in her case, she had snatched at this chance of showing her
false lover how little she was troubled by his defection. With her
consent, Mr Lake had written to her guardian; and her guardian,
for reasons which he had omitted to disclose to her, had replied,
refusing to receive the fellow or countenance his suit. Thereupon
Mr Lake had proposed the elopement, and in despair she had
consented.

They had set out from Petersfield soon after dawn that day. Mr
Lake had made arrangements for their marriage at Guildford. But
with every mile that they rode together the sense of what she was
doing, and the fear of it, increased in the heart of Miss Helston,
until in the end, being fully if tardily awake to the folly of entrust-
ing her life to a man of whom, after all, she knew nothing, and for
whom she felt no more than a simulated affection, having its roots
in pique, she frankly told him so, and begged him to order the
chaise to be put about, and either to conduct her or send her back
to her guardian. It was then that Mr Lake revealed himself for the
adventurer that he really was. Miss Helston was—or would be
presently, on attaining full age, to which she was very near—a

lady of very considerable wealth, and so you conceive the rage and chagrin begotten in the heart of our gentleman, who had been congratulating himself upon the snug acquisition of her fortune. His conduct had been abominable. He had allowed her to perceive that he would stop at no violence short of murder to compel her to carry out her undertaking to marry him, and but for the captain's very timely arrival on the scene Miss Helston trembled to think what might have become of her.

It was a very moving tale, and Captain Evans, who was a little prone to sentiment, was deeply touched. Then he grew practical.

'And what's to be done now?' quoth he.

Miss looked at him with those melting, questioning eyes of hers. They had clattered through Godalming while her tale was a-telling, and were holding amain on the road to Guildford, the unreflecting postboy intent upon carrying out his original instructions, without regard to the change of passengers that had taken place.

'What—what do you advise?' she asked pathetically.

'Why, that you carry out your earlier intention of returning to Petersfield and your guardian. What else can you do, whatever?— unless you have friends with whom you would prefer to stay awhile until you can make your peace with Sir Henry.'

'No, no!' she said. 'I'll go back to him. I'll go back to Petersfield.'

Greatly relieved, the captain gave the necessary order. The chaise went about, and set out to return in its tracks. And then the captain bethought him of that important engagement of his for noon that day with the ostler of the Fox and Hounds at Petersfield—an engagement blown out of his mind by the events, and no longer to be kept with any degree of punctuality. It was striking one as they clattered for the second time over the cobbled streets of Godalming.

'I—I am very hungry,' says miss pathetically. It was not a cry to which a man of heart could close his ears. 'I haven't tasted food today,' she added. And at that he called himself a brute, and awoke to the fact that his own appetite was keen enough.

They drew up, by his order, at the Swan—a house at which he was unknown—and in a private room which he commanded above-stairs they sat down a half-hour later to the best dinner the house could provide and a bottle of the landlord's best Burgundy. Having drunk a generous share of it, Captain Evans came to account the time well lost, and the business appointment at Petersfield a matter of small consequence compared with the sweet delight of protecting and ministering to this choice, helpless wisp of womanhood. That satisfaction with things as they were was soon to increase to thankfulness, and he was to see in all that had happened the hand of Providence befriending him. It was the chamberlain of the inn who came presently to enlighten him.

'I hear, sir,' he said, in the course of his ministrations, 'that the Portsmouth Road will be safer for travellers after today. That pest of the highway, Captain Evans, is likely to be laid by the heels before night.'

'And is that so?' says the captain, with sharp interest. 'Now, that's mighty good hearing—yes, indeed.'

'You're right, sir. A gentleman just arrived from Petersfield tells me that the sheriff and his men had spread a net for the rascal, in which he must have been taken before this.'

The captain poured himself the remainder of the wine with a steady hand.

'Yet what all the world knows Captain Evans himself may discover,' said he.

'Too late for that, sir. He'll be took by now,' said the chamberlain with confidence as he withdrew.

The captain raised his glass to pledge the lady who all unconsciously had been the means of saving him from what he now surmised to be a bait trapped for him by that scoundrel Tim. Aloud, he toasted her safe return, a toast to which she responded almost gaily.

Her spirits, too, had improved under the invigorating influence of meat and wine, and the dark cloud that had hung over her since morning began at last to lift. She took an optimistic view of the future, and envisaged a return to Sir Henry's house without any serious misgivings. When he knew all he would forgive the escapade. What troubled her far more at the moment, she confessed, was how adequately to return thanks to her preserver.

'You have been to me the best friend that ever I had,' she told him, 'for you came to me in the hour of my greatest need, and never hesitated to afford me your assistance.'

He looked into the dainty face, with its so delicate complexion and eyes of blue, over which the lids were shyly and alluringly fluttering, and heaved a sigh.

'I am thinking we have been good friends to each other,' said he. 'It will be something for me to remember afterwards.'

'Afterwards?' says Miss.

'To be sure, afterwards—when you and I have gone our separate ways again, having each of the other just the memory of this day.'

'It will be a very grateful memory to me,' said she; and he saw the faintest cloud gathering again about her eyes.

'And a sweet one to me,' said he, and sighed again.

Now, it may have been that sigh of his that touched her, or the Burgundy that had emboldened her, or both working conjointly.

'We shall meet again, of course,' says she. 'We—we should be friends after what has happened—after the way in which you have befriended me.' And she looked at him with such ravishing candour for a moment that he was put out of breath and out of countenance.

'You—you make too much of the little service I have done you,' said he, faltering.

She frowned, and as her eyes were lowered he observed a sudden deepening of the colour in her cheeks, and realized how ungracious his words must have sounded. She pushed back her chair and rose.

'Miss Helston,' he exclaimed, 'you must not misunderstand. I——'

'I do not, sir. Your honest sincerity is very charming to me after what I have suffered at the hands of your sex. I could not fail to appreciate it deeply.'

But the sarcasm in the words cut him sharply, the more sharply because he must suffer it in silence. What was there he could say?

She crossed to the window and looked out upon the sunlit inn-yard. A coach came clattering into it at that moment.

'Shall we be resuming our journey, sir?' said she. 'We have some way to ride—that is, if I may still count upon the honour of the escort.'

He got to his feet.

'Now, why do you say that to me?' he growled, half resentfully, 'Can't you see that I would——'

Her sharp outcry interrupted him. She swung to him, showing a white, scared face: her bosom raced.

'Sir Henry—my guardian!' she cried. 'He is here! He saw me! And there are people with him!'

Captain Evans received the news with positive relief. It would make an end to a situation that was beginning to occasion him some anxiety.

'In that case, ma'am, your troubles will be at an end.'

'Will they?' She looked at him, and then the door opened, and from the threshold a tall, lean, sardonic gentleman stood regarding them with a smile that was not quite pleasant.

Captain Evans blenched. But it was not the sardonic countenance of Sir Henry that occasioned his disorder; it was another face perceived over Sir Henry's shoulder, the round, jolly face of Sir Thomas Blount, the sheriff of the county; nor did he pause to think under the moment's shock that his own face could not be as well known to Sir Thomas as was Sir Thomas's to him. He saw that behind the sheriff there were several men, and he accounted himself lost. Somehow they had trapped him when he failed to walk into the trap at Petersfield. Perhaps they had come upon Mr Lake, and he had assisted them with information. With his glance he measured the distance to the window, mentally calculated its height from the ground, and strove to imagine what might await him in the inn-yard should he take the desperate decision to go that way. Meanwhile the drawling voice of Sir Henry Wood-bridge—a voice that sorted excellently with the gentleman's sardonic countenance—was speaking.

'It would appear, then, that we arrive in time. I say it would appear so. And for your sake, Mr Lake, I sincerely trust that appearances do not deceive me, otherwise it will be for my friend Sir Thomas Blount to deal with you.'

He sauntered forward. The more corpulent sheriff rolled after him.

'Egad, yes, my buck,' gurgled the latter. 'Ye're caught red-handed in the hideous act of abduction. I've heard of you. I know something of your affairs, Mr Lake, and if you've had the services of a parson with this lady I promise you it shall go hard with you.'

Then forth trilled Miss Helston's laugh, and there was no mis-taking its naturalness and freedom from anxiety.

'Why, Sir Henry,' she addressed her guardian, 'this is not Mr Lake——'

'Of course not,' sneered Sir Henry the sardonic, and from that Captain Evans, whose courage had revived upon discovering that he was not himself the object of the sheriff's pursuit, very promptly took his course.

'My dear,' he said, on a note of romantic sorrow, 'what purpose can it serve to deny my identity?'

'But——' she began, and there she checked. Something compelling in her preserver's glance interrupted her, and imposed—almost seemed to beg—silent acquiescence. And meanwhile there was Sir Henry sneering.

'No purpose at all, sir. You very foolishly left the gentleman's letter behind you, Mary. It only remains for you to tell me whether you are yet married, whether this'—and he waved a slender hand towards the table from which they had risen—'was the wedding feast which we so inconsiderately interrupt?'

'We are not, sir,' said the captain, and, remembering what she had told him, added, 'We were to have been married at Guildford.'

'I remember that you mentioned it in your letter, Mr Lake. I am relieved by the tense you employ. It is very well for you, sir, that you can place it in the subjunctive and conditional perfect. My dear——' He crooked his arm, and proffered it to his ward, with something between mockery and command. Then, melting a little from his sarcastic haughtiness, 'Come, child,' he added, 'you shall yet come to thank me for saving you in time from this broken gamester.'

'Ay, ay; but are ye sure that you can take his word for't?' broke in the bustling little sheriff. 'I've been bubbled once today, when I should have been able to put my hand on that rascal Evans——'

'I am sure that I can take hers,' Sir Henry interrupted. He stood squarely before his errant ward, and looked into her pale face with its troubled eyes, that were now aswim with tears. 'Tell me, Mary—in a word, yes or no—are you married to him?'

'No,' she faltered. 'I am not.'

'That is enough, then. Let us be going.'

'Faith, it may be enough for you, Sir Henry,' quoth the officious Blount, 'but it's not enough for me. Abduction is a serious crime, Mr Lake, as you shall learn. Fetch him along, my lads,' he bade his men. 'We'll lodge him snugly in Guildford Gaol for tonight. He's a poor substitute for Captain Evans, but we'll take him along.'

At that she flung away from her guardian's arm, and came

running to her preserver, fear, misery, and bewilderment all blending in the appealing eyes she lifted to him.

'Oh, why——' she was beginning, when again he checked her.

'Believe me, my dear, Sir Thomas knows his business. Protests
would never avail to turn him aside from it. He is, as you observe,
a very conscientious and perspicacious gentleman. Pray let him
have his way without waste of words. Good-bye!'

He bore her hand to his lips, and felt it tremble almost convulsively in his grasp. More than his actual words, his glance, so
pregnant with a meaning that she could not read, commanded her
silence, and—whatever else might baffle her—made her realize
that this was the course which he desired that things should take.

And so they parted, she to return to Petersfield in her guardian's
coach, he to be haled away a prisoner in a hired chaise to Guildford. Until they had left Godalming behind them, it had been his
dread lest Sir Thomas should summon and question the postboy
who had driven him that morning. Fortunately, the bustling sheriff
neglected that detail as of no account, never conceiving that the
postboy's story could do other than confirm the matter which the
runaways themselves did not attempt to deny.

Captain Evans spent the night in Guildford Gaol, wondering
where exactly his knight-errantry would land him. He was visited
on the following morning by the sheriff. Sir Thomas was not in the
best of humours.

'You are in luck, Mr Lake,' he said sourly.

'I've not yet perceived it,' said the captain.

'But you will. I cannot proceed against you unless Sir Henry
Woodbridge prosecutes, and Sir Henry declines to do so.'

The captain sighed relief.

'That's vastly kind of him.'

'Kind! He doesn't do it to be kind to you, sir. He declines to
prosecute because he realizes that to do so would be to blow upon
the fair fame of his ward, Miss Helston. Out of consideration for
the lady he must forgo demanding upon you the punishment you
deserve. It was a fortunate thing for you, my lad, that he overtook
you in time to prevent the marriage. If he had found her your
wife, I believe she would have been your widow by now. Sir
Henry can be mighty hot, for all his cool ways. Remember that,
sir, and let it serve as a warning to you in the future. And now be

off. I've work to do. I've to be on the heels of that dammed tobyman Evans, who gave me the slip yesterday, and you're partly to blame for that.'

'Oh, Sir Thomas!' cried the captain, and his tone was pained. 'I swear you do me an injustice there. It's no fault of mine if you didn't gaol your highwayman.'

'It will be if you keep me talking here,' snapped Sir Thomas, and on that departed.

Captain Evans went off in a hired chaise to Godalming once more, and there sought his brother Will at the Black Boar. His arrival startled Will out of the deep dejection into which he had sunk, and he came to his feet with an oath at sight of his brother.

'How did you escape?' he cried.

'Escape?' echoed the captain. It was impossible that Will should have knowledge of his adventure. 'Escape what?'

'The trap that was laid for you at Petersfield.'

'Trap! Was it a trap?'

'Of course it was. That scoundrel Tim had sold you to the sheriff, and his men were waiting for you until night at the Fox and Hounds. Indeed, for all I know, they may be waiting for you still. Gadslife, Tom, I'd forsaken all hope of ever seeing you again. Where have you been?'

'With the sheriff,' says the captain.

'With the sheriff?'

'Ay—Sir Thomas Blount. I slept in Guildford Gaol, and parted from him there two hours ago. Let me explain.'

'I confess it's necessary.'

The captain told his story. 'So that, you see,' he ended, 'what time the sheriff and his men were waiting to take me, there was I safely hidden in the sheriff's own hands. Humorous, wasn't it?'

But Will was blind to the humour of it. He looked reproachfully at his brother.

'I suppose this ninny of a runaway girl beglamoured you, till you nearly lost your neck in the business.'

''Pon my soul, Will, that's ungracious, seeing that she saved me.'

'Saved you? Pshaw! If you hadn't allowed her to get you into danger there would have been no need for her to have saved you. You're an incorrigible sentimentalist.'

'I admit it. But it's been the salvation of me this time. And you're not to suppose that I neglected business completely. You'll remember that I came off with Mr Lake's coat.'

'Oh, Lake's coat!' sneered Will.

The captain dropped a bag of soft leather on the table. It squelched down with a melodious chink.

'There's fifty guineas in that; it was in one of his pockets. And here's a snuff-box—a pretty thing of gold and brilliants worth at least half as much. I thought I'd like it as a keepsake. Perhaps I am a sentimentalist.'

Will was mollified.

'But you've nothing of the girl's,' he complained.

'Nothing—tangible,' said the captain, and sighed. 'After all, you're no doubt right. I am an incorrigible sentimentalist. I must be.' And he sighed again.

Duroc

DUROC came down the Rue de la Harpe so stealthily that his steps scarcely made a sound. He moved like a shadow, and when at last he came to a halt before the house of the Citizen Representative Clairvaux it was as if he had totally effaced himself, as if he had become part of the general gloom.

There he paused considering, his chin in his hand; and perhaps because the ground-floor windows were equipped with bars, he moved on more stealthily than ever along the garden wall. Midway between two of the lanterns slung across the narrow street and shedding a feeble yellow light he paused again.

He stood now at a point where the shadows were deepest. He listened intently for a moment, peered this way and that into the night, and then went over the wall with the swift silent activity of an ape. He found the summit of that wall guarded by a row of iron spikes, and on one of these, for all his care, Duroc left a strip of his breeches.

The accident annoyed him. He cursed all *chevaux de frise*, pronouncing them a damnably aristocratic institution to which no true patriot could be guilty of having recourse. Indeed from the manner in which the Citizen Representative Clairvaux guarded his house it was plain to Duroc that the fellow was a bad republican. What with bars on its windows and spikes on its wall, the place might have been a prison rather than the house of a representative of the august people. Of course, as Duroc well knew, the Citizen Representative had something to guard. It was notorious that this modest dwelling of his in the Rue de la Harpe was something of a treasure-house, stored with the lootings of many a *ci-devant* nobleman's property, and it was being whispered that no true patriot— and a Citizen Representative into the bargain—could have suffered himself to amass such wealth in the hour of the nation's urgent need.

Duroc advanced furtively across the garden, scanning the silent, sleeping house. Emboldened by the fact that no light or faintest sign of vigilance showed anywhere, he proceeded so adroitly that within five minutes he had opened a window and entered a room that was used by the deputy as his study.

Within that room he stood quite still, and listened. Save for the muffled ticking of a clock no sound disturbed the silence. He turned and very softly drew the heavy curtains across the window. Then he sat down upon the floor, took a small lantern from his breast and a tinder-box from his waistcoat pocket. There was the sharp stroke of steel on flint, and presently his little lantern was shedding a yellow disc of light upon the parquetry floor.

He rose softly, placed the light on a console, and crossed the room to the door which stood half open. He listened again a moment then closed the door and came back, his feet making no sound upon the thick and costly rugs that were flung here and there.

In mid-chamber he paused, looking about him, and taking stock of his luxurious surroundings. He considered the painted panels, the inlaid woods, the gilded chairs and the ormolu-encrusted cabinets—all plundered from the hotels of *ci-devants* who were either guillotined or in flight, and he asked himself if it was in this sybaritic fashion that it became a true republican to equip his home.

He was a short, slender man, this Duroc, whose shabby brown garments looked the worse for the rent in his breeches. He wore a fur bonnet, and his lank black hair hung in wisps about his cheeks and neck. His face was white and wolfish, the jaw thrust forward and ending in a lean square chin; his vigilant quick-moving eyes were close-set and beady as a rat's; his thin lips were curled now in a sneer as he considered the luxury about him.

But that attitude of his was momentary. Duroc had not come there to make philosophy but to accomplish a purpose, and to this he addressed himself forthwith. He took up his lantern, and crossed to a tall secretaire that was a very gem of the court-furnisher's art in the days of Louis XIV. Setting the lantern on top of it, he drew from his pocket a bunch of skeleton keys, gripping them firmly so that they should not rattle. He stooped to examine the lock, and then on the instant came upright again, stiff and tense in his sudden alarm.

A knock had fallen upon the street door, and the echo of it went reverberating through the silent house.

Duroc's lips writhed as he breathed an oath.

The knock was repeated, more insistent now. To the listening Duroc came the sound of a window being thrown up. He heard voices, one from above, the other replying from the street, and guessed that the awakened Clairvaux was challenging this midnight visitor before coming down to open.

Perhaps he would not come. Perhaps he would dismiss this inopportune intruder. But that hope was soon quenched. The window rasped down again, and a moment later the flip-flop of slippered feet came shuffling down the stairs and along the passage to the door. A key grated and a chain clanked—this Clairvaux made a Bastille of his dwelling—and then voices sounded in the passage. The door of the house closed with a soft thud. Steps and voices approached the room in which Duroc still stood immoveable, listening.

At last he stirred, realizing that he had not a moment to spare if he would escape detection. He turned, so that his back was to the door, snatched up his lantern and pressed it against his breast, so that while it might still light him forward, its rays should not strike backwards to betray him. Then in three strides he gained the shelter of the heavy velvet curtains that masked the window. Behind them, his back to the casement, he extinguished at last the light.

The door opened an instant later. Indeed had Clairvaux who entered, candle in hand, in nightcap and quilted dressing-gown, bestowed an attentive look upon the curtains he would have detected the quiver that still agitated them. After him came a tall young man in a long black riding-coat and a conical hat that was decorated by a round tricolour cockade to advertise his patriotic sentiments. Under his arm he carried a riding-whip, whose formidable quality as a weapon of offence was proclaimed by its round head in plaited leather with silver embellishments. He placed it upon a table beside his hat, and the thud with which it dropped to the wood further announced its quality.

The Citizen Representative, a short, stiffly built man whose aquiline face was not without some resemblance to that of his visitor, flung himself into a gilt armchair upholstered in blue silk near the secretaire that but a moment ago had been the object of Duroc's attention. He threw one knee over the other and drew his quilted dressing-gown about his legs.

'Well?' he demanded, his voice harsh. 'What is this important communication that brings you here at such an hour as this?'

The man in the riding-coat sauntered across to the fireplace. He set his back to the overmantel, and the ormolu clock with its cupids by Debureau, and faced the deputy with a smile that was almost a sneer.

'Confess now,' he said, 'that but for your uneasy conscience, my cousin, you would have hesitated to admit me. But you live in the dread of your own misdeeds, with the blade of the guillotine like a sword of Damocles suspended above you, and you dare refuse no man—however unwelcome in himself—who may be the possible bearer of a warning.' He laughed an irritating laugh of mockery.

'Name of a name,' growled the deputy, 'will you tell me what brings you, without preamble?'

'You do not like preambles? And a representative! Now that is odd! But there, Etienne, to put it shortly, I am thinking of emigrating.'

It was the deputy's turn to become mocking.

'It was worth while being aroused at midnight to hear such excellent news. Emigrate by all means, my dear Gustave. France will be well rid of you.'

'And you?' quoth Gustave.

'And I no less.' The deputy grinned sardonically.

'Ah!' said his cousin. 'That is excellent. In such a case, no doubt, you will be disposed to pay for the privilege. To carry out this plan of mine I need your assistance, Etienne. I am practically penniless.'

'Now that is a thousand pities.' The deputy's voice became almost sympathetic, yet slurred by a certain note of sarcasm. 'If you are penniless, so am I. What else did you expect in a member of the National Convention? Did you conceive that a representative of the sacred people—an apostle of Liberty, Equality, and Fraternity—could possibly have money at his disposal? Ah, my good cousin, I assure you that all that I possessed has been offered up on the sacred altar of the nation.'

Gustave looked at him, and pursed his lips. 'You had better

reserve that for the National Assembly,' he said. 'It may sound
convincing from the rostrum. Here—' he waved a hand about him
at all the assembled splendours, 'it sounds uncommonly like a
barefaced lie.'

The deputy rose with overwhelming dignity, his brows
contracted.

'This to me?' he demanded.

'Why not?' wondered Gustave. 'Come, come, Etienne. I am not
a child, nor yet a fool. You are a man of wealth—all the world
knows it, as you may discover to your cost one fine morning. These
are days of fraternity, and I am your cousin——'

'Out of my house,' the deputy broke in angrily. 'Out of my
house this instant.'

Gustave looked at him with calm eyes. 'Shall I then go and tell
the National Assembly what I know of you? Must I denounce you
to the Committee of Public Safety as a danger to the nation? Must
I tell them that in secret you are acting as an agent of the emigrés,
that you plot the overthrow of the august republic?'

Clairvaux's face was livid, his eyes were bulging. He mastered
himself by an effort. 'Denounce all you please,' he answered in a
suffocating voice. 'You'll leave your own head in the basket. Sainte
Guillotine! you fool, am I a man of straw to be overthrown by the
denunciations of such a thing as you? Do you think to frighten me
with threats of what you will do? Do you think that is the way to
obtain assistance from me?'

'Seeing that no other way is possible,' flashed Gustave.

'Out of my house. Go, denounce me! Go to the devil! But out of
here with you!'

'Take care, Etienne!' The other was breathing hard, and his eyes
flamed with anger—the anger of the baffled man. 'I am desperate,
I am face to face with ruin. I need but a thousand francs——'

'Not a thousand sous, not a single sou from me. Be off!' And
Clairvaux advanced threateningly upon his cousin. 'Be off!' He
caught him by the lapels of his riding-coat.

'Don't dare to touch me!' Gustave warned him, his voice shrilling
suddenly.

But the deputy, thoroughly enraged by now, tightened his grip,
and began to thrust the other towards the door. Gustave put out a
hand to the table where his hat and whip were lying, and his

fingers closed upon that ugly riding-crop of his. The rest had happened almost before he realized it; it was the blind action of suddenly overwhelming fury. He twisted out of his cousin's grasp, stepped back, holding that life-preserver by its slender extremity, swung it aloft and brought the loaded end whistling down upon the deputy's nightcapped head.

There was a horrible sound like the crunching of an egg-shell, and the Citizen Representative dropped, fulminated by the blow, and lay in a shuddering, twitching heap, whilst the colour of his nightcap changed slowly from white to crimson under the murderer's staring eyes.

Gustave stood there, bending over the fallen man, motionless whilst you might count ten. His face was leaden and his mouth foolishly open between surprise and horror of the thing he had done.

Not a sound disturbed the house; not a groan, not a movement from the fallen man. Nothing but the muffled ticking of the ormolu clock and the buzzing of a fly that had been disturbed. Still Gustave stood there in that half-crouching attitude, terror gaining upon him with every throb of his pulses. And then quite suddenly a voice cut sharply upon the stillness.

'Well?' it asked. 'And what do you propose to do now?'

Gustave came erect, stifling a scream, to confront the white face and beady eyes of Duroc, who stood considering him between the parted curtains.

In a long silence he stared, his wits working briskly the while.

'Who are you?' he asked at last, his voice a hoarse whisper. 'How come you here? What are you? Ah! A thief—a housebreaker!'

'At least,' said Duroc drily, 'I am not a murderer.'

'My God!' said Gustave, and his wild eyes turned again upon that tragically grotesque mass that lay at his feet. 'Is he—is he dead?'

'Unless his skull is made of iron,' said Duroc. He came forward in that swift, noiseless fashion of his, and dropped on one knee beside the deputy. He made a brief examination. 'The Citizen Representative represents a corpse,' he said. 'He is as dead as King Capet.' He rose. 'What are you going to do?' he asked again.

'To do?' said Gustave. 'Mon Dieu! What is there to do? If he is dead——' He checked. His knavish wits were racing now. He looked into the other's round black eyes. 'You'll not betray me,' he cried. 'You dare not. You are in no better case than I. And there is no one else in the house. He lived all alone. He was a miserly dog, and the old woman who serves him will not be here until morning.'

Duroc was watching him intently, almost without appearing to observe him. He saw the man's fingers suddenly tighten upon the life-preserver with which already he had launched one man across the tide of the Styx that night.

'Put that thing down,' he commanded sharply, 'put it down at once, or I'll send you after your cousin.' And Gustave found himself covered by a pistol.

Instantly he loosed his grip of his murderous weapon. It fell with a crash beside the body of the man it had slain.

'I meant you no harm,' panted Gustave. 'Do you know what wealth he hoards in these consoles, in that secretaire? You do, for that is what you came for. Well, take it, take it all. But let me go, let me get away from this. I—I——' He seemed to stifle in his terror.

Duroc's lipless mouth distended in a smile.

'Am I detaining you?' he asked. 'Faith, you didn't suppose I was going to drag you to the nearest *corps-de-garde*, did you? Go, man, if you want to go. In your place I should have gone already.'

Gustave stared at him almost incredulously, as if doubting his own good fortune. Then suddenly perceiving the motives that swayed the other, and asking nothing better for himself than to be gone, he turned and without another word fled from the room and the house, his one anxiety to put as great a distance between himself and his crime as possible.

Duroc watched that sudden scared flight, still smiling. Then he coolly crossed the room, took up the dead man's candle and placed it upon the secretaire. He pulled up a chair—there was no longer any need to proceed with caution—sat down, and producing his keys and a chisel-like instrument he went diligently to work to get at the contents of this secretaire.

Meanwhile Gustave had gone like a flash the length of the Rue de la Harpe, driven ever by his terror of the consequences of his deed. But as he neared the corner of the Cordeliers he was brought suddenly to a halt by the measured tread of approaching steps. He knew it at once for the march of a patrol, and his consciousness of what he had done made him fearful of meeting these servants of the law who might challenge him and demand to know whence he was and whither he went at such an hour—for the new reign of universal liberty had imposed stern limitations upon individual freedom.

He vanished into the darkness of a doorway, and crouched there to wait until those footsteps should have faded again into the distance. And it was in those moments as he leaned there panting that his fiendishly wicked notion first assailed him. He turned it over in his mind, and in the gloom you might have caught the gleam of his teeth as he smiled evilly to himself.

He was his cousin's heir. Could he but fasten the guilt of that murder upon the thief he had left so callously at work in the very room where the body lay, then never again need he know want. And the thief, being a thief, deserved no less. He had no doubt at all but that the fellow would never have hesitated to do the murder had it been forced upon him by circumstances. He reflected further, and realized how aptly set was the stage for such a comedy as he had in mind. Had not that fool compelled him to drop the very weapon with which the deputy's skull had been smashed?

No single link was missing in the chain of complete evidence against the thief. Gustave realized that here was a chance sent him by friendly fortune. Tomorrow it would be too late. In seeking his cousin's murderer the authorities would ascertain that he was the one man who stood to profit by the Citizen Representative's death, and having discovered that they would compel him to render an account of his movements that night. They would cross-question and confound him, seeing that he could give no such account as they would demand.

He was resolved. He must act at once. Not three minutes had sped since he had left that house, and it was impossible that in the meantime the thief could have done his work and taken his departure.

And so upon that fell resolve he flung out of his concealment, and ran on up the street towards the Cordeliers, to meet the advancing patrol, shouting as he went—

'Au voleur! Au voleur!'

He heard the patrol quickening their steps in response to his cry, and presently he found himself face to face with four men of

the National Guard, who, as it chanced, were accompanied by an
agent of the section in civilian dress and scarf of office.

'Down there,' he cried, pointing back down the street. 'A thief
has broken into the house of my cousin—my cousin the Citizen
Representative Clairvaux.' He gathered importance, he knew, from
this proclamation of his relationship with one of the great ones of
the Convention.

But the agent of the section paused to question him.

'Why did you not follow him, citizen?'

'I am without weapons, and I bethought me he would probably
be armed. Besides I heard you approaching in the distance, and I
thought it best to run to summon you, that thus we may make sure
of taking him.'

The agent considered him, his white face—seen in the light of
the lantern carried by the patrol—his shaking limbs and gasping
speech, and concluded he had to deal with an arrant coward, nor
troubled to dissemble his contempt.

'Name of a name!' he growled, 'and meanwhile the Citizen
Representative may have been murdered in his bed.'

'I pray not! Oh, I pray not!' panted Gustave. 'Quickly, citizens,
quickly! Terrible things may happen while we stand here.'

They went down the street at a run to the house of Clairvaux,
whose door they found open as Gustave had left it when he
departed.

'Where did he break in?' asked one of the guards.

'By the door,' said Gustave 'He had keys, I think. Oh, quick!'

In the passage he perceived a faint gleam of light to assure him
that the thief was still at work. He swung round to them, and
raised a hand. 'Quietly!' he whispered. 'Quietly, so that we do not
disturb him.'

The patrol thrust forward, and entered the house in his wake.
He led them straight towards the half-open door of the study, from
which the light was issuing as if to guide them. He flung wide the
door, and entered, whilst the men crowding after him came to a
sudden halt upon the threshold in sheer amazement at what they
beheld.

At their feet lay the body of the Citizen Representative Clairvaux
in a raiment that in itself seemed to proclaim how hastily he had
risen from his bed to come and deal with this midnight intruder;

and there at the secretaire, now open, its drawers broken and their contents scattered all about the floor, sat Duroc, white-faced, his beady rat's eyes considering them.

Gustave broke into lamentations at sight of his cousin's body.

'We are too late! Mon Dieu! We are too late! He is dead—dead. And look! Here is the weapon with which he was slain. And there sits the murderer—caught in the very act—caught in the very act. Seize him! Ah, *scélérat*,' he raged, shaking his fist in the thief's white, startled face. 'You shall be made to pay for this!'

'Comedian!' said Duroc shortly.

'Seize him! Seize him!' cried Gustave in a frenzy.

The guards sprang across the room, and laid hands upon Duroc to prevent him having recourse to any weapons.

Duroc looked up at them, blinking. Then his eyes shifted to Gustave, and suddenly he laughed.

'Now see what a fool a man is who will not seize the chances that are offered him,' he said. 'After that scoundrel had bludgeoned his cousin to death I bade him go. He might have made good his escape, and I should have said no word to betray him. Instead he thinks to make me his scapegoat.'

He shrugged, and rose under the hands of his captors. Then he pulled his coat open, and displayed a round leaden disc of the size of a five-franc piece bearing the arms of the republic.

At sight of it the hands that had been holding him instantly fell away.

The agent of the section stepped forward frowning.

'What does this mean?' he asked, but on a note that was almost of respect, realizing that he stood in the presence of an officer of the secret service of the republic, whom no man might detain save at his peril.

'I am Duroc of the Committee of Public Safety,' was the quiet answer. 'The Executive had cause to doubt that the Citizen Representative Clairvaux was in correspondence with the enemies of France. I came secretly to examine his papers and to discover who are his correspondents. Here is what I sought.' And he held up a little sheaf of documents which he had separated from the rest. 'I will wish you good-night, citizens. I must report at once to the Citizen-Deputy Marat. Since that fellow has come back take him to the Luxembourg. Let the committee of the section deal with him tomorrow. I shall forward my report.'

Gustave shook himself out of his sudden paralysis to make a dash for the door. But the guards closed with him, and held him fast, whilst Duroc of the Committee of Public Safety passed out, with dignity in spite of his torn breeches.

Kynaston's Reckoning

U NDER the date of the 18th August 1660, you will find the
following entry in the diary of Mr Samuel Pepys: 'Captain
Ferrers took me to the Cockpitt play, the first that I have had time
to see since my coming from sea, "The Loyall Subject," where one
Kinaston, a boy, acted the duke's sister, but made the loveliest
lady that ever I saw in my life.'

Edward Kynaston was short of stature, and of a lithe and stripling grace, golden-headed, with a milk-and-rose complexion that
any woman might have envied, and a countenance so delicately
beautiful that it provoked from Mr Pepys the above ejaculation,
and, further (on the 2nd of January following), this tribute: '. . . I
and my wife to the theatre, and there saw "The Silent Woman."
Among other things there Kinaston, the boy, had the good turn to
appear . . . in fine clothes, and in them was clearly the prettiest
woman in the house.'

This Kynaston had been discovered by Sir William Davenant—
the same who boasted himself to be the son of Master William
Shakespeare—and such were his histrionic gifts and personal
beauty that even when women were admitted at last to the English
stage he continued for some time thereafter to be entrusted with
the principal female roles, since no woman could be found to
compare with him in the performance of them.

Some years later (on the 9th February, 1669) we find Mr Pepys
writing as follows: 'To the King's Playhouse, and there saw "The
Island Princesse," which I like mighty well as an excellent play;
and here we find Kinaston to be well enough to act again; which he
do very well after his beating by Sir Charles Sedley's appointment.'

It is with this beating and its consequences that my story is
concerned. Ned Kynaston was by now in his twenty-second year,
and whilst he was still engaged in the main for female parts, yet
upon occasion he would play the youthful gallant—and have every
woman in the house enamoured of him.

In what way Sedley offended him we do not know, nor does it greatly matter. We do know that Sedley was very prodigal of offence, and although at this time a man well advanced in the forties, yet age had not sobered him or given him dignity. He was still quite the most outrageous of all the rakes about the court of that prince of rakes, their sovereign. The audacity of his intrigues was second only to that of his royal master. It has been made the subject of a lampoon by his brother rake, my Lord Rochester. Once when, as a result of what Anthony Wood calls his 'indecent and blasphemous behaviour', he had raised a riot in the Cock Tavern in Covent Garden, and had been haled, together with my Lord Buckhurst and some others, before Sir Robert Hyde— Lord Chief Justice of the Common Pleas, sitting in Westminster Hall—Sir Robert caustically commended to him the perusal of a book entitled *The Compleat Gentleman*—a recommendation which galled him worse than the fine of £500 by which it was accompanied.

Pepys, too, tells us of a 'frolic and debauchery' of Sedley's and Buckhurst's, 'running up and down all the night, almost naked in the streets, and at last fighting and being beat by the watch and clapped up all night'.

It is not difficult to conceive that so turbulent a rake may have got foul of the players at the King's Theatre, and thus provoked Kynaston. Be that as it may, Kynaston chose to appear on the stage made up in so life-like a portrait of Sir Charles, and so naturally counterfeiting his accent and his posturings, that the whole house was convulsed with it when it had assured itself that it was not Sir Charles himself who strutted there upon the boards.

You imagine, I hope, the fine passion into which Sedley was flung when he knew of it. Those who overheard his threats to have the actor's life say that he foamed at the mouth in uttering them. But he did not take the direct way to achieve his purpose expected by those who were witnesses of his ravings. He did not send his friends and the length of his sword to Kynaston. How could he? Blackguard though he was by instinct and behaviour, it yet remained that by birth he was a gentleman; and it could not have become a gentleman to have so forgotten what was due to himself as to have condescended to cross swords with a rogue and a vagabond of an actor. Besides, Kynaston, for all his slight frame

and almost womanish beauty, was of an extremely virile spirit, and
of a singular address in all the exercises of his age. He played—as
indeed you shall see—as pretty a rapier as any man in these
islands.

So Sir Charles took another way—the way of the gentleman
with the plebeian. He sent a couple of hired bullies to waylay
Kynaston in the park one morning. They fell upon him, broke his
sword with their cudgels, and so belaboured him that he was left
almost for dead when they made off before the advent of those who
ran belatedly to the poor actor's assistance.

Such was the resentment of town and Court—for Kynaston was
a universal favourite—that for once the King frowned upon one of
those who modelled their conduct upon his own august pattern.
But beyond a transient coolness, his Majesty did not see fit to visit
any other punishment upon Sedley, and Kynaston, seeing that
there was none to avenge him, considered, so soon as he was
restored to health, how best he might avenge himself.

The cowardly assault had raised in him such a thirst for vengeance as naught but Sedley's blood could assuage. He must take
steps to make it impossible for the rake to do aught but set aside
his gentleman's estate and measure swords with him; that much
accomplished, at whatever cost or consequences, Kynaston was
resolved to kill him without mercy.

He was about his murderous purpose on that sunny February
morning on which Sir Lionel Faversham tells us that he met him
outside the Dolphin in the Strand. He was dressed in a black
camlet suit, very sober and simple, yet of an elegance that heighted
his distinguished air. 'Actor though he was,' says Faversham, 'I'll
swear that no courtlier figure might you see in Whitehall.'

Faversham found him pacing there like a sentry, with a heavy
riding-whip tucked under his arm.

'Whither away, Ned?' he greeted him.

Kynaston tossed his golden curls, and with his whip he pointed
across to the Dolphin.

'I am staying for Sir Charles Sedley,' he replied in that gentle
and wonderfully musical voice of his. 'If you'll tarry here awhile,
you'll see a reckoning paid, and a rakehell carried home to bed.
'Twill divert you, Sir Lionel.'

'Odds my life, lad! Are ye clean mad?' cried Faversham.

Having a very real affection for the young man, and foreseeing for him the worst possible consequences from such an affair, he set himself urgently to turn him from his purpose. They wrangled there awhile, and in the end, Sir Lionel's good sense prevailing, Kynaston suffered himself to be led away. Faversham carried him off to his own lodging in King Street, and kept him there out of mischief until the morrow. By then the actor's rage had so far cooled that he lent an ear to the reasonable counsel of his host.

'I'll be advised by you, Sir Lionel,' he said at parting, 'and I abandon all thought of repaying him in his own coin. 'Tis stupid currency when all is said. Yet, sink me, it shall be the worse for him! For you are not to suppose that I shall forgo the reckoning. I'll present it in another form, and, when I do, you shall see Sedley pilloried to the mock of the town.'

Faversham accounted all this to be no more than the vapourings of a histrionic temperament, the last flicker of the flame of the actor's resentment; and he deemed himself confirmed in this judgement when, as the weeks went by, the whole affair was permitted by Kynaston to fall into oblivion. Confidently he accounted the incident closed, which but shows that, despite his friendship for Kynaston, his knowledge of him did not go very deep.

It would be about a month after these events that town and Court were set agog by the advent of a new beauty at Whitehall in the person of Caroline Countess of Chesterham. Her coming had been heralded in advance in a letter from the septuagenarian Lord Chesterham to his old friend Faversham, who had been cornet of horse in a regiment commanded by his lordship at Naseby. He wrote from the remote wilds of Cornwall, whither he had retreated some years before, to announce that he had married a young wife.

What the town said of it is neither here nor there, and, in any case, is very readily imagined. Also, it is readily imagined with what curiosity the town looked forward to his announced visit, and to see this girl whose beauty he extolled at such length in another letter addressed to Lady Denham. His lordship wrote that, although he had never thought to forsake his hermitage again, yet having taken so young a bride he was sensible of the duty that he owed her, and that since it was her desire to see something of the great world, he could not find it in his heart to deny her.

A handsome house was made ready for them in Pall Mall by a

steward, and a posse of servants sent ahead. And a few days later the news was put about that they had arrived.

Among the first to pay their devoirs were, of course, Sir Lionel Faversham and Sir John and Lady Denham. To receive them they found, however, none but the bride, installed in a nobly proportioned drawing-room whose windows looked out upon the park.

They had naturally assumed from his lordship's letters that she would be country-bred, but they found little to confirm the assumption in her appearance and her manners. She was of striking, of superb beauty—tall, straight, and slender, with a carriage of such grace and supple dignity that a queen might have been proud of it. If a fault there was in that glorious, gipsy-tinted face it was that it too closely matched her bearing. It was cold and proud, and it derived a something almost of boldness from the steady glance of her magnificent sombre eyes. Her gown was in the very latest mode of France, and her abundant, lustrous black hair, intertwined with a string of pearls, was dressed in the very noontide of fashion, whilst a round black patch—that very latest of fashion's mad conceits—sat roguishly upon her chin, and yet another on her cheek 'neath her left eye. Her voice was low and cultured and very rich, and none could have been more infinitely and nobly at ease than she when she explained the absence of her septuagenarian bridegroom.

She informed her visitors that within ten miles of town they had been overtaken by a courier, who brought them word that his lordship's brother had a seizure, and was not expected to live, whereupon his lordship had gone posting back at once, leaving his wife to end the journey alone and to await him in London, whither he would follow as soon as might be. She brought a little note from him to Lady Denham, in which he implored the latter's good offices of her—a charge which Lady Denham very amiably accepted, entirely ravished by the grace and dignity of Lady Chesterham.

Faversham tells us that he withdrew perturbed in spirit. He had conceived his old friend to have committed the regrettable imprudence of giving rein to an infatuation for some rustic Hebe, whereas instead he was driven to fear that he had fallen a prey to an adventuress of talent, who would not be long in covering him with that ridicule which so often falls to the lot of the old man who marries a young wife—the Pantaloon in the Comedy of Life.

The events most certainly nourished these fears of his, and did credit to his discernment. Presented at Whitehall by Lady Denham, Lady Chesterham created a greater sensation than in its day had been caused by the advent there of Barbara Palmer. Her triumph was to be read in the hostility with which the women received her. Metaphorically they recoiled before her. That cold assurance, amounting almost to boldness, which Faversham had detected in her bearing, proved repellant to the majority of her own sex. They discovered in her something almost approaching raffishness, which disconcerted their own more veiled immodesty. And then there was her astounding popularity with the men to quicken the venom of the ladies of the Court. The latter looked on with noses at a disdainful angle, whilst they stripped her character to its last rag, tore her reputation into tatters.

Yet she thrived amazingly in the assiduous court that was paid her by the brothers, fathers, and husbands of her instinctive enemies. The sultan Charles himself was vastly taken with her—which, after all, considering his temperament, was not wonderful. He went the length of visiting her in her splendid mansion in Pall Mall, a matter which caused Faversham to wring his hands in despair, and pray that her husband's brother might get his dying done with as much despatch as possible.

But there was worse to follow. All day, and often far into the night, a line of chairs and coaches stood before her doors, and in her ante-chambers, such was the press of courtiers that you might have deemed yourself at Whitehall.

In her social tastes she proved herself extremely catholic. Not merely were beaux and men of fashion welcomed; soon her rooms were thronged with wits and poets, painters, writers of plays, and even one or two actors haled thither in the train of Sir George Etheredge, who himself belonged to two worlds. To all she was alike gracious, until in the end, inevitably, she came to manifest to one a special favour. And this one, to Faversham's dismay, was none other than Sir Charles Sedley, that devourer of hearts, that heartless blighter of reputations. And the worst of it was that the first advances came undoubtedly from her. She it was who ogled the rake and lured him on to pay his assiduous court.

Soon her name, coupled with Sedley's, was on the gay town's lips. Faversham—immensely daring—breathed a warning to her. She measured him with her bold black eyes, 'twixt raillery and scorn.

'I protest I find him vastly amusing,' said she.

'I pray Heaven, madam, you may always say so.' said Faversham impressively.

'You are more devout than witty, sir, which is to say, you are a dullard,' was the fleeting answer with which she quitted him.

Some days later, in the Rhenish Wine House, which was full of company at the time, Sir Lionel came face to face with Ned Kynaston. The actor had a flushed, excited air, and his eyes were bright.

'What's this I hear of Sedley, Sir Lionel?' he cried out, in a voice that drew attention. 'They are coupling his name with Lady Chesterham's. But an hour ago I all but had a duel on my hands through it.'

Faversham's lips tightened. He froze. Were matters indeed gone so far that her name was thus flung about a wineshop? Yet because of his affection for Kynaston he tempered the rebuke that had arisen to his lips.

'Lady Chesterham's affairs,' he replied gravely, 'are her own and Lord Chesterham's, who, no doubt, will demand an account of any who presumes to lend her name to scandal-mongers.'

'Faith, then, he'll need to be returning soon, or he'll find his work done for him by another. Curse me, Sir Lionel, I tell you no man shall say a word against her ladyship in my hearing but I'll ram his lies down his dirty throat with the point of my cane!'

Faversham took him by the arm.

'Be silent, Ned!'

'Silent?' roared Kynaston. 'Shall I be silent what time that foul fellow Sedley's verses upon her are being sung up and down the town? I'll do more than write verses in her honour to prove myself her slave!' And he declaimed, adapting:

> I'll sing my praise of thee in trumpet sounds,
> And write my homage down in blood and wounds.

Faversham's grip upon his arm tightened. He dragged him out of the tavern into the pale February sunshine.

'Art mad, Ned?' he growled. 'Another word in that strain in public, and I shall quarrel with you. If you respect the lady as you pretend, afford by silence some testimony of that respect.'

But the mischief was done. Kynaston had been abundantly over-heard. His words were, of course, repeated. The women got hold of the story, and it suffered nothing in their fierce retailing of it. This bold wanton was so lost to decency, so greedy of admirers, that even players were admitted to sun themselves in her smiles. As for Kynaston, there were no limits to what was said of him. It was most plausibly suggested that, availing himself of the oppor-tunity her lack of circumspection was affording him, he meant to oust Sedley from her favour, and thus take vengeance upon Sedley for the beating he had received by his appointment. Since her tastes were admittedly base, it was deemed not impossible that he might prove victorious in this contest, though, to be sure, it would be a victory that could bring him but little glory. Thus the ladies.

That pretty tale overran the town like wildfire. It came to Sedley's ears, and set him in a seething passion. In this he went off to Lady Chesterham's.

'Madam, what is't I hear?' he burst out at sight of her.

From the couch where she reclined she eyed him languidly.

'I see that you are come to set me riddles,' she drawled. 'But I warn you that they weary me.'

'Riddles?' quoth he. 'Ay, a riddle in sooth. 'Tis said that you favour that low fellow Kynaston; that you receive him here; that he has the temerity to proclaim himself the champion of your good name!'

'Does he so?' she cooed. 'I vow 'tis vastly sweet in him.'

'Vastly sweet?' he roared. 'Fan me, ye winds! Do you real-ize what it means? Would you have him blast your fair repute, madam?'

She considered him with half-closed eyes, smiling insolently over the edge of her gently moving fan.

'Do you desire to be alone and absolute in the enjoyment of that privilege?' quoth she.

He looked at her blankly a moment, speechless. Then he stamped his foot.

' 'Tis not to be borne!' he cried.

'Who bids you bear it, sir, whatever it may be?' she countered scornfully. 'Did I bid you to come pestering me with your sheep's eyes and your sighs and your silly speeches? If the dear lad please me, what is't to you, pray? Who gave you rights upon me? La, now! I protest you weary me.'

'Caroline!' he began unsteadily. He advanced and stood over her, glowering down into that mocking, gipsy-tinted face. He swallowed, and began again. 'You are to understand, madam, that it is not safe to play fast-and-loose with me.'

The jewelled fingers of her fine long hand moved her fan gently to and fro again. Her lip curled.

'You are a mirror of the politenesses, sir.'

'Curse me, madam, I do not aim at politeness!'

'In that case you will be the less put about.'

'Ha! You rally me! You make a mock of me!' he raved, beside himself with anger. 'You have brought me to this—to this! And now——'

He flung his arms wide and let them fall again, his face very pale.

She sat bolt upright.

'Sir Charles,' said she, 'I was warned of your presumption and your ill-repute.'

'If that dog Kynaston has dared malign me——'

'Believe me, 'twere impossible—beyond the compass of his invention. It is time, Sir Charles, you understood that you have no right or claim upon me beyond such as it may be my pleasure to confer. Such rights belong only to my husband.'

'Damn your husband, madam!' he snapped in his rage.

She rose, frowning.

'Sir Charles, you forget the respect due to me,' she rebuked him, with a great dignity, her face forbiddingly cold. 'You have my leave to go.'

He gaped foolishly, stricken by her sudden iciness.

'Forgive me!' he pleaded. 'I—I am a little disordered. I——'

'Faugh!' she broke in. 'I could forgive your being disordered, but I cannot forgive you for being maudlin and tiresome. Heaven be my witness I never could endure a tiresome man. I give you good-day.'

He flung out in a rage, not trusting himself to say another word. In his heart he cursed her for a wanton who had but lured him on that she might subject him to this humiliation. But anon, as he cooled, he came to consider that perhaps he had been precipitate. His vanity argued that her self-respect must have compelled her to resent the too-masterful tone he had taken with her. He had been foolish; he had displayed no more tact or judgement than an oaf.

Hence it happened that he came contritely to her house upon the following morning, intent to make his peace with her, confident of his power to do so. He reflected that no cloud would ever have troubled their relations but for that rascal Kynaston. The very thought of the fellow was enough to fling Sir Charles into a fresh passion. But he curbed his mood, bethinking him that to give way to it was to suffer defeat in the end. After all, Kynaston was most rarely handsome, and he had gifts—Sir Charles deemed it prudent to admit his enemy's strength—which might entrap the heart of a wilful, headstrong woman such as Caroline Chesterham. Women were such fools in these matters, he considered. They never could distinguish between a rogue and a gentleman.

He entered the spacious hall at the foot of the main staircase—a hall which served the purpose of the mansion's principal ante-chamber. Here he found the usual company assembled, but, if anything, more numerous than usual, which put him out of temper. Yet perhaps she would do him the honour of granting him im-mediate and private audience?

He approached one of her splendid servants, and slipped a guinea into the fellow's hand and a message into his ear. The lackey pocketed the coin, and vanished. He returned almost at once.

'Her ladyship's compliments, Sir Charles, and she desires to be private until she announces herself disposed to receive.'

Vexed, Sir Charles turned aside, and fell into absent-minded talk with Buckhurst. Ten minutes passed, and then there was a sudden stir in the courtly groups about the hall.

Down the stairs, serene and graceful, came a young man in a suit of heliotrope satin edged with silver, a wealth of lace at wrist and throat, his plumed hat under his right arm, and an ebony cane dangling from his left wrist. His hair fell in a shower of golden ringlets, a bunch of them caught in a heliotrope ribbon on a level with his left ear.

It was Ned Kynaston. As Sir Charles stared incredulously he

could scarcely believe his eyes. A red mist rose at last before them; he felt a tightening at the throat. He and some twenty of the first gentlemen of the town were left there to cool their heels like lackeys whilst she was private with this low-born fellow, who descended now as self-assured and supercilious as though the house belonged to him.

Men nudged one another, and Sir Charles felt every eye turned upon him. He told himself that he was become their laughing stock.

Then, on the fourth step from the foot of the stairs, Kynaston paused.

'Her ladyship's compliments, gentlemen, to you all,' he announced—ladies there were none present at this levee—'and she bids me beg you to hold her excused, as she desires to rest herself this morning.'

This was too much for Sedley. Rudely he shouldered his way through the throng to the foot of the stairs, and every eye was upon him, every face betrayed its gleeful expectancy of a scene.

'So,' he growled, hoarse with passion, 'you play the lackey, do you, Kynaston? Faith, I never saw you better fitted with a part to suit you.'

The actor, still on that fourth step—a position which gave a certain advantage over his enemy—paused to take snuff daintily before replying.

'Ha, Sir Charles!' he said, in his clear, bell-like voice, and never had an audience hung more intently upon his words. 'I have a word for you in addition to what I have announced already.' He shut his snuffbox with a snap, and dusted fragments of the Burgamot from his ruffles. 'If her ladyship does not receive this morning the fault, Sir Charles, is yours. I see no reason to spare you the humiliation you seek when you thrust yourself in here despite her ladyship's definite dismissal of you yesterday. Yet her ladyship would have spared it you, and 'twas to that end—that she might not be forced to single you out—that she determined today, being informed of your presence, to deny herself to all.'

Mad with anger and mortification, intent only upon insult, Sir Charles flung forward with the retort:

'You lie, you dog of a play-actor!'

That was Kynaston's great opportunity. In a flash he took it; took it like one who has been waiting in leash for it. His right hand swung up, and he caught Sir Charles a buffet full upon the cheek, that knocked him into the arms of Sir John Ogle.

There was a pause until Sedley recovered from his astonishment. Then, bellowing blasphemy, he lugged at his sword. Instantly a dozen hands fastened upon him.

'Not here, Charles!' cried Buckhurst. 'We'll not suffer it in her ladyship's house. You shall not make her name the talk o' th' town. Elsewhere, Charles! Elsewhere! Not here!'

Thus they—his own friends—committed him to it. He glared at Kynaston, who, leaning now upon his cane, looked down upon him with a crooked smile.

'You dog!' he roared. He was foaming at the mouth, his handsome, dissipated face aflame with passion. 'I'll kill you for this! My friends shall wait upon you!'

'You sent your friends to me once before. Faith, they were the friends I should expect in you,' drawled the actor.

Through Sedley's furious mind there flashed then a suspicion that all this was an elaborate trap in which he was caught. But still he did not realize its details.

'It shall be cold steel this time!' he bellowed. 'Get measured for your coffin.'

The meeting took place at eight o'clock next morning in Leicester Fields, and it presented some unusual features. In the first place, Ned Kynaston did not come to the ground with his friends, as is prescribed by all sound authorities on the formalities of the duello. And when Faversham and Etheredge, who had consented to act for him, made their joint appearance at five minutes to eight, their principal was not yet come.

Sedley, stripped to shirt and breeches, was already there with Buckhurst and Ogle. Also there was such a throng of spectators that every rank of life was represented. This was a matter that increased Sedley's fury. If he must disgrace himself and soil his sword in the blood of an actor, he would, at least, have desired to have been private. However, being thrust into so unworthy a position, he must perforce bear himself as best he could. He turned to Faversham with a sneering laugh.

'Odds death, Sir Lionel!' quoth he. 'Is your friend like to keep us waiting longer? I've gotten an appetite from this early rising, and I'm in haste to get to breakfast.'

That taunt was followed by others that became more and more barbed as time passed and still there was no sign of Kynaston. Faversham tells us that, mortified, he was on the point of offering to take his principal's place when at last a chair was espied advancing from St Martin's Lane.

It must be Kynaston at last! But when the bearers had set it down and raised the roof, out stepped, not Kynaston, but Lady Chesterham, to the dumbfoundering of every man present. Instantly she ran to Sedley.

'Sir Charles!' she cried, a note of appeal in her voice, and tears in her lovely eyes. 'Forgive me for what I have done. There will be no fighting this morning.'

Sir Charles looked down at her. He was very white, and his lips were twitching.

'Madam,' he muttered at last, 'let me beg you to take some thought for your name, and to withdraw.'

'My name!' she cried. 'What care I for my name? I can take thought for nothing but his life, Sir Charles.' (A spasm rippled over Sedley's face.) ''Tis all my fault. 'Twas I bade him bear that message to you. I'll not have him murdered for what was of my doing.'

'Did he send you hither?' snapped Sedley.

'Send me? Not he, poor lad. He's safe enough, and no harm can come to him. But you shall not fight him.'

'By Heaven, madam, shall I take a blow? And from such a dog as that?' quoth he. 'The quarrel was of his seeking.'

'Nay, 'twas of yours; 'twas you gave him the lie. What could he do, poor boy?' She looked up at him in distress and appeal; but he remained unmoved before it, mindful only of his wrongs.

'Madam, let me entreat you to withdraw.'

'Not until I have your promise that you will spare him. Why are you so set on killing him? What is his life to you?'

'What is it to you, madam?' countered Sedley fiercely, himself forgetful now of spectators.

But if he was lost to shame she was a thousand times more so.

'He is everything to me,' she answered; 'and I care not who

hears me! If he dies, I shall die. If you wish to kill me, kill him. Ah, bethink you, he is so young, so gentle, and so lovely——'

Perhaps that plea was ill-considered. Sir Charles stepped back, his face set and scowling.

'This is idle, madam. Worse than idle. You humiliate yourself in vain.' And he waved a hand to the assembled throng, all greedily watching this extraordinary scene.

'You are resolved to fight, in spite of all that I have said?' she demanded tragically.

'Madam, I am!'

'Be it so, then!' she answered, in a sudden fury. 'In that case you shall fight me!' And before Faversham knew what she was about she had snatched the sword from his side. Flourishing it, she advanced upon Sedley. 'On guard, sir!' she challenged him.

'Madam, you are mad,' he answered; and he believed it. 'I implore you to be more circumspect. There are those who hear you——'

'I desire them to hear me,' she answered, and her voice seemed to take on a deeper note. 'And they shall see me, too,' she added.

And then the amazing thing took place. She tore off her plumed hat, and with it tore away her lofty mass of lustrous black hair, leaving in its place a ripple of golden locks about her neck. She flung off the long black cloak in which she had been wrapped; her furbelow fell away about her feet; and forth from that burst chrysalis, under the eye of the gaping company, stepped Ned Kynaston himself.

Kynaston indeed it was, and yet even now the face was hardly his own: it was still in part transformed by the darkened eyebrows, the olive-tinted cheeks, the patches under lip and eye, and other cunning touches which the theatre had taught that masterly player of feminine roles, and which had gone to make him in real life what so often he had been upon the stage—the loveliest lady that ever Mr Pepys saw in all his life.

Like a ripple over water ran the truth through the assembled crowd, and after its first gasp under the shock of that revelation a great peal of laughter broke upon the morning air.

Sedley looked on, white to the lips, cut and wounded to the very soul of him. He had no delusions on the score of the laughter. It was himself was the object of it; he it was who had been fooled

to the very top of his bent; he who must die under the ridicule that
would convulse the town. Had he not made love to Caroline
Chesterham? Had he not written verses in her honour? Had he
not languished and sighed and fondled her hand by the hour? Had
he not come to fight this very duel out of jealousy aroused by her?

With a snarling cry he hurled himself upon the actor. But
meanwhile Kynaston had kicked aside the discarded furbelow and
cloak, and stood free to receive this onslaught—graceful, alert, and
poised like a fencing-master.

Faversham would have interposed. But the actor waved him
away.

'In Heaven's name,' he laughed, 'let him have what he came
for.'

The blades met and jarred, then Sedley's was deflected; there
was a twinkling disengage, and Kynaston's point flew straight and
unhampered at the region of his opponent's heart. Within an inch
of the body it paused, and Kynaston drew back his arm. As all saw,
he had spared his enemy. Sedley came on again, and for the
second time the actor got within his opponent's guard, yet again he
checked his point in the very moment of touching the other's
body. If aught had been wanting to complete Sedley's humiliation
it was afforded in that fine display of fence, and the almost contemptuous mercy with which it was accompanied.

The end came soon. Kynaston, supremely the master, made a
fresh opening, went in for the third and last time, and transfixed
his adversary's sword-arm.

Perforce that was the end, and Kynaston went off to breakfast
with his seconds; whilst the crowd dispersed to put this amazing
story about the town.

'I shall look to you, Sir Lionel,' said the actor, when they had
got to table, 'to make my peace with my Lord Chesterham should
this affair ever come to his ears. You'll have guessed by this that
'twas I, myself, who wrote the letters of introduction which I
brought to you and to Lady Denham. No doubt 'twas a gross libel
on his lordship, who, belike, has no thought whatever of marrying
again.' Then he sighed and laughed in one. 'Odds life! That house
in Pall Mall and the rest of it will cost me a year's earnings. But
Sedley's is the heavier reckoning. I promised you it should be
heavy.'

Heavy it was, indeed. Sedley left town immediately, unable to face the ridicule in store for him, and for a year thereafter he abode quietly in the country, no man knowing where. Nor does it transpire that he ever attempted to pit himself against Ned Kynaston again.

The Abduction

MR GRANBY came away from the Manor and his interview with his old friend, Squire Clifford, in anything but the most satisfied frame of mind. He was face to face with a very knotty problem—for a lover. However much the squire might favour his suit, the fact remained that sweet Jenny Egerton—the squire's ward—whilst very friendly disposed towards Granby, was obviously careful to be nothing more.

Mr Granby strode through the dusk kicking the snow before him and making for the lights of the town at the foot of Manor Hill, and as he went his thoughts were very busy with what Squire Clifford had said. Jenny's nature was romantic, and if Mr Granby would win her heart as well as her hand the squire opined that he might be well-advised to present himself romantically to her consideration. But Granby, for all that he was a stolid, unimaginative man, realized that, rising forty as he was and being a shade wider at the waist than at the shoulders, in aiming at the romantic he might achieve no more than the ridiculous.

Still brooding, with hands deep in the pockets of his riding-coat, whip under his arm, and three-cornered hat pulled down over his brows, he strode on through the town, where the snow was becoming slush under the traffic that was toward. He made his way up the High Street with ears deaf to the shouts of the busy shopkeepers and busier vendors at the booths of the Christmas fair, and, still deep at his thoughts, he turned into the King's Arms. He nodded carelessly to the drawer in the tap-room, and his ill-fortune guided his steps to the bar-parlour and into the company of three graceless young neighbours of his, who sat with wigs awry and coats unlaced in a cloud of smoke over a bowl of punch.

He stood in the blaze of candlelight, the fine powder of snow that had gathered on the shoulders of his scarlet coat being rapidly transmuted by the warmth of the room into glittering diamonds of water, whilst those merry bloods hailed him noisily. Mr Granby had long been a choice butt for the practical jokers of the countryside, though he had never yet perceived it.

They haled him to the fire; they gave him punch to drink—a hot, delicious beverage of brandy, muscadine, lemon, and spices—which so warmed his heart and choked discretion that, when presently they toasted Jenny Egerton, and drank to her speedy union with Mr Granby, he must needs pour out the whole story of his unprospering love affair and the quandary in which he now found himself, winding up with an appeal to those merry jesters for advice and guidance in the pursuit of the romantic.

Their response was prompt and hilarious. As with one breath, they urged him to carry his tale to Ned Pepper, who, they swore, was the very man to help him.

'You couldn't find a better man for your business in the whole country,' one of them assured him. 'Ned Pepper's the most romantic young dog in England.'

'And he's upstairs now,' added another, 'drinking himself out of his senses in solitude.' And so they urged him noisily to go up at once.

'But if I should intrude,' he faltered. 'Mr Pepper and I are but slightly acquainted.'

'Ned Pepper will give you a warm welcome,' they assured him amid fresh laughter; and so, persuading and pushing, they got him above-stairs to the room where Ned Pepper sat wondering what might be the source of the bursts of merriment that floated up to him through the floor.

Granby found Mr Pepper—a comely young gentleman, with a good chin and a roguish eye—very much at his ease before a blazing fire. He was comfortably ensconced in a spacious oak chair, and rested the shapeliest silk-cased legs in Surrey upon a second one. There was a bowl of steaming punch at Mr Pepper's elbow, a pipe between his fingers. His head was rested against one of the wings of his chair, his peruke—which he had doffed for greater comfort—was perched upon the other, his broidered vest was open, and he had undone the silver buckles of his lacquered shoes. As I have said, Mr Pepper was very much at his ease.

At the foot of the stairs the young bloods stood grouped expectantly, with smirks and nudges and smothered guffaws. They knew

Ned Pepper to be as peppery as his name implied, and they had reason to believe that he would presently be kicking Mr Granby downstairs. Therefore they waited.

But they were disappointed. At sight of Mr Granby hesitating in the doorway a flicker of interest had for a moment lighted Mr Pepper's dark eyes; then he smiled lazily, and as lazily invited him to come inside.

'A cold night, Mr Pepper,' said Granby civilly.

'Ring for another glass,' said Mr Pepper, like a man taking a hint, and with the stem of his long pipe he pointed to the brew, thus clearing up any obscurity in his meaning.

The glass was brought, and, having helped himself, Granby drew up to the fire and took a pipe.

'I hope,' said he, 'I'm not intruding, though I must confess that I am taking a great liberty. I have come to you for advice. I have been advised to do so.'

Mr Pepper took the pipe from between his teeth, and gave his guest every encouragement to proceed. They were alone in that cosy parlour. The punch warmed and expanded Granby's simple nature, and he remembered the assurances he had received that Mr Pepper was the very man to help him in his quandary. So out came the whole story, all but the names, which, with a remnant of discretion, Granby thought better to omit.

'And do you tell me you were sent to me for advice in this matter?' quoth Mr Pepper, whose eyes had now lost all sign of drowsiness. 'By whom?'

Granby told him, and Pepper nodded with a slow smile.

'I am sore perplexed,' added the luckless lover earnestly. 'I don't know whether you have ever been in the like position.'

'I have, indeed,' answered Mr Pepper, 'with this difference that with me the maid was willing, but the father, who accounted me a hairbrain, wouldn't hear of it. I carried her off: we were overtaken, and I was laid by the heels for a time. Her father was too friendly with the sheriff.'

'You carried her off,' mused Granby. 'Now that was a romantic enough thing to do!'

Mr Pepper stared at him. 'If it's romance you want, you may do the same. As for me, I prefer to wait until the lady is of age. The county gaol cured me of any leanings towards romance.'

'But our cases are hardly parallel.' Mr Granby reminded him. 'I have no pursuit to fear since her guardian is my friend.'

'True,' said Pepper with a roguish smile, 'but, then, you say the lady isn't, and you'll hardly make her so by a display of violence.'

'Ah!' sighed the unimaginative Granby, and his honest, rugged face grew clouded. Pepper puffed in silence for a moment or two; then spoke.

'To abduct her forcibly, and against her will, were to do a monstrous ill thing. Your suit thereafter must be hopeless and deservedly. But——' And he paused solemnly, raising a delicate white hand that sprouted from a cloud of lace, and poising it in line with Granby's suddenly uplifted eyes—'but if someone else were to do the thing, and you were to prove the heroic rescuer——'

'Gad!' cried Granby, and the pipe slipped from his fingers, and was shivered on the floor.

'You would reap the heroic rescuer's reward,' concluded Pepper. 'By your promptness of action you would inspire gratitude; by your ready courage—there might be a little sword-play in the comedy—admiration; and by your restraint and courtesy to the lady in her plight, you should awaken confidence and trust. These, my friend, are the compounds that go to make up that poison men call love.'

'Yes, yes,' gasped Granby, in some amazement at the other's fertility of imagination. 'But how would you go about it, Mr Pepper?'

Mr Pepper pondered awhile, puffing vigorously. Then, setting down his pipe, he leaned forward, and propounded the result of his cogitations. On the morrow there was a Christmas dance to be held at Sir John Tyler's, two miles away, to which, no doubt, Squire Clifford and his ward would be going.

'Clifford?' gasped the startled Granby, leaping to his feet. 'How guessed you I spoke of them? I never mentioned——'

'The whole countryside knows all about it,' said Pepper shortly, and Granby sat down again. Pepper proceeded with his expounding. At Kerry's Corner Mr Granby was to post some obliging rogue who would play the highwayman for him; he would hold up Mr Clifford's coach, but at sight of the lady be so taken with the jewels that were her eyes, as to have no thought for other riches. The highwayman should request her to alight, and then make off

with her on his crupper, the Squire being forewarned to offer
no resistance.

'Away goes the amorous highwayman,' Pepper proceeded,
'whereupon the lady lets out a cry or two, which attracts the
attention of a very staid and sober gentleman riding in the opposite
direction. That gentleman is yourself. You call upon the ruffian to
stand; he rides on, and you give pursuit. A pistol shot or two—in
the air, of course—will add effect, and show the general earnest-
ness of the affair. And now you are racing through the night, and
the highwayman is racing ahead of you; the race must be protracted. To overtake him too soon would be injudicious. You must
wait until the lady's feelings of terror have been wrought to their
highest pitch. She knows a rescuer is behind, and when, towards
dawn, that rescuer comes up, and compels the highwayman to
mend his manners and deliver up the lady, lo! she discovers that it
is the man to whose gallantry, courage, and resource she has so
long and so foolishly been blind. If she does not promise to marry
you there and then, you are the most hopeless bungler that ever
tired of being a bachelor.'

In a burst of enthusiasm Granby tore at the bell-rope; then he
crossed the room, and grasped one of Mr Pepper's slender hands
in his own massive fist.

'You're a man of heart and brain, Mr Pepper,' said he; 'a man
I'm proud to call my friend.' Then, to the drawer who entered,
'Another bowl of punch,' he ordered. And with that the enthusiasm
went out of him as suddenly as it had flared up.

'But, rat me!' he cried, 'where am I to find a man who will play
the highwayman for me?'

'Surely,' said Pepper, 'that should not be difficult. You'll have
some friend——'

'But the task asks more than friendship. It asks tact, it asks
resource, it asks—I scarce know what.' And then he grew inspired. 'Now, if you, Mr Pepper——'

'Alas!' sighed Pepper. 'It is just such a frolic as would sort well
with my rascally instincts, such a night ride as I should relish. But,
unfortunately, I am bidden, myself, to Lady Tyler's ball.'

'If that be all, surely the difficulty might be overcome. But
perhaps I make too bold, sir. I presume, maybe, when I consider

that you might stand my friend. Our acquaintance is, after all, but slight.'

'A misfortune which the years may mend,' said Pepper pleasantly.

'You mean that?' quoth the simple Granby.

'If you need proof of it—why, I am your man in this affair.'

Thus was it planned, and on the following night—or, rather, towards two o'clock of a sharp and frosty Christmas morning—was the plan put into execution.

Half a mile from Kerry's Corner—which was a mile, or so, from Tyler Park—Mr Granby walked his horse up and down in the moonlight, waiting.

A coach rolled past him, followed soon after by another, whereat realizing that these were homeward bound guests from Lady Tyler's, Mr Granby waxed impatient for the arrival of Mr Pepper. Presently hoofs rattled in the distance, growing rapidly louder and nearer, and ringing sharp and clear on the still, frosty air. A horseman riding madly down the road loomed black in the moon-light, and Mr Granby rode to meet him.

Affairs had sped well with Mr Pepper. He had held up Squire Clifford's coach, and carried off Squire Clifford's ward, what time the Squire, instructed in his role, bellowed and trumpeted, but took care to do nothing that might hinder the make-believe high-wayman in his task. The girl had not gone without a struggle, it is true. But in the end, masterful Mr Pepper had swung her to the withers of his horse, and dashed off, his left arm embracing and supporting her, and her head—for she seemed to have lapsed into a half-stupor—fallen back against his breast. Thus they rode until they came upon Mr Granby ambling in the opposite direction. The girl struggled, and let out a cry or two for help as she was swept past that bulky figure, and Mr Granby, taking his cue from that, wheeled about, and called upon the abductor to stand. Mr Pepper laughed for answer, and rattled on. Shots went off in the night, with no hurt to anyone, and Mr Granby flung himself into hot and gallant pursuit.

He gained on them too quickly at first, so he slackened his pace, mindful of Pepper's instructions that the chase should be a long one. Suddenly something stirred by the roadside; a third horseman loomed on that lonely road, barring Mr Granby's path; a pistol barrel gleamed before him, and——

'Stand!' thundered a gruff voice.

Mr Granby stood. He was not by nature foolhardy, and his common sense told him that a man with a levelled pistol was a man to be obeyed. He slipped a hand towards one of the holsters, furtively, to withdraw it again as he remembered that he had discharged both pistols at the commencement of his chase of Mr Pepper.

'If it's my purse you want——' he began, in haste to push on.

'I want more than that,' came the answer, interrupting him. And then, in the politer manner affected by gentlemen of the road, 'Sir, it grieves me vastly to put you to discomfort. But the messengers are after me, and my horse is spent. I'll trouble you to dismount.'

'But——' began Granby in dismay.

'Dismount!' bellowed the highwayman, dropping all courteous affectations. 'Dismount this instant, or I'll blow your brains out.'

Mr Granby came quickly to the ground. In an instant the toby-man was beside him. Another moment, and he had swung himself into Granby's empty saddle, and was off at a gallop into the night.

There stood Granby—Granby, the heroic rescuer of distressed dames—on the white, sparkling snow, in sore perplexity, anger, and chagrin. Then, in a spirit of philosophy, determining to make the best of matters, he mounted the spent horse that had been left him, the sorriest nag that ever wore a saddle, and gave it a touch of the spur. After all, his loss amounted to no more than a horse, and Mr Granby was wealthy enough to envisage that loss without great concern. But what of Pepper and the lady he was to rescue? Surely Pepper would lag behind, and wait for him. But soon— being unable to get more than a walk out of the animal he be-strode—he realized that unless Pepper came to a standstill, there was no chance of his being overtaken; and if he were so foolish as to come to a standstill to wait for Granby to come up with him, then the whole scheme would be betrayed, and must miscarry. The horse staggered a quarter of a mile or so under the stimulus of Granby's frantic spurring; then it foundered altogether, and Granby was forced to dismount.

He pondered the matter as best his rage would let him. To take the horse further was out of the question. There was no choice but to leave the beast and push on afoot, trusting to Mr Pepper's ingenuity to afford him an early opportunity of coming to that pretty swordplay they had agreed upon. Mr Granby set off at a run, taking the road that led to Guildford, for Guildford was the goal arranged. But Guildford was twenty miles away, and it was not until after eight o'clock of that Christmas morning that Mr Granby dragged his weary body over the bridge that spans the Wey, and up the precipitous High Street of that ancient town.

He was a man utterly disillusioned, a man in whom the thought of his own physical discomforts had quenched all amorous aspirations, a man whose only remaining ambition was to dry his sodden boots in some comfortable inn parlour and mend his physical discomforts with an ample breakfast. If a thought he gave to any other matter, it was to curse the idiotic Pepper for having ridden on, as he appeared to have done, heedless of whether Mr Granby was in pursuit or not.

He stamped wearily into the yard of the 'Black Bull', swung into the inn, and making his way down a passage, opened the first door he came upon. A lady and a gentleman were at table there, and Mr Granby, realizing that he intruded, was for withdrawing hastily, when a cheery voice hailed him.

'Mr Granby! Gad! You're come at last!'

Mr Pepper had risen from the table, and was advancing towards him with a smile upon his pleasant young face. Granby gasped, and looked at the lady. It was Jenny.

'At least,' cried slow-witted Granby, thinking that matters were to be righted after all, 'it seems I am not come too late.' And he put his hand to the hilt of his small-sword. But Pepper only laughed.

'If it's the pretty show of swordplay you're thinking of, you're too late altogether. Come in, man, and break your fast with us. I make no doubt you'll be nigh dead of hunger.' And he drew Granby, despite himself almost, into the room.

'What—what do you mean?' he demanded, scowling, for he noticed now that Jenny's air was not such as her position should inspire; her cheeks were red, and she seemed a prey to laughter.

'Why,' said Mr Pepper airily, advancing a chair for his guest, 'when you never came, what was I to do with this lady on my hands? I ask you, what would you have done in my place?'

The question quenched all Mr Granby's vexation. Engrossed as
he had been in his own calamities, he had given no thought to Mr
Pepper's quandary.

'You'll agree,' continued Mr Pepper, 'that I could scarce ride on
with her after daylight. We should have been stopped. Besides,
there are limits to a horse's endurance, and to a man's. We must
stop somewhere. At the first inn would be Miss Egerton's opportunity. She has but to call for help, and in what case should I find
myself? I have been in gaol once, as I have already had occasion to
inform you, and I have little fancy for repeating the experience. I
hope, sir, that you realize my delicate position.'

'Indeed, sir,' murmured the confused and bewildered Granby, 'I
own it must have been trying. I——'

'You see, then,' Mr Pepper cut in, 'that it was necessary to do
something that should put me in shelter from the law.'

'And he did,' Jenny explained, laughter sparkling in her eyes
and dimpling her smooth, fresh cheek, 'what you will agree was
the only thing to do. He told me the truth. Oh, shame, Mr
Granby! Shame on you for setting such a scheme on foot and
subjecting a poor girl to so much misery and discomfort.'

'But, madam——,' groaned Mr Granby, unable to say more.

'Mr Pepper was wise to tell me the truth, and cast himself, as he
did, upon my mercy,' she concluded.

Mr Granby said nothing. He sat nursing his hat, his gaze
averted, abashed like a child caught in a naughty act. How different
was all this from the brave plan they had made!

'Miss Egerton very charitably forgave us,' said Pepper, 'and we
determined to break our fast here whilst awaiting you.'

Granby screwed up his courage to ask: 'And now?' in a very
sheepish voice.

'You see,' Pepper explained confidentially, 'even having made
my peace with Miss Egerton, I felt myself far from secure.
You'll remember why I was in gaol two years ago. I told you the
reason.'

Granby nodded.

'Therefore,' put in Jenny, 'it became necessary for Mr Pepper
further to protect himself.'

'In her mercy,' Pepper resumed, 'she realized how unpleasant it
might be for me if I were discovered here—by her guardian,

say—alone with a child upon whom I had no claim of kinship. Besides, the lady has a reputation, and I could not in honesty have called myself your friend if I had allowed the reputation of a lady whom you had thought of making your wife to be placed in jeopardy. So while breakfast was cooking we stepped across the street, and were quietly married by the most civil person in the world.'

'Odso!' roared Granby. 'You are fooling me, then?' And he got heavily to his feet, his face purple with indignation.

'Fooling you?' cried Pepper. 'Not I. I am telling you the truth. I ask you what else was I to do? You yourself forced the situation upon me. What other way out of it had I? And, rat me, sir, where have you tarried all night that you never overtook me as we had arranged?'

'Bah!' said Granby, who was now beginning to understand things. 'I have been walking a matter of twenty miles since the knave you hired deprived me of my horse.'

He paused, summoning invective to his aid, his wits now penetrating to the very heart of this situation. It flickered in that moment through his mind that Squire Clifford had made some allusion to a spark for whom his ward was suspected of a fancy. This, then, was the spark in question, and Granby had been fooled by him. And it was into the keeping of this hairbrained young scapegrace—who had been gaoled already for running off with some girl or other—that Jenny had given her sweet young life! Granby felt naturally vindictive. He planted himself squarely on his feet, and dully eyed the couple at the table.

'Will you tell me,' he asked with grim unction, 'the name of the lady for whose abduction you were gaoled two years ago, Mr Pepper?'

Mr Pepper looked disconcerted, Granby thought with relish.

'It's something of an ordeal, sir, to be forced to confess to such follies in the presence of my wife, and—and on my bridal morning. Still, if you insist——'

'I do,' said Granby firmly. 'She shall know what manner of man she had wed.'

'It's two years ago, and that's a long time in a young man's life,' said Pepper. 'My memory may be at fault, but I believe it was a Miss Egerton, of whom you may have heard, sir.' And from the ripple of laughter that broke from Jenny's lips, Granby knew that he was being mocked with the truth.

It was more than he could bear. He swung out of the room, and out of the inn, and tired, damp and hungry though he was, he determined to get a horse and ride back to Clifford Manor to tell the squire what had befallen. He realized with angry shame how those merry young gentlemen at the 'King's Arms' had fooled him the night before when they sent him to Pepper for guidance in this delicate matter.

While he waited in the yard for a horse, he could not resist a peep through the window of the room where the bridal couple were at table. A bright firelight played upon walls and ceiling, and relieved the lingering gloom of that Christmas morning. Jenny, he noticed, sat with a kerchief to her eyes, and Mr Pepper with an arm round her neck strove to console her. The sight affected Granby oddly. Maybe she was weeping out of pity for the treatment he had received; maybe she was thinking of her guardian and the trouble he would make for them. Mr Granby was honestly fond of the child, and he felt a lump in his throat as he pondered the matter of her tears. Tears on her wedding-day!

He noticed now how well-matched they were in youth and looks, and he realized how ill-matched would she have been had she wedded him as was intended. He remembered, too, now that his mood was softening, that, after all, Pepper was little to blame for what had happened. It was those rascally wags at the 'King's Arms' who had fooled him rather than Pepper. In Pepper's place he might himself have done just what Pepper had done.

And then a peal of joybells crashed suddenly upon the morning air to remind Granby of what day it was, and what the message of that day was.

He straightened himself. He may have been dull, podgy and unimaginative, but he was a good fellow at heart. Back into the inn and into their parlour he strode, and so full of purpose was his step that Jenny looked up in alarm as he thrust wide the door. He advanced, his face rather red, his eyes more sheepish than ever.

'I forgot,' said he, 'to wish you a merry Christmas, and I've come back to do it. If you'll ride to Clifford Manor with me, I think I can persuade the squire to let us all spend this bridal Christmas happily together.' And he held out a hand to each of them.

Jack o'Lantern

JACK O'LANTERN was the name bestowed upon him by the Bow Street runners whom his elusiveness was exasperating. His real identity was as unknown to them as his countenance, which he covered with a black visor, whenever operating. The speed of his movements was such that he seemed to multiply himself. No sooner was the hue-and-cry raised in Kent for the robbery of a nobleman on Gad's Hill at noon, than they heard of him holding up the Oxford coach beyond Watford in the evening. They identified him by a general description: his genteel methods; his good shape and his military exterior; a laced hat cocked over the right eye, an elegant, full-skirted coat, a stein-kirk and so on. He rode a bay mare, presenting, however, no peculiar characteristics.

On that afternoon in May when just beyond Kentish Town he relieved Squire Kendrick of a purse of fifty guineas, a gold snuff-box, a diamond ring of price and a handsome small-sword that took his fancy, he was led by his ill-starred meeting with Mr Richard Lessingham to depart from his usual practice of setting out at once to put a score of miles between himself and the scene of the outrage.

He could not have chosen a worse moment for the encounter. At the best of times Mr Richard Lessingham would have proved an awkward customer, for, like most men endowed with a strong dash of rascality, he was a considerable fellow of his hands. Today he happened to ride in a furious temper, feeling that life had declared war upon him, and all but looking for an opportunity to deliver battle.

He was the nephew and heir presumptive of that wealthy nawab Sir John Lessingham, who, following a fashion and a taste for the district, common in his day with so many of his kind, had built himself out of the plunder of the Indies a handsome house in a handsome park on the north side of Highgate Hill. For any inheritance beyond the baronetcy and the little estate that went to adorn it, Richard Lessingham must depend upon the relations between his uncle and himself. Sir John had been more than generous with him. He desired that his nephew and heir presumptive should cut a prominent figure in the world of fashion wherein, himself, he had failed. For English Society looked askance on these nawabs and their suspiciously acquired wealth. To this end he made the lad a princely allowance. But it had not proved liberal enough to meet the extravagances of a vain, ostentatious, and fundamentally worthless nature. Horses and cards and other extravagances had run Mr Richard heavily into debt.

On the first occasion the nawab had relieved the obligations with a laugh. The name of Lessingham would gather lustre from being well gilded. Later he had relieved obligations again, but he had not laughed. Later still he had stormed whilst paying, and warned his nephew that he would pay no more excesses of the allowance. The warning, however, was powerless to curb extravagances that by this time had become settled habits. All that had resulted was that when next Richard found his debts submerging him, instead of seeking his uncle, he had sought—on the advice of a fellow-member of White's to whom he had lost a deal of money at ombre—a certain Mr Nicholas Magdalen, who in a back office in Essex Street was amassing an incalculable fortune by the benevolent assistance of young gentlemen of quality in financial distress.

Mr Magdalen, an elderly little man with a moist, red face and greasy black hair that straggled untidily about a skull-cap, had displayed a solicitude of the friendliest. He could not have been more distressed over his new client's plight if Richard had been his own child. He invited him to dismiss all concern. There was neither sense nor right in that a fine young gentleman of his quality and a future baronet should be plagued over a matter of a mere couple of thousand pounds. His little short-sighted eyes beamed through his horn-rimmed spectacles as he thanked his gods that it was in his power to play the fairy godfather. The money should be paid to Mr Lessingham's bankers without fail in the morning. He would, of course, make a charge for the accommodation. One had to live. But—again thanking his gods—Mr

Magdalen was no usurer, like some that he could name. Thirty per centum was the uttermost interest he would consent to take, considering how good must be the security that Mr Lessingham would supply.

It became necessary to explain to the ignorant but immensely relieved Mr Lessingham the exact meaning of the term 'security'. His relief was diminished by the explanation. Dismay finally replaced it.

'But I have no property. No property whatsoever.'

Mr Magdalen's smile was reassuring. 'Not *in esse*, as we say. No. But *in posse*, my dear sir, there is Lessingham Park, which your uncle has entailed to go with the title.'

'But that's not mine yet.'

The benign smile of Mr Magdalen became broader. 'The prospect is enough, my dear sir. It would not be enough for everybody. Nor would I do this for everybody; for, of course, the risk is considerable. If you should predecease your uncle, the post-obit will be so much waste paper. But we can provide for that risk in the rate of interest. I am afraid I must make it sixty per centum. But, then, you'll not account that unreasonable, considering . . .'

'What is a post . . . What d'ye call it?'

Mr Magdalen gently explained the nature and effect of the post-obit.

'Ecod!' said Mr Lessingham to this wealth of instruction into mysterious and unsuspected ways of finance.

He departed with the assurance that the cash would be at his disposal on the morrow, and he came back again in six months' time not only gloomily to confess that he could not find a matter of twelve hundred pounds due for interest, but that he had pressing debts for another thousand and didn't know where the devil to seek it.

Mr Magdalen's undiminished benignity at once dispelled his apprehensions.

'No cause to distress yourself, my dear young friend. We add the interest to the principal, and that's the end of the matter. Forget it. Amuse yourself. As for your present debts, I will provide the thousand pounds at once.'

Six months later, Mr Lessingham found himself owing something over two thousand pounds for interest, whilst one or two creditors were pressing him for debts which in all amounted to about eight hundred pounds. It began to be borne in upon the dull wits of the nawab's nephew that a morass awaited him at the bottom of the easy slope to which he had set his feet. The benignity of Mr Magdalen on this occasion did not suffice to allay his very real anxieties, especially when he discovered that whilst Mr Magdalen would again be content to add interest to principal, he was by no means prepared to advance the further moneys so immediately necessary. The little estate, he pointed out, was not worth above twenty thousand pounds, and the risks attached to post-obit made it impossible to increase the capital liability already incurred.

Mr Lessingham was appalled. He made a mental calculation and presented the result to Mr Magdalen. That he was capable of it shows the extent to which his education in financial matters had lately improved.

'Ecod, sir! At this rate in a couple of years' time Lessingham Park will be your property, and all that I'll have had will have been a matter of three thousand pounds. Blister me!'

'Sir John may die before then,' said Mr Magdalen hopefully.

'Damme! Sir John won't die in the next ten years. God knows he's hale enough for another twenty.' Mr Lessingham sucked his breath in sudden terror. 'What'll be owing you in twenty years at this thieving rate?'

With pursed lips Mr Magdalen opined that it might be rather more than the whole fortune of the nawab. But he begged Mr Lessingham to dismiss such gloomy conjectures. Mr Lessingham, however, could not dismiss them.

'Sold myself for a mess of pottage, ecod!' said he, and black, vicious despair looked out of his livid face at the benevolent little usurer. A snarl crept into his voice. 'I've a mind to . . .'

'Now wait a moment. Wait a moment,' Mr Magdalen begged him. 'Between friends there are always ways of arranging matters, and I hope, Mr Lessingham, sir, that you will consider me your friend. There's a proposal I might make to you that I give you my word I wouldn't make to another man living. 'Pon honour I wouldn't. Have you . . . hem . . . have you ever thought of marriage, Mr Lessingham, sir.'

'Marriage!' sneered the young gentleman. He became cynical. 'I've never met a lady well enough dowered.'

'That,' said Mr Magdalen, 'is where I might help you.'

'Faith, ye're a marriage-broker, then, as well as a moneylender? If your rate of interest is as unconscionable . . .'

'There's no rate of interest at all. The lady is perhaps the wealthiest heiress in England, and her dowry will be . . . ah . . . princely.'

Mr Lessingham's handsome face was darkened in a scowl.

'Let me know more of this. Be plain with me.'

Mr Magdalen was plain. And forth came a proposal which had already been made to a half-dozen other young gentlemen of title, actual or prospective, in straitened circumstances. Mr Magdalen possessed a daughter who would one day inherit the ill-gotten millions in which his only joy had been that of accumulating them. It would, however, he felt, be vain to leave her the wealthiest woman in England unless at the same time he could assure for her a place in those exalted social circles where wealth enabled life to be lived at its fullest and most brilliant.

It had become an obsession with the little usurer. The fact that in the past five years the proposal had been declined by the needy noblemen to whom it had been made, had merely served to sharpen Mr Magdalen's desire to a desperate keenness.

On the understanding that he made the offer subject to the lady's own consent—a consent which he opined, with an appreciative eye for Mr Lessingham's attractive exterior, was not likely to be refused—he invited Mr Lessingham to consider how happy an issue from all his troubles lay for him in marriage with so well-dowered a lady. He did so with confidence, gloating secretly over the fact that Mr Lessingham was in a vice far tighter than that in which he had held any of the gentlemen who had declined. Nevertheless Mr Lessingham was prompt, outraged and virulent in damning the moneylender for his impudence. As foul-mouthed as a drayman, he practised no decency in his comments upon Mr Magdalen's probable ancestry. But when he came to express assumptions concerned with Mr Magdalen's only descendant, the moneylender checked him suddenly.

'Say nothing that will make it impossible for you to change your mind,' he warned him, in a thin, hard voice from which all benignity had departed. And at once he turned the screw of the vice in which he held his debtor. 'There's a matter of two thousand five hundred pounds for interest that was due from you yesterday. I don't wish to be hard, Mr Lessingham, sir, but unless I have the money by four o'clock this afternoon, I shall wait upon Sir John with the post-obit in the morning, and ask him if he would wish to redeem it.'

To Mr Lessingham this was a blow between the eyes. For a moment it almost stunned him. Recovering, he was first violent, then plaintive, then violent again. But Mr Magdalen, now tight of lip and hard of eye, remained unmoved, and the end of the matter was that Mr Lessingham went off to Highgate and Sir John with ruin staring him in the face. For he knew his uncle too well to doubt that the disclosure of how he had raised money on the prospect of the nawab's death would put on end to all his hopes of inheriting a shilling beyond the wretched little estate that went with the title.

At all costs that knowledge must be kept from Sir John.

In sheer despair, rather than consent to marry the daughter of that greasy little thief in Essex Street he chose the lesser evil of an appeal to the already exasperated nawab.

He may or may not have been mistaken in making his prayer more or less in the form of an accusation. It was Sir John's hardness towards him, he urged, that had driven him into the clutches of a rascally moneylender. To extricate himself completely he needed at once a matter of six or seven thousand pounds. The nawab's reply amounted to a sketch of his nephew's character as succinct as it was accurate and blistering, at the end of which he bade him go to the devil.

Mr Lessingham accounted that to marry Magdalen's daughter would be tantamount to obeying this injunction. But if he was to avoid the ruin of his hopes and the immediate possibility of a debtor's gaol, there was no choice but to consent to make this probably greasy wench the future Lady Lessingham. It would be necessary to humble himself to the dust so as to obtain from Mr Magdalen a renewal of the offer he had so insolently rejected; and he must lose no time. It must be done at once if he would prevent Mr Magdalen's journey to Lessingham Park tomorrow with the post-obit.

He came raging to the summit of Highgate Hill. Without eyes for the fine prospect, with London under a haze at his feet, and the broad ribbon of the Thames visible for a dozen miles with its burden of shipping, he spurred his big black horse down the slope towards Holloway.

It was at the foot of the hill that Jack o'Lantern met him, and, to his undoing, was tempted to arrest his headlong course.

At the sight of the black-visored horseman and the levelled pistol, Mr Lessingham stood, as he was bidden. But as for delivering, it came to him as a climax of irony to swell his already excessive rage that such an invitation should be issued to a man in his desperate case.

Jack o'Lantern was, of course, not to know this. Nor had he any means of perceiving that the horseman he had brought to a standstill was a reckless, dangerous fellow at the best of times, and in particularly savage mood this afternoon. By the time he might have suspected it, he was beyond suspecting anything. For, with sudden, lightning speed, Mr Lessingham's heavy riding-crop had crashed into his temple and knocked him senseless from the saddle.

When the highwayman recovered consciousness, he was lying on the turf of a meadow beyond a belt of trees by which the horses were tethered, with his assailant sitting cross-legged and watchful beside him.

Mr Lessingham had taken the natural precaution of depriving him of his weapons. He had drawn a second pistol from its holster, and he had removed the sword the highwayman was wearing, a pretty piece of workmanship with a mother of pearl handle and for pummel a milky crystal of the size of a pigeon's egg, that might have been a moonstone. It was attached to a baldrick of red Spanish leather adorned with a pattern of oak-leaves in gold bullion, and by this it was now slung from Mr Lessingham's own shoulder. To make sure that the rascal had no other weapon about him, Mr Lessingham had gone through his pockets. Amongst some lesser effects, he had found a gold snuff-box, and a heavy purse of red silk mesh that was stuffed with guineas and contained in addition a diamond ring of price. Perceiving no sin in robbing a thief, Mr Lessingham's easy conscience regarded these valuables as a windfall, and he transferred them to his own pocket. After that he sat down to await the man's recovery, and he smiled as he waited, for it seemed to him that nothing could have been more opportune. The encounter which had so infuriated him had ended by bringing inspiration. It prompted an easier way to deliverance from his difficulties than that to which he had been so dejectedly riding.

Jack o'Lantern sat up, straightened his wig on an aching head and in doing so became aware of the lump on his brow. He looked about him with eyes that were still dazed, met the derisive smile of Mr Lessingham and awakened a little further.

'What the devil . . .' he began, and checked there.

'Give yourself no concern, my friend,' said his captor. 'The worst has happened to you, unless you show no more sense than a woodcock.'

The highwayman's eyes alighted on the baldrick with the oak-leaves pattern. He felt in his pockets. Then his lip curled.

'So that's what you are,' said he. 'A dog that eats dog.'

Mr Lessingham laughed joyously, as a man will whose soul has suddenly been delivered of a burden of care. 'A mastiff that dines on poodles, if you will. But a tobyman by proxy, and that for one occasion only, provided you show sense. In that case you may go your ways to the devil when you've served my turn. In any other you'll ride with me to the Bridewell.'

Jack o'Lantern gathered up his legs and embraced his knees. Out of a lean, keen young face, wide of mouth and tip-tilted of nose, a pair of astute eyes calmly took the measure of Mr Lessingham. Whatever the rascal's emotions, he kept a mask upon them, and fear was certainly not amongst them.

'Could you be plainer?' he asked.

'As plain as you please. Early tomorrow we take the road together, hereabouts. That belt of trees will supply the screen we'll need, and we'll wait for a certain hackney coach that'll be coming from London on its way over the hill there. There'll not be many hackneys come as far as this, so we're not likely to be mistook, besides ye'll not stir until I've seen who rides in it. When I give you the word, you'll halt it. You'll require the traveller to strip himself and hand you his clothes besides anything else in the way of baggage that he may have with him. When you've delivered these to me, you may go your ways. Is it clear?'

'Clear enough, codso! I'm to pull chestnuts from the fire for you, so as if any fingers is burnt it'll be mine. But what do I get for doing it?'

'It's what'll you get for not doing it. The gallows. That's what you'll get.'

'Spoke like a gentleman,' said Jack. Then he passed a hand over an aching brow. 'Ye've got a pistol at my head. I must stand and deliver, I suppose. Do the dirty work ye're too fine to do for yourself.'

'I'm glad ye're sensible. And speaking of pistols, an empty one will serve your turn tomorrow. Our subject is an old man, and the hackney driver's only thought will be to keep a whole skin. So don't be building any false hopes.'

'Ye take no chances,' said Jack with the suspicion of a sneer.

'None, as you'll find. Remember it. For tonight you'll be my guest for bed and supper.'

'I had a notion that it was you might be mine, being as ye've filched my purse,' said Jack.

Mr Lessingham got up. 'I'll trouble you to keep a civil tongue, my lad. Get that into your brain-pan, and let it simmer there. Come on now. Up with you.'

Jack o'Lantern came slowly to his feet. He stood swaying a little, a hand to his head again.

'Odsbud! I'm giddy. Lend me your arm, sir.'

A smile twisted Mr Lessingham's full, cruel lips. 'I'll lend you nothing. Step out ahead, and no tricks, you rogue, or you'll forfeit your only chance of postponing acquaintance with the gallows. You'll not slip through my fingers; not if you were as slippery as Jack o'Lantern himself.'

Jack's only answer to that was a wistful smile. He went forward staggering a little, Mr Lessingham following closely, his riding-crop in readiness. Thus they reached the horses, untethered them, mounted, and picked their way through the trees to the road.

With the highwayman leading by half a length, so that the eye of this captor who took no chances was upon his every movement, they came, as dusk was closing in, to the Bull at Islington, where Mr Lessingham had resolved that they should lie the night, in readiness for the morrow's business of waylaying Mr Magdalen.

They left their horses with the ostler in the yard, and strode forward towards an open side-door from which the light was shining, the highwayman leading ever, with Mr Lessingham close upon his heels. Voices met them, coming from a room at the far end of the passage by which they were advancing, and what Jack o'Lantern heard made him check in his stride. The movement was instinctive, but so momentary that he seemed merely to have stumbled.

'And a bay mare, ye say, sir? I'll wager my bones that'd be Jack o'Lantern, as sure as my name be Tom Bowles.'

Impelled by his follower, Jack perforce went on, and as he reached the open door, the answer came delivered in a voice that was shrill with rage.

'Jack o'Lantern or another. What's the odds? A crying scandal to you all that such things should be done in daylight. In broad daylight. On the King's highway. It shows the worth of your vigilance. It shows the worth of all these measures of which Sir Henry Fielding makes a boast. Measures that were to clear the country of this vermin. Why, things were no worse a hundred years ago.'

The speaker was still inveighing when Jack came to the doorway. And Jack was not encouraged when in this speaker, a portly gentleman in high leather gaiters and a short skirted frock under the tails of which his hands were now thrust, he recognized the victim of his robbery that afternoon.

Squire Kendrick's face was inflamed with the anger into which he had lashed himself whilst denouncing the outrage suffered. For audience he had a couple of rustics, the landlord in shirt sleeves and apron, a man who held a constable's staff and a couple of tough-looking fellows who at a glance might be recognized for Bow Street runners.

It was not the sort of company into which Jack o'Lantern would normally have cared to thrust himself. Yet now he swaggered in, a smile on his lips, a jauntiness in his step, fully approved by Mr Lessingham who followed more closely than ever upon the parlour's sanded floor. Heads were turned to see who came, and the landlord was detaching himself from the group to give welcome to these new guests, when Jack's hearty hail momentarily arrested them.

He had taken a swift step aside, away from his companion, and tossed up his head with a laugh of satisfaction.

'Well met, my hearties,' he greeted the Bow Street men, 'and in the very nick of time. If it's Jack o'Lantern ye're hunting, I'll be claiming the reward. For here you have him, led by the nose into your very arms for you.' And he flung out a hand to indicate Mr Lessingham.

There was a moment's silent, round-eyed amazement. Then it was Squire Kendrick who moved. His head craned forward on his stout neck, and his eyes bulging, he advanced on Mr Lessingham. Mr Lessingham, more taken aback than any of them by what he accounted a futile impudence, was uttering a fleeting laugh when Squire Kendrick flung out an accusing arm.

'Seize him,' he roared. 'I recognize him.' And at the word the Bow Street runners were upon Mr Lessingham like hounds upon a stag.

He struggled, panting and snarling in their arms, turning a face of fury upon the squire.

'What do you mean, you pot-bellied dotard? You recognize me?' The Squire was upon him, whilst the runners held him.

'I mean this, you impudent rogue. This!' He seized the sword-belt of Spanish leather with the pretty oak-leaf pattern, upon which the ready-witted Jack o'Lantern had counted when he so boldly made his staggering announcement. 'I may not recognize your face, for that was masked; but, ecod! I recognize my own baldrick, ay, and the sword of which you robbed me this very afternoon, you damned hedge-creeper.'

The constable rolled forward importantly. 'Here. Give way whiles I search him.'

Lessingham abandoned the struggle, commanding himself now that he began to recognize that violence would not get him out of this trap. Forth from his pockets they brought a gold snuff-box on the lid of which was the squire's crest, a hand holding aloft an oak-leaf, and a heavy purse in which, in addition to the guineas, there was a diamond ring of price which had left the squire's finger three hours ago.

Mr Lessingham strove desperately to be calm. 'It looks like evidence, but it isn't. I can explain it all.'

'Ecod! so you shall,' chortled the squire. 'At Bow Street tomorrow morning. Keep your lies for the magistrate. Away with him.'

'Tomorrow morning will be too late, you fools.' Lessingham was suddenly beside himself, thinking of what would happen in the morning. 'I have an engagement to keep tonight. An important engagement. You shall hear me now, sir.'

They drove him to frenzy with their mockery until the squire, wearying of the sport, bade them away with the rascal.

The constable was looking round. 'But where's the gentleman that took him?' he asked.

He was answered by a clatter of departing hoofs on the kidney stones outside. Jack o'Lantern was proving true to his fame. And it was on the big black horse that he rode away, leaving the bay mare as further evidence against Mr Lessingham.

The Fortunes of Casanova

Giacomo di Casanova, the greatest of Italian—perhaps of all—adventurers, was born in Venice in April of 1725, the son of an actor of the San Samuele Theatre and the lovely daughter of a Venetian cobbler, who, as a result of her marriage, became herself an actress of some note. Clever, unscrupulous, and audacious, well-endowed by nature with a good exterior, a magnetic personality and a lively wit, he chose to make the world his oyster. By temperament something of a poet, something of a philosopher, something of a soldier, and entirely a gamester in every sense, he was a rogue by accident rather than design. A doctor of canon law, he knew Horace by heart, was familiar with natural science, richly stored with unusual knowledge, and as learned in the tricks of sharpers of all degrees. He accepted all adventures that came his way, rubbed shoulders with princes, and lay down with thieves, and was equally at home in palace and hovel.

R.S.

The Alibi

THERE can be little doubt—although it is not explicitly so stated in his memoirs—that it was the sight of the mast of a fruit-boat before the window of his prison that first aroused the notion in his fertile brain.

But let us begin at the beginning of this story of one of the earliest exploits of that Giacomo di Casanova who has been so aptly called the Prince of Adventurers, and whom some have accounted the very Prince of Scoundrels.

He was at the time in the eighteenth year of his age, but with the appearance of at least some five-and-twenty, extremely tall and personable, and already equipped with that air of a man of the great world which later—and coupled with his amazing impudence and undoubted talents—was to stand him in such excellent stead in the exploitation of his fellow-man.

To Casanova this was perhaps the most critical stage of his life. The career of the priesthood for which he had been intended by his mother—and for which, surely, there never lived a man less suitable—had rejected him. The seminary at Padua, in which he had been qualifying for holy orders, outraged by the wildness of his almost pagan nature, had just expelled him. He had accepted that expulsion in the spirit of philosophy for which he is so remarkable, accounting all things for the best. In this instance no doubt he was justified. He had doffed his seminarist's cassock, replacing it by a laced coat bought at second-hand, and the steel-hilted sword of the ruffler. Thus he had returned, in the summer of that year 1743, to Venice, the city of his birth, intent upon following his destiny—*sequere deum*, as he puts it himself.

There he had eked out, by gaming, the slender allowance which his mother made him out of her earnings on the trestles of a *forain* theatre at Warsaw; and we perceive already the beginnings of that extraordinary success of his at faro and kindred games of cards—a success so constant that, in spite of his emphatic and repeated assurances, we cannot avoid a suspicion on the score of the methods he employed.

But that is by the way. His trouble came to him through one Razetta, a Venetian of some substance and importance, of whom he has many evil things to say, some of which we are disposed to credit. In what Razetta first provoked his hostility we are not permitted to perceive. But we do know that such was his hatred of the man that, although Razetta must undoubtedly have been accounted an excellent match for Casanova's sister, our young adventurer would have none of it.

His sister dwelt—as did Casanova himself in the early days of that sojourn of his in Venice—at the house of the Abbé Grimani, the kindly old tutor appointed to the pair of them by their absent mother. At this house Signor Razetta was a constant visitor, and our shrewd ex-seminarist was not long in perceiving the attraction that drew him thither and in deciding that the matter must end. He began with his sister, whom he addressed in that pseudo-philosophic strain peculiar to him—if his memoirs are a faithful mirror of his utterances—a habit of speech acquired, we suppose, in the course of his preparation for a pulpit which he was, fortunately, never destined to disgrace. He reduced her to tears, he tells us—which is not in the least surprising. Indeed, we marvel that anyone should ever have listened to him without weeping. That done, he flung out after her lover, who had just taken leave of Grimani. He overtook him on the Rialto as dusk was falling. Accompanied by a servant Signor Razetta was on his way to a café in the neighbourhood where it was his habit to spend an hour or two before going home to bed.

Casanova demanded two words in private with him. Razetta—a corpulent and uncomely gentleman of some thirty years of age, deeming it as well to use civility towards the brother—and such a brother!—of the lady to whose favour he aspired, bade his lackey draw off across the bridge out of earshot.

Casanova used, as was the fashion with him, many words, and but little tact.

'It afflicts me, Signor Razetta,' said he, 'that a gentleman of my condition should be reduced to the necessity of discussing with an animal of yours, so delicate a matter as his own sister. But the fault, sir, is not mine. You have been wanting—as, after all, perhaps, was but to be expected—in that fine feeling which might have saved us both from the humiliations inseparable from this interview.'

'Sir!' roared Razetta, his great face aflame. 'You insult me!'

'I congratulate you upon a susceptibility to insult which I should never have suspected in a man of your deplorable origin and neglected breeding,' said Casanova. 'Since it is so, you afford me some hope that we may yet understand each other without the necessity being thrust upon me of proceeding to harsher measures.'

'Not another word, sir,' blazed the other, 'I will not listen to you further!' And he swung on his heel.

But Casanova took him by the shoulder. I have said that he was tall. It remains to add that he was of a prodigious strength. Razetta's soft flesh was mangled in that iron grip, his departure arrested.

Casanova turned him about again, and smiled balefully into his empurpled face.

'It is as I feared,' he said. 'Indeed until you spoke of insult I had not conceived that words could be of the least avail with you. Nor indeed was I prepared to employ with you any argument whatsoever. My sole intent was to command you never again to show your face at the Abbé Grimani's while my sister is in residence there, and to assure you that in the event of your disobedience—a folly to which I implore you not to commit yourself—I shall be put to the necessity of thrashing you until there is not a bone left whole in your body.'

Razetta shook with blending rage and fear.

'By the Madonna!' he swore. 'I go straight to the Signoria to inform the Saggio of your threats and demand his protection. You shall be laid by the heels, my fine cockerel. There is law and order in Venice, and——'

'Alas!' Casanova interrupted, 'you precipitate the inevitable.'

He raised his cane, and fell to belabouring with it the unfortunate Razetta. Razetta struggled, struck out in self-defence as best he could, and yelled to his servant.

Over the kidney stones of the bridge the man came clattering to his master's aid. Casanova, ever gripping his victim's shoulder, pulled him back to the foot of the bridge, where there was a gap in the parapet. Through this he flung him into the canal.

When the servant came up, our ex-seminarist was straightening his cravat and smoothing his ruffles. He pointed quite unnecessarily to the water where Razetta was floundering and gurgling in danger of drowning.

'You'll find your master down there,' said he. 'No doubt you will wish to fish him out for the sake of what wages he may owe you. But you would be doing humanity a nobler service if you left him where he is.' And he went home to supper, conscious that he had borne himself with infinite credit.

The sequel was, of course, inevitable. Razetta, rescued from drowning, smarting with pain and choler, went to lay his plaint before the chief notary—the Saggio della Scrittura—who was responsible for the preservation of order in the city.

Next morning Casanova awakened to find his chamber invested by officers of justice. They hauled him into a great black gondola, and so to the palace of the Signoria and the presence of the magistrate. There he found Razetta, who poured out his denunciation with a volubility marred by frequent sneezings, and Razetta's servant, who affirmed on oath the truth of his master's statement.

'What have you to say?' demanded the scowling Saggio of Casanova.

Casanova's swarthy, masterful face was a study in scorn; his full red lips curled contemptuously.

'I have to say, excellency, that these villains make a mock of your credulity and abuse your justice. Let me throw light upon their motives. That rogue Razetta, there, permits himself the effrontery of paying his addresses to my sister. I have signified to him my distaste of this, and my desire that he shall set a term to it. His retort, excellency, is this false accusation, and he has bribed and suborned his servant to confirm the lies with which he has insulted you.'

That was but the beginning. His volubility was never at fault, and whatever the Church may have gained when he was expelled the seminary, there can be little doubt that she lost a famous preacher. His was a fervour that carried conviction, and he might have carried it now but for the testimony of Razetta's back and shoulders, which were black and blue from last night's drubbing.

The end of it was that Casanova was taken back to the black gondola. This headed towards the Lido, and brought up a half-

hour later at the steps of the fort of Sant' Andrea, fronting the
Adriatic on the very spot where, annually, on the Feast of the
Ascension, the bucentaur comes to a halt when the Doge goes
forth to wed the sea. A year's sojourn in this prison was the heavy
penalty imposed upon Casanova in expiation of his offence against
the peace of Venice.

The place was garrisoned by Albanian soldiers, brought from
that part of Epirus which belonged to the most serene republic. Its
governor was a Major Pelodero, by whom Casanova was amiably
received and given the freedom of the entire fortress. The major, it
would seem, took a lenient view of the offence which the young
man was sent to expiate, and he came, no doubt, under the
influence of that singular charm and personal magnetism which
was one of this rogue's chief assets. He was given a fine room on
the first floor with two windows, and it was from these that he first
espied the masts of those fruit-sellers' boats, and so—after a week's
residence in the fort—came to conceive the first notion of enlisting
their service to help him effect his escape.

That, of course, was no more than the first, crude, germinal and
somewhat obvious idea that leapt to his mind. Another in his place
might have been content to act upon it. Not so Casanova. He
considered that merely to escape could, after all, profit him but
little. Perforce he must remain an outlaw, a fugitive from justice,
unable to show his face again in Venice without the certainty of
being sent to the galleys. A door was open to him, and he were a
fool not to avail himself of it. Yet he were a greater fool to avail
himself of it in the crude fashion that first suggested itself. He sat
down to think, and at last he discovered a way by which he might
bring about his honourable enlargement, the discomfiture of
Razetta, and, perhaps, his own considerable profit as well.

The result of his consideration was that when, at dawn on the
morrow, the gentle splash of an oar reached him from below, he
slipped from his bed, and gained the window. The single mast of a
fruit barge came level with it at that moment. He thrust his head
between the bar and the sill, and called softly to one of the
boatmen.

'Hola, my friend! Have you any peaches?'

'Peaches? Certainly, excellency. At once!' And whilst one of the
men steadied the vessel against the wall of the fort, the other

swarmed up the short, stout mast with a basket on the crook of his arm.

Casanova stretched out to reach it. He emptied out the peaches on to the floor of his room, put a gold coin in the basket and so returned it to the man, who broke into protestations of gratitude at such munificence, and summoned every saint in the calendar to watch over this princely consumer of peaches.

'That,' said Casanova, indicating the shining ducat, 'is a fruit culled from the Tree of Wisdom. So that you are wise you may fill your basket with the like.'

'Show me but where the tree grows, excellency!' was the fruiterer's prompt reply.

'What would you do for ten ducats?' enquired the prisoner, and in naming that amount he named almost all the money he had in his possession.

'Anything short of murder,' replied the other, dazzled by the mention of a sum which to one of his modest estate amounted to a fortune.

Casanova pondered him, smiled and nodded.

'Be here at ten tonight,' he said. 'Now go.'

Protesting that he would not fail, the boatman slithered down his mast again, and the barge moved on past the fort towards the city, all gilded now by the sun new-risen from the Adriatic.

Casanova looked at his peaches, and his first notion was to send them as a present to the governor's wife. But he thought better of it. They might afford a trace, however slender, to what he had planned should follow. So, one by one, he dropped them into the sea.

Later that morning, as he was taking the air with Major Pelodero's aide-de-camp, he happened to leap down from one of the bastions of the fortress. As his foot touched the ground he cried out, staggered, and fell in a heap, clapping his hand to his knee. Stefani, the aide, ran immediately to his assistance.

'It is nothing,' said Casanova, and sought to rise unaided, but found the thing impossible.

He availed himself, then, of the hand solicitously held out to him, and came to his feet; or rather, to his left foot, for he found it quite impossible to put his right to the ground. He must have wrenched his knee, he declared, clenching his teeth in his effort to

master the pain from which Stefani perceived him very obviously
to be suffering. Then leaning heavily upon his cane, and assisted
on the other side by the aide's arm, he hobbled painfully within
doors and straight to his room, where presently he was attended
by the surgeon of the fort. His knee was examined, and although
no swelling was visible as yet, its sensitiveness was apparent from
the manner in which the patient winced under the pressure exerted
by the doctor on his knee cap.

'A slight strain of the muscles,' the latter concluded. 'Not very
serious, although undoubtedly painful. You have had a narrow
escape, sir. As it is, a few days' rest and bandages, according to a
fashion of which I possess the secret and you will be yourself
again.'

Thereafter the knee was tightly bound in bandages soaked in
camphorated spirits of wine, and Casanova sat for the remainder
of the day with the ailing limb stretched across a chair. Major
Pelodero and some other officers of the garrison, taking pity upon
his helpless plight, spent a portion of the evening at cards with
him; and whatever the condition of his leg, his wits had clearly
suffered no damage, for despite the modesty of the points, he
contrived to win a matter of six ducats from them. When they left
him, towards eight o'clock, he begged that his servant might be
sent to him and permitted to spend the night in his room, lest in
his present crippled state he should have need of assistance.

This servant was a new acquisition of Casanova's. He was a
temporary valet, one of the soldiers of the garrison whose services
the prisoner was permitted to hire for a few coppers daily. The
fellow's chief recommendation to the ex-seminarist lay in the fact
that he had been a hairdresser before enlisting, and Casanova's
hair—as he tells us himself—required rescuing from the effects of
the neglect which it had naturally suffered in the seminary. It is
obvious to any reader of his memoirs that he was at all times
extremely vain of his personal appearance, and it is easy to imagine
how highly he valued, and how assiduously he employed, the
services of this fellow.

On the present occasion it would seem that the sometime hairdresser had another quality which recommended him to his temporary master. He was a famous drunkard. Casanova, in a more
than ordinarily indulgent mood, now afforded him the means to

gratify his inclinations on that score. He gave him money, and bade him procure three bottles of a full-bodied Falernian from the canteen. Further, he insisted that the fellow should drink them, although I confess that 'insisted' is hardly the word in which to describe such mild persuasion as he found it necessary to employ.

By half-past nine the soldier-valet was snoring most unpleasantly, reduced to a stupor. By ten o'clock the whole fort was wrapped in slumber, for strict discipline prevailed, and early hours were kept. By five minutes past ten came the splash of an oar under Casanova's window, and but for the darkness, a mast might have been seen to come to a halt before it.

Casanova slipped from his bed and into his clothes with a nimbleness that was miraculous, and still more miraculous was the cure that appeared to have been effected; for as he crossed to the window there was no slightest sign of lameness in his agile gait. A single bar was set horizontally across the window, but there was room for a man of ordinary proportions to pass above or below it; and Casanova, though tall and strong, was of slender—almost stripling—proportions at this time of his life. He tied a sheet to the bar, twisted it into a rope, slipped through, and a moment later he was standing amid the decaying vegetable matter in the barge. There he found but one man, the fruiterer with whom he had that morning come to an understanding. He pressed five ducats into the rogue's hand.

'The other five when the thing is done,' said he. 'Now push off!'

The boatman plied his single oar, gondolier-wise in the stern, and stood off from the fort.

'Whither now, excellency?' he enquired.

'Hoist your sail,' said Casanova—for the breeze was fresh—'and steer for Venice.'

They had words, of course. The boatman had conceived that here was a simple matter of assisting a gentleman to escape from prison, and that Casanova would desire him to make for the open sea beyond the Lido, and so head for the mainland. This going to Venice was fraught with danger, and he spoke of the risk he ran of being sent to the galleys if he were caught with an evaded prisoner.

Casanova took up a stout oak cudgel that he found in the bottom of the boat. He was ever a violent man, in words and in deeds. On this occasion his threats were sufficient, especially as they were seconded by a reminder that ten ducats was a sum worth some risk.

By his directions, then, the boat came to moor at the Schiavoni. He leapt ashore, bidding the fruiterer await him there. Thence he walked quickly to San Stefano, roused a dozing gondolier, and had himself borne to the Rialto.

It was striking eleven when he stationed himself upon the bridge to wait. It was a little before the hour at which Razetta usually returned from that obscure café which he frequented and whither commonly he was wont to go upon leaving the Abbé Grimani's. Leaning upon the parapet, Casanova waited patiently, smiling grimly down at the black, oily waters in pleasurable contemplation of the business they were to do.

He had not very long to wait. At about a quarter-past eleven he beheld his victim emerge from one of the narrow side-streets on the right of the bridge, accompanied, as on another similar occasion, by a lackey, who now bore a lantern. Casanova quitted his position and moved down to meet him.

They came face to face at the foot of the bridge, Casanova walking in the middle of the road and receiving the full glare of the lantern as he advanced. He halted, and Razetta stared at him, first in incredulity, and then in terror.

'Do you bar my passage?' Casanova thundered truculently, affecting to suppose the other to be the aggressor, and a whirling blow of his cudgel shivered the lantern into a thousand atoms.

'Seize him!' cried Razetta to his lackey. But his lackey was deaf to the command. His hand was still tingling from the blow that had swept the lantern from it. 'Body of Satan! You have broken prison! You shall go to the galleys for this!'

'You mistake me, I think,' said Casanova.

'Mistake you? Not I! You are that villain Casanova! Seize him, I say!'

'If you will insist upon hindering me I must defend myself as best I can!' replied Casanova, and he plied his cudgel.

On the occasion of their last meeting he had been armed with a slender cane capable of comparatively light punishment. But the stout oaken club he wielded tonight went near to endangering the very life of Razetta. Its smashing blows fell upon his shoulders, upon his limbs, and finally upon his head. He screamed, and his servant roared for help, until the matter ended as it had ended on that other occasion. Razetta was knocked into the canal.

Casanova flung his cudgel after him, and in a voice of thunder ordered the servant to be silent.

'Instead of squalling there go and fish him out,' he said, 'so that I may have the pleasure of throwing him in yet again some other evening.'

Steps were approaching down the street by which Razetta had come. Casanova waited for no more. He flung swiftly across the bridge and down a narrow by-lane. He made a detour that brought him out at the spot where his gondola was waiting. He jumped in, and was carried back to San Stefano—the pursuit, meantime, having been arrested by the more urgent need to rescue the drowning man.

So quickly had he acted that in less than ten minutes of flinging Razetta into the water he was once more aboard the fruit barge, speeding towards the Lido and the Fort of Sant' Andrea. Five minutes before midnight he was climbing back through the window of his prison. Another three minutes and he was in bed, considering his soldier-servant still asleep in his chair. To rouse him, Casanova flung first one boot at his head, and then the other, cursing him volubly the while, and in his loudest tones.

The fellow awoke with a yell when the heel of the second boot caught him so shrewdly on the forehead that it drew blood.

'What is it, sir? What is it?' he babbled, still half-bewildered from sleep and wine.

'What is it, you drunken dog?' roared Casanova, in a mighty passion. 'Do you think you were sent hither to spend the night asleep on a chair? I suffer. My knee burns. My head throbs. I have a fever! I cannot sleep! Go, fetch the surgeon. Tell him I am in agony!'

The soldier protested that it was midnight—through the stillness of the night came the boom of the hour from St Mark's even as he spoke—and that the surgeon would be abed. But Casanova was so fierce and bloodthirsty in his reply that the man departed at a run. He was back in five minutes, accompanied now by the surgeon in nightcap and bed-gown.

Casanova lay back moaning, his eyes had closed. The haste he had made had drenched him in a perspiration which admirably answered his present purposes, whilst his general agitation set up an irregularity in his pulse sufficient to deceive the incompetent man of medicine of the fort.

'Do you suffer?' quoth the surgeon sympathetically.

'Like the damned!' groaned Casanova, through clenched teeth. 'This bed is become a bed of pain. I burn, my knee throbs; I cannot sleep. If I could but sleep!'

The surgeon went to mix a drug. On the way he roused the governor with the news that Casanova was taken seriously ill. The governor cursed Casanova and the surgeon jointly and severally for disturbing his rest and went to sleep again most unsympathetically.

Casanova swallowed the drug when it was brought him. The surgeon sat with him until he announced that he felt easier, and that, if the light were extinguished, he thought he might now be able to sleep.

In the morning he was much better. Supported by his servant and leaning upon his cane, he hobbled to breakfast in Major Pelodero's dining-room—for the genial governor had made him free of his table—and he congratulated the surgeon in very graceful and flattering terms upon his skill, and the efficacy of his drug. His fever had entirely abated, and his knee was much less painful. The surgeon recommended care and rest for a few days yet, when he was sure that all would be well.

But it would seem that there was to be no rest for Casanova just yet.

They were still at breakfast when a soldier came with the announcement that an officer sent by the Chief Notary of Venice had just arrived at the fort. The governor went instantly to receive that envoy.

'His excellency the Saggio, sir,' said the officer, 'has sent me to receive your explanation of a circumstance by which he is greatly exercised. He desires to know how it happens that news of the evasion of your prisoner, Signor Giacomo di Casanova, should have been communicated to him in the first instance by others than yourself?'

The officer's tone was extremely frosty. Major Pelodero's reply was of the hottest.

'What the devil may be the meaning, sir, of this impertinence? I resent your manner, and as for your news, it is as foolish as is, apparently, its bearer!'

'Sir!' cried the officer, in a very big voice.

'Bah!' The major swung on his heel. 'Desire Signor Casanova to attend us here,' he bade the orderly.

The officer's eyes grew round; his mouth itself kept them some sort of company.

'Do I understand that Signor Casanova is still here? That the report which has reached his excellency the Saggio is false?'

'You shall see!' was the peppery governor's curt answer.

Casanova came in, hobbling and assisted. Looking from one to the other of those present, he courteously announced himself their servant. The major sneered at the officer, and waited for him to speak. The officer stared from Casanova to the major, and said nothing. It was Casanova, himself, at last, who broke the silence:

'May I hope, sir, that your presence here, and the governor's request for my presence signify that the truth of the matters with which I am charged has at last been brought to light, and that you are come to announce me my release? Since I am suffering in health, as you may see, such news were very welcome. Though, considering my crippled condition, and that I am unable to walk without assistance, I am less vexed at the moment by my incarceration than I might be at another time.'

'I—I don't understand!' stammered the officer.

'So I had thought,' snapped the major testily.

'Perhaps—perhaps I had better explain,' said the officer.

'I confess it is not unnecessary,' agreed the major.

Forth came the explanation. Razetta and his servant had been before the Saggio that very morning to lay a second plaint against Casanova, the details of which the officer now expounded.

'But this is incredible,' said Casanova, his face blank.

'Not merely incredible, but impossible,' said the governor, still smarting under the memory of the tone the officer had taken at the outset of their interview.

'Would it not be best that I should go before the Saggio at once, sir?' said Casanova.

It was, of course, the only thing to do. The prisoner accompanied the officer back to Venice, and with them went the governor, the surgeon, and Casanova's servant.

Casanova's arrival in such company at the palace of the Signory surprised the Saggio as much as his appearance in the fort had surprised the Saggio's envoy.

Casanova bowed as gracefully as his crippled condition would permit him, a twinge of pain crossing his features as he did so. The Saggio was solicitous, and ordered a chair to be set for him. He sank into it gently, assisted by the surgeon and the governor, his leg stretched stiffly in front of him. Then he made one of his famous speeches to the bewildered magistrate.

Somewhere in his voluminous memoirs he protests that a gentleman should never have recourse to anything but the truth save only when he deals with rogues, with whom it would be unavailing. It would seem to follow that he had a good many dealings with such rogues in his time, and that he took the liberty of placing the Saggio himself in that category.

'I understand, excellency,' he said, 'that it is alleged by Signor Razetta and his servant that last night, near the bridge of the Rialto, at about midnight, I fell upon him with a cudgel, belaboured him, and flung him again into the canal—all, in fact, as precisely as before.'

The Saggio nodded without interrupting, and Casanova proceeded, his bold black eyes full upon the other's countenance.

'When last before your excellency I had the honour to inform you that your credulity was being abused, and your high office mocked by those two villains. It is not for me to blame your excellency for having been their dupe. They were two, and I was but one; and the law—of which you are so exalted and worthy an administrator—runs that the testimony of two persons must outweigh that of one. But there is another justice more discerning and far-reaching than that human justice of which your excellency is so noble and shining a dispenser. That justice, it would appear, has led these villains to overreach themselves and betray their falsehood. If your excellency's renowned perspicuity should ever plumb the depths of this infamy, it will, I have no doubt, be discovered that Signor Razetta, misled by some false rumour that I had broken prison, has come to you with this fresh lie that he might thus spur you on to my recapture.'

'And yet, sir,' the Saggio interrupted, 'Messer Razetta's condition and the testimony of several other witnesses prove beyond all doubt that he was most cruelly beaten and thrown into the canal.'

'Since that is so, I can but suppose that he is in error—an error quickened by his malice. I do not need to plead my case today. The facts plead for me more eloquently and irrefutably than would be possible to any words of mine. Not only—as your excellency sees—have I not broken prison, but I have been crippled these four-and-twenty hours, unable to walk without assistance. If more were necessary, this good fellow here, who tended me all night, can inform your excellency that precisely at the hour in which I am accused of having committed this offence on the Rialto I was in bed at Sant' Andrea, in extreme pain and beset by fever. Further this learned doctor will tell you that, summoned by my servant, he came to ease my sufferings at that hour; and the governor here will add that he was informed of my condition at the time. Never in all the history of justice was an accused man furnished with so complete an alibi. I leave it to your excellency's acute penetration to lay bare the truth of this affair.'

The Saggio heard the other three in turn, each and all of them emphatically bearing out Casanova's statement.

'It is enough,' he said in the end. 'It is but logical to assume that, whatever the motives that may have actuated him, since Messer Razetta was mistaken in his assailant last night, he must similarly have been mistaken before.'

'Mistaken!' quoth the rogue Casanova, with a wry smile.

The Saggio made him no reply. He took up a pen, and wrote rapidly.

'You will be restored to liberty at once, sir,' he announced, 'and Signor Razetta shall be dealt with. You are free to return home.'

But Casanova had not yet quite reached the end of his rascally purpose.

'I go in such dread of the rancour of that villain Razetta,' said he, 'that I will implore your excellency to afford me the State's protection until I am restored to such vigour as will enable me to protect myself. I shall be eternally grateful for your permission to return with the major to Sant' Andrea until my knee is completely mended—a matter of a week or so, as the doctor here informs me.'

His excellency graciously gave his consent to this, and would thereupon have dismissed them but that still Casanova had not done.

'I most respectfully submit to your excellency that some amend is due to me for what I have suffered morally and physically: the indignity, extremely painful to a man of my sensitive honour; the duress in which I have been kept; and finally my present crippled condition, arising directly out of my imprisonment.'

The Saggio frowned.

'The State, sir——' he was beginning coldly.

'Ah, sir, your indulgence!' Casanova interrupted him. 'It is not from the State that I suggest any amend should come. It is not the fault of the State that these things have come to pass. The fault is entirely Razetta's, and I submit—most respectfully and humbly— that it is from Razetta should proceed the adequate compensation which I solicit.'

The Saggio reflected.

'It is but just,' he agreed at last. 'At what sum do you estimate your inconvenience?'

Casanova sighed reflectively.

'It is not in ducats and sequins, excellency,' said he, 'that a gentleman of my condition can estimate the damage to his honour and his body. To do so were to affront the one and the other. Not then to compensate me, for that is impossible, but to punish Razetta do I suggest that he should be mulcted in my favour to the extent of—shall we say?—a hundred ducats.'

The magistrate pursed his lips. The sum was heavy.

'I should say,' he answered deliberately, 'that fifty ducats were a just fine.'

'Your excellency is the best judge,' said Casanova, with angelic submission. 'Fifty ducats be it then—to teach him the way of truth and honesty.'

Thus ended the matter, in spite of all that Razetta had to say, which was a deal, and all of it so offensive and profane that it confirmed the Saggio in his conviction that he was dealing justly.

With the fifty ducats Casanova set up a faro bank, and prospered so well that in the end Venice became dangerous for him, and he was compelled to seek fresh pastures for his splendid talents.

The Augmentation
of Mercury

I WARN you at the outset not to take him for a vulgar rogue. A rogue he was undoubtedly, but vulgar never. Himself, for all his frankness, he would not admit even so much. He discriminates finely. Indeed, as a splitter of hairs Casanova is unrivalled among all those who have made philosophy. 'The honest ruse,' he says somewhere in the course of his voluminous memoirs, 'may be taken to be the sign of a prudent spirit. It is a virtue, true, which resembles rascality. But he who cannot in case of need exercise it with dignity is a fool.'

Lest even after this warning you should be disposed to pass a harsh judgement upon the exploit I am about to relate, let me make clear the desperate position in which he found himself.

He had embarked at Venice for Ancona two days ago with fifty gold sequins in his pocket. And in a cellar at Chiozza—the first port of call—he had been so soundly drubbed at faro that he had lost not only that fifty, but a further thirty sequins yielded by the sale of his trunk of clothes.

Disconsolate, and very hungry—not having tasted food for four-and-twenty hours—he sat now upon a bale of cordage in the vessel's waist, reckoning up his assets.

Besides the semi-clerical but becoming garments in which he stood, he was possessed of a handsome figure, an iron constitution, an effrontery that was proof against all things, a doctor's degree in canon law, some very considerable learning for his eighteen years, a remarkable histrionic talent inherited from his parents, both of whom had achieved some renown upon the stage, and a letter of introduction to the Bishop of Martorano in Calabria, who was to advance him in the ecclesiastical career to which he was destined.

Casanova's tastes, heaven knows, were far from ecclesiastical. He had wished to study medicine, having indeed a certain taste for chemistry, and a perception that of all professions medicine offers the greatest scope to empiricism. But his mother, now a considerable actress in Dresden, and those whom she had made responsible for his education, had insisted that he should study not merely law, but canon law, and that he should take holy orders. He submitted in obedience to the *sequere deum* of the Stoics, which he had taken for his own motto; and as you behold him now upon the threshold of his career, you shall judge how justified were the instincts that warned him that he was as little likely in the end to become a priest as a physician.

He sat there on his bale of cordage, lugubriously looking out across the sunlit waters to the receding coast of Istria. Despite the genial warmth of the day—for it was August, of 1743—he was shivering with cold from lack of nourishment.

A shuffling step approached him. A voice deep and harsh, yet vaguely solicitous, enquired:

'Are you ill, sir?'

He turned slowly to survey a tall, vigorous young Franciscan with a coarsely pleasant countenance, whose tonsured head was fringed with tufts of coarse red hair. Small, dark, inquisitive eyes met Casanova's bold magnetic glance.

'I am troubled,' he answered shortly.

'Troubled?' quoth the friar. 'I have medicine here that will dispel trouble—a capon, sausages, a bottle of good wine, and my own company if you'll suffer it.' And out of one of the amazing sack-like pockets of his habit he produced the articles he named.

Casanova frowned, considering him. The invitation came so pat upon his urgent need. Had the shaveling been spying upon him? And if so what profit did the fellow look to make? This misanthropical suspicion proceeded from a cynicism newly begotten of his Chiozza adventure. Still his need was urgent.

Rising, he accepted the invitation, but with condescension rather than gratitude. Already at that early age he had some of the lordly airs that were later to distinguish him, a gift of accepting favours with all the appearance of bestowing them.

Together they sat down to dine, and as they ate and drank, Casanova's dignity lessening, he listened more and more affably to the garrulous confidences of the friar. Brother Stefano—as he was called—displayed with ostentation treasures of bread and wine,

cheese, sausages and a ham which he had received as alms in
Orsara, and with which the unfathomable pockets of his habit were
now cumbered.

'Do you receive money as well?' quoth Casanova, genuinely
interested.

'God forbid!' cried the friar. 'It is against the rules of our glorious
order. Besides,' he added slyly, 'if I asked for money what should I
receive? A few coppers, of which you behold here ten times the
value. St Francis, believe me, was a shrewd fellow.'

To this he added an invitation, which Casanova was but too
willing to accept, that for the two days remaining of the journey he
should allow himself to be provided for by St Francis.

Not until they had landed at Ancona, and found themselves
lodged in the lazaret with the prospect of twenty days of quarantine
imposed upon all who came just then from Venice, did Casanova
discover the motive he had been seeking of the friar's spontaneous
generosity. He was requesting for himself a room with a bed,
table, and some chairs, agreeing to pay the hire on the expiry of
the term, when Stefano sidled up to him.

'Sir,' he said, 'if of your benevolence you would allow me to
share your room, I should require only a truss of straw for my
bed.'

Casanova agreed, and perceiving now how they might inter-aid
each other he took the friar fully into his confidence, telling him
that he was going to Rome, where a secretarial appointment awaited
him, but that until he got there he would be in need of everything.
He had expected acquiescence, but hardly the eager gladness with
which Stefano received the news.

'Count on me,' he said. 'Provided you will write some letters for
me, I will see you safely as far as Rome at the expense of St
Francis.'

'But why don't you write your own letters?' wondered Casanova.

'Because I can write only my own name. True, I can write it
with either hand, but what advantage is that?'

Casanova stared at him as at a portent. 'You amaze me,' said he.
'I thought you were a priest.'

'I'm not a priest; I'm a friar. I say Mass. Consequently I can
read. St Francis, whose unworthy child I am, could not read,
which is why he never said Mass. But since you can write, you
shall write to the persons whose names I will give you, and I

promise you we shall have enough to feast upon to the end of the quarantine.'

Here Casanova perceived the second chief reason why Stefano had befriended him—that he might act as his secretary during those twenty days in which the friar, being unable to leave the lazaret, must have gone hungry without somebody to discharge this office. Forthwith he wrote eight letters—eight because, according to the oral tradition of the order, when a Franciscan shall have knocked at seven doors and been refused he is to knock at the eighth with confidence of response. These letters, dictated by the friar, were interlarded with scraps of Latin, which he ordered Casanova to supply, and packed with foolish and unnecessary falsehoods. Thus, to the Superior of the Jesuits Stefano bade him say that he was not writing to the Capuchins because they were atheists, which was the reason why St Francis could not endure them.

'But that is nonsense,' cried Casanova. 'For in the time of St Francis there were no Capuchins or friars of any kind.'

'How do you know that?' quoth Stefano.

'It's a matter of history.'

'History!' snorted the friar. 'What has history to do with religion? You're very ignorant for a doctor. Did they teach you no better than that at Padua? Write as I tell you, and don't argue with me.'

Casanova shrugged and wrote, persuaded that such letters would be ignored as those of a knave and a madman. But he was mistaken. They were deluged with hams and capons, sausages and eggs, fresh meat and wine, and thus those three weeks in the lazaret of Ancona were a time of plenty.

At the end of the quarantine Casanova repaired to a minorite convent, where the further funds for the journey to Rome were to be supplied to him. He received there, together with the Bishop of Martorano's address, the sum of ten sequins. Out of these he paid for the hire of the room and furniture at the lazaret, bought himself a handsome long coat and a pair of strong shoes, and set out for Rome in Stefano's company.

It was an eight days' journey on foot, but not as the friar understood it. Stefano's notion was to travel three miles a day, at which rate they would have been two months upon the road. Casanova being now sufficiently in funds to defray his travelling expenses, said frankly that this rate of travelling would not suit him, and proposed to leave the friar. But the friar would not be left.

'Carry my cloak,' said he, 'and I will walk at least twice the distance daily. Thus St Francis shall defray us both.'

Our young doctor agreed, taking Stefano's cloak, which was a mule's load, its pockets stuffed as they were with victuals of all descriptions, sufficient for a fortnight.

Sweating and toiling along the dusty road under this burden, Casanova developed a natural curiosity.

'When travelling,' he asked, 'why don't you seek food and shelter in the convents of your order?'

Stefano looked at him owlishly, and winked.

'Because I am not a fool,' said he. 'In the first place I shouldn't be received because, being a fugitive, I have no written obedience card, such as they always insist upon seeing. I might even risk being sent to prison; for they are an evil lot of dogs. In the second place, it is never as comfortable in a convent as in the house of a benefactor.'

'Why are you a fugitive?' asked Casanova, and knew that the unintelligible, incoherent answer he received about imprisonment and escape was all compounded of falsehood.

He was growing a little weary of this harlequin of a Franciscan, and it is small wonder that in the end they quarrelled. The thing began on the following morning. Stefano led the way to a handsome house standing back from the high-road near Macerata. There was a small chapel attached to it, arguing piety on the part of the inhabitants, and acting as a beacon to the friar.

He strode boldly in, pronouncing a sonorous benediction, which brought the family clustering about him to kiss his unwashed hand. Then the mistress of the house invited him to say Mass, and hearing him consent, Casanova clutched his arm in horror.

'Have you forgotten that we have breakfasted?' he whispered.

'That's none of your business,' growled the friar. 'Be quiet.'

The Mass was said, and Casanova's amazement and disgust were increased to perceive that Stefano was very indifferently acquainted with the ritual. But there was worse to follow. The friar went to the confessional, and summoned the family to confession. And there the evil fellow took it into his head to refuse absolution to the youngest daughter, a lovely child of thirteen, whose budding beauty was moving Casanova to tenderness.

From his earliest years he had been inordinately susceptible to the charms of the other sex, and that susceptibility, no doubt, was one of the chief factors in his eventual decision to abandon the ecclesiastical career.

Stefano scolded the child publicly, threatening her with hell-torment, until bewildered and agonized by shame she ran to shut herself up in her room.

The event threw a gloom over the repast that followed, spread expressly to regale this holy man, and it profoundly angered Casanova, the more because the victim of that loutish caprice was so sweet and lovely.

'You infamous, ignorant impostor!' he denounced the friar, to the horror and amazement of all present, his dark eyes blazing, the veins of his temples swollen. 'You impudent lout! How dared you so treat that child?'

Stefano looked at him, his little eyes very evil. But he exercised sufficient self-control to render his voice meek and gentle.

'I forgive your heat, my son. I understand your feelings. They are a snare set for you by the devil. Beware of them.'

'Beware of me, rather,' roared Casanova, 'for I propose to thrash you into a state of decency. On what grounds did you refuse that child absolution?'

Stefano cast his eyes to heaven in afflicted protest.

'Ignorant and heedless youth,' he answered sadly, 'what are you saying? Are you bidding me betray the secret of the confessional? Are you?' His voice swelled up on a note of sudden wrath.

Casanova looked round, and everywhere met eyes that dis-approved of a provocation so strange and so distressing. It was enough. He got up, and went out without another word.

A couple of hours later, as Stefano was slowly trudging along the road, Casanova surged suddenly out of a hedge before him.

'Ha! Ha!' laughed Stefano, full of the mirth that excess of wine engenders. 'We meet again, as I expected.'

'We meet to part,' said Casanova, who had been nursing his anger.

'Why to part?' bubbled the friar.

'Because I'll not travel further with a rogue, lest I be condemned with him to the galleys.'

Stefano's round genial face grew sinister. He gripped his staff more firmly. 'You say that to me?' he growled.

'I do. You are an unwashed scoundrel, ripe for gaol.'

'And what are you, my pretty gentleman? A needy beggar, who have been living upon me for a month.'

For answer Casanova soundly boxed the friar's ears. The friar swung his heavy staff, and caught the young doctor a blow across the head that sent him reeling into the ditch.

When Casanova recovered consciousness it was approaching noon. He rose from the depths of the dry ditch into which he had rolled, the grasses of which had concealed him from the eyes of wayfarers, and collected his wits. His head was aching villainously, and under the lustrous chestnut hair which he wore clubbed, and in which he took great pride, he discovered a lump as large as a pigeon's egg—the Franciscan's parting gift.

He felt that he had not come as well out of the encounter as he intended. But he took comfort in the thought that he was well rid of an evil travelling companion, who had served his turn. After all, he had seven gold sequins in his pocket, enough to carry him with ease and dignity to his patron, the Bishop, who would place him beyond the reach of all anxiety.

The distance to Macerata was not far—a mile or so—and there he would dine well, and sleep between clean sheets, setting out refreshed upon the morrow. He picked up his hat, and stepped out whistling. Suddenly he checked in his stride. His whistling stopped. His hands were racing and fumbling through the pockets of his handsome coat. Conviction followed swiftly upon apprehension. His purse containing the seven sequins was gone.

Solemnly, terribly, and most uncanonically did the pale lips of our young doctor of canon law anathematize the scoundrelly Franciscan who had picked his pocket. Then he sat down on a mound of stones by the roadside to contemplate his case. It was desperate indeed. Save for a few pieces of silver and some copper *paoli* in his breeches pocket, which the friar had missed, he was utterly destitute. Regretfully he thought of the good dinner and the good bed he had promised himself. And then in rebellion against fate he decided that, come what might, dinner and bed should not be forgone. To pay for them he would, if necessary, pawn his handsome coat. An hour later he was striding across the threshold of Macerata's best inn, mustering those almost unsuspected histrionic gifts of his to explain away his lack of luggage.

'I am the Bishop of Martorano's secretary,' he announced, 'travelling to Rome. Has my servant arrived?'

'Your servant, excellency?' quoth the landlord eagerly, impressed by the tall figure and boldly handsome face, the luxuriant well-coiffed hair, and the handsome coat—a compromise between clericalism and modishness.

'I sent him ahead of me in the chaise. I needed exercise, and preferred to walk the last two miles.'

The landlord understood. The gentleman's dusty legs and shoes were at once explained. He shook his head.

'Not here,' he was beginning. Then he checked. 'Would it be a yellow chaise?' he asked.

Guessing the drift of the question, Casanova decided that the chaise must have been a yellow one. It was a common enough colour after all.

'A yellow chaise drove through the town at a great rate a half-hour ago. The postilion, excellency, was in green.'

'In green—that's it. And he drove on, do you say? He drove on?'

The landlord admitted it, and grew terrified before Casanova's tempestuous anger. Roundly he cursed all valets, and all postilions. Had he not told them plainly enough that this was the inn he would honour with his patronage? He could forgive the valet for misunderstanding him, the valet being not merely a Frenchman, but an idiot as well. But the postilion was an Italian, of Ancona— that is, if the inhabitants of Ancona were Italian, a fact which he began seriously to doubt. Himself he was a Venetian, he announced in passing, secretary, he repeated, to the Bishop of Martorano. Explosively, he desired the host to tell him what he was to do.

'Your excellency will pardon the suggestion that you might have fared worse. This is a comfortable house, and my beds. . . .'

'I know, I know,' Casanova broke in impatiently. 'Give me a room, and if those sons of dogs come back with the chaise whilst my anger endures, I'll crack their empty skulls one against the other.'

It was a piece of acting that earned him more than he had reckoned. His loud, angry voice had drawn people from the common room, and indeed from every part of the inn. Now among the guests there was a Greek trader, distinguished by his Oriental gabardine, who had pricked up his ears when our gentleman announced himself a Venetian. The citizens of the Republic were notoriously wealthy and lavish—which was precisely why Casanova had mentioned his origin—and the Greek made wealthy, lavish gentlemen his prey.

It would be an hour or so later, when Casanova, washed and brushed, showed himself once more below, that our Greek approached him.

'I think, sir,' he ventured, 'that I heard you say you are a Venetian.'

Casanova flashed him a sidelong glance, and wondered.

'I certainly said so. What you may have heard is your own affair,' he answered dryly.

But a trader with business to do is not easily disconcerted.

'I am myself a subject of the Republic,' the Greek announced, 'and so in some sort your excellency's compatriot. I am from Zante. My name is Panagiottis, and if I can serve you in the inconvenience caused you by . . .'

Under Casanova's cold stare the trader spread his hands, and left the offer there. But, persistent of purpose, he remained and chattered amiably awhile, Casanova compelling him at first to pursue a monologue. Little by little, however, the young doctor's manner became less frosty. Panagiottis began by dilating upon the glories of Venice, passed on to deplore at length the inconvenience of travel, and then by way of manners and customs adroitly reached his objective, the comparative merits of Italian and foreign wines. Finding his listener interested, he touched at last the very bull's eye of the matter.

'After all,' he said, 'and with all due praise to Tuscan vintages, there are wines of the Levant that stand almost unrivalled. Now I have with me some Muscadine—some of which, by the way, I could sell you cheaply—which is of rare excellence.'

'I might buy some, if it is as good as you say,' said Casanova grandly. 'I know something of wine.'

The Greek rubbed his hands. 'So much the better. I have some excellent Cerigo, some wine of Samos, and some Cephalonian. If you will do me the honour to dine with me you shall have an opportunity of tasting them.'

'*Fata viam inveniunt,*' said Casanova to himself. Here had fate provided him with a dinner. But it was only when the Greek had used polite insistence that Casanova yielded, gracefully condescending.

It is inconceivable that he could have had any intention of exploiting the Greek beyond this matter of dinner. What followed was entirely unpremeditated. The repast served in the Greek's private room proved excellent, and the Cerigo was quite the best that Casanova had ever tasted.

The Greek's conversation was naturally of his trade. He mentioned that he had acquired a considerable quantity of minerals: vitriol, cinnabar, antimony, and a hundred quintals of mercury. At the mention of mercury Casanova bethought him of an amalgam of bismuth and lead, by which that mineral can be augmented by one quarter. I have said that he was interested in chemistry. It occurred to him that if the Greek were not acquainted with this mystery here was a chance of profit.

'These minerals are for sale?' he enquired.

'Of course; but they would hardly interest you.'

'On the contrary, I might buy some mercury.' He smiled darkly. 'I do a curious trade in mercury myself,' he added.

Panagiottis became inquisitive, but Casanova was not disposed to gratify him. Address was necessary. The mere offer to sell the secret would lead to nothing. He must astonish Panagiottis by effecting the augmentation, laugh at the Greek's amazement when manifested, and so lure him on to desire the secret for himself.

At the end of dinner Panagiottis invited him to inspect the wares displayed in an adjoining room. They made up a heterogeneous collection: flasks of Levantine wines, assorted Eastern fabrics and metal ware, minerals and dried fruits, and four large flagons containing each 10 lb of mercury. Casanova purchased one of these flagons—on credit, of course, since he was without the means to pay for it—and took it to his room.

He went out to find the only druggist in Macerata, and laid out most of his slender stock of silver and copper on the purchase of two and a half pounds each of bismuth and lead. Returning to the inn, he procured himself two empty bottles, proceeded to make his amalgam, and decanted it into these.

That evening he invited Panagiottis to sup with him in his own room. Before sitting down he placed on the table the Greek's mercury, divided into two bottles, and from these he now re-filled the original flagon, observing with secret delight the merchant's mystification at sight of 5 lb of fine mercury remaining over.

Answering Panagiottis' insistent questions with a laugh, Casanova called the inn boy, and handing him the quarter flagon of mercury bade him go and sell it to the druggist. The boy returned with fifteen carlini, which Casanova pocketed. In itself that sum would more than suffice to pay Casanova's score at the inn. But he aimed much further.

The Greek begged for the return of his flagon, which was worth sixty carlini, and Casanova at once restored it to him, with laughingly-expressed thanks for having allowed him so easily to earn fifteen carlini.

Then he called for supper, sat down, and talked of other things. But Panagiottis was visibly preoccupied, and he betrayed alarm when his host announced that he would be leaving early on the morrow, travelling post if necessary until he overtook his chaise and servant.

'Why don't you stay tomorrow, and earn a further forty carlini on the other three flagons?' he asked unsteadily.

Casanova shrugged. 'I am in no need of money. I augmented one flagon merely to amuse and surprise you.'

Panagiottis' glance was laden with envy and wonder.

'You must be very wealthy,' he said.

'I should be were it not that I am working at the augmentation of gold, which is a very costly operation.'

'But where is the need? The augmentation of mercury should suffice any man. Tell me, what does the augmentation cost?'

'One and a half per cent.'

'And would that which you have increased be susceptible of further increase?'

'Oh, no. If that were so, it would be an inexhaustible source of wealth.'

And thereupon, to play out his part, Casanova rose, called the landlord, paid for the supper, and ordered a carriage and a pair of horses for eight o'clock next morning. Bidding good-night to the chagrined and reluctant Panagiottis, and promising to send him an order for a barrel of Muscadine later, Casanova went to bed, convinced that the Greek would not close his eyes all night.

He was in the act of dressing next morning when Panagiottis invaded his chamber, after due apology. Casanova received him cordially, and invited him to share his morning coffee, which stood steaming on the table.

Panagiottis came straight to business. 'I have come to ask you if you could be induced to sell me your secret,' he announced.

'Why not?' was the genial answer. 'When next we meet. . . .'

'When next we meet?' cried the Greek in panic. 'But when will that be?'

'Why, when you will. Should you come to Rome. . . .'

Again Panagiottis interrupted. He was trembling with excitement.

'But why not now? Why not now?'

'Now?' Casanova stared. 'My horses are harnessed. I am expected in Rome, and already I have delayed upon the journey.'

'But surely no great delay can be entailed in what I ask.'

He was in dread lest fortune should elude him after being brought within his reach.

Casanova became grave.

'That depends,' said he. 'My secret is expensive and, after all, I do not really know you.'

Standing, he sipped his coffee calmly.

The Greek sat down. The truth is that his legs were yielding under him. Beads of perspiration gleamed on the arch of his heavy, pendulous nose—the brand of the acquisitive. He drew his gabardine about his slender shanks, and stroked his thinning black hair with an unsteady hand.

'But these are not reasons for delay,' he protested in distress. 'I am sufficiently well-known here, and my credit is good. Do you need an earnest of it?'

A gesture of lofty deprecation was Casanova's only answer.

'How much would you want for your secret?' Panagiottis asked point-blank.

Casanova's answer was as prompt as it was calm.

'Two thousand gold ounces.'

At the mention of so vast a sum the Greek gasped like a fish. Casanova smiled and reached for his hat.

'You see,' he said. 'Besides, it is striking eight, and my horses are waiting.'

Panagiottis swallowed audibly. 'I will p-pay it,' he stammered, 'provided that I, myself, augment the 30 lb I have here with the ingredients you shall name, which I myself shall purchase.'

'The condition is natural,' Casanova agreed. 'But a contract would be necessary.'

'You shall have it, sir. It is what I should myself desire.'

'But it will need time, and my horses——'

'Put off the journey for an hour or two,' the Greek besought him.

Casanova took a turn as if considering.

'Sir, sir, your hesitation wounds me!' burst from his agonized companion. 'Look!' He snatched up a pen and wrote swiftly. 'Take this. The banker de Laura lives a hundred yards from here. Present it and ask him for information of my credit.'

Casanova took the note. It was draft running as follows:

Pay the bearer at sight fifty gold ounces for account of

PANAGIOTTIS.

He smiled almost wistfully. 'Really,' he was beginning, 'so much is not necessary to——'

'Take it, please—please. I insist.'

'Very well.'

Casanova went, came back, and placed the fifty ounces on the table.

'Your banker's account of you is quite satisfactory,' said he. 'To oblige you—since you are so set on it—I have bidden the landlord put back the horses until noon, so that we may conclude the transaction.' And drawing up a chair, he sat down facing the Greek.

Panagiottis expressed his relief by a sigh, and insisted that as a preliminary Casanova should pocket the fifty ounces. Casanova did so, under protest, and they proceeded to draw up the contract. It ran as follows:

I agree to pay Messer Giacomo di Casanova the sum of two thousand gold ounces when he shall have taught me how and by what ingredients I may augment mercury by one quarter, without deterioration of its quality, equal to that which he sold at Macerata in my presence on the 25th of August, 1743.

Having signed it, Panagiottis delivered it to Casanova, together with a bill of exchange for two thousand ounces on a Roman banker, which, if necessary, he said, de Laura would discount at once upon a word from himself. So much being concluded, Casanova proceeded to impart the secret, naming the ingredients— lead and bismuth, the first which by its nature amalgamates with mercury, the second which restores its fluidity, impaired by the amalgamation.

The Greek went off perform the operation, on the understanding that they should dine together, when he would report upon the results. He returned at noon, a pensive, saddened man, which was quite as Casanova had expected. Nevertheless he hailed his pupil heartily.

'Well?' he cried.

Panagiottis shook his head. 'It is not well at all,' he said gloomily, 'The augmentation is made, but the mercury is not perfect.'

Casanova's tone and manner betrayed impatience. 'It is equal to that which I sold yesterday at Macerata, as the contract stipulates.'

'Ah, but the contract also says that there must be no deterioration of quality. And you must confess that the quality has deteriorated. So true is this that no further augmentation is possible.'

'Did I not tell you so at the beginning?' Casanova reminded him. 'I stand by the condition of equality to that which I sold yesterday. You will force me to go to law with you, and the case will go against you.' He displayed a nice blend of regret and indignation. 'Should you happen to win, you may congratulate yourself upon having obtained my secret for nothing—though it will be worthless then to both of us, since it will be a secret no longer. I did not dream you capable of resorting to such trickery.'

Panagiottis rose, indignant. 'Sir, I am incapable of trickery, or of taking an unfair advantage of any man.'

'Have you learnt my secret or have you not?' demanded Casanova. 'And should I have imparted it to you without the contract? Sir, the world would laugh, and lawyers will make money out of us. I am distressed to think that I should so easily have been deluded. Meanwhile, here are your fifty ounces.'

And he smacked the money on the table bravely, though inwardly fainting from terror lest Panagiottis should take it.

But Panagiottis, shamed by the reproachful gesture, indignantly refused the money, and rose to leave the room. This was a declaration of war. But Casanova smiled, confident that peace would be easily concluded.

You are not to suppose that he ever dreamed of obtaining the two thousand ounces. He had foreseen precisely such a situation as had since arisen, and he was fully prepared to moderate his pretensions very considerably. He detained Panagiottis.

'It is necessary sir, that you should take this money,' he insisted. 'It belongs to you.'

Between misery and indignation Panagiottis again refused.

'You have placed me in an impossible situation,' he protested.

'Did I invite you to buy my secret? Or did you pester me into selling what you now refuse to pay for?'

'But you must confess that it is not worth two thousand ounces.'

'Yet that is the amount in the contract you have signed.'

They sat down to argue, the Greek as before insisting upon the condition that the mercury should present no deterioration of quality, Casanova urging the condition that it should be equal to the 15 lb he had sold yesterday. Thus was half an hour consumed.

'We appear,' said Casanova at length, 'to have reached a deadlock which only the lawyers can resolve, and you should be as reluctant as I am to appeal to them. I will make sacrifices rather than take that course. Have you any adjustment to propose?'

Panagiottis considered. 'You shall retain the fifty ounces. I will pay you an additional fifty, and you shall surrender to me the contract and the bill of exchange.'

Casanova was more than satisfied, but his face remained grave, even sorrowful. Appearances demanded that he should yield reluctantly, and he did so only at the end of arguments which endured for another hour and a half. But when he did yield it was gracefully and graciously. Having pocketed the hundred ounces, he invited Panagiottis to dine with him, and they sat down together like the best of friends, despite the Greek's uneasy feeling that he had taken a certain unfair advantage of a too confiding young cleric. To make amends he presented Casanova at parting with a case of beautiful razors and an order on his Naples warehouse for a barrel of the Muscadine the Venetian had praised. Thereupon they embraced and parted, thoroughly pleased each with the other.

Two days later, as Casanova, travelling now in state, was approaching Cesena, his carriage overtook a group that attracted his attention. Four papal guards were conducting a big, red-haired man in the habit of a brother of St Francis. The prisoner walked dejectedly, his head sunk upon his breast, his wrists pinioned behind him.

Looking more closely at that familiar figure, Casanova recognized his sometime travelling companion, Brother Stefano. He bade the postilions slacken to a walk.

'What's this?' he asked the leader of the guards.

'A rascally bandit who goes about disguised as a monk to rob honest folk. We heard of him at Ancona, where he had a companion who has given us the slip. But we've got this one at least, and he'll go to the hulks where he belongs.'

Casanova's eyes met Stefano's, and he saw recognition and amazement dawning in them. In the circumstances Casanova thought it best not to mention his seven sequins.

As he was whirled away in a cloud of dust, he reflected that dishonest practices must sooner or later bring a man to the galleys, congratulated himself upon the incident which had separated him from Stefano, and reclining luxuriously in his chaise considered how—as in his own case—rectitude of behaviour is properly rewarded sooner or later.

The Priest of Mars

IT was in Bologna in the spring of the year 1744, that Casanova took the great resolve to exchange his abbé's dress and his prospect of Holy Orders for the military coat, and the only priesthood to which his adventurous spirit could conceivably be a credit—the priesthood of Mars.

He was in his twentieth year at the time, tall, vigorous, handsome and magnetic; and to the audacity that was natural to him he gathered additional assurance from the fact that he was well-equipped with funds, having left Rome with two hundred sequins in gold and a letter of credit on Ancona for five hundred more.

He sought a tailor, and issued presently from his hands in a handsome military coat of heavy white cloth with silver lace and gold and silver shoulder knot, and a pale blue silk waistcoat descending half-way to his knees; lacquered canon boots, a rakishly looped hat displaying a black cockade, a long rapier and a long cane completed his equipment, and in this guise he paraded the town and ruffled it in the cafés of Bologna, enjoying the sensation of drawing admiring, questioning glances such as he had never attracted in his modest clerical garments.

Thus arrayed, and carrying himself with the proper degree of insolence, he reappeared in his native Venice a week later, to the scandal of all those who had seen him depart thence for Rome, and were conceiving him by now to be well on the way to politico-ecclesiastical advancement. None was more scandalized than the old patrician abbé Grimani, who had acted in some sort as his guardian; yet seeing him well supplied with funds and coming to consider his unruly nature, he ended by confessing that perhaps this young doctor of canon law had chosen wisely, and presented him with a strong recommendation to the Venetian Secretary for War. This recommendation was supported by that of Casanova's own bold martial bearing and intrepid air. Further still, Grimani had presented him to a lieutenant in the Venetian service, who was anxious from motives of ill-health to sell his commission and prepared to take a hundred sequins for it, and the Secretary for War being informed of all this and having talked a while with Casanova, agreed that he should enter the service, acquiring the lieutenant's commission, but on condition that he served first as an ensign with however the promise that he should be promoted lieutenant within the year.

Thus the matter was settled, and Casanova embarked on the *Europa*, a fast frigate of seventy-two guns, which landed him eight days later at Corfu, to the garrison of which he was appointed.

He found it an agreeable place with no lack of society, whose head was the Proveditor-General of the Republic, an officer exercising a sovereign authority, and keeping splendid state, in which he was supported by three admirals of Venice, a dozen governors of galleys, as many chiefs of the army ashore and half that number of civil officers, all of whom were Venetian nobles, and most of whom had with them their wives and families.

The office of Proveditor-General was filled by General Dolfino, a well-preserved patrician of seventy-five, ignorant, vain, obstinate and choleric, who kept open house, holding a reception every evening, and at whose table twenty-four covers were always laid for chance guests.

There was a theatre at Corfu, which was intermittently supplied with a company of comedians, and no lack of gaming houses, for no restraints were placed upon gaming, and play was inclined to run high. The faro tables proved an immediate attraction to Casanova. Although what little past experience he had of them had been disastrous, yet the instincts of play were in his blood.

It took him three months to lose some six hundred sequins, yet whatever his losses he never lost his magnificent calm. Those inherited histrionic talents of his stood him in good stead, and even when staking his last sequins, despite the agony of apprehension in his soul, he preserved a careless smile, and when they were swept away he rose with an indifferent air and a stifled yawn. He had beggared himself of all but his jewels, worth some hundred sequins, but he had not done it quite in vain. The indifference with which he lost had earned him the reputation of a *beau joueur* and a man of wealth, since he allowed none to guess that he had ruined himself. Now the world loves wealth and it loves good losers; when, in addition, a man is young, handsome, and witty, he will find all doors opening before him. Thus it came about that Casanova found himself high in the esteem of Corfu society.

He was still wondering how to turn this circumstance to advantage when Major Maroli, a professional gamester at whose faro bank Casanova had lost most of his money, meeting him one day, reproached him with coming no more to play.

'I am tired of losing,' said Casanova.

'Why not come and win?'

'Because it is always the bank that wins.'

'Then why not join the bank?'

Casanova stared. Maroli explained himself. His explanation was a proposal of partnership. He saw in Casanova, with his reputation for wealth, his popularity, his easy, laughing ways, his magnificent insouciance as a player, the ideal partner of a bank which was beginning to excite suspicion. Casanova desired a little while in which to consider a proposal he had instantly determined to accept.

He pawned his jewels for a hundred sequins, and with this sum acquired a partnership in the major's bank. Thus came about his association with Maroli. He acted as croupier when the major dealt, and when he dealt himself the major performed the like office by him. Now Maroli handled the cards in a fashion that inspired terror, whilst Casanova on the contrary was always easy and gay, winning without avidity and losing without regrets, a bearing always pleasing to punters. The consequence was that Casanova came to deal oftener than Maroli, and that the bank—as the latter had shrewdly expected—increased rapidly in popularity and prosperity.

We gather that Maroli initiated him into the secrets of success. But he does not betray those secrets; in fact he does little more then hint at their existence.

'Those addicted to games of chance,' he says, 'will always lose unless they know how to captivate fortune by playing with real advantages dependent upon calculation or dexterity, but independent of luck. I believe that a wise and prudent player may avail himself of the one and the other without incurring blame or without rendering it possible to impugn his honour.'

Such a wise and prudent player it is evident that Casanova now became, for he grew wealthy rapidly—prodigally spending his money with almost equal rapidity—and acquired great fame as a gamester. He saw himself now the idol of the ladies, the envied of the men, once more upon the high road to fortune. In the following September he received the honour of being appointed adjutant to the Marquis Rinolfo, the Admiral-in-Chief of the Galeasses— those almost obsolescent vessels with the body of frigates and the benches of galleys, each rowed in calm weather by five hundred convicts. With the appointment he took up his abode at the residence of the Marquis.

But Fortune, into whose hands he had come to abandon himself with more than Oriental fatalism, was preparing him a fall even whilst exalting him.

From Camporese, his captain, Casanova had obtained as a valet a French soldier named La Valeur, a drunken, libertine rascal whose vices Casanova overlooked in consideration of his talent as a hairdresser. Towards the middle of November La Valeur caught a chill which resulted in congestion of the lungs. Casanova sent him to hospital, and informed his captain. Four days later, happening to meet Camporese, he learnt that La Valeur was dying.

'I am afraid you will not see him again,' said the captain. 'He has already received the last sacrament.'

Casanova was therefore, if grieved, not at all surprised to receive from Camporese that evening the news that the man was dead. But he was very much surprised by what accompanied the announcement.

The captain handed him a letter, a baptismal certificate, and a copper seal bearing a coat-of-arms under a ducal coronet. The letter was in French, of which Camporese had no knowledge, and he came now to beg Casanova to translate it.

'I have received it,' he said, 'from La Valeur's confessor.'

Casanova took it, marvelling, for he knew that the rude Picardy peasant could hardly write. With a growing amazement he read the following document:

It is my will that this paper, written and signed by my own hand, shall be delivered to my captain only after my death. Until then my confessor can make no use of it, since he receives it from me under the seal of the confessional. I beg my captain so to bury me that my body may be exhumed should the Duke, my father, desire to remove it to France. I also beg him to send to the French Ambassador in Venice the enclosed baptismal certificate, the seal with the arms of my family, and a certificate of my death in proper form, so that all may be forwarded to my father, and that my rights of succession may pass to the prince, my brother. In witness whereof I append my signature.—François VI, Charles Philippe Louis Foucaud, Prince of La Rochefoucauld.

The baptismal certificate, dated from St Sulpice, bore the same name; that of the Duke, his father, was given as François V, and that of his mother as Gabrielle du Plessis.

Casanova read it through twice, once to himself, and once aloud to the captain, his amazement steadily increasing. He had in his time seen many forms of imposture, and at need practised one or two, but he could never have conceived any swindle at once so ridiculous and gratuitous as this, since the letter was not to be published until after the man's death, and could therefore profit him nothing.

He smiled as he returned the letter to Camporese, but observing the captain's awe-stricken gravity his smile incontinently became a burst of laughter.

'I see nothing to laugh at,' the captain rebuked him, scandalized.

'That is what I find so amusing,' said Casanova disconcertingly. 'What are you going to do with the letter?'

'There is only one thing to do: Take it to his excellency at once.'

'You will probably succeed in amusing him also,' said Casanova, on which the captain departed, too dignified to ask for explanations.

A half-hour later, as Casanova at Maroli's side was in the act of tearing the covers from a pack of cards with which to open the bank, Sanzonio, his fellow adjutant in the Admiral-in-Chief's service, entered the café with the news of the real identity of La Valeur. He had just heard it at the residence of the Proveditor-General, who was even then issuing instructions for a funeral becoming the exalted rank of the deceased.

Casanova smiled quietly to himself, but said nothing. He had never held a great opinion of General Dolfino's intelligence, but he had certainly never supposed it to be as limited as Captain Camporese's. After all, it was none of his business; his business at present was to empty the pockets of the eager punters facing him across the green table, and to this he applied himself with a diligence and an amiability which left nothing to be desired.

But at the height of the game, an hour or so later, someone

touched him on the shoulder. It was Lieutenant Minotto, the Proveditor's aide-de-camp, who announced that his excellency was asking for Casanova.

Casanova calmly finished the deal, then invited Maroli to take his place. The Major did so with an ill grace, cursing the dead lackey, to whom he attributed the interruption of a game running so smoothly in favour of the bank.

At the Proveditor's Casanova found a considerable company, all pervaded by an air of excitement. It was soon made evident to him that they had swallowed La Valeur's posthumous imposture at a gulp, and he was beginning to conclude that he was the only person in Corfu with a proper complement of wits.

Conscious that he was being stared at as the man who had committed the sacrilege of owning a prince for his hairdresser, he advanced through the throng towards the beckoning Proveditor.

'So,' his excellency greeted him, 'your lackey was a prince.'

Casanova looked into the wrinkled, arrogant, rather vulturine old face under its heavily powdered wig. He smiled quietly.

'I should never have suspected it whilst he lived, and I don't believe it now that he's dead,' he answered.

It was an answer that sent a rustle through the company, and seemed to put his excellency out of countenance. The great man frowned.

'How? You don't believe it, and the man dead! You have seen his coat of arms, and his birth certificate, as well as the letter written in his own hand, and you must know that the hour of death is not the time to turn comedian.'

'If your excellency believes all that to be so, then my duty is to say no more.'

His excellency was annoyed. He was not accustomed to contradiction, and here was a form of contradiction that wounded his vanity by an implied reflection upon his acumen.

'It can't be other than true,' he insisted. 'Your doubt amazes me.'

'It springs from the fact that I am well acquainted with the man.'

His excellency snorted. He permitted himself sarcasm.

'And you are, of course, a connoisseur in princes?'

'Thanks to my opportunities of consorting with men of your excellency's quality.'

The old eyes looked sharply, but vainly, into the bold, hand-some young face to see whether any glint of mockery lurked behind the suspicious smoothness of that courtly answer.

'Have you not seen his arms, under a ducal coronet? But per-haps you are not aware that M. de La Rochefoucauld is a duke and a peer of France?'

'On the contrary, excellency. I am fully aware of it. I even know that François VI was married to a demoiselle de Vivonne.'

'Bah! You know nothing.'

Before that rude utterance into which his excellency's exaspera-tion had betrayed him, Casanova contented himself with bow-ing, and, as if seeing in it his dismissal, he withdrew into the background.

He read in the eyes of some of the men about him satisfaction at what they accounted the discomfiture of a young man who was altogether too presumptuous.

Conversation broke out about him. He heard one praising the handsome looks and noble air of his late valet; another extolled the rascal's wit, and marvelled at the talent with which he had played his part so that none had ever guessed his real identity. A lady exclaimed that had she known him she would have succeeded in unmasking him, another proclaimed him always gay, amiable, and obliging, without arrogance towards his fellows, in all things a great gentleman. And then Madame de Sagredo, the wife of one of the sea-lords of Venice, turned provokingly upon Casanova.

'You hear, sir, what is being said of him. Surely in all the time he was with you, you must have perceived something of this kind?'

But she was very far from putting Casanova out of countenance.

'I can only report him to you, madam, as I found him,' he answered, with a respectful inclination of his handsome head, 'and I found him very gay, as has been said, often indeed to the point of idiocy. His only faults were that he was dirty, drunken, dissolute, obscene, quarrelsome, and a thief. I endured him because he dressed my hair as I like it.'

A resentful silence greeted that bold speech which so flatly contradicted the expressed opinion of the assembly, and then before anyone could answer him, Captain Camporese entered suddenly in a great state of excitement, and approached his excellency with the news that the prince still breathed; that the announcement of his death had been premature.

In a flash Casanova saw light. The imposture—how contrived he could not think, nor did he ever discover—was not so gratuitous as he had imagined. He saw indeed how shrewdly La Valeur had made sure of its succeeding. And then he met the eye of General Dolfino fixed grimly upon him.

'I shall hope,' said his excellency, with a malicious air of challenge, 'that the prince may revive completely.'

'I do more than hope, excellency,' was the confident, smiling answer. 'I am convinced he will.'

They stared at him, as if to plumb the exact depth of his meaning. His bold, dark eyes swept slowly over those almost hostile faces.

'Gentlemen,' he said slowly, 'I offer you here a wager of one hundred sequins that this rascal will recover, and a further hundred that his imposture will be revealed, though perhaps not before he shall have made you the dupes of it.'

General Dolfino found that wager so offensive that he turned his back upon the speaker. But Sanzonio, his fellow adjutant, an ill-favoured, knock-kneed youngster, urged at once by his sycophancy and his jealousy of Casanova's popularity and fame, immediately took up the challenge.

'I will accept both those wagers,' he cried, and as a result found himself noticed for the first time since his coming to Corfu a year ago.

Smiling, Casanova bowed to him, took out a pocket-book, and made a note of the bet. But as he left the Proveditor's house he no longer smiled. He began to reflect that by his assumption of wisdom in the face of gullible ignorance he had given offence to many, including the Proveditor himself, upon whose favour he was dependent for the promotion that he awaited. He wondered whether he had not been imprudent in placing so heavy a strain upon his popularity. Positive, however, that time would prove him right, he was convinced that the winning of the wager would re-establish him more firmly than ever. He did not realize for all his precocious wisdom that this was precisely what would ruin him. Could they laugh at him in the end for having been mistaken they would forgive him. But that he should have the last laugh as well as the first would be more than their vanity could endure. And already he had made a mortal enemy of the Proveditor, who was of that unforgiving temper which goes with arrogance and vanity.

The recovery of the Prince de La Rochefoucauld was a very rapid one. Casanova heard on the morrow that he was out of danger, and on the next day that he had been conveyed to the house of General Dolfino, where he was lodged in a fine suite of rooms, with servants of his own, and otherwise treated as an honoured guest. No sooner was he pronounced convalescent than all the admirals, galley-commanders, and officers of the garrison, following the example set by the Proveditor-General, went with their ladies to pay their respects to him.

Soon Casanova heard that he was going about. He was dressed like a prince, served like a prince, and housed like a prince, and he was well supplied with money—all delightedly provided by his host, General Dolfino. Within a week it was whispered that he was making flagrant love to Madame Sagredo, and that Admiral Sagredo was beginning to display anxiety.

Casanova ceased to attend the Proveditor's receptions, and at last he was taxed with it one day by Madame Sagredo herself.

'Having said what I have said of the man,' he made answer frankly, 'I have neither the vileness not the courage to contradict myself. Therefore it is better that I should not come face to face with him.'

Meanwhile he reminded Sanzonio that he owed him a hundred sequins—the amount of the first of the two wagers.

'You shall be paid by the loss of the second one,' Sanzonio assured him.

'At your pleasure, sir,' was the easy answer. 'You are no doubt wise to be confident. It is reported to me that he gets drunk regularly twice a day, and falls asleep and snores in public every evening at his excellency's receptions.'

'What of that?'

'Oh, a princely custom, no doubt. I also gather that his conversation is condescending to the point of lewdness, and that to put you all at your ease he is so free in his habits and table-manners that were he not a prince one must pronounce him a pig.'

'You may mock as you please, but you'll pay in the end,' Sanzonio

answered. 'These things are nothing. If he were an impostor would
he be awaiting the reply to the General's communication to the
French ambassador in Venice?'

'You will see that he will contrive to disappear the day before it
arrives,' laughed Casanova.

'Of course you would say that. But do you know that the confessor who, he says, betrayed him, is in prison, and that the prince
is appealing to the bishop to have him unfrocked?'

'Shrewd of him, that,' said Casanova, and went his way.

And then one day, going to visit Madame de Sagredo, he came
face to face with his sometime hairdresser in that patrician lady's
salon. At first he scarcely knew him, so complete was the meta-
morphosis wrought by his great wig and splendid garments.

He smiled at Casanova, and advancing confidently, leaning upon
a ribboned cane, reproached him with not having been to visit
him.

Casanova laughed in his face.

'You would be well advised, you rogue,' he said uncompromis-
ingly, 'to disappear before the arrival of news about you that will
compel the Proveditor-General to send you to the hulks.'

'You insult me,' said the prince, turning pale.

'On the contrary,' said Casanova, 'I give you this advice because
my nature is kind and my judgement sane.'

For answer the prince boxed his ears so soundly as to leave him
half-stunned for a moment. Recovering, Casanova performed the
miracle of retaining his dignity. He bowed profoundly to Madame
Sagredo, and in the general silence—for there were at least a score
of persons of quality present—he walked slowly out, his face very
white and wicked. As the door closed behind him, he heard
Admiral de Sagredo's voice raised in anger.

'These manners in my house, sir. . . .' The rest was lost to him.

He left the house, and for half an hour paced the esplanade in
the autumn sunshine. At last he beheld his sometime servant leave
Sagredo's house to return home to the Proveditor's, accompanied
by two officers of the garrison. Casanova went after him with
lengthening stride, caught him up, and hailed him, at the corner of
the esplanade.

'A moment, sir.'

La Valeur turned. He was pale, but very haughty, depending no doubt on his companions to see that he suffered no violence. Casanova took a grandiloquent tone.

'No man shall live,' he said, 'who can boast of having struck me. I rejoice to see that you wear a sword. If you will have the goodness to follow me, you shall have an opportunity of using it. These gentlemen will no doubt be good enough to act as witnesses.'

'Sir,' said La Valeur, in a voice that might have been steadier to match his general haughtiness. 'I have no satisfaction to render you. I owe you none.'

'Let me then become the debtor in that respect,' replied Casanova, and struck him sharply with his cane.

The officers attempted to intervene. But Casanova with swinging cane waved them impatiently aside.

'Sirs, this is an affair between gentlemen. The prince will no doubt require your services.'

But the prince was reduced by now to a state of terror.

'I take you to witness, gentlemen . . .' he was beginning, when Casanova's cane descending a second time swept off his hat and knocked his wig awry.

'Your highness is desired to fight, not to make speeches. But if you prefer to be caned, that is your own affair. Which shall it be?'

La Valeur appealed in terror to his companions. The officers remained contemptuously unresponsive. He proclaimed himself a prince, and wore a sword, yet did not draw it when struck by a cane. His bearing now did more to convince them that he was an impostor than any formal proofs that could have been urged. Far from intervening, they drew aside. The prince's remedy lay in his sword. If he chose to draw it, they would see that he had fair play, but until he did so they did not consider that by the code of honour they had any right to interfere after what already had occurred.

And so it befell that La Valeur found himself entirely at the mercy of his aggressor, an aggressor who knew no mercy. The cane, smartly wielded, descended again and again with ever-increasing force. At first each blow was followed by an invitation to him to draw his sword. Then the invitations ceased, and the blows continued, until howling from pain and terror La Valeur went down under them, and lay moaning on the ground, half-stunned and smothered in blood.

Then at last Casanova paused, perhaps from sheer weariness. He readjusted his ruffles, doffed his hat to the two officers, and passing through the crowd of spectators that had meanwhile assembled, he went to the café and called for a glass of lemonade without sugar to precipitate the bitter saliva which his rage had excited.

He was very shortly followed by Lieutenant Minotto, the Proveditor's adjutant, who brought him an order from his excellency to report himself immediately under arrest to Captain Foscari on board the *Bastarda*. Now the *Bastarda* was a galley where all under arrest were chained like convicts.

Casanova turned pale and stiffened at that command. It was an infamy on the part of General Dolfino, a vile, tyrannical abuse of power to satisfy a personal spite. The degradation of the *Bastarda* was not for officers in the service of the Republic, and certainly not for an officer who had committed no offence against the laws of honour, whether La Valeur were a hairdresser or a prince. He quivered with rage, and I doubt if there were enough lemons in Corfu to correct his present condition. Yet after a moment's silence he controlled himself.

'Very well, sir,' he answered stiffly. Whereupon Minotto, who was himself ill at ease, made haste to withdraw.

Casanova went out a moment later, but at the end of the street, instead of turning towards the esplanade he made straight for the beach. Come what might, he would not submit to being chained like a convict, with all the accompanying degradation. In his rage he could not reason beyond that point.

Striding along the beach he came presently upon an empty boat. A mile or so out to sea a fishing vessel was lazily drifting. Casanova pushed the boat into the water, jumped in, took up the oars and rowed out to the vessel. Boarding it, and abandoning the boat, he bribed the skipper to hoist sail and take him away, anywhere. The result was that they landed him at midnight on the island of Casopo, twenty miles from Corfu.

It may be that his aim was to remain there for a few weeks, until he judged that the imposture of La Valeur should have been discovered, or it may be that he had no plan at all, and simply abandoned himself to the winds of chance, as was his custom when in difficulties. He is not clear on the point, and as for the ridiculous story of how he spent the time on Casopo, I do not believe a word of it. The real truth of the matter, as is established from another source, is that he spent the fortnight during which his visit lasted as the guest of the Greek priest, who was in a way the governor of that romantic island.

And then one day at the end of that fortnight, an armed sloop dropped anchor in the bay, that was overlooked by the priest's house; a boat put off, and brought Lieutenant Minotto ashore. Casanova went to meet the visitor.

'I suppose you have come for me?' he said.

'That is so,' the lieutenant replied, 'and I am glad to find you looking so fresh and well.'

'What exactly is your business with me?'

'In the first place to ask you for your sword. You are under arrest as a deserter.'

'That is serious,' said Casanova. 'So serious that I might decide to defend myself, yielding only to force.'

Minotto smiled in deprecation. 'That would be foolish on two counts. In the first place, I have ample force with me to compel you. I refrained from bringing my men ashore, because I preferred to come as your friend. In the second place, you have really nothing to fear. Your arrest is a formal matter. General Dolfino will wish to avoid the publicity which proceedings against you would entail, as in view of all that has happened he would cover himself with ridicule.'

'What has happened?'

'Four days ago a frigate came from Venice with letters from the French Ambassador, as a consequence of which the prince, your hairdresser, was promptly placed under arrest on board a galley bound for home.'

Casanova was surprised.

'How came the rascal to wait for that to happen?'

'He couldn't help himself. He was still in hospital as a consequence of the thrashing you gave him. You broke one of his arms. The General, of course, has divulged nothing of what was in the Ambassador's dispatches. But Corfu has guessed the truth, and you will find yourself more esteemed than ever as the only man who had the wit not to be deceived by that impostor. So that in returning with me you have nothing to fear.'

Thus Casanova was persuaded, and the more readily since he

was practically without means. His funds in Maroli's faro bank amounted at the moment to some three thousand sequins. But in the haste of his departure he had neglected to obtain supplies from him, and of course from Casopo there had been no means of communicating with his partner. In this connection a desolating shock awaited him. One of the first pieces of news Minotto gave him of events at Corfu since his departure was that there had been a horrible fracas one evening at the faro table, one of the punters who had been losing heavily accusing Major Maroli of dishonest play, and threatening to bring the matter to the attention of the Proveditor-General. As a consequence the major had decamped from Corfu next day, leaving a mass of unpaid debts behind him.

The news was within an ace of turning Casanova physically sick. At a blow he had lost three thousand sequins, which in itself was a considerable fortune, and he could blame only himself for having left his funds so trustingly in the bank of a professional gamester. His resilient nature, however, did not long permit him to remain downcast. There was at least the wager of two hundred sequins which Sanzonio had lost to him; in his clever hands that sum should become the seed of a fresh fortune in which he would have no partners.

Immediately on landing he was conducted by Minotto to the Proveditor's residence. General Dolfino received him with hostile coolness, being rendered the more resentful by the fact that he dare not now openly punish Casanova without overwhelming himself with a ridicule even greater than that under which he lay already on the score of the false prince.

'So,' the General welcomed him, 'to the offence of disobedience you have now added the crime of desertion.'

'The circumstances, I respectfully submit to your excellency, are extenuating.'

'No circumstances, sir, can extenuate insubordination. I should be within my rights in sending you to the galleys. If out of several considerations I decline to do so, at least I cannot permit you to remain in Corfu. You disobeyed me once. You certainly shall have no chance of disobeying me again.'

'I do not think, excellency,' said Casanova coolly, feeling himself entirely master of the situation, 'that you show a proper gratitude. In what case would you be now if I had obeyed you, if I had submitted to the unjust punishment to which through a misapprehension you condemned me?'

'Do you presume to question me?'

His excellency's face turned purple.

'Hardly. But I venture to hope that when your excellency shall have considered further, you will decide to reward me with the lieutenancy that was promised me some time ago.'

'The lieutenancy?' said the General, and he laughed maliciously. 'It fell vacant in your absence, and has been conferred upon your fellow ensign, Sanzonio, who understands better than yourself the duties of an officer. He left yesterday for Constantinople on an important mission.'

That was a blow that struck Casanova's confidence dead. It was not so much the loss of the lieutenancy as that Sanzonio had gone without paying him the two hundred sequins—all that had stood between himself and destitution. Looking into the evilly smiling old eyes of Dolfino, Casanova knew that the General had deliberately done this vindictively to rob him. Instinctively, he realized too that the fracas which had resulted in Maroli's flight was also of his excellency's contriving to the same purpose, and almost his excellency's next words confirmed it.

'Then there is this unsavoury business of a faro bank which you ran in partnership with Major Maroli.' Dolfino leered. 'It has transpired that all was not conducted honestly at that bank, and Maroli has confirmed the charge by decamping.'

Casanova stiffened: his eyes blazed.

'If any man dare to impute dishonest practices to me I'll ram the imputation down his dirty throat with my sword.'

'Well, well,' said his excellency coolly, 'that is no affair of mine. But it is my affair to see discipline observed here, and one so careless of it as yourself cannot remain. You will therefore return to Venice at once, and report yourself there to the Secretary for War. In my own opinion,' he ended contemptuously, 'the profession of arms is little suited to a man of your character.'

Casanova looked him steadily in the eye for a long moment. Then with a wicked smile, 'Of course your excellency,' he said, 'is an unerring judge of character and of men, even of princes, as I shall assure them in Venice when I get there.'

It was all the vengeance that it lay within his power to take for so much harm suffered. But seeing the general white and trembling, mouthing and snarling like an infuriated but infirm old mountain cat, he departed satisfied for the moment.

He returned to Venice, a simple ensign, as he had left it nine months earlier, as a result of knowing some men too well and others not well enough. He was forced for the second time to sell his jewels to defray the expenses of the journey, and finding himself without funds soon after his arrival he was obliged to sell his commission for rather less than he had paid for it.

Thus ended his priesthood of Mars.

The Oracle

IN April 1746, Casanova's declining fortunes reached their nadir. After months of vicissitudes, in which he had snatched a precarious livelihood by lowly and often questionable means, he found himself reduced to scraping a fiddle in the orchestra of San Samuele. The fortuity which rescued him justified him of his unfaltering fatalism.

The orchestra of which he was an incompetent member—for his talents, great and varied as they were, did not lean towards fiddling—was engaged for a ball at the patrician house of Soranzo. He was departing thence alone an hour before daybreak, and chanced to descend the staircase in the wake of a gentleman wearing the scarlet robes and full-bottomed wig of the senator. A letter fluttered from the great man's pocket. Casanova picked it up, and quickening his steps, restored it to its owner as he was on the point of entering a magnificent gondola, manned by liveried gondoliers.

The senator, a tall man of a noble, handsome countenance, turned kindly eyes upon the fiddler in his rusty, threadbare garments, thanked him as one thanks an equal, and having asked him where he lived, proposed to carry him home.

Gratefully Casanova stepped on board, and took the place to which the senator invited him on the cabin seat. Swiftly the swan-like boat glided from the radiance of the illuminated palace into the deep shadows of the Canal Regio. Awhile they sat in a silence broken only by the creak and swish of the great oars and the gurgle of the water at the prow. Then the patrician, stirring in the gloom, complained of a numbness in his left arm, and begged his companion to rub it. Scarcely had Casanova begun to comply when the senator hurtled heavily against him.

'The numbness,' he said, articulating indistinctly, 'is spreading to the whole of my left side. Oh, my God!' he groaned. 'I think I am dying.'

Alarmed, Casanova sprang up, swept aside the leather curtains, and snatched the lantern from the poop. Holding it aloft, he beheld the patrician huddled on the seat, ghastly of countenance, with twisted mouth and moribund eyes.

In the course of his considerable studies Casanova had dabbled in medicine, and had learnt enough to recognize here a case of apoplectic seizure.

He shouted to the gondoliers to land him and wait. He leapt ashore and almost dragged a reluctant surgeon from his bed, and drove him out into the chill air of dawn in night-cap, dressing-gown and slippers to the waiting gondola.

There he ordered him at once to bleed the stricken senator, whilst tearing his own shirt into strips to provide bandages. That done, he commanded the gondoliers to make for home at the double. Soon they skimmed alongside of a handsome palace at Santa Marina, and servants were roused to carry their almost lifeless master to bed, Casanova following and superintending, so authoritative in manner that none dared question his right.

The famous and popular Senator Bragadino, a bachelor, enjoying a reputation for wit and learning and a leaning towards abstract science, had no family. He lived alone with a retinue of servants becoming his rank, and these servants no doubt welcomed the orders of one who obviously assumed responsibility in this crisis.

The senator's own physician, Doctor Terro, when fetched, prescribed at once a further blood-letting, thus approving what Casanova had already done. When Terro departed, Casanova remained on watch by the bedside, and there he was found an hour later by two patrician gentlemen, named Dandolo and Barbaro, who were Bragadino's closest friends, and who had been hurriedly summoned.

Although no more aware than the servants of Casanova's identity, and although his presence surprised them, and his appearance, rendered shabbier than ever by the sacrifice of his shirt, was hardly prepossessing, they hesitated to question him, so imposing was his manner, so bold and masterful his glance.

At noon he dined in the palace with the two patricians, and few were the words exchanged. But towards evening they came to him, and Messer Dandolo spoke for both.

'As no doubt, sir, you will have affairs of your own,' he said, 'and as we shall spend the night in the patient's room, you may depart when you please.'

Casanova considered them gravely. Fate had thrust him into this strange position, and he would not have Fate thwarted in her intentions concerning him, whatever they might be.

'Sirs,' he answered them, 'I shall spend the night by the bedside. For if I depart the patient will die; and I know that he will live so long as I am here.'

They stared at him, and then at each other, in utter stupefaction; but there was no further talk of his departure. Later, he was to learn how calculated was his sententiousness to impress these two gentlemen who with Bragadino composed a trinity secretly devoted to the study of the occult.

That evening Doctor Terro prescribed applications of mercury for the almost lifeless senator stretched on that magnificent cano-pied bed. The immediate result of this violent treatment was a reanimation of the patient, which greatly delighted the two friends, whilst vaguely alarming Casanova. His uneasiness increased his watchfulness. By midnight, finding Bragadino all on fire, so ex-hausted that he scarcely breathed, his staring eyes dull and lack lustre, he roused the slumbering friends.

'Unless relieved of these infernal plasters he will die,' he pro-nounced, and at once uncovered the patient's breast, removed the plasters, and bathed him gently with warm water. Relief followed immediately, Bragadino's breathing became regular and free, and within a few minutes he had fallen into a peaceful sleep.

The delight of the patricians was as great as the anger of Terro next morning. Storming that this audacious interference with his treatment was enough to kill the senator, he demanded to know who was guilty of it. It was Bragadino himself who answered the angry question.

'Doctor,' he said gently, 'I was delivered from your plasters, which were suffocating me, by a greater physician than yourself,' and he indicated Casanova, who stood by.

'In that case,' said Terro, 'I had better relinquish my place to him,' and on that he departed livid with mortification.

Thus you behold Casanova physician to one of the most illus-trious members of the Venetian Senate. His self-assurance did not suffer the responsibility to alarm him. He assumed it readily, assuring the patient that now that the best season of the year was approaching careful dieting was the only medicine he required. That he was right was proved by the rapidity of Bragadino's recovery.

One day a cousin of the senator's who came to see him professed amazement that Bragadino should have chosen a fiddler for a doctor. Bragadino, who had already exchanged his bed for an armchair, looked gravely at his cousin.

'If he is a fiddler, as you say, he is a fiddler who knows more medicine than all the physicians in Venice: a fiddler who has twice saved my life by the promptitude and soundness of his judgement—once in the gondola, when he had me bled, and again here when he relieved me of Terro's plasters, which were killing me. Tell that in Venice, cousin.'

But when the cousin had departed, Bragadino turned to Casanova and invited him to explain himself. Briefly Casanova sketched his story to the senator and the two patricians, who were present. How at the age of sixteen he had taken a doctor's degree in canon law; how it had been intended that he should enter the Church; how, discovering in himself no vocation, he had acquired a commission in the army of the Republic; how, fortune abandoning him, he had sold his commission and gone from bad to worse, until for all his talents and his learning he was obliged to scrape a fiddle for a livelihood. Of his humble origin—that he was the son of an actor and a cobbler's daughter—he said no word, and from his appearance now none would have suspected it. The fiddler's rags had given place to a handsome satin suit, provided him by order of his illustrious patient, which did justice to his fine, tall figure. His luxuriant chestnut hair was becomingly coiffed and clubbed, and his swarthy aquiline young face was of an ultra-patrician haughtiness. But his physical attractions were overshadowed by his mental gifts, and his ability in parading them. He was beginning to wonder how this rather extraordinary adventure would end for him when at last Chance pointed out the way. It is not every man would have been as quick to perceive the pointing finger, or to follow the road it indicated.

'Do you know,' said Dandolo, one day, 'that for so young a man you are too learned. There is something unnatural in your knowledge.'

Barbaro nodded his head approvingly. But Bragadino went further; he smiled the smile of the man who knows.

'I have long since reached a conclusion,' he announced. 'I am convinced that he owes it to supernatural agency.' He turned to Casanova. 'Will you not be frank with us, my friend?'

I have said that Bragadino dabbled in abstract sciences. Yet this was the first hint of it that Casanova had received. The discovery coming so abruptly, conveyed in that direct question, left him for a moment speechless.

'You hesitate to answer me, I see,' said Bragadino.

Upon the instant the young adventurer took his resolve.

'Why should I, after all?' he said, and without further reflection embarked upon the most flagrant imposture he had ever perpetrated. 'I possess the secret of a numerical calculation by which I can learn whatever I desire to know!'

'A numerical calculation?' echoed Bragadino. He seemed disappointed.

Casanova elaborated, inventing briskly. 'By means of a question, which I write down and convert into numbers, I obtain, similarly in numbers, an answer which gives me whatever information I seek, information which no one in the world could supply me.'

'That,' said Bragadino, further revealing his vulnerability, 'must be *The Clavicula of Solomon*, vulgarly termed the Cabala.'

'Where did you learn this science?' asked Barbaro.

'From an old hermit who lived on Mount Carpegna,' Casanova lied glibly.

'Ah!' cried Bragadino, after the fashion of one who suddenly sees light. 'The hermit taught you the mode of calculation, but since simple numbers of themselves cannot reason, it is clear that he attached to you without your knowledge an invisible intelligence to be your real guide.'

Casanova's fine eyes kindled as with sudden understanding.

'You may be right. The hermit spoke of one Paralis who would answer. It must be as you say. Paralis is the tutelary spirit, the invisible intelligence, of which you speak.'

He was excited by the discovery, and they shared his excitement, particularly the senator, who took visible pride in having made it.

'You possess,' he told Casanova, 'a wonderful, inestimable treasure, and it is for you to turn it to account.'

'But how?' said Casanova, as indeed he was wondering. 'On the few occasions when I have tried it, the replies have been often so obscure as to discourage me. And yet,' he added thoughtfully, 'if I had not had recourse to it when last I did, I should never have had the good fortune to know and serve your Excellency.'

The three sat forward intrigued, begging him to explain.

'I asked my oracle whether at the Soranzo ball I should meet anyone who mattered to me. I obtained this answer. "Leave the ball at the tenth hour of night." I obeyed, and—you know the result.'

Those amiable, credulous gentlemen were petrified. Then Messer Dandolo stirred himself.

'Will you obtain me an answer to a question I shall set you on a matter known only to myself?' he asked.

Casanova was taken aback. But having rashly engaged himself, he must summon effrontery to carry the thing through.

'Why not, sir?'

He drew a gilded chair to the handsome ormolu-encrusted secret-aire, sat down and took up a pen.

Messer Dandolo propounded a question so obscure that Casanova had no inkling of what was at issue. No matter. He wrote it down, translated it (quite arbitrarily) into numbers, and set down the answer also in numbers, pyramidically arranged. And now his general learning, and in particular his intimacy with the classic authors, served him well. He was familiar with the pronounce-ments of the Delphic oracle, and its machinery of ambiguity. Gradually he evolved an answer as cryptic as the question itself.

Messer Dandolo conned it slowly twice; then the meaning which only himself could read into it must have been revealed to him, for he cried that this was wonderful, divine, incredible.

Bragadino sagely nodded his handsome head.

'It is as I said,' he reminded them. 'The numbers are a mere vehicle. The reply itself proceeds from an immortal intelligence.' And he added: 'Let me ask a question.'

Casanova perceived that there is no more insidious form of self-delusion than the over-eagerness of the fervent student of occultism to discover occult manifestations, and so gathered courage. After Bragadino's test came Barbaro's, and so shrewdly ambiguous were Casanova's answers that both were at least as convinced as Dandolo of the divine nature of Paralis.

And then Bragadino evinced a desire very natural in a student of abstract sciences whose studies had hitherto yielded him no practical return.

'How long,' he asked, 'would it take you to teach me the calculation?'

'Not long. But—' and Casanova hung his head, 'there is an obstacle. The hermit warned me that if I ever divulged the secret my death would follow within three days.' They stared at him in awe. 'After all,' he added 'the threat may have been an idle one.'

'You are very wrong to assume that,' Bragadino gravely answered him, 'and you would be mad to incur the risk.'

There was no further question of his teaching them the calculation. And he shrewdly foresaw that if they could not possess the secret they would seek at least to possess the holder of it. In Casanova they believed they had found the means of communicating with supernatural intelligences, celestial and infernal, and of mastering all the secrets of the world, and soon he found himself established as the hierophant of these three wealthy and potent gentlemen.

They made frequent demands upon Paralis now, and Casanova with practice became more and more skilled in answering after the Delphic manner.

One day of early summer, by when the senator's recovery was so complete that he was able to resume his attendance at the senate, he set a hand upon Casanova's shoulder, and affectionately addressed him.

'Whoever you may be, I owe you my life and more. Those who sought to make of you a doctor, a lawyer, a priest, a soldier, were fools who did not know you. Heaven ordained that you should come to me, who know and appreciate you. If you will become my adopted son you have but to recognize in me your father, and in my house your home. You shall have apartments, servants, and a gondola of your own, a place at my table, and ten sequins a month, which is more than my father allowed me at your age. The future need give you no concern.'

Casanova went down on his knees and kissed the hand of that noble, kindly gentleman, who thus raised him to the rank of a gentleman of the Serene Republic. I hope he felt ashamed of himself. But I doubt it.

And then as if to provide him with the means of affording a crowning proof of the omniscience of his oracle, he met the Countess Angela. He was taking the air one afternoon on the Square of St Mark, pleasantly conscious that his whaleboned coat became him, when he saw her alight from the Ferrara barge. She was dressed in a long blue travelling-cloak, her face lost in the shadows of a hood. He observed her hesitating, uncertain attitude as she stood there, a small valise in her hand, and he was utterly taken by surprise when suddenly she started towards him, and he heard her pronounce his name. The voice at least being pleasant, off came his laced hat, and he made her a leg very gracefully, whilst those fine eyes of his stabbed the depths of the concealing hood.

'Heaven,' she cried, 'must surely have sent you to assist me.'

'Not a doubt of it,' he said promptly. Since his discovery of Paralis he was growing accustomed to being regarded as a celestial envoy. And then at last he knew her for a noble Roman child whom he had met once or twice at the receptions given by Cardinal Acquaviva when, a year or so ago, he had been one of that prelate's secretaries. But this acquaintance had naturally been of the slightest; between him and the young women of the Roman aristocracy intimacies were not at all encouraged. It amazed him that he should remember her, but not at all that she should remember him. You see, he never suffered from any lack of self-esteem.

He desired her to command him, and tremulously she answered that she would be profoundly in his debt if he would escort her to the house of Messer Barbaro, her uncle.

Now it happened that Messer Barbaro was away in Padua, and not expected to return for a week or two. He told her so.

'In Padua? What then am I to do? I am in sorest trouble. Where can I go?'

She stood, white and faltering, and Casanova observed her lip to tremble. That and her soft young loveliness undid him.

'Would it help you to confide in me?' he gently invited.

'If I dared!'

He relieved her at once of her ridiculous valise.

'Come this way,' he said, 'and keep your hood close.'

At the same time he covered his face with a mask, too common a Venetian custom with men of fashion, especially when escorting ladies, to provoke much notice.

He led her to an obscure wine-shop mid-way down a narrow street. There, across an isolated table, they faced each other and she told her story.

'Sir,' she said, by way of preface, 'you'll think me mad or abandoned to have thrust myself so shamelessly upon you. But I am at the point of despair, in a strange city where I know none but my uncle, Messer Barbaro, and even of his welcome I can be none too sure, considering the manner of my coming. In addressing you, I acted upon impulse, believing in my distraught condition that a miracle had brought you to my aid. Say, sir, that you forgive me.'

'I should find it harder to forgive you had you neglected to obey an impulse that was so clearly an inspiration.'

'You might not have known me again,' she murmured, trembling.

'In that case I should not have deserved the honour of your confidence, which I am now awaiting.'

'Tell me first: do you know here in Venice a young patrician named Zanetto Steffani?'

'There is a young noble of that name who enjoys the reputation of being the most dissolute scoundrel in the Republic. I believe him to be absent from home just now. He is not, I hope, a friend of yours?'

Her answer staggered him. 'He is my lover—my affianced husband.'

Then came her piteous story. She was to have made a marriage arranged for her by her father, Count Tagliavia; but heeding instead what she believed to be the call of love, she had secretly fled from Rome with the scoundrel Steffani, who was to bring her to Venice, and there make her his wife. But at Ferrara they encountered a young gentleman towards whose sister Steffani had already con-tracted a similar obligation, a young gentleman who had been seeking Steffani up and down Italy for months. Through a thin partition dividing her room from that in which this meeting took place, the Countess Angela overheard the young champion of his sister's honour give Steffani to choose between death and marriage. A blow was struck, and Steffani fled the place, leaving the young man unconscious. (Casanova did not see what else Steffani could have done in the circumstances.) Thus the too confiding young

Countess found herself alone in Ferrara, with her discovery of her
lover's perfidy.

'What was I to do?' she cried. 'Return home to my father I dared
not, as you will perhaps understand. So I came on to Venice,
hoping for the protection of my uncle until I can avenge myself
upon the monster who has ruined my life.'

And she drew from her massed black hair a slender blade some
eight inches long. Casanova shivered to discover such blood-thirst
in so lovely a child. Then, as he watched her, the fierceness died
out of her glance. It became troubled, and it was with fumbling,
unsteady fingers that she re-sheathed the stiletto in her hair.

'But now you tell me that Messer Barbaro is away from Venice.
What am I to do?'

The sympathetic Casanova addressed himself at once to the task
of soothing her.

'But he will return—in a week perhaps. You must wait for him.'

'Where can I wait? Who will take me in?'

'I know a widow of unimpugnable respectability with lodgings to
let not far from here.'

It was settled—what choice had she?—and he presented her to
the widow as a niece of Messer Barbaro, who sought lodgings for a
few days. At mention of that patrician name, and observing that
this masked gentleman was richly dressed, and the lady of an air
and carriage that bore out the tale of her high connections, the
widow became at once solicitous.

Casanova left the Countess in her care, and departed thoughtful.
He had protected the girl partly because she was Barbaro's niece,
and partly because her romantic air and delicate loveliness assured
him that it would be pleasant to protect her. And as the days
passed, and as each day he went to visit her and beguile for an
hour or so the tedium of her waiting, he began to wish that Messer
Barbaro's return might be indefinitely postponed. She was in need,
poor child, of consolation, and he began to see himself in the role
of the consoler. Also because he found himself more gladly welcomed each day, and this friendship grew apace, he walked with
his head in the clouds and began to dream dreams, until, confronted
suddenly with brutal reality, he awakened from them, and came
sharply down to earth again.

The brutal reality took the shape of her father. One day, a week after Angela's coming, on returning home from his daily visit to her, he was summoned to the presence of his adoptive father, and found in his company a tall, stern-faced old gentleman whom he was startled to hear announced to him as Count Tagliavia.

'The Count,' said Messer Bragadino, 'has sought me in the absence of his kinsman Barbaro to assist him in a very delicate matter. His daughter ran away from home three weeks ago, leaving a letter announcing that she was going to the man she loved. He has traced her to Venice, and discovered that on landing here she was met by a man who was presumably her lover. The Count desires to place the matter before the Council of Ten. But it has occurred to me that you, my son, might assist him first to track the fugitives. I have told him of your gift—under pledge of secrecy, of course.'

You conceive how taken aback he was, and what doubts he conceived on the score of his position. Let it be known that Angela was living, in a sense, under his protection, and would any explanation persuade this austere, fire-breathing parent that Casanova was not himself the guilty man? Was he not persuaded already that the man who met her was her lover?—And was not that man indeed Casanova himself? It was even possible that he had been seen and recognized. He perceived here two necessities equally urgent—to protect himself and to serve the young Countess.

Slowly, at last, he propounded a question.

'Will the Count tell me precisely what information he desires from Paralis, and how he proposes to use it when obtained?'

'In the first place,' said the Count, speaking haughtily and half-contemptuously, as if he did this thing but out of courtesy to humour Bragadino, 'I desire to know the name of the villain who has abducted her, and where they are to be found. Then if he be of worthy rank either they shall be married at once, or I will kill the man and bury the girl in a convent for the remainder of her days.'

'And if his rank should not fit him for the amende?' quoth Casanova.

The Count's face empurpled, the veins of his forehead stood out like strands of whipcord. His answer came in a roar of fury.

'It is impossible my daughter should have abased herself to that extent, but if it should prove so, then—God helping me—I will efface the dishonour by killing both.'

Here, thought Casanova, was an amiable gentleman with whose

daughter to have made free. He sat down, took up a pen, and wrote down his double-question, converting it into numbers under their eyes—Bragadino's eager, the Count's scornfully sceptical. He built his numbers into a pyramid, and extracted the reply in numbers, which once more he converted into words.

For once Paralis discarded all Delphic obscurities. The answer ran thus:

'I will reply completely when the father is disposed to seek his daughter in a spirit of forgiveness, abandoning all intentions of wedding her to the patrician Zanetto Steffani who carried her off, but from whom she fled in time to save herself; nor need he trouble himself with vengeance, for Steffani is condemned to death by the will of Heaven.'

This last daring sentence Casanova was inspired to add by a sudden vision of a young champion of a sister's honour, scouring Italy athirst for Steffani's blood.

As Tagliavia read, the scorn and scepticism perished from his face. A blank amazement overspread it.

'Steffani!' he cried. 'Zanetto Steffani! Why, how blind I have been! He was in Rome for a month before she disappeared. He saw her frequently, and he quitted Rome at the same time.'

Bragadino rubbed his hands. 'You see, you see!' he purred delightedly. Affectionately he patted the shoulder of his adopted son. 'Did I not say that Paralis is divine?'

'It transcends belief!' cried the stupefied Count. 'But my daughter? Where is she?'

'Paralis promises to tell you when you abandon your present project.'

His face grew overcast, his mouth stern. 'Paralis asks too much,' he answered. 'The honour of my family demands the marriage, the world demands it.'

'A man may be too much concerned with worldly considerations,' the philosophical Bragadino reproved him gently. But no persuasions could alter the Count's fixed intent. It was idle to remind him that here was a heavenly command. His feet were firmly planted upon earth, and so in the end he departed to seek worldly aid to recover his daughter.

'At least your oracle has shown me where to look,' he said at parting. 'I will begin with the Palazzo Steffani.'

He went his ways, leaving Bragadino saddened by this instance of obstinate obtuseness, and Casanova uneasy as to the results that might attend the Count's enquiries, so uneasy indeed that on the morrow, for once, he denied himself the joy of visiting Angela, fearful lest he should be detected. But whilst he sat in his rooms a servant came to summon him to the senator. Tagliavia was come again, and with him now was his kinsman Barbaro, who had that day returned to Venice.

The Count turned to Casanova as he entered. 'The mystery, sir,' he announced, 'is deeper than your oracle would seem to imply. I have made further enquiries. Steffani is not in Venice, nor has been for the last two months.'

Casanova frowned as if puzzled. 'Perhaps your daughter is not in Venice?'

'I have it positively from the master of the Ferrara barge that she landed here. It was he who told me that she was joined immediately on landing by a man who must have been her lover. He tells me now this man was tall; whilst Steffani is short.'

'You assume too much, I think,' said Casanova coldly. 'Appearances can be deceptive; and whilst your information depends upon human perception, mine is derived from a supernatural intelligence which cannot err.'

The Count dismissed this interjection with a gesture of impatience.

'Four persons who saw them together claim to have recognized the man, although he wore a mask. Unhappily, each gives a different name. But I intend to denounce the names of all four to the Council of Ten. Here is the note.'

And he read out the names of the men alleged to have been seen with the Countess. The last name he pronounced was Casanova's own.

Hearing it, Casanova threw back his head in a gesture of well-feigned indignant surprise, whilst peals of laughter broke from Barbaro and Bragadino. Amazed, the Count stared at them. 'You find it amusing?' he said icily.

It was Bragadino who explained. 'I did not tell you that this my son is so only by adoption. The last name on that paper is his own—Giacomo di Casanova. And what should he know of your daughter, who has not been in Rome for over a year, and who for the last three months has scarcely been out of my house, and certainly never out of Venice?'

Tagliavia was overwhelmed with confusion. Unreservedly he accepted the explanation, and as unreservedly tendered his apologies.

'Let it be a lesson to you, Count,' said Casanova, 'of the error to which human perception is prone. Can you seriously oppose such testimony to my oracle's infallible pronouncement?'

'Then I will not rest,' cried Tagliavia, 'until I have found Steffani, and compelled him to confess and atone.'

'But if not dead already the man soon will be,' Bragadino said. 'You remember the oracle's pronouncement? Will you avenge yourself upon your daughter by compelling her to marry a notorious scoundrel doomed by the justice of heaven?'

The Count's affection for his daughter struggled with his pride of family. And if affection did not yet carry the day, Casanova, assured that he must come to it in the end, confidently planned the issue. He whispered at parting to Barbaro to bring the Count again next day. Then, after they had left he went out in his turn and, changing gondolas three times so as to throw off any possible pursuit, reached the widow's house.

He threw Angela into a panic by announcing her father's presence in Venice. But he made haste to convince her that he was working diligently to obtain her pardon, and without divulging too much yet knew in his compelling way how to persuade her to be guided absolutely by his counsel.

'You will take a gondola at nightfall,' he instructed her, 'and go straight to your kinsman Messer Barbaro, who has returned and who will gladly give you shelter.'

'But he will betray my presence to my father!'

Her lovely eyes dilated in alarm.

'He will not,' Casanova assured her confidently. 'He knows your father's frame of mind, and he will say no word of your presence until the Count's humour has become entirely one of forgiveness, as I promise you that it shall.'

Thus he succeeded in persuading her.

'You will tell Messer Barbaro that you followed Steffani to Venice, that he had promised to marry you on your arrival, but that you have not seen him since you came. All this is true, remember. Say further that you awaited him in the house of a respectable widow. Avoid divulging her name, and above all make no slightest mention of me lest you ruin everything.'

'Ah, never that!' she cried. 'You must remain my friend. My father shall thank you for all that you have done for me. What might I not have become if you had not come to my aid?'

'The thanks your father would render me might considerably discompose me,' said Casanova grimly. 'You could do nothing so likely to make me regret befriending you as that. Promise me, then, that my name shall never cross your lips; that you will forget the insignificant part I have played in this.'

'How can I ever forget . . .' she began, and faltered. Her lids fluttered down over her eyes, a faint surge of colour showed itself in her cheeks, and with a sigh she ended by promising to do his will. He departed in a dangerous state of emotionalism, convinced that it was high time to set a term to his odd relations with the too tender daughter of the fire-eating Count.

Next day precisely at noon Barbaro came again to Bragadino's with Tagliavia. Casanova observed in Barbaro a vague uneasiness, a furtiveness of glance, that told him all had fallen out as he had planned. The Count looked pale and harassed, and he had lost all the ferocity of manner that had earlier marked him.

'I have sought all day and almost all night in vain,' he announced brokenly. 'My daughter!'

They comforted him, and gradually Bragadino suggested he should consult Paralis once more. He consented, and Casanova sat down to make his pyramid. He laboured awhile at his numbers, then threw down the pen.

'There is no answer,' he announced. 'It must be because your intentions are not yet what Paralis demands.'

The Count protested that he was ready to pardon his daughter.

'But Paralis demands that your spirit shall be purely one of forgiveness.'

'I am but human,' said the Count impatiently, thereby confirming Casanova's doubts.

For three days he was not seen again. And when at last he came his mood appeared so thoroughly chastened that Casanova produced from his oracle the following revelation:

'Angela, who was lured away by arts of magic, has for the past four days been safe in her kinsman's house, where the father may embrace her when he will.'

The Count read it aloud, his eagerness changing to disappointment and contempt. 'But this is nonsense,' he cried, and Bragadino looked alarmed.

'It is not nonsense,' answered Barbaro, in a voice that quivered with excitement. 'It is the truth most wonderfully revealed. She has been at my house since Wednesday night, poor child.'

'And you never told me?'

'She implored me in terror not to do so.'

The Count looked round. Then slowly his lips parted in a bitter smile.

'The oracle is explained,' he sneered.

But Barbaro and Bragadino pledged their honour that he was mistaken, that he wronged them grossly by this suggestion, that the oracle's pronouncement was a pure miracle.

And then a miracle happened indeed. Came Messer Dandolo into the room in a breathless state, with dilating eyes.

'Did not Paralis foretell the speedy death of Steffani? Well, he is dead—I have just heard the news.'

'Dead!' they all echoed, awe-stricken, and none more deeply than Casanova himself.

'Dead to the world at least,' Dandolo explained. 'He has become a monk!'

Then Bragadino gave vent to his wonder, seeing in this constructive death a greater mark of the divine wisdom of Paralis than if Steffani had actually perished in the flesh. 'The actual words of Paralis were that he was sentenced by the will of Heaven! How true, how wonderfully true that was! And how slow we are to read the divine messages of our oracle.'

Casanova's first shock of surprise gave way to self-complacency. His prophecy had been a shrewd inference of what must inevitably happen to a man in Steffani's position, pursued by the avenging brother of one woman and the avenging father of another. Only in the cloister or the grave could he find refuge, and it was his own wit, thought Casanova, that had drawn from the oracle this culminating proof of its supernatural nature.

Under the Leads

A N oft-told tale is that of Giacomo di Casanova's escape from the Prison of the Piombi. Not so that of his first and frustrated attempt at evasion. And yet, of the two, this is in my opinion the more entertaining, not only because of the extraordinary resourcefulness with which he went about the task, but also for the ready wit which showed him a way out of the ghastly peril that attended its discovery.

His arrest took place in July of 1755. Early one morning the terrible Messer Grande and his tipstaves broke into Casanova's lodging, aroused him from his slumbers, and bade him dress and go with them.

'In whose name do you command me?' quoth the startled Casanova.

'In the name of the Inquisitors of State.'

Casanova realized that it was not a season for argument. He rose, and what time the apparitors were ransacking his rooms, he dressed with care. He selected a suit of blue taffeta with silver lace, in which he had intended that day to visit and conquer a certain lady at Murano. He clubbed his luxuriant hair becomingly, and drew on a pair of white silk stockings. Lacquered red-heeled shoes with steel buckles, and an elegant new hat laced with point of Spain completed his toilet. He announced himself ready.

Messer Grande led him below, thrust him into a gondola, and carried him off to prison. He was accounted, it seems, a disturber of the public peace; he was notoriously a libertine, a gamester, and heavily in debt; also—and this was more serious, matter indeed for an *auto de fé*—he was accused of practising magic. To establish this grave charge, Messer Grande found in his lodging, and carried off thence, various forbidden works—copies of *The Clavicula of Solomon*, the *Zecor-ben*, a *Picatrix*, and a very full *Instruction on the Planetary Hours*, giving the necessary incantations for raising devils of all varieties.

These works were part of his adventurer's stock in trade, the plinth upon which he erected his reputation for supernatural powers, whereby he exploited to his own profit the credulity of simpletons of all degrees. In all Europe there was no man with a greater contempt for those horn-books of chicanery, no man more convinced than Casanova that they were written by knaves for fools. He would have explained to the Inquisitors of State that he collected works of magic as curiosities of literature, as instances of pitiful human aberration. But the Inquisitors of State would not have believed him, for the Inquisitors were of those who took magic seriously. And anyhow they never asked him to explain. They had him lodged without any sort of trial in the Prison of the Piombi, the garret under the leads of the palace of the Doges of the Most Serene Republic.

There in the care of a villainous gaoler named Lorenzo, Casanova inhabited a miserable cell some twelve feet square by five and a half feet high—so low that a man of his fine height could not move upright in it. No table or toilet implement was allowed him beyond an ivory spoon bought at his own charges. The cell was lighted (very occasionally) by a window two feet square, criss-crossed by six iron bars each an inch thick, and even then the light was blocked by an exterior baulk of timber some eighteen inches wide that crossed the aperture at close quarters. During the summer months, when first he occupied that cell, there was light enough by which to read for some five hours daily. This period decreased as the year advanced, until when winter came and the mists from the lagoon hung over Venice, the daily hours of darkness numbered twenty-four, which is to say that he lived in perpetual night, that he was left in perpetual darkness to sit and think and go mad, for no lamp was permitted him.

The days passed, and grew into weeks; the weeks accumulated into months, and he abode there in that unspeakable cell under the leads, scorched—and devoured by insects—in summer; frozen almost to death when winter followed, without books—save two works of a religious character—without exercise of any kind, or any means of beguiling the endless tale of days. There, gaunt now and hollow-eyed, indescribably filthy, with matted beard and unkempt hair, lay the once elegant, flamboyant adventurer, forgotten, as it seemed to him, by God and man.

It was a cruel, subtle torture, calculated to break the health and destroy the sanity of any normal man. But Casanova's constitution was of iron, his nerves of steel, and his sanity was kept whole by his faith in himself and his confidence that his wits must sooner or later discover him a way to escape. That he should even think of escaping from such a place reveals the high quality of his courage; that he should come to find the means, fashioning himself the implements out of nothing, as it were, proves how incomparable was his resource. Indeed, in none of the many adventures with which his life was filled did he ever display in so high a degree his audacity, inventiveness, and cunning. Be you the judge.

He was allowed for a few minutes daily, whilst his cell was being swept, to walk in the attic upon which his prison opened—a gallery some twelve feet wide by thirty feet in length. Here one day he espied in a pile of rubbish in a corner a small slab of black marble. He picked it up, thinking that it might in some way prove useful. That was in the spring of 1756, by when he had been some six or eight months in prison. A few weeks later, in the same place, his eye was attracted by a discarded door-bolt—a stout bar of iron measuring a couple of feet in length. He appropriated it, with a vague sense that at last he had brought the possibility of escape within his reach.

His imagination had been busily at work, and he was well served by his knowledge of the ducal palace—for this prison of the Piombi is, as has been said, simply the extensive garret of the Palace of the Doges, deriving its name from the lead with which the roof immediately above is covered. His window faced the west, and from this and other observations and deductions he knew that his cell was immediately above the noble chamber in which the Council of Ten held its sittings.

Long ago he had come to the conclusion that the only possible way of escape lay through that chamber, and the only way into it through the floor of his cell. He had dreamt of cutting a hole in the floor, through which he might lower himself, but that was a dream that had been dismissed again and again by his despair of ever obtaining the tools to effect such an operation. Now, at last, he possessed the tools, or at least the material out of which he could fashion them.

He set about this task at once, and for days thereafter he laboured almost unremittingly to sharpen one end of the bolt, using the slab of marble as a whetstone. It was a test at once of patience and of endurance. Progress was almost imperceptibly slow, and meanwhile the palm of his right hand became a mass of sores from the ceaseless contact with, and the chafing of, the iron. In the end, however, he found himself armed with a sharp, octagon-pointed spontoon, which he concealed in the upholstery of the armchair that had been supplied him.

But it was one thing to have fashioned himself an implement with which to cut his way through the floor, and quite another to carry out undiscovered a task that must entail at least a couple of months' work.

He was visited each morning by Lorenzo, who brought him food for the day. His gaoler came attended on these visits by a couple of archers, whose chief duty it was to sweep out the cell. It follows that any attempted excavation must immediately be revealed to them, and unless he could discover some good reason why this daily task of essential cleanliness should be permanently abandoned, it must remain impossible for him to put his project into execution. A reason might seem beyond discovery, yet his inventiveness and histrionic ability discovered it.

He began by peremptorily forbidding the archers to sweep, without advancing any reason. For a week he was obeyed without question, then at last Lorenzo made the enquiry Casanova had been expecting into the reason for this strange order.

'They raise the dust,' said Casanova, 'and the dust chokes me. I cough so violently that I fear serious—even fatal—consequences.'

Lorenzo wrinkled the ape-like features of his leathern face, and peered suspiciously at his prisoner.

'I will have the floor sprinkled with water,' he announced.

'That would be worse, Messer Lorenzo,' cried Casanova. 'The damp might give me congestion of the lungs.'

The gaoler said no more. He withdrew in silence, and for another week there was no sweeping. But Casanova waited inactive, and on the eighth day Lorenzo came, attended again by his archers. He ordered them to sweep the cell, and that this might be done with thoroughness he lighted a couple of candles, and bade them carry the bed out into the gallery.

Casanova perceived quite plainly from this—as he had fully

expected—that Lorenzo's suspicions had been aroused, and he smiled to himself as he submitted without protest. But when the gaoler came to visit him next morning he found his prisoner abed in an exhausted condition, holding a blood-drenched handkerchief to his lips. (He had contrived to scratch his arm some hours earlier.)

'What's this? What ails you?' he cried in alarm.

'You would sweep,' Casanova reproached him, fighting for breath. 'Behold the consequences. I have had so violent a cough that I must have broken a blood-vessel.' A paroxysm of coughing interrupted him at the moment. He lay back gasping. 'It is very likely I shall die of it,' he groaned.

In terror, Lorenzo ran to fetch a doctor, who when he came prescribed some medicine, and ordered a blood-letting. To him Casanova complained bitterly.

'It is this gaoler who is to blame for my condition,' he said. 'I warned him of what would happen if he insisted upon sweeping my cell.'

He had expected sympathy from the doctor, but hardly that the fellow should reproach Lorenzo as he did, denouncing the gaoler's obstinate ignorance, and relating a sad story of a young man who had died as a result of breathing dust when troubled in the chest.

Lorenzo defended himself by protesting that his sole intention had been to render service to the prisoner, and he ended by swearing that in view of what had happened the cell should be swept no more. When the doctor had departed Lorenzo humbled himself still further by begging Casanova to forgive him.

'How was I to know,' he ended, 'that it would have such serious consequences for you?'

'I warned you,' Casanova answered feebly from his bed.

'But I sweep the cells of other prisoners, and they remain sound and healthy.'

'Perhaps their lungs are not as delicate as mine,' was the plaintive explanation, accepted without further question by the gaoler. And thus Casanova won immunity from the main danger of having his work discovered whilst in progress.

He had decided to make the excavation under his bed, moving this aside for the purpose, and then replacing it so as to conceal what was done. He commenced operations at once, but progress was slow because, as we have seen, he was in darkness for all but some five hours out of the twenty-four, and in darkness it was impossible to work. Unless he was to take a year over his labours, he must fashion himself a lamp. Courageously he addressed himself to the problem. For a vessel there was the little pan in which eggs were cooked for him; oil he procured by doing without it in the salad served him daily; a wick was easily fashioned out of strands taken from the bedclothes and the lamp was ready. But the lamp was nothing without light, and how was light to be obtained?

The crowning-piece of the inventiveness he displayed in this affair is afforded by the manner in which he went about the Promethean task of assembling the elements of light.

Luck helped him a little by providing him with one of the ingredients. Under each arm of the coat of that brave summer suit of taffeta in which, you will remember, he had gone to prison nearly a year ago, he had ordered his tailor to place a patch of amadou, so as to prevent the delicate material from being stained by perspiration. Thus he found himself supplied with tinder, or at least with that which would become tinder when sulphur was added to it. To obtain the sulphur he used his considerable medical knowledge. He feigned indisposition, and complained of an irritation of the skin, begging Lorenzo to ask the doctor for a prescription. Came next day a recipe, recommending a diet and—as he had reckoned—an unguent of flower of sulphur.

In common with all those confined by order of the Inquisitors, Casanova lived upon a daily allowance—graduated to the social position of the prisoner—spent for him by the gaoler in accordance with his own instructions.

'Go and buy me the unguent,' he bade Lorenzo, 'or rather—go and buy me the sulphur. I'll mix it with butter, and so make my own unguent.'

Lorenzo obeyed him, and thus he was provided with the sulphur with which to prepare the tinder. For steel he bethought him of the stout buckle of his belt, which would answer admirably. It but remained to obtain a flint. Again he feigned indisposition, and employed his wits to play upon the ignorance of Lorenzo. He complained of a raging toothache, and begged for some pumice-stone to soak in vinegar, which, applied to the tooth, he claimed, would immediately ease the pain.

'But if you haven't any pumice-stone,' he added, cunningly, 'a gun-flint would do as well.'

He knew, of course, that Lorenzo must carry flints in his pocket. If that was all the prisoner needed, his wants could soon be supplied. Lorenzo flung him three or four flints, and went out.

That night Casanova lighted his lamp. He was vain of the achievement. To use his own words, he had created light out of darkness.

It was a fortnight after Easter when he eventually got to work on the task of breaking through the floor, and he toiled thereafter slowly and assiduously with his improvized spontoon for only implement, covering the hole each day with his bed. Progress was at first dishearteningly slow, and the labours of the first few days were represented by a handful of grains of wood dug from the uppermost plank. Under that, when at last he had cut through it, he came upon a second plank, and under that again a third. Laboriously he cut through the three successive planks, to find himself confronted next by a layer of marble tiles, which for a moment caused him to despair. But he went on, and whilst the weeks were growing into months, he persistently dug at the cement in the interstices until he had extracted one of the marble squares. After that it was a simple matter to prize up the others, and at last he had cleared a space sufficient for the passage of his body, and laid bare yet another layer of planks. Persuaded that this formed the ceiling of the Council Chamber, he went to work with extremest care, excavating the timber of these last planks until no more remained than a mere film of wood, which half a dozen blows would smash away. He pierced a hole, and, applying his eye to it, verified with joy that his calculations were correct, and that the room immediately below was indeed the Council Chamber of the palace.

That was on the 23rd August, and having made all other preparations, he then determined to leave his prison on the 27th. He chose this date because he knew it for the eve of the feast of St Augustine, a day on which the rooms below were most likely to be utterly untenanted. His plan was to smash away the remaining film, and lower himself by means of a rope improvised from his bedclothes. He would choose an hour of early morning, and once in the Council Chamber he did not apprehend any serious obstacle to his escape.

Confidently then he waited, within sight now of the salvation for which he had laboured so strenuously and patiently, and then, with brutal suddenness, the thunderbolt fell from the clearest of skies.

Precisely at noon on the 25th he heard the sound of bolts being withdrawn, a thing so unusual at such an hour that at once it filled him with terror. He had just time to drag his bed into its normal position, so that it covered the gaping hole and the debris of the excavated floor, and to fling himself into his armchair, before the apish face of Lorenzo grinned at him through the Judas-hole in the door.

'I congratulate you, sir, upon the good news I bring you,' was the gaoler's greeting, in accents of unusual joviality.

For an instant Casanova's heart seemed to stop beating. He imagined at once that Lorenzo was the bearer of an order for his release; and release so ardently desired through so many months of horror was the last thing he could now wish to see effected in this manner. For it must inevitably entail the discovery of the way of escape he had prepared, and this in itself must suffice to cancel the boon.

Lorenzo came in. 'You are to come with me,' he announced.

'Wait until I dress myself,' said Casanova weakly.

'That's of no consequence,' he was answered. 'You are to leave this filthy hole for a fine new chamber, lofty and airy, with two windows from which you will be able to see the half of Venice.'

Casanova sank limply back into the depths of his chair. He felt as if he would swoon.

'Fetch me some vinegar,' he begged faintly. 'Then go tell his Excellency the Secretary that I am grateful to the Tribunal for this mercy, but that I beg their Excellencies to leave me where I am.'

Lorenzo stared at him in amazement a moment, then flung back his head and laughed aloud.

'Are you mad, sir?' he asked, not unreasonably. 'I offer to transplant you from hell to heaven, and you refuse! Come, come! The Tribunal must be obeyed. Take my arm. I will have your things removed at once.'

Seeing that remonstrance would be futile, and resistance more futile still, Casanova rose heavily to his feet. The only ray of light in the darkness of his despair at that moment was afforded him by Lorenzo's command to one of the archers to take up the prisoner's armchair, and carry it ahead of them. For this meant that the precious spontoon, concealed in the upholstery, would accompany him. If only he could have taken with him that precious hole as well, the object of so much wasted labour and vain hopes, all would have been well.

He went, leaning on Lorenzo's shoulder and leaving, as he says, his soul behind him in that place of horror. He was conducted to a room on the other side of the palace, certainly more airy and spacious than the kennel he had left, with a large barred window, through which he saw two other windows also barred, beyond a narrow corridor which they lighted. Through these there was a pleasant view extending to the Lido, and the air was clean and fresh. But these were matters which he scarcely noticed at the moment. He sank limply into the armchair, which the archer had set down, and, whilst Lorenzo went to see to the removal of his effects, he sat there waiting for the storm to burst.

He tells us that in that hour he was able to attach faith to the boast of the philosopher Zeno that he had discovered the secret of suppressing pallor, blushes, laughter, and tears. Casanova sat immovable as a statue, awaiting the storm, as I have said, but with a calm that amazed even himself.

Two of the archers entered carrying his bed, which they set down, and then went out again without a word, after which he was left alone for two whole hours or more. This delay in bringing the remainder of his effects was entirely unnatural, but not at all surprising. He knew, of course, what the removal of his bed must have revealed, and he sat there, all power of emotion numb, considering in a curiously detached and dispassionate manner what consequences must follow upon that discovery. He had no illusions on the score of those consequences. He knew that in the foundations of the ducal palace there were prisons even more horrible than the attics of the Piombi, prisons appropriately known as the Pozzi—the wells—foul, subterranean, and subaqueous dungeons, below the level of the canals, invaded by water at high tide, rat-infested *oubliettes* to which the light of day never pierced —prisons in which men died quickly, after first going mad.

He knew of these prisons, and knew that they were reserved for grave offenders, and for men guilty of his own offence of attempting to escape; and he saw that it must now be his fate to be flung into one of them, whence evasion would be impossible. He was irrevocably lost.

At last Lorenzo came. He entered quickly, followed by a couple of his men, his countenance—repulsive at its best—disfigured now by anger. He stood there foaming at the mouth, raging and blaspheming horribly, what time Casanova considered him with a detachment of spirit that almost permitted him to derive an on-looker's amusement from this crisis.

When at last Lorenzo had sufficiently mastered his passion to become coherent——

'You will,' he said, 'deliver to me at once the axe and other implements with which you were breaking through the floor, and you will also give me the name of the archer who supplied you with them.'

'I don't know what you are talking about,' was the answer, so calm that Lorenzo flung into a fresh passion, and ordered him to be searched.

Before that threat Casanova rose, and, with the imposing dignity of which he was master, he commanded the archers to wait whilst he stripped off his gaments and flung them down.

'Do your duty,' he bade them, 'but let none of your dirty hands touch me.'

They searched his clothes, tore open the mattress and pillow of his bed, and even the cushion of his armchair, but without success.

'If you will not answer my questions of your own free will,' stormed the furious Lorenzo, 'we have the means at hand to loosen the most stubborn tongue.'

And then, at grips with the issue, face to face with that threat of torture, and worse to follow, Casanova's incomparable resource rose admirably to the occasion.

Lorenzo himself may unconsciously have pointed the way out of this overwhelming peril when he demanded the name of the archer who had supplied the prisoner with the prison-breaking tools. Casanova knew exactly how hard it must have gone with such a man had he existed and been denounced. If he escaped hanging, which was improbable, he would at least be sent to the galleys, there to toil at an oar for the remainder of his days. And the punishment that would overtake an archer guilty of assisting a

State prisoner to escape would overtake Lorenzo himself no less if he were the offender.

This reflection dictated Casanova's answer.

'If it is true that I have made this hole you talk about, it must have been yourself who supplied me with the means. In fact, now that I come to think of it, that is what happened.'

Lorenzo stared at him for a moment with dilating eyes, whilst the colour receded from his face, leaving it deathly pale. In the background, behind him, the archers grinned and nudged one another.

'From me?' spluttered at last the stupefied gaoler. 'You had the means from me?' Indignation succeeding panic, the blood flowed back into his face. His eyes blazed. 'You had a lamp. I found it. How did you come by that?'

'Why, it was you who supplied it me.'

'Bah! Lies!' roared Lorenzo. 'Tell me when—where?'

'You have forgotten, I see,' said Casanova quietly, smiling now.

'Forgotten! You impudent scoundrel——!'

'A little calm, Messer Lorenzo, a little calm,' Casanova enjoined. 'Bethink you now: the oil—from my salad; the sulphur—to make an unguent for a rash; the flints—to dissolve in vinegar for the toothache. Ah! I see that you remember. The other things necessary I already possessed.'

Lorenzo understood, and understanding he grew really afraid. He had been imprudent, and culpably negligent, and if these details should come to the knowledge of the Inquisitors of State it was likely to go very hard with him. He trembled now with very real apprehension. He drove out the archers, bidding them go fetch the remainder of the prisoner's effects, and Casanova conceived that he had Lorenzo at his mercy, and that the danger of the dungeons was less imminent.

'But the axe, and what other tools you had?' the gaoler demanded, when they were alone. A perceptible change had come over his tone and bearing; it was as if he feared to learn that in some similarly unconscious manner he had himself purveyed the implements.

'I had them also from you,' was the stolid answer.

Lorenzo tore his hair, and stamped about the room in a state of frenzy. At length he made an effort to recover his calm.

'I admit that you were right about the lamp,' he said. 'But can you convince me as easily that I supplied you with the tools you required to make that hole?'

'Assuredly. To begin with I swear to you solemnly that I received nothing from anyone but you.'

'*Misericordia!*' Lorenzo flung up his arms in a gesture of protest to Heaven. 'But how—tell me how and when I supplied you with an axe.'

'You shall know everything—if you insist—the whole truth. But I will tell you only in the presence of the Secretary of the Inquisitors. Take me before him, if you please.'

For a moment Lorenzo stood white and shaking before him. Then, without another word, he turned on his heel and departed, locking the door after him. And he took with him a considerable part of the load of dread that had earlier oppressed Casanova.

For two days the gaoler sulked, and refused to open his lips when he paid his morning visit to the prisoner. But on the third day his manner had completely changed, and he stood before Casanova as a suppliant, imploring him at length to say nothing of what had passed.

'For myself,' said Lorenzo, 'I am content to believe what you have told me, and I ask you no more questions as to how you obtained the means to excavate the floor. All I now beg of you to consider is that I am a poor devil with a wife and children, and that I should be ruined if the matter came to the knowledge of the Inquisitors.'

You conceive that it was not difficult for Casanova to yield to these intercessions. Graciously he gave the required promise, congratulating himself inwardly not only upon having escaped the imminent peril of the dungeons, where death must soon have followed, but also upon having obtained a dominion over the scoundrelly Lorenzo, which should ensure him better treatment in the future.

These considerations compensated him in some measure for the cruelty of fate which had foiled in the eleventh hour, and by the merest chance, his project of escape. And for further comfort he had the reflection that the spontoon was still safe in his chair, and that it was now for him to begin all over again, if he desired to regain his liberty.

How he did so, and how some months later he contrived to make good his escape from the Prison of the Piombi, is another story.

The Night of Escape

PATRICIAN influence from without had procured Casanova's removal, in August of that year, 1756, from the loathsome cell he had occupied for thirteen months in the Piombi—so called from the leaded roof immediately above those prisons which are simply the garrets of the Doge's palace.

That cell had been no better than a kennel seldom reached by the light of day, and so shallow that it was impossible for a man of his fine height to stand upright in it. But his present prison was comparatively spacious, and it was airy and well-lighted by a barred window, whence he could see the Lido.

Yet he was desperately chagrined at the change, for he had almost completed his arrangements to break out of his former cell. The only ray of hope in his present despair came from the fact that the implement to which he trusted was still in his possession, safely concealed in the upholstery of the armchair that had been moved with him into his present quarters. That implement he had fashioned for himself with infinite pains out of a door-bolt some twenty inches long, which he had found discarded in a rubbish-heap in a corner of the attic where he had been allowed to take his brief daily exercise. Using as a whetstone a small slab of black marble, similarly acquired, he had shaped that bolt into a sharp, octagonal-pointed chisel or spontoon.

It remained in his possession, but he saw no chance of using it now, for the suspicions of Lorenzo, the gaoler, were aroused, and daily a couple of archers came to sound the floors and walls. True they did not sound the ceiling, which was low and within reach. But it was obviously impossible to cut through the ceiling in such a manner as to leave the progress of the work unseen.

Hence his despair of breaking out of a prison where he had spent over a year without trial or prospect of a trial, and where he seemed likely to spend the remainder of his days. He did not even know precisely why he had been arrested. All that Giacomo di

Casanova knew was that he was accounted a disturber of the public peace. He was notoriously a libertine, a gamester, and heavily in debt; also—and this was more serious—he was accused of practising magic, as indeed he had done, as a means of exploiting to his own profit the credulity of simpletons of all degrees. He would have explained to the Inquisitors of State of the Most Serene Republic that the books of magic found by their apparitors in his possession—*The Clavicula of Solomon*, the *Zecor-ben*, and other kindred works—had been collected by him as curious instances of human aberrations. But the Inquisitors of State would not have believed him, for the Inquisitors were among those who took magic seriously. And, anyhow, they had never asked him to explain, but had left him as if forgotten in that abominable, verminous cell under the leads, until his patrician friend had obtained him the mercy of this transfer to better quarters.

The same influence that had obtained him his change of cell had also gained him latterly the privilege—and he esteemed it beyond all else—of procuring himself books. Desiring the works of Maffai, he bade his gaoler purchase them out of the allowance made him by the Inquisitors in accordance with the Venetian custom. This allowance was graduated to the social status of each prisoner. But, the books being costly and any monthly surplus from his monthly expenditure being usually the gaoler's perquisite, Lorenzo was reluctant to indulge him. He mentioned that there was a prisoner above who was well equipped with books, and who, no doubt, would be glad to lend in exchange.

Yielding to the suggestion, Casanova handed Lorenzo a copy of Peteau's *Rationarium*, and received next morning in exchange, the first volume of Wolf. Within he found a sheet bearing in six verses a paraphrase of Seneca's epigram, *Calamitosus est animus futuri anxius*. Immediately he perceived he had stumbled upon a means of corresponding with one who might be disposed to assist him to break prison.

In reply, being a scholarly rascal, he wrote six verses himself. Having no pen he cut the long nail of his little finger to a point, and, splitting it, supplied the want. For ink he used the juice of mulberries. In addition to the verses, he wrote a list of the books in his possession, which he placed at the disposal of his fellow captive. He concealed the written sheet in the spine of that vellum-bound volume; and on the title-page, in warning of this, he wrote the single Latin word *Latet*. Next morning he handed the book to Lorenzo, telling him that he had read it, and requesting the second volume.

That second volume came on the next day, and in the spine of it a long letter, some sheets of paper, pens, and a pencil. The writer announced himself as one Marino Balbi, a patrician and a monk, who had been four years in that prison, where he had since been given a companion in misfortune, Count Andrea Asquino.

Thus began a regular and very full correspondence between the prisoners, and soon Casanova—who had not lived on his wits for nothing—was able to form a shrewd estimate of Balbi's character. The monk's letters revealed it as compounded of sensuality, stupidity, ingratitude, and indiscretion.

'In the world,' says Casanova, 'I should have had no commerce with a fellow of his nature. But in the Piombi I was obliged to make capital out of everything that came under my hands.'

The capital he desired to make in this instance was to ascertain whether Balbi would be disposed to do for him what he could not do for himself. He wrote, enquiring, and proposing flight.

Balbi replied that he and his companion would do anything possible to make their escape from that abominable prison, but his lack of resource made him add that he was convinced that nothing was possible.

'All that you have to do,' wrote Casanova in answer, 'is to break through the ceiling of my cell and get me out of this, then trust to me to get you out of the Piombi. If you are disposed to make the attempt, I will supply you with the means, and show you the way.'

It was a characteristically bold reply, revealing to us the utter gamester that he was in all things.

He knew that Balbi's cell was situated immediately under the leads, and he hoped that once in it he should be able readily to find a way through the roof. That cell of Balbi's communicated with a narrow corridor, no more than a shaft for light and air, which was immediately above Casanova's prison. And no sooner had Balbi written, consenting, than Casanova explained what was to do. Balbi must break through the wall of his cell into the little corridor, and there cut a round hole in the floor—precisely as Casanova had done in his former cell—until nothing but a shell of ceiling remained—a shell that could be broken down by half a dozen blows when the moment to escape should have arrived.

To begin with, he ordered Balbi to purchase himself two or three dozen pictures of saints, with which to paper his walls, using as many as might be necessary for a screen to hide the hole he would be cutting.

When Balbi wrote that his walls were hung with pictures of saints, it became a question of conveying the spontoon to him. This was difficult, and the monk's fatuous suggestions merely served further to reveal his stupidity. Finally, Casanova's wits found the way. He bade Lorenzo buy him an in-folio edition of the Bible which had just been published, and it was into the spine of this enormous tome that he packed the precious spontoon, and thus conveyed it to Balbi, who immediately got to work.

This was at the commencement of October. On the eighth of that month Balbi wrote to Casanova that a whole night devoted to labour had resulted merely in the displacing of a single brick, which so discouraged the faint-hearted monk that he was for abandoning an attempt whose only result must be to increase in the future the rigour of their confinement.

Without hesitation, Casanova replied that he was assured of success—although he was far from having any grounds for any such assurance. He enjoined the monk to believe him, and to persevere, confident that as he advanced he would find progress easier. This proved, indeed, to be the case, for soon Balbi found the brickwork yielding so rapidly to his efforts that one morning, a week later, Casanova heard three light taps above his head—the preconcerted signal by which they were to assure themselves that their notions of the topography of the prison were correct.

All that day he heard Balbi at work immediately above him, and again on the morrow, when Balbi wrote that as the floor was of the thickness of only two boards, he counted upon completing the job on the next day, without piercing the ceiling.

But it would seem as if fortune were intent upon making a mock of Casanova, luring him to heights of hope, merely to cast him down again into the depths of despair. Just as upon the eve of breaking out of his former cell mischance had thwarted him, so now, when again he deemed himself upon the very threshold of liberty, came mischance again to thwart him.

Early in the afternoon the sound of bolts being drawn outside froze his very blood and checked his breathing. Yet he had the presence of mind to give the double knock that was the agreed alarm signal, whereupon Balbi instantly desisted from his labours overhead.

Came Lorenzo with two archers, leading an ugly, lean little man of between forty and fifty years of age, shabbily dressed and wearing a round, black wig, whom the tribunal had ordered should share Casanova's prison for the present. With apologies for leaving such a scoundrel in Casanova's company, Lorenzo departed, and the newcomer went down upon his knees, drew forth a chaplet, and began to tell his beads.

Casanova surveyed this intruder at once in disgust and in despair. Presently his disgust was increased when the fellow, whose name was Soradici, frankly avowed himself a spy in the service of the Council of Ten, a calling which he warmly defended from the contempt universally—but unjustly, according to himself—meted out to it. He had been imprisoned for having failed in his duty on one occasion through succumbing to a bribe.

Conceive Casanova's frame of mind—his uncertainty as to how long this monster, as he calls him, might be left in his company, his curbed impatience to regain his liberty, and his consciousness of the horrible risk of discovery which delay entailed! He wrote to Balbi that night while the spy slept, and for the present their operations were suspended. But not for very long. Soon Casanova's wits resolved how to turn to account the weakness which he discovered in Soradici.

The spy was devout to the point of bigoted, credulous superstition. He spent long hours in prayer, and he talked freely of his special devotion to the Blessed Virgin, and his ardent faith in miracles.

Casanova—the arch-humbug who had worked magic to delude the credulous—determined there and then to work a miracle for Soradici. Assuming an inspired air, he solemnly informed the spy one morning that it had been revealed to him in a dream that Soradici's devotion to the Rosary was about to be rewarded; that an angel was to be sent from heaven to deliver him from prison, and that Casanova himself would accompany him in his flight.

If Soradici doubted, conviction was soon to follow. For Casanova foretold the very hour at which the angel would come to break through the roof of the prison, and at that hour precisely— Casanova having warned Balbi—the noise made by the angel overhead flung Soradici into an ecstasy of terror.

But when, at the end of four hours, the angel desisted from his labours, Soradici was beset by doubts. Casanova explained to him that, since angels invariably put on the garb of human flesh when descending upon earth, they labour under human conditions. He added the prophecy that the angel would return on the last day of the month, the eve of All Saints—two days later—and that he would then conduct them out of captivity.

By this means Casanova ensured that no betrayal should be feared from the thoroughly duped Soradici, who now spent the time in praying, weeping, and talking of his sins and of the inexhaustibility of divine grace. To make doubly sure, Casanova added the most terrible oath that if, by a word to the gaoler, Soradici should presume to frustrate the divine intentions, he would immediately strangle him with his own hands.

On October 31 Lorenzo paid his usual daily visit early in the morning. After his departure they waited some hours, Soradici in expectant terror, Casanova in sheer impatience to be at work. Promptly at noon fell heavy blows overhead, and then, in a cloud of plaster and broken laths, the heavenly messenger descended clumsily into Casanova's arms.

Soradici found this tall, gaunt, bearded figure, clad in a dirty shirt and a pair of leather breeches, of a singularly unangelic appearance; indeed, he looked far more like a devil.

When he produced a pair of scissors, so that the spy might cut Casanova's beard, which, like the angel's, had grown in captivity, Soradici ceased to have any illusions on the score of Balbi's celestial nature. Although still intrigued—since he could not guess at the secret correspondence that had passed between Casanova and Balbi—he perceived quite clearly that he had been fooled.

Leaving Soradici in the monk's care, Casanova hoisted himself through the broken ceiling and gained Balbi's cell, where the sight of Count Asquino dismayed him. He found a middle-aged man of a corpulence which must render it impossible for him to face the athletic difficulties that lay before them; of this the count himself seemed already persuaded.

'If you think,' was his greeting, as he shook Casanova's hand, 'to break through the roof and find a way down from the leads, I don't see how you are to succeed without wings. I have not the courage to accompany you,' he added. 'I shall remain and pray for you.'

Attempting no persuasions where they must have been idle, Casanova passed out of the cell again, and approaching as nearly as possible to the edge of the attic, he sat down where he could touch the roof as it sloped immediately above his head. With his spontoon he tested the timbers, and found them so decayed that they almost crumbled at the touch. Assured thereby that the cutting of a hole would be an easy matter, he at once returned to his cell, and there he spent the ensuing four hours in preparing ropes. He cut up sheets, blankets, coverlets, and the very cover of his mattress, knotting the strips together with the utmost care. In the end he found himself equipped with some two hundred yards of rope, which should be ample for any purpose.

Having made a bundle of the fine taffeta suit in which he had been arrested, his gay cloak of floss silk, some stockings, shirts, and handkerchiefs, he and Balbi passed up to the other cell, compelling Soradici to go with them. Leaving the monk to make a parcel of his belongings, Casanova went to tackle the roof. By dusk he had made a hole twice as large as was necessary, and had laid bare the lead sheeting with which the roof was covered. Unable, single-handed, to raise one of the sheets, he called Balbi to his aid, and between them, assisted by the spontoon, which Casanova inserted between the edge of the sheet and the gutter, they at last succeeded in tearing away the rivets. Then by putting their shoulders to the lead they bent it upwards until there was room to emerge, and a view of the sky flooded by the vivid light of the crescent moon.

Not daring in that light to venture upon the roof, where they would be seen, they must wait with what patience they could until midnight, when the moon would be set. So they returned to the cell where they had left Soradici with Count Asquino.

From Balbi, Casanova had learnt that Asquino, though well-supplied with money, was of an avaricious nature. Nevertheless, since money would be necessary, Casanova asked the count for the loan of thirty gold sequins. Asquino answered him gently that, in the first place, they would not need money to escape; that, in the second, he had a numerous family; that, in the third, if Casanova perished the money would be lost; and that in the fourth he had no money.

'My reply' writes Casanova, 'lasted half an hour.'

'Let me remind you,' he said in concluding his exhortation, 'of your promise to pray for us, and let me ask you what sense there can be in praying for the success of an enterprise to which you refuse to contribute the most necessary means.'

The old man was so far conquered by Casanova's eloquence that he offered him two sequins, which Casanova accepted, since he was not in case to refuse anything.

Thereafter, as they sat waiting for the moon to set, Casanova found his earlier estimate of the monk's character confirmed. Balbi now broke into abusive reproaches. He found that Casanova had acted in bad faith by assuring him that he had formed a complete plan of escape. Had he suspected that this was a mere gambler's throw on Casanova's part, he would never have laboured to get him out of his cell. The count added his advice that they should abandon an attempt foredoomed to failure, and, being concerned for the two sequins with which he had so reluctantly parted, he argued the case at great length. Stifling his disgust, Casanova assured them that, although it was impossible for him to afford them details of how he intended to proceed, he was perfectly confident of success.

At half-past ten he sent Soradici—who had remained silent throughout—to report upon the night. The spy brought word that in another hour or so the moon would have set, but that a thick mist was rising, which must render the leads very dangerous.

'So long as the mist isn't made of oil, I am content,' said Casanova. 'Come, make a bundle of your cloak. It is time we were moving.'

But at this Soradici fell on his knees in the dark, seized Casanova's hands, and begged to be left behind to pray for their safety, since he would be sure to meet his death if he attempted to go with them.

Casanova assented readily, delighted to be rid of the fellow. Then in the dark he wrote as best he could a quite characteristic letter to the Inquisitors of State, in which he took his leave of them, telling them that since he had been fetched into the prison without his wishes being consulted, they could not complain that he had departed without consulting theirs.

The bundle containing Balbi's clothes, and another made up of half the rope, he slung from the monk's neck, thereafter doing the same in his own case. Then, in their shirtsleeves, their hats on their heads, the pair of them started on their perilous journey, leaving Count Asquino and Soradici to pray for them.

Casanova went first, on all-fours, and thrusting the point of his spontoon between the joints of the lead sheeting so as to obtain a hold, he crawled slowly upwards. To follow, Balbi took a grip of Casanova's belt with his right hand, so that in addition to making his own way, Casanova was compelled to drag the weight of his companion after him, and this up the sharp gradient of a roof rendered slippery by the mist.

Midway in that laborious ascent, the monk called to him to stop. He had dropped the bundle containing the clothes, and he hoped that it had not rolled beyond the gutter, though he did not mention which of them should retrieve it. After the unreasonableness already endured from this man, Casanova's exasperation was such in that moment that, he confesses, he was tempted to kick him after his bundle. Controlling himself, however, he answered patiently that the matter could not now be helped, and kept steadily amain.

At last the apex of the roof was reached, and they got astride of it to breathe and to take a survey of their surroundings. They faced the several cupolas of the Church of St Mark, which is connected with the ducal palace, being, in fact, no more than the private chapel of the Doge.

They set down their bundles, and, of course, in the act of doing so the wretched Balbi must lose his hat, and send it rolling down the roof after the bundle he had already lost. He cried out that it was an evil omen.

'On the contrary,' Casanova assured him patiently, 'it is a sign of divine protection; for if your bundle or your hat had happened to roll to the left instead of the right it would have fallen into the courtyard, where it would be seen by the guards, who must conclude that someone is moving on the roof, and so, no doubt, would have discovered us. As it is, your hat has followed your bundle into the canal, where it can do no harm.'

Thereupon, bidding the monk await his return, Casanova set off alone on a voyage of discovery, keeping for the present astride of the roof in his progress. He spent a full hour wandering along the vast roof, going to right and to left in his quest, but failing completely to make any helpful discovery, or to find anything to which he could attach a rope. In the end it began to look as if, after all, he must choose between returning to prison and flinging himself from the roof into the canal. He was almost in despair when, in his wanderings, his attention was caught by a dormer window on the canal side, about two-thirds of the way down the slope of the roof. With infinite precaution he lowered himself down the steep, slippery incline until he was astride of the little dormer roof. Leaning well forward, he discovered that a slender grating barred the leaded panes of the window itself, and for a moment this grating gave him pause.

Midnight boomed just then from the Church of St Mark, like a reminder that but seven hours remained in which to conquer this and further difficulties that might confront him, and in which to win clear of that place, or else submit to a resumption of his imprisonment under conditions, no doubt, a hundredfold more rigorous.

Lying flat on his stomach, and hanging far over, so as to see what he was doing, he worked one point of his spontoon into the sash of the grating, and, levering outwards, he strained until at last it came away completely in his hands. After that it was an easy matter to shatter the little latticed window.

Having accomplished so much, he turned, and, using his spontoon as before, he crawled back to the summit of the roof, and made his way rapidly along this to the spot where he had left Balbi. The monk, reduced by now to a state of blending despair, terror, and rage, greeted Casanova in terms of the grossest abuse for having left him there so long.

'I was waiting only for daylight,' he concluded, 'to return to prison.'

'What did you think had become of me?' asked Casanova.

'I imagined that you had tumbled off the roof.'

'And is this abuse the expression of your joy at finding yourself mistaken?'

'Where have you been all this time?' the monk counter-questioned sullenly.

'Come with me and you shall see.'

And taking up his bundle again, Casanova led his companion

forward, until they were in line with the dormer. There Casanova showed him what he had done, and consulted him as to the means to be adopted to enter the attic. It would be too risky for them to allow themselves to drop from the sill, since the height of the window from the floor was unknown to them, and might be considerable. It would be easy for one of them to lower the other by means of the rope. But it was not apparent how, hereafter, the other was to follow. Thus reasoned Casanova.

'You had better lower me, anyhow,' said Balbi, without hesitation; for no doubt he was very tired of that slippery roof, on which a single false step might have sent him to his account. 'Once I am inside you can consider ways of following me.'

That cold-blooded expression of the fellow's egoism put Casanova in a rage for the second time since they had left their prison. But as before he conquered it, and without uttering a word he proceeded to unfasten the coil of rope. Making one end of it secure under Balbi's arms, he bade the monk lie prone upon the roof, his feet pointing downwards, and then paying out rope, he lowered him to the dormer. He then bade him get through the window as far as the level of his waist, and wait thus, hanging over and supporting himself upon the sill. When he had obeyed, Casanova followed, sliding carefully down to the roof of the dormer. Planting himself firmly, and taking the rope once more, he bade Balbi to let himself go without fear, and so lowered him to the floor—a height from the window, as it proved, of some fifty feet. This extinguished all Casanova's hopes of being able to follow by allowing himself to drop from the sill. He was dismayed. But the monk, happy to find himself at last off that accursed roof, and out of all danger of breaking his neck, called foolishly to Casanova to throw him the rope so that he might take care of it.

'As may be imagined,' says Casanova, 'I was careful not to take this idiotic advice.'

Not knowing now what was to become of him unless he could discover some other means than those at his command, he climbed back again to the summit of the roof, and started off desperately upon another voyage of discovery. This time he succeeded better than before. He found about a cupola a terrace which he had not earlier noticed, and on this terrace a hod of plaster, a trowel, and a ladder some seventy feet long. He saw his difficulties solved. He passed an end of rope about one of the rungs, laid the ladder flat along the slope of the roof, and then, still astride of the apex, he worked his way back, dragging the ladder with him, until he was once more on a level with the dormer.

But now the difficulty was how to get the ladder through the window, and he had cause to repent having so hastily deprived himself of his companion's assistance. He got the ladder into position, and lowered it until one of its ends rested upon the dormer, whilst the other projected some twenty feet beyond the edge of the roof. He slid down to the dormer, and placing the ladder beside him, drew it up so that he could reach the eighth rung. To this rung he made fast his rope, then lowered the ladder again until the upper end of it was in line with the window through which he sought to introduce it. But he found it impossible to do so beyond the fifth rung, for at this point the end of the ladder came in contact with the roof inside, and could be pushed no further until it was inclined downward. Now, the only possible way to accomplish this was by raising the other end.

It occurred to him that he might, by so attaching the rope as to bring the ladder across the window-frame, lower himself hand over hand to the floor of the attic. But in so doing he must have left the ladder there to show their pursuers in the morning not merely the way they had gone, but, for all he knew at this stage, the place where they might then be still in hiding. Having come so far, at so much risk and labour, he was determined to leave nothing to chance. To accomplish his object then, he made his way down to the very edge of the roof, sliding carefully on his stomach until his feet found support against the marble gutter, the ladder meanwhile remaining hooked by one of its rungs to the sill of the dormer.

In that perilous position he lifted his end of the ladder a few inches, and so contrived to thrust it another foot or so through the window, whereby its weight was considerably diminished. If he could but get it another couple of feet further in he was sure that by returning to the dormer he would have been able to complete the job. In his anxiety to do this and to obtain the necessary elevation, he raised himself upon his knees.

But in the very act of making the thrust he slipped, and clutching wildly as he went, he shot over the edge of the roof. He found himself hanging there, suspended above that terrific abyss by his hands and his elbows, which had convulsively hooked themselves on to the edge of the gutter, so that he had it on a level with his breast.

It was a moment of dread the like of which he was never likely to endure again in a life that was to know many perils and many hairbreadth escapes. He could not write of it nearly half a century later without shuddering and growing sick with horror.

A moment he hung there gasping, then, almost mechanically, guided by the sheer instinct of self-preservation, he not merely attempted but actually succeeded in raising himself so as to bring his side against the gutter. Then continuing gradually to raise himself until his waist was on a level with the edge, he threw the weight of his trunk forward upon the roof, and slowly brought his right leg up until he had obtained with his knee a further grip of the gutter. The rest was easy, and you may conceive him as he lay there on the roof's edge, panting and shuddering for a moment to regain his breath and nerve.

Meanwhile, the ladder, driven forward by the thrust that had so nearly cost him his life, had penetrated another three feet through the window, and hung there immovable. Recovered, he took up his spontoon, which he had placed in the gutter, and, assisted by it, he climbed back to the dormer. Almost without further difficulty, he succeeded now in introducing the ladder until, of its own weight, it swung down into position.

A moment later he had joined Balbi in the attic, and together they groped about it in the dark, and finding presently a door, passed through into another chamber, where they discovered furniture by hurtling against it. Guided by a faint glimmer of light, Casanova made his way to one of the windows and opened it. He looked out upon a black abyss, and, having no knowledge of the locality, and no inclination to adventure himself into unknown regions, he immediately abandoned all idea of attempting to climb down. He closed the window again, and going back to the other room, he lay down on the floor, with the bundle of ropes for pillow, to wait for dawn.

And so exhausted was he, not only by the efforts of the past hours, and the terrible experience in which they had culminated, but also because in the past two days he had scarely eaten or slept, that straightway, and greatly to Balbi's indignation and disgust, he fell into a profound sleep.

He was aroused three and a half hours later by the clamours and shakings of the exasperated monk. Protesting that such a sleep at such a time was a thing inconceivable, Balbi informed him that it had just struck five.

It was still dark, but already there was a dim grey glimmer of dawn by which objects could be faintly discerned. Searching, Casanova found another door on the opposite to that of the chamber which they had entered earlier. It was locked, but the lock was a poor one that yielded to half a dozen blows of the spontoon, and they passed into a little room beyond which by an open door they came into a long gallery lined with pigeon-holes stuffed with parchments, which they conceived to be the archives. At the end of this gallery they found a short flight of stairs, and below that yet another, which brought them to a glass door. Opening this, they entered a room which Casanova immediately identified as the ducal chancellery. Descent from one of its windows would have been easy, but they would have found themselves in the labyrinth of courts and alleys behind St Mark's, which would not have suited them at all.

On a table Casanova found a stout bodkin with a long wooden handle, the implement used by the secretaries for piercing parchments that were to be joined by a cord bearing the leaden seals of the Republic. He opened a desk, and rummaging in it, found a letter addressed to the Proveditor of Corfu, advising a remittance of 3,000 sequins for the repair of the fortress. He rummaged further, seeking the 3,000 sequins, which he would have appropriated without the least scruple. Unfortunately they were not there.

Quitting the desk, he crossed to the door, to find it not merely locked but to discover that it was not the kind of lock that would yield to blows. There was no way out but by battering away one of the panels, and to this he addressed himself without hesitation, assisted by Balbi, who had armed himself with the bodkin, but who trembled fearfully at the noise of Casanova's blows. There was danger in this, but the danger must be braved, for the time was slipping away. In half an hour they had broken down all of the panel it was possible to remove without the help of a saw. The opening they had made was at a height of five feet from the ground, and the splintered woodwork armed it with a fearful array of jagged teeth.

They dragged a couple of stools to the door, and getting on to these, Casanova bade Balbi go first. The long, lean monk folded his arms, and thrust head and shoulders through the hole; then Casanova lifted him, first by the waist, then by the legs, and so helped him through into the room beyond. Casanova threw their bundles after him, and then placing a third stool on top of the other two, climbed on to it, and, being almost on a level with the opening, was able to get through as far as his waist, when Balbi took him in his arms and proceeded to drag him out. But it was done at the cost of torn breeches and lacerated legs, and when he stood up in the room beyond he was bleeding freely from the wounds which the jagged edges of the wood had dealt him.

After that they went down two staircases, and came out at last in the gallery leading to the great doors at the head of that magnificent flight of steps known as the Giant's Staircase. But these doors—the main entrance of the palace—were locked, and, at a glance, Casanova saw that nothing short of a hatchet would serve to open them. There was no more to be done.

With a resignation that seemed to Balbi entirely cynical, Casanova sat down on the floor.

'My task is ended,' he announced. 'It is now for heaven or chance to do the rest. I don't know whether the palace cleaners will come here today as it is All Saints, or tomorrow, which will be All Souls. Should anyone come I shall run for it the moment the door is opened, and you had best follow me. If no one comes, I shall not move from here; and, if I die of hunger, so much the worse.'

It was a speech that flung the monk into a passion. In burning terms he reviled Casanova, calling him a madman, a seducer, a deceiver, a liar. Casanova let him rave. It was just striking six. Precisely an hour had elapsed since they had left the attic.

Balbi, in his red flannel waistcoat and his puce-coloured leather breeches, might have passed for a peasant; but Casanova, in torn garments that were soaked in blood, presented an appearance that was terrifying and suspicious. This he proceeded to repair. Tearing a handkerchief, he made shift to bandage his wounds, and then

from his bundle he took his fine taffeta summer suit, which on a
winter's day must render him ridiculous.

He dressed his thick, dark brown hair as best he could, drew on
a pair of white stockings, and donned three lace shirts one over
another. His fine cloak of floss silk he gave to Balbi, who looked for
all the world as if he had stolen it.

Thus dressed, his fine hat laced with point of Spain on his head,
Casanova opened a window and looked out. At once he was seen
by some idlers in the courtyard, who, amazed at his appearance
there, and conceiving that he must have been locked in by mistake
on the previous day, went off at once to advise the porter. Meanwhile, Casanova, vexed at having shown himself where he had not
expected anyone, and little guessing how excellently this was to
serve his ends, left the window and went to sit beside the angry
friar, who greeted him with fresh revilings.

A sound of steps and a rattle of keys stemmed Balbi's reproaches
in full flow. The lock groaned.

'Not a word,' said Casanova to the monk, 'but follow me.'

Holding his spontoon ready, but concealed under his coat, he
stepped to the side of the door. It opened, and the porter, who
had come alone and bareheaded, stared in stupefaction at the
strange apparition of Casanova.

Casanova took advantage of that paralysing amazement. Without
uttering a word, he stepped quickly across the theshold, and with
Balbi close upon his heels, he went down the Giant's Staircase in a
flash, crossed the little square, reached the canal, bundled Balbi
into the first gondola he found there, and jumped in after him.

'I want to go to Fusine, and quickly,' he announced. 'Call
another oarsman.'

All was ready, and in a moment the gondola was skimming the
canal. Dressed in his unseasonable suit, and accompanied by the
still more ridiculous figure of Balbi in his gaudy cloak and with
out a hat, he imagined he would be taken for a charlatan or
an astrologer.

The gondola slipped past the custom-house, and took the canal
of the Giudecca. Halfway down this, Casanova put his head out of
the little cabin to address the gondolier in the poop.

'Do you think we shall reach Mestre in an hour?'

'Mestre?' quoth the gondolier. 'But you said Fusine.'

'No, no, I said Mestre—at least, I intended to say Mestre.'

And so the gondola was headed for Mestre by a gondolier who professed himself ready to convey his excellency to England if he desired it.

The sun was rising and the water assumed an opalescent hue. It was a delicious morning, Casanova tells us, and I suspect that never had any morning seemed to that audacious, amiable rascal as delicious as this upon which he regained his liberty, which no man ever valued more highly.

In spirit he was already safely over the frontiers of the Most Serene Republic, impatient to transfer his body thither, as he shortly did, through vicissitudes that are a narrative in themselves, and no part of this story of his escape from the Piombi and the Venetian Inquisitors of State.

The Rooks and the Hawk

IT was in March of 1760 that Casanova's roving spirit and evil genius between them took him to Stuttgart in a well-appointed chaise of his own, attended by an efficient bodyservant, as became a man of his importance. For now, in his thirty-fifth year, he found himself hoisted into wealth and fame. Taking advantage of an introduction to the French Minister of Finance, he had, without the least knowledge of the subject, undertaken to organize the State lotteries in France. So impressed was the Ministry by the result that he was sent to Holland to negotiate a State loan. Again thanks to his impudence and resourcefulness, he not only succeeded in this mission, but in the course of it amassed for himself a fortune of upwards of half a million francs. Another might have settled down to easy respectability. But that was never Giacomo di Casanova's way. He set out again upon his travels, and came presently to Stuttgart, where he put up at 'The Bear'.

Having dined, he dressed with care, and went forth to study the manners of the capital of Würtemberg. He began by going to the handsome playhouse built and managed by the Grand Duke, for the theatre was the chief hobby of this ridiculous prince, pursued at enormous cost. He imported the best comedians from France and Italy; his *corps de ballet* consisted of a score of the leading Italian dancers of the day, supported by at least a hundred coryphées; the famous Novers was his ballet-master; the composer Jumella was in his service; and some of the ablest painters available were employed as his scenographers. To pay for these and other kindred extravagances, this luxurious, debauched prince enjoyed not only the heavy revenues extracted from his long-suffering subjects, but a considerable subsidy paid him by the King of France for maintaining a force of ten thousand Würtembergers in the service of the French armies.

From his seat in a box in the first tier, Casanova considered with interest the ruler who wasted upon frivolous amusements the fruits of that unworthy traffic in the flesh and blood of his subjects. He beheld him standing before the orchestra surrounded by a knot of courtiers, a tall, florid man in a heavy wig, with the flabby, gross habit of body that results from excesses, hard blue eyes and a sneering, sensual mouth. Casanova, himself a libertine, thought him rather disgusting, and turned his attention to the music. His Italian enthusiasm being presently aroused by the performance of a singer, he broke suddenly into applause, and as suddenly checked upon perceiving that he was applauding alone, and that the Grand Duke was directing upon him a stare of haughty displeasure.

A moment later his box was invaded by an officer who, assuming him to be a stranger, informed him in French that the sovereign being in the theatre no one was permitted to applaud unless his highness applauded.

Casanova rose with dignity.

'In that case,' said he, 'I shall come some other time, when the sovereign is absent, so that I may be at liberty to express my appreciation.'

And upon that he went out, his head in the air, and called for his carriage. But as he was in the act of stepping into it, came the same officer to inform him that his highness desired to speak to him.

Entirely master of himself, Casanova re-entered the theatre, and was presently bowing perfunctorily before the Grand Duke, whilst stared at from every quarter.

Expressionless hard blue eyes considered him.

'You are, I believe, Monsieur Casanova,' said a guttural voice.

'Yes, monseigneur.'

'Is this your first visit to Stuttgart?'

'Yes, monseigneur.'

'Do you intend to make a long stay?'

'Of a week or so, if your highness will permit me.'

'Readily. And I further permit you to applaud whenever you are so inclined.'

'I am grateful, your highness. I shall take advantage of the permission.'

'Very well.'

Thick lips smiled faintly, sneeringly, as was their habit, a fat hand waved dismissal, and Casanova bowed and stepped back out of the circle of intimates.

He sat down at the end of a bench a little behind the court group, and the curtain rose upon the second act. Presently his highness quitted the orchestra, and went up to a box on the first tier to kiss the hand of a magnificent, bejewelled lady before leaving the theatre.

Casanova looked up. The lady's shoulder was towards him, and he obtained no more than a fleeting glimpse of her profile, yet something familiar about it drew his attention and piqued his curiosity. He turned to an officer sitting on his right to enquire her identity. With unconcealed surprise at Casanova's ignorance the Würtemberger answered that she was 'Madame'.

'Madame!' said Casanova, staring. 'Madame what?'

'Why, Madame—the prince's *maîtresse-en-titre*; that is the title by which the lady occupying that exalted position is always known. She was once a famous dancer, and for a time charmed us all from the stage. But the prince fell in love with her, and——' The officer waved a hand towards the box. 'It oftens happens,' he added, casually.

'What is her name?' quoth Casanova.

'In the theatre she was known as La Gradella. She was, I believe, a countrywoman of your own.'

Ten years ago Casanova had known a girl of that name who danced in the theatre of San Samuele in Venice. But she had been an indifferent dancer of notorious conduct and low extraction—the daughter of a gondolier named Gradello. It was inconceivable that she should be this 'Madame' of the Grand Ducal court. But even as he gazed upwards with increasing intentness the languorous beauty turned her head, fully revealing her face to him, and he recognized indeed the boatman's daughter.

'Since you have had the honour of being presented to the prince,' the officer was saying, 'you may permit yourself the further honour of kissing Madame's hand.'

Despite himself, Casanova burst out laughing. The officer frowned and stiffened. Our Venetian realized the ambiguity of his laughter, and hastened to explain it.

'I laugh, sir, because I perceive in Madame an old acquaintance.' The officer's deepening frown warned Casanova that he had made matters worse. 'A relation, I should say,' he corrected, too hastily, and could at once have bitten out his tongue.

The officer rose, bowed, smiling now, and withdrew to reappear in the box above. Presently Casanova saw Madame turn to stare in his direction. Then, smiling languidly, she beckoned him with her fan. He was relieved that she did not utterly disown him. He went up, and as the officer withdrew, bowed over the hand she graciously extended.

'Did you announce yourself as my cousin to his highness?' she asked him.

'I did not, Madame.'

'That is an omission that I shall repair,' she drawled, whilst he repressed an inclination to laugh at the lazily insolent air of this once free-and-easy ballet-girl of San Samuele. 'Come and dine with me tomorrow, my cousin,' she invited him, and rose to leave.

When he had escorted her to her carriage he took his way to the stage, for Casanova, who enjoyed the freedom of the green-rooms of Europe, had recognized one or two of his acquaintances among the performers, La Toscani, the singer, La Binetti, the famous dancer, and young Baletti, who was later to become one of the greatest mimes of the Italian Comedy. He was joyously hailed, and carried off to a gay supper-party at Baletti's, graced by the presence of Count von Schultz, the Austrian envoy.

Next day, Casanova, dressed with the splendour of a Versailles courtier, went to dine with the favourite. Here a setback awaited him. La Gradella had not yet seen his highness, who must meanwhile have heard from others of the relationship claimed with her by Casanova, and she expressed anxiety on the score of how he might take that little pleasantry.

'But, my dear,' said Casanova, undismayed by the state in which he found her and the airs she gave herself, 'why admit that it was a pleasantry? Why not allow the belief that we are cousins to persist?'

'I would suffer it willingly to avoid unpleasantness,' was the answer. 'But there is my mother to consider.'

'Your mother?'

'She lives with me. She will not hear of the relationship.'

And then the mother entered—a shapeless woman dressed in all the colours of the rainbow, with a coiffure half a yard high surmounted by a couple of nodding green plumes. Her reception of him was so frosty as to make it obvious to Casanova that the foolish head of this boatman's widow had been turned by her daughter's equivocal exaltation.

'We cannot admit relationship,' she told him, in answer to his question, 'with one whose parents were comedians.'

He was more amazed than offended. 'If the theatre is so dishonouring a profession, Madam, what of your own daughter here?'

'The question is indiscreet and insolent,' she answered, reddening under her rouge. 'It was against my wishes that my daughter trod the stage.'

'Yet but for that, you will confess, she might have trodden barefoot all her life,' he answered brutally.

A scene might have ensued, but at that moment a couple of officers were announced, and dinner was served. Casanova was so angry and contemptuous that he could not eat. But he dissembled his temper until the elder La Gradella began to boast of the patrician state of her relations in Venice. Disgust mounted to his thin lips, his saturnine face became alight with wicked mockery.

'And your sister?' he asked suddenly. 'Is she still alive?'

She quivered and stiffened, and her little eyes considered him malevolently. 'I don't know what sister you mean,' she answered him, since she must answer something.

'I mean the blind beggar of the little bridge behind St Mark's.'

There was a deathly silence. The two officers stared at him, their eyebrows raised, and from him to La Gradella, whose bosom heaved tumultuously. Beads of perspiration broke upon the mother's brow.

'It is a curious jest, sir,' she answered acidly.

'No jest at all,' he assured her, 'Many a copper paolo have I dropped into her lap as I went that way in the old days.'

'If you do not jest, sir, then you are mistaken,' she said, and Casanova bowed his head with a sardonic smile, and left the subject there, satisfied that the whole town would hear of it before nightfall.

After that, you conceive, the meal proceeded with some constraint, and La Gradella was very chilly towards him when he took his leave. As he left the house a magnificent lackey informed him that in future he would not be admitted. He was not surprised. On his way home he came to the conclusion that Stuttgart was a very unattractive place and that he would resume his journey to Zürich on the morrow.

At nightfall, however, he was visited at his hotel by the two officers with whom he had dined at La Gradella's—Captain von Reuss and Captain Stoffel—accompanied by a third, whom they presented to him as Lieutenant von Diesenheim. Casanova received them stiffly, conceiving they might be come to demand satisfaction for the affront he had put upon the favourite and her mother. Far from it, however; they were come to laugh with him over the affair, which did not seem to Casanova very noble on the part of men who habitually enjoyed the favourite's hospitality; but he excused them on the ground that no doubt all Germans were disgusting, and that one cannot expect the habits of a beast to differ from those of the herd.

They proposed to show him some of the amusements of Stuttgart, and he yielded against his inclinations. As he says, it was written that in Stuttgart he was to commit blunder after blunder. They began—and, indeed, ended—by leading him to an evil-looking gaming-house in a back street, kept by an Italian named Peccini with the assistance of a couple of raddled daughters who, as Casanova surmised, performed the office of decoys.

A vile supper was served on an unclean cloth, which in itself was sufficient to turn the stomach of our fastidious Venetian. He was ill at ease, and not without his suspicions both of the Peccini family and of the Würtemberg officers. Already he repented having yielded to their invitation, and on no account would he consent to eat. But to avoid giving offence he drank one or two small glasses of Tokay.

Anon, the cloth being cleared, a game of faro was proposed, and half-a-dozen packs of cards were produced. Peccini took from a strong box five rouleaux, each of twenty louis, and made a bank with these. To a player of Casanova's calibre such a game seemed puerile, but he began to punt in the hope that after an hour or so of this bagatelle, he might be permitted to depart. Within half-an-hour he had lost the fifty or sixty louis that his purse contained, and announcing himself cleaned out he rose to withdraw.

But the officers would not hear of it. They were distressed, particularly von Reuss—a lean, sinister-looking man of thirty—at his ill-fortune, and anxious to give him the opportunity of retrieving his loss. His word, they swore, was good for any amount with them. He yielded, sat down, and lost another hundred louis on credit within half that number of minutes. One of the Peccini girls had pressed upon him another glass of Tokay, insisting that he should drink her health. Again he would have withdrawn, but again he was persuaded to remain, and invited now to make a bank himself. The very manner in which he yielded shows that he was no longer master of his wits, proves, as he afterwards claimed, the Tokay to have been drugged. It was the invariable rule of his life that in whatever company he played he never made a bank without calling for a fresh pack at every deal, himself tearing off the envelope. Yet in this obviously disreputable company he was content to use these greasy cards that had been doing duty for over an hour already; and with a boastfulness entirely foreign to him he announced, merely to startle these players for crowns, that he would make a bank of a thousand louis.

How long the game went on he never knew. His intoxication increased until active consciousness faded out.

Next morning when his valet Le Duc awakened him he learnt that he had been brought home dead drunk at midnight in a sedan chair. Through gaps in the fog that clouded his memory of last night's events, he saw flushed, leering, wicked faces confronting him about a table, heard the soft slither of cards, and his own voice laughing recklessly.

Le Duc informed him that his pockets had been picked, and that his gold snuff-box and both his watches were missing. That loss, though considerable, was trifling by comparison with another which was about to be disclosed to him. His three companions of yester-night were announced, and he received them in his dressing-gown.

They came full of condolence. They were beyond words distressed that his initiation into play in Stuttgart should have been so exceedingly costly. But he had certainly proved himself the formidable gamester which rumour named him, and they hoped it would not inconvenience him unduly to liquidate at once the debt incurred.

He listened with a growing sense of uneasiness.

'What is the sum total of my debt?' he asked.

'You lost last night, playing on your pledged word, a hundred thousand francs,' he was coolly informed by von Reuss, who showed him his note for that amount signed in a hand that he hardly recognized for his own.

A smaller sum might have angered him. But this amount by its very enormity merely amused him. His bold, dark eyes played over that scoundrelly trio with deadly derision. Did they really know him so little, he who for fifteen years and more had been a hawk among rooks, to think that he was to be plucked in this fashion? Did they really think he would disgorge a hundred thousand francs, or any part of that sum, to thieves of their low kind? He drew himself up, tall, lithe, and virile, despite his aching head.

'Sirs,' he answered them very coldly, 'there are two ways in which you may obtain payment. One is by an appeal to the law, which I hardly think you will dare, the other is by an appeal to arms, in which case I shall be happy to pay you one at a time—not in gold, but in steel.'

'Sir,' cried von Reuss, 'this is unworthy! We deemed you a gentleman, else——'

'Oh no,' Casanova broke in, his brown, aquiline face infinitely mocking, 'you deemed me a pigeon to be plucked by any dirty fingers. And so you lead me to an infamous gaming-den, where I am drugged, and cheated, and my pockets are picked. Between the fifty or sixty louis I had on me, and the valuable objects stolen from me, I have lost some three hundred louis. I am content to suffer that loss as the price a man must pay for his follies. But when you ask me to pay a single sou of this sum out of which you tell me that you have swindled me amongst you, why, sirs, you have knocked at the wrong door.'

There was a moment's pause, then all together the three gentlemen of Würtemberg broke into menaces and insults. The storm was at its height when the door opened, and in came Baletti and some half-dozen players from the Grand Ducal theatre, whom Casanova had invited to breakfast.

Still muttering threats the three officers withdrew. The players had heard enough to gather what was in the wind. At table, Casanova, who save for his headache was now serene and calm again, gave them what further enlightenment they craved. Some laughed, but Baletti thought the matter serious.

'My dear Baletti,' laughed Casanova, 'do you think I have roamed the world these years without meeting their kind before, and knowing how to deal with them? I tell you the matter is at an end.'

'You may find yourself at fault,' Baletti answered. 'Von Reuss is a friend of La Gradella's, you know. He may induce her to exert her influence with the Grand Duke to your undoing.' Casanova became thoughtful. 'If you will heed my advice,' Baletti continued, 'you will not lose a moment in informing his highness of the event before they have time to tell their story.'

'I am not sure,' said Casanova, 'that I made a very good impression on his highness.'

He was really thinking of what had occurred at La Gradella's house, and wondering how much of this might have been reported to the Grand Duke; how far, indeed, La Gradella herself might be responsible for what had happened.

'No matter,' replied Baletti. 'His highness has a rough sense of justice. It was these officers who led you to this gaming-house, and engaged you to gamble in spite of the prince's edict forbidding it, which they knew, and you did not; it was whilst in their company that your pockets were picked, and you were first drugged, then swindled. The prince must give you justice, otherwise he is himself dishonoured by an offence committed by officers in his service.'

Thus persuaded, Casanova, as soon as breakfast was done, dressed himself and set out for the Palace. He contrived without difficulty to penetrate as far as the last ante-chamber. Here a chamberlain listened deferentially to his request for an audience, and having heard his name and grounds of complaint, assured him that the Grand Duke would receive him presently.

But whilst he waited in that ante-chamber among a few other petitioners, in swaggers Captain von Reuss to engage the chamberlain in close and intimate talk. Casanova had not the least doubt that he had been spied upon and followed, and that he himself was the object of that intimate conversation. He was still meditating a course of action when von Reuss saluted lightly, and withdrew. Casanova continued to wait, but no longer sanguine. The chamberlain presently vanished into the prince's room. He returned soon after, and crossed to Casanova.

'You may return home, sir,' he said 'His highness cannot see you now. But he is informed of the whole affair, and will see that justice is done you.'

Our Venetian was very angry. But as he was not the man to break his head against obstacles, he withdrew, determined to leave Stuttgart at once.

Instead of going straight back to 'The Bear', however, he bent his steps towards Baletti's, to inform the actor of what had happened and to take his leave of him. Baletti kept him to dine. The actor was lodged in a house on the very walls of the city, and the window of his dining-room was some sixty or seventy feet above the old moat—now waterless—a circumstance which Casanova was to find singularly propitious later. Whilst they were at table Le Duc, who had been hunting up and down the town for his master for the last hour, brought the ominous news that an officer and two soldiers awaited Casanova at the inn. This could only mean his arrest. The affair began to look ugly.

'I have been a fool throughout,' Casanova confessed. 'I have made enemies everywhere, and von Reuss has procured the interest of La Gradella against me.'

Baletti determined to invoke the aid of his friend the Austrian envoy, and carried Casanova off at once to the house of von Schultz. The Count received them cordially, and was indignant when he heard what was afoot.

'But you must do justice to his highness,' he said. 'It is inconceivable that he should know the truth. Sit down, Monsieur Casanova, and write me a brief account of the affair. You may depend upon me to see that it reaches the prince's hands tomorrow.'

Nor did the Austrian's kindess end there. Since Casanova could not return to his inn without being arrested, or indeed show himself abroad without incurring that same danger, von Schultz insisted that he should remain in his house, where no officer of justice might seek him without violating ambassadorial privileges. On the morrow Casanova's memoir was placed in the Grand Duke's hands, and three days further Casanova remained the envoy's guest, discharging the debt as best he could by entertaining the Count with tales of his adventures.

But on the fourth day the envoy received a letter from the Secretary of State requesting him in the name of the Grand Duke to order M. Casanova to leave his house at once, since his remaining there prevented the course of justice in an action invoked against him by three officers in the Grand Duke's service. The letter concluded with the assurance that complete justice should be done M. Casanova.

Von Schultz placed the letter in the hands of his guest. 'I am sorry, my friend,' he said. 'But you will realize that I cannot keep you here against the wishes of the sovereign.'

Casanova understood, and with gratitude for all that the Count had already done for him he returned to his quarters at 'The Bear', where an officer and two soldiers awaited him.

The officer was courteous, but firm. Casanova must not be surprised to be placed under arrest in his own room, since his opponents in the action pending against him were within their rights in demanding precaution against his possible evasion. He ended by politely requesting Casanova's sword, which the Venetian regretfully surrendered.

Forbidden now to leave his chamber, with a sentry on guard day and night in the ante-room, and another under his window, Casanova was nevertheless permitted to receive visitors, and of this permission his friends of the Italian Comedy availed themselves to the full.

He was visited also by the three officers. They came to persuade him to be reasonable and to pay the sum required, thus avoiding heavy legal charges and perhaps a heavy fine as well as imprisonment.

'You talk in vain,' Casanova told them. 'I have not such a sum at hand. My wealth has been grossly exaggerated to you.'

'We should be willing, all things considered, to compromise with you,' von Reuss suggested. 'We would accept your jewels, lace, travelling chaise, and other effects on a valuation, and for any balance remaining we would take bills from you of a reasonable term. We desire to assist you in this.'

'So I perceive,' was the tart answer. 'I will say this in your favour—that you are the most impudent and shameless swindlers I have ever met—and I have met many. You may go to the devil!'

They promised him they would have the pleasure of killing him for his insolence after he had paid his debt to them.

'Quite so,' said he. 'Business first; honour afterwards. That is the motto of your kind. And when the business is done the honour as a rule may go hang!'

'You realize what will happen when sentence is pronounced against you?' said von Reuss from the doorway. 'Your effects will be sold, and the money realized will be applied towards the payment of this debt. For what may still be lacking you will have to contribute your person; you will be enrolled as a soldier in the army of his serene highness, and you will pass to the service of France for a yearly sum of six louis. You will continue to serve until the debt is entirely extinguished.'

On that von Reuss went out, having shattered at last Casanova's composure. For awhile the Venetian stood there petrified by fear. Here was something he had left out of the reckoning. To be swindled by rooks, to have his pockets picked, to be embroiled in legal proceedings was bad enough. But to contemplate in addition the fate of becoming a soldier in the service of a princeling such as the Grand Duke of Würtemberg, who existed only by virtue of his horrible traffic in flesh and blood with France, was more than his fortitude could contemplate. He broke into a cold sweat, and then sat down to think of a way out, cursing himself for having remained so long inactive. Even if he could escape from the inn it would be impossible to leave the city now, since the guard at all the gates would have been warned.

Baletti came presently to visit him, and the sight of the actor was in itself an inspiration. Casanova spoke of his peril. Baletti was aghast with horror. Then Casanova invoked his aid, and Baletti unconditionally promised it, and departed almost at once to invite half the female members of the Italian Comedy to sup that evening with Casanova.

They were a jovial company, and the supper was of the best 'The Bear' could yield. Towards the end of the repast Casanova informed them of the danger in which he stood.

'You must pay,' they cried.

'Not a copper,' said he, and snapped his lips. 'I am determined that these Würtemberger swine shall not have a rag of mine. I have jewels here worth three-quarters of the total amount claimed, and laces worth at least fifty thousand francs at an honest valuation—such as I am persuaded they would not receive at the hands of these thieves. In any case I do not propose to wait for it. I intend to make my escape at the sacrifice of nothing more than my travelling chaise, which the host may keep in discharge of my debt here at "The Bear". My jewels are easily portable, but it is in the matter of my laces that I implore, ladies, your assistance. If you will dispose of them under your hoops, and so carry them away from here, you will leave me eternally in your debt.'

He had chosen his moment well, after the wine had been circulated freely and produced that expansion which disposes us to take generous risks. When an hour later the ladies took their departure there was about their figures a matronliness which had not earlier been apparent, yet which went unperceived in the uncertain candlelight. They were to leave the laces, linen, silk stockings, and other fripperies—a whole wardrobe, in fact—with Baletti, who would know how to dispose of them.

Two days later—on the 1st of April, the eve of the trial— Casanova had another visit from von Reuss, who made a last appeal to him.

'Your persistence,' Casanova mocked him, 'implies doubt of the issue of your action.'

'We shall see tomorrow,' snarled the Würtemberger as he stamped out.

'You shall,' laughed Casanova.

That night Casanova sat at supper alone, Le Duc behind his chair. The door of his room stood open to the ante-room, where the sentry himself was supping. Le Duc was pouring wine from a freshly uncorked bottle. Casanova stayed his hand.

'Desire the sentry to drink a glass with me since this is my last night in these quarters.'

Le Duc went out, and returned, his priestly face composed and solemn. The sentry thanked his excellency, and would be greatly honoured.

'Take him the bottle,' said Casanova grandly.

Half-an-hour later the sentry was snoring.

'He's a noisy devil, Le Duc,' said Casanova. 'But, you see, the gentlemen of Würtemberg are not the only men who can play tricks with wine. Let us be stirring, my lad. I'll leave my travelling-chaise to pay the bill.'

He took up cloak and hat, thrust a brace of pistols into his pockets, and a hunting-knife into his belt. His jewels were already securely disposed about his person. He took a last look round at the empty travelling bags, and they went out softly, locking the door after them, and removing the key. They tiptoed across the ante-room, past the drugged sentry, and unperceived gained the stair-case that led down to the side entrance. Three minutes later they were in the street, muffled to the eyes against the night air.

The sentry pacing under the window of Casanova's room gave them good-night as they passed him. It was his business only to see that nobody escaped by the window. In less than a quarter of an hour they were in Baletti's house on the walls. There they were received by La Binetti and Toscani, who trembled with excitement.

'All is ready,' said Toscani. 'A travelling carriage is waiting on the Fürstenberg road, already laden with the valises containing your laces and effects.'

'And Baletti? Where is he?'

'In the moat, awaiting you.'

They stepped to the window which stood open. Seventy feet below, knee-deep in the mud, stood Baletti invisible. But a soft whistle announced his presence the moment Casanova's head was thrust from the window.

A rope was ready, and by this first Casanova and then Le Duc were gently lowered by the women to the moat. Having clam-bered out to the far side at considerable damage to their garments, they set out, led by Baletti, across a stretch of waste land to the road where a carriage waited near a wayside tavern. Baletti halted.

'There lies your way,' he said. 'I come no further. I was disguised when I hired the chaise in Fürstenberg, and I would not have the postilion see me, lest he should recognize me again, and thus dispel the mystery that must overhang your escape. He has his orders. He is to drive you over the frontier straight to Fürstenberg.'

They embraced each other, and Casanova profusely thanked the comedian, to whom and to the accidental situation of whose lodg-ings he owed it that his escape was possible.

Five minutes later they were driving briskly through the night, away from Stuttgart and its disgusting court. Next morning from Fürstenberg, safe beyond the reach of the Grand Duke of Würtem-berg, Casanova wrote to the three scoundrelly rooks. He told them that persisting in his intention of paying them in steel, he would await them for seven days in Fürstenberg, where the ægis of their obscene prince would no longer shield them. Should they fail to come, he would publish them as cowards in every city of Europe.

They never came, of course; nor did he ever trouble to publish them, or to give them another thought.

Stuttgart was left gaping at the mystery of his escape, until it was remembered that he had dabbled at different times in magic, and it was concluded that he had employed the agency of the devil to pass unperceived through the barred gates of the city. Of those in the secret not one dared breathe a word of the truth, for Casanova had taken care to make each of them an accomplice.

The Polish Duel

CASANOVA possessed in a pre-eminent degree the adventurer's faculty of drawing fortune from misfortune, and sometimes, too, he was well served by his luck to the same end, but never so well as on the occasion of his brief but chequered sojourn in Warsaw in the winter of 1765.

You see him now a hard-bitten man of forty, already conscious that his best years lie behind him, yet of a *verve* as vigorous as his constitution. The fortune amassed in Holland some years before, which would have kept an ordinarily extravagant man in luxury for the remainder of his days, he had by now entirely dissipated. Already he was beginning to have recourse to the questionable shifts by which he had kept himself in funds in his early years. Outwardly, however, he still contrived to maintain the splendour of the great gentleman, and though his purse grew light and his creditors in Warsaw impatient, his air and manner were as haughty and imposing as in his most affluent days.

He had come to the Polish capital armed with those letters of introduction with which he was invariably able to provide himself. They led to his being presented to the witty, scholarly Stanislas-Auguste, and a happy quotation from Horace established him in the royal favour. Also, the king—like most monarchs of the day—was avid of news of the doings of Catherine of Russia, and Casanova, fresh from St Petersburg, where he had wintered, was not only able to gratify his curiosity, but did so with all the piquant humour in which he knew how to array his impudence. Stanislas-Auguste was very pleased with him, providing him with some work of a literary character, to which Casanova devoted himself with assiduity, being led to hope that it would lead to his being appointed the King's private secretary. Thence he hoped that Fortune, following the royal example, would smile on him once more. And with that end in view he was as prudent now in his mode of life as it lay within his nature to be. He avoided gaming-

tables, and strove to keep himself clear of intrigues. Yet in the end
an intrigue of the vainest character caught him in its toils almost
despite himself.

It happened early in February that the famous Italian dancer, La
Binetti, with whom Casanova had been acquainted for some years,
halted at the Polish capital on her way to Russia. Tomatis, the
enterprising director of the Warsaw Opera House, engaged her for
a week, and so well did she acquit herself that she was offered, and
accepted, a year's engagement, to the dismay not only of La Cataï,
who had hitherto reigned unrivalled in the Warsaw theatre, but
also of Tomatis himself, who was La Cataï's best friend, and who
had been far from foreseeing such a consequence to his speculation.

Very soon La Binetti was the rage, languidly receiving the
homage of a multitude of adorers. Yet since La Cataï continued
still to have her partisans, it followed that the frequenters of the
Warsaw theatre were divided now into two parties, so that the
rivalry between the two dancers became more and more acute.

Considering that Casanova was an old acquaintance, it was natural that La Binetti should expect to find him in the ranks of her
followers. But his new mood of prudence, and his resolve to avoid
intrigues, kept him aloof from all partisanship. He tells us that La
Binetti scolded him for his aloofness, and that she was almost as
annoyed with him as with Tomatis. But I hesitate—for reasons that
will presently become apparent—to accept that statement. Besides,
there was no parallel between his friendly neutrality and Tomatis's
avowed hostility towards her. For Tomatis was by now bitterly
repenting that he should himself have afforded La Binetti the
opportunity of conquering rather more than the half of Warsaw.
He made no secret of this, but worked quite openly in the interest
of La Cataï, and missed no occasion to manifest how greatly superior he considered her to La Binetti. As a consequence it was no
long before La Binetti came to hate Tomatis, and to look round for
a weapon with which to avenge herself upon the luckless director.
That weapon—and a very ready one—she found presently in
Xavier Branicki, who, deeply enamoured of her unquestionable
charms, was prepared to go any lengths to win her favour.

This Count Branicki was a handsome, vigorous man of thirty
newly returned from Berlin, where he had been as ambassador to
the court of Frederick. He was Grand Chamberlain of the kingdom

a colonel of Uhlans, and a close friend of the king's. A man
therefore of some weight and consequence in Warsaw, as you can
conceive, yet not above becoming a bully in the service of a
dancer, as you shall see.

At her imperious behest, he addressed himself to the punishing
of Tomatis for the latter's preference of her rival. One night at the
opera, during the performance of the second ballet, in which La
Binetti was appearing, Branicki amazed the audience by entering
the box occupied by Tomatis and La Cataï. It was the first time
that either in public or in private he had paid the slightest attention to the rival dancer, and before the present homage of his
words and bearing both La Cataï and her friend Tomatis could
conclude only that he had quarrelled with La Binetti. He took a
seat beside the lady, and was assiduous in his attentions throughout the remainder of the evening. At the end of the performance
he begged to be permitted to conduct her to her carriage, which in
reality was the carriage of Tomatis. Even then he did not take his
leave of her; having handed her into the vehicle, he followed, and
seated himself beside her. Tomatis, who under the eyes of the
courtly throng that filled the vestibule had followed the pair between satisfaction and mistrust, stepped forward now to enter the
carriage in his turn. But he found his way barred by the arm which
Branicki suddenly shot forward.

'Take another carriage, and follow us,' the Grand Chamberlain
commanded, much as he might have commanded a lackey.

Stung by the tone, Tomatis was so imprudent as to display a
dignified insistence. 'I am not accustomed, Count,' he said, 'to
travel in any carriage but my own.'

'Drive on!' shouted Branicki to the coachman.

'Stay where you are!' Tomatis commanded, and since Tomatis
was the master it was Tomatis who was obeyed.

The scene promised to become interesting; it began to look as if
the Grand Chamberlain were about to be made ridiculous. But
Branicki played with loaded dice. The thing had gone as far as he
intended, and Tomatis had afforded him the pretext he required.
Compelled by the director's firmness to alight from the carriage,
he did so with every appearance of anger, and called to an orderly
who stood by to box the director's ears. The orderly, with perfect,
mechanical military obedience, dealt Tomatis a resounding buffet.

The director reeled, half-stunned by the blow. Then, partly recovering himself, but lacking the wit or the courage to drive his sword through the body of his assailant, he plunged into the carriage, and was driven home to eat, as Casanova says, his *soufflet* for supper.

The unfortunate director was so crushed by the affair that for a time he hardly dared to show himself. He appealed to the king for justice; but Stanislas-Auguste was reluctant to take action against his friend and Grand Chamberlain. To Casanova, who had been a witness of the affair, and who was filled with indignation against the aggressor and sympathy for Tomatis, the director confided bitterly that vengeance on Branicki was too costly a luxury for him. It would entail his departure from Poland, and the loss of some 40,000 sequins which he had invested in the theatre.

Heaven knows I do not wish to add to the catalogue of rogueries to which Casanova confesses. Yet I suspect him of a certain lack of candour in his account of what followed. We know that he was extremely hard-pressed for money at this moment; that he was of a resolute courage, and a useful man of his hands; we know that Tomatis was tolerably rich, and burning to punish Branicki, if it were possible to do so without his own agency being revealed. Is it therefore unreasonable to suspect that more passed at his interview with Tomatis than Casanova reveals, and that the sequel did not fall out exactly as he would have us believe?

He says, for instance, that he had reason to suspect that La Binetti intended to have him similarly dealt with. But he can have had little grounds for this suspicion, considering how friendly had been his relations with the dancer until then. What is far more probable is that he now deliberately provoked her resentment by ostentatiously joining the party of her rival, in the hope that she would send Branicki to box his ears. He admits, indeed, that not having 40,000 sequins to lose like Tomatis, he had no occasion to fear her lover. He tells us, too, that she was radiant now, whilst hypocritically affecting regret for the misfortune of her 'friend' Tomatis, and that her falseness disposed him against her. Is it too much to suppose that he deliberately expressed his feelings; and short of supposing this, how is one to account for what followed?

It happened that a little while later—on the feast of St Casimir, to be precise—Casanova was of the king's party at the theatre. Stanislas-Auguste left after the second ballet, and Casanova went behind to congratulate a young Piedmontese dancer, named La Caracci, whose performance had greatly pleased his majesty. Passing La Binetti's dressing-room, the door of which stood open, he paused to exchange a greeting with her, and had got no further when Count Branicki arrived. To Casanova this was the signal for departure. Frigid and distant, he bowed to the Polish nobleman, his chill and deadly politeness an insult in itself, and went his way to convey to La Caracci the pleasing news of the royal approbation. He was still delighting her with this, when to his amazement—as he says—the dressing-room was unceremoniously invaded by Branicki. Casanova's bold dark eyes played over the Count with a glance that was haughty and challenging. Branicki laughed. He was a handsome fellow, tall and florid, with keen blue eyes, and a sneering mouth.

'Confess, M. Casanova,' he cried, 'that I am inopportune.'

If Casanova did not confess it, neither did he deny it. He just stood there drawn to his full height—and, tall man though Branicki was, the Venetian stood an inch or so taller—and stared at the intruder as one stares at something curious, unusual, and not quite pleasant. His swarthy, aquiline face was disconcertingly contemptuous. The Count should have discerned that here was a man of a stamp very different from Tomatis, a man ready to go more than half-way to meet him if his purpose were a quarrel. Perhaps Branicki did discern it.

'Your silence admits it,' he cried. 'I do not wonder. This lady is so amiable that—that, faith, I am deeply in love with her, and I intend to suffer no rival. You understand me?'

Casanova smiled, but it was a crooked smile. He looked at the bewildered little dancer, whose cheeks were flushed with dawning indignation, and then bowed too elaborately to Branicki.

'In that case,' he said, 'I must renounce all pretensions.'

Branicki sneered. He does not appear to have possessed a keen ear for irony. 'You are a prudent man, M. Casanova.'

'Who could be so ill-advised as to enter into rivalry with a man of your excellency's quality?' quoted Casanova. But now the mockery of his voice was more pronounced, and his smile more wickedly sardonic.

'I account anyone a coward,' said Branicki, 'who abandons his ground at the first threat of danger.'

Despite his iron self-control, Casanova quivered under the whiplash of those words. Mechanically, his hand was half-way to his sword before he recollected himself. Turning, he bowed profoundly to the scared and breathless girl, who stood leaning for support against her dressing-table. Then holding himself stiffly erect, he walked past the Count, so closely as almost to touch him. For an instant he paused face to face with the Pole, and looked deep into the man's eyes, unpardonable contempt in his glance, in the curl of his lip, and in the slight shrug of his shoulders. There is no doubt that he intended to give Branicki ample rope; I suspect that he deliberately tempted the Count to slap his face, so that the affront might be complete. But as Branicki did not appear disposed to do so, Casanova passed out.

Instantly the Count sprang after him, and his voice hoarse with anger rang down the corridor.

'Venetian coward!' he shouted.

Casanova checked in his stride, and turned. Dressing-room doors stood open on either hand, and in the corridor loitered several officers of the court. There was no lack of witnesses that the Pole was the aggressor.

'Count Branicki,' said our adventurer, in a steady voice, 'I will prove it on your body when you please and where you please that a Venetian coward does not fear a Polish nobleman.'

Thus was the quarrel engaged between these two men, one of whom had for only aim to salve the wounded vanity of an empty-headed dancer, the other to avenge the wrongs of a theatrical director. That at least is my own conclusion so far as Casanova is concerned. But even so, I am very far from wishing to impute that he descended on this occasion—or was even capable of descending—to the level of the hired bully. I am convinced that nothing would have induced him to espouse Tomatis's quarrel had he not been deeply in sympathy with the director, and contemptuous of the nobleman who had so unworthily used him. I suggest then, no more than that he combined chivalry with profit, each acting as a spur to the other. Meanwhile, he went home to await developments.

Early next morning Prince Lubomirski, with whom he was on terms of friendship, went to visit him. Casanova was elegantly lodged in a small suite of rooms in the house of Campioni, the dancing master. There Prince Lubomirski found him still abed, but sitting up and writing busily. He laid down his pen, and gave the Prince a hearty welcome. Lubomirski sat down, and came straight to the matter on his mind.

'Branicki had been drinking last night,' he said. 'I hope that a man of your experience is above being offended by the indiscretions of a gentleman in his cups.'

'To be sure I am,' said Casanova genially, 'provided that being sober this morning the Count will have the discretion to apologize.'

'That is a great deal to expect of Branicki,' opined the prince.

'So I had imagined,' Casanova agreed, 'for which reason I have just written him a letter. Let me read it to you.' And he read it:

Your excellency insulted me yesterday, and as I can discern no reason why you should have done so, I can only assume that you dislike me. In the circumstances I have the honour to place myself at your disposal. To settle the matter I am ready to meet you under conditions in which my death could not be considered an assassination, and in which I might kill your excellency without being guilty of the same offence against the law. This proposal should prove to your excellency the high regard in which I hold you. I have the honour to enclose the length of my sword, and venture to hope that you will appoint a meeting for tomorrow.

Aghast at the letter, Lubomirski broke into protestations calculated to dissuade Casanova from his purpose. Failing, he departed in despair, and Casonova at once dispatched a messenger with the letter. Within an hour it was answered by Count Branicki in person.

Admitted to Casanova's bedchamber—for the Venetian was still abed engaged in correspondence—the Count locked the door, and came unceremoniously to seat himself upon the bed. Finding this proceeding not merely irregular in the circumstances, but a thought too intimate, and not knowing what might follow out of it, Casanova prudently reached for a pistol.

'I haven't come to kill you in your bed,' Branicki assured him pleasantly, 'but merely to tell you that I never postpone a duel to the morrow. Either we fight today or we do not fight at all.'

He spoke of it lightly, much as he might have discussed a visit to the opera.

'Today is impossible, Count,' Casanova answered. 'I am at work, as you see, and I must finish these letters—they are to go by a courier leaving Warsaw tonight.'

'You can finish them afterwards.'

'I might conceivably not be in case to do so.'

Branicki laughed. 'That is unlikely. But if so—the dead need fear no reproaches on the score of unanswered letters.'

'But I don't understand,' protested Casanova, 'why your excellency should refuse to wait until tomorrow.'

'Don't you see that if we wait you will miss the satisfaction you desire of me. His majesty is sure to hear of it, and will have us both placed under arrest.'

Branicki was today as charming and amiable as he had last night been insolent and overbearing. Then, too, in his florid, blond way, he was a handsome man, and a handsome face in either man or woman was ever an irresistible recommendation to Casanova. He says somewhere that a handsome face is a draft at sight, which all the world is prepared to honour. Thus it happened that he found himself liking Count Branicki, whose acquaintance he was really only just beginning to make. And there is little doubt that the feeling was reciprocated by the Pole. It is curious but undeniable that these two odd fellows were actually in course of becoming friends whilst arranging to cut each other's throats.

'Very well,' said Casanova, at length. 'I consent, since I cannot neglect anything that should afford me the privilege of a meeting with you. If therefore you will call for me after dinner I shall be ready.'

'You are very kind, sir. I hoped that you would accompany me at once.'

'Not that,' said the Venetian. 'I must dine first.'

'Each to his taste,' was the reply. 'Myself I prefer to fight fasting. But I will wait. Meanwhile, sir, why send me the length of your sword? I never consent to meet a stranger with any weapons but pistols.'

This was a shock to Casanova, who was confident of his swordsmanship.

'I do not fight with pistols,' he protested, 'and in all the circumstances I have the right to the choice of weapons.'

'Perhaps; but you are, I am sure, too gallant a man not to accept the weapon I propose.'

Conquered by the fellow's amiability and good looks, Casanova yielded the point.

'So be it,' he said. 'You will bring a brace of pistols to be loaded in my presence, and I will choose my own. Should we miss each other, perhaps I shall have the honour of crossing swords with you, until one of us draws first blood—that is all.'

'Excellent.' Branicki rose to depart. 'I shall call for you at three o'clock. Until then not a word to anyone. And now let us shake hands. It will be an honour to meet you.'

Entirely charmed with him, Casanova shook his hand effusively, and so they parted for the moment, completely pleased with each other.

Casanova, who, like your true man of the world, was a complete epicurean, prepared himself for the ordeal by ordering and sitting down to a succulent dinner and the choicest of wines. He sent for Campioni to keep him company, but found Campioni—who more than suspected what was in the wind—dull and preoccupied. Nevertheless, Casanova ate heartily, and drank as heartily, but with discretion.

Precisely at three o'clock Branicki arrived in a berline drawn by six horses, followed by two led horses in the charge of two order-lies and a couple of mounted hussars. Moreover, the Count was accompanied by his aide-de-camp and a General in full dress uniform. He was conducting the affair in the grand manner, you see.

Casanova, dressed with care and wrapped in a valuable fur pelisse—for which I am sure that he had not paid—entered the carriage, and took the seat beside Branicki to which the latter invited him. Branicki suggested that he might wish to bring a friend of his own.

'I have made no such provision,' he answered, 'nor do I now see the need, since we have witnesses enough, and I leave myself with confidence in your hands.'

The Count acknowledged the compliment by tightly pressing Casanova's hand, and they drove off. For awhile there was silence. Then Casanova felt it necessary to make polite conversation.

'Do you expect to spend the summer in Warsaw, Count?' he asked.

'Yesterday that was my intention. But today—it is possible that you are about to prevent it.'

'I trust sincerely that our little affair may not disturb any of your plans.'

'I reciprocate the wish with regard to yourself. You have been a soldier, Monsieur Casanova?'

'I have. But why do you ask?'

'Oh, merely to keep the conversation going.' And Branicki laughed frankly and pleasantly.

The carriage rolled through the snow-clad suburbs, and came to a halt at the gates of a park. They alighted, and made their way through the trees to a clearing in which there were a seat and a table of stone. On this one of the hussars placed a brace of pistols, each a couple of feet in length, and set himself to load them.

When they were ready, and even as Branicki was inviting his opponent to make his choice, there occurred the first discordant note in an affair hitherto conducted, you will agree, in the sweetest harmony. This was precipitated by a well-meant, but ill-advised, attempt on the part of the General to compose the quarrel.

'After all, gentlemen,' said he, 'would it not be wiser to appeal to the king to settle your dispute, rather than fight each other?'

'For my part,' said Casanova, 'I should be charmed to have his majesty arbitrate between us, provided that his excellency here will express regret for having insulted me yesterday.'

Branicki flushed with sudden anger. 'Have we come to fight or to talk?' he asked, and, proffering the pistols for the second time: 'Choose, sir,' he cried.

'You will bear witness hereafter, sir,' said Casanova to the General, 'that I have done all that my honour will permit to avoid the duel.' And, tossing back his fur-lined cloak, he seized one of the pistols. Momentarily he was angered.

'You will find it a good weapon,' said Branicki.

'I shall test it on your brain,' answered Casanova, and saw Branicki turn pale with anger. Without answering, the Count stepped back, and Casanova now did the same, until they stood some twelve paces apart. The trees on either side of the clearing prevented a wider distance. A moment they stood regarding each other, then Branicki raised his pistol slowly. He was deliberately covering Casanova, when the latter's arm shot up with disconcerting suddenness—a shrewd trick this to disturb the other's aim— and he fired so abruptly that the two shots made but one report.

Branicki staggered, reeled, and fell, whereupon Casanova, flinging away his weapon, sprang forward with real concern to the

Count's assistance. He assures us that he had fired without aiming, and that he was filled with dread lest he should inadvertently have killed the Count.

Suddenly he found his way blocked by Branicki's hussars, their sabres gleaming lividly in the wintry sunshine, and murder in their eyes. He judged that his last hour had come, as undoubtedly would have been the case if Branicki had indeed been slain. As it was, the Count's voice rang out hoarsely to arrest this murderous intent.

'Hold, dogs! Respect Monsieur Casanova—on your lives!'

They fell back at once, and Casanova went forward to assist his adversary to rise from the snow, which his blood was already flecking. It was only then that our Venetian discovered that he was wounded himself, and that the other's bullet was lodged in his left hand.

Branicki was carried to an inn a hundred yards from the park, Casanova walking beside him, and the two looking at each other ever and anon, but no word passing between them. At the inn the Count was put to bed and his wound examined. The bullet had passed through him, from right to left below the ribs, and there was reason to fear that his intestines were perforated.

He looked up at Casanova, and a faint smile crossed his white face.

'You have killed me, my friend,' he said, without resentment. 'Therefore make haste to save yourself. My purse is at your disposal if you have need of money.'

Overcome with grief, and deeply touched by the other's gallantry and magnanimity, Casanova thanked him effusively, refused the purse, embraced him, and stumbled out of the inn blinded by tears. All Branicki's people had gone off in quest of surgeons, priests, and friends, and Casanova now found himself alone, wounded, without weapons, on foot in a snow-clad country that was unknown to him. Fortunately, he met a peasant in a one-horse sleigh. Holding up his hand to stop him, he showed him a ducat, uttered the single word 'Warsaw', and thus was driven back to the city.

There, instead of going to his lodgings, he repaired to the Franciscan monastery, deeming it wise—in view of the sample the hussars had afforded him of Polish ways—to claim sanctuary until he should know, in the event of Branicki's death, what might be intended against himself. He was kindly received by the aged Prior, who placed a room at his disposal, and sent at once for Campioni, a surgeon, and Casanova's servant. The surgeon fetched was a clumsy performer, who miserably lacerated the patient's hand in the course of extracting the bullet.

Casanova assigns it to vanity that while the operation was being performed he, dissembling his pain, related the details of the affair to those who were present. Headed by Prince Lubomirski, and attracted by the news which had gone through Warsaw like a ripple over water, they made already a considerable crowd. Others came on the morrow; indeed not an enemy of Branicki's remained absent, and from the solicitude they displayed, and the readiness with which they offered him their purses, he was able to judge how detested the Count's eminent position and arrogant ways had rendered him. Knowing how pressed he was for funds, I conceive him to have been very sorely tempted by their offers. But he set a high price upon his dignity, and perceiving that only by a sacrifice of this could he accept what was tendered out of hate for Branicki rather than of love for himself, he refused with the careless air of one who has inexhaustible resources at his command. He confesses that he regretted it later.

But if Branicki had enemies, he had friends as well, and these were moving vigorously to avenge the Count—whose life hung for days in the balance. The Grand-Marshal, acting upon orders from the king, who esteemed Casanova, had the convent guarded by a detachment of dragoons on the pretext of making sure that the Venetian did not escape, but in reality to protect him from any desperate attempts to seize his person. Then, too, the wound in Casanova's hand producing considerable inflammation, three surgeons in consultation decided that it must be amputated to save his life. But Casanova, suspecting that they were the agents of Branicki's avengers, and that their object was really to offer up his hand in sacrifice to their rancour, boldly played his life against his hand, and saved it by refusing to submit to the amputation.

He remained with the Franciscans until Easter, by when Branicki was pronounced out of all danger—and it was believed that the Count owed his life to having adhered to his practice of fighting on an empty stomach. However that might be, Casanov.

was really relieved and thankful not to have slain a man whom he
had found so very estimable.

Nevertheless, there was still a good deal of feeling against him in
certain sections of Warsaw society, and upon the advice of the
Russian ambassador Casanova decided to absent himself from the
Polish court for a couple of months. It was to be expected that by
the end of that time this feeling would have died down, and that
he might return and assume the office of secretary to his majesty,
upon which his heart was set.

Accordingly he set out for Kieff, mysteriously supplied with two
hundred ducats for the journey, and I find it difficult to believe
that this sum was other than a mark of gratitude from Tomatis,
whom he was constantly seeing at this time. And Tomatis had
more reason to be grateful than he knew as yet. For in avenging
him upon Branicki, Casanova had also avenged him upon La
Binetti, who had been the unworthy cause of the whole affair. Her
relations with Count Branicki were at an end. Perceiving into what
unworthy courses her vanity had led him, and how near it had
been to costing him his life, the Grand Chamberlain broke with
her completely, and refused to see her again.

Realizing that as a consequence of this her reign in Warsaw was
at an end, she took her departure while Casanova was absent in
Kieff. But before she went she sowed a seed that should yield her
a rich harvest of vengeance upon the Venetian, to whom she
attributed her misfortune.

That harvest the unsuspecting Casanova returned to gather,
after an absence of six weeks. He came back to find himself
shunned on every hand, and since not only Branicki's friends, but
his very enemies—those who lately had been most assiduous in
their attentions to himself—now received him with the most studied coldness, he came to conclude that some cause other than the
duel was responsible for this.

Everywhere the same impolite phrase greeted him: 'We did not
expect to see you in Warsaw again. Why have you returned?'

'To pay my debts,' was the invariable answer with which he
turned his back upon his questioners.

He went to court. The Russian ambassador, with whom he had
been on very friendly terms, bowed frigidly and passed him. The
king, from whom he had looked for so much, looked through him

as if he were made of glass, whereupon he withdrew, dissembling his chagrin.

Branicki had left Warsaw, and Tomatis, too, was absent, but Lubomirski remained, and from Lubomirski, who had been his friend, Casanova sought an explanation. But even Lubomirski had changed, though not to the extent of the others.

'It is merely a manifestation of the national character,' the prince informed him in answer to his questions. 'We are an inconstant people. Your fortune was made if you had known how to seize the opportunity. Now it is too late, and there is only one course open to you——'

'To depart,' Casanova interrupted angrily. 'Very well.'

But it was one thing to talk of going, and another thing to go. He had not the means. The two hundred ducats with which he had gone to Kieff he had spent with characteristic prodigality, assured that his purse would be amply replenished on his return to Warsaw. He went home to find an anonymous letter, which repeated Lubomirski's advice, and gave him at last the explanation of the attitude towards him of Warsaw society. It informed him of certain things that the king had been told concerning him; that he was a sharper and a rogue; that he had been burnt in effigy in Paris on account of certain malpractices in connection with his organization of the State lotteries, with which he had laid the foundations of his sometime fortune—now notoriously dissipated in evil living; that he had been guilty of innumerable swindles in London, which had necessitated his abrupt departure from England; and that for similar reasons he dared not show his face in Italy, and much also beside of a like nature.

He suspected—no doubt with reason—that this letter was from La Binetti, and that it was she herself who had put about these calumnies. Calumnies they were, all the more deadly and insidious because in each statement made there was just a grain of truth and of all lies none is so difficult to refute as a truth untruly told. He must go; there was no alternative. Yet how was he to go in the present state of his finances?

To aggravate his despair, he was visited next morning by Sulaskowski, the General who had acted as Branicki's second, with a message from his majesty, ordering Casanova to leave Warsaw within eight days.

Stung by the order, Casanova angrily replied that he was not disposed to obey. 'If the king should employ force to compel me, I shall protest against his violence before all the world. Pray tell him so.'

'Sir,' was the calm reply, 'I am not instructed to convey any answer of yours to the king, but merely to acquaint you with his majesty's order.' And upon that Sulaskowski ceremoniously took his leave.

When Casanova had mastered his rage he sat down and composed a letter to the king.

'My honour,' he wrote, 'does not permit me to obey, as I should wish, your majesty's order to quit your capital, as I have had the misfortune to contract here some debts which must be satisfied before I leave, and I do not at present possess the necessary resources.'

This letter Casanova sent to the king by the hand of Prince Lubomirski. On the morrow Lubomirski brought him the royal answer.

'His majesty wishes me to say that in sending you his order to quit Warsaw he was far from suspecting that you were short of money. I am to add that this order is given to you entirely in your own interest, and that his majesty is anxious to know you safely out of a capital where your enemies are multiplying daily, and where you are daily receiving provocations. His majesty commends the prudence with which you have ignored these provocations, but realizing that there must be a limit to your patience desires you to accept this slight recompense for the services you rendered him before your unfortunate affair with Count Branicki.' And he handed Casanova an order on the treasury for 1,000 ducats.

This was so liberal a sugar-coating to the pill that Casanova swallowed it now with gratitude. He wrote a letter of sincere thanks to Stanislas-Auguste, accepted the travelling-chaise which Lubomirski offered him as a parting gift, and set out in it next day, taking the road to Würtemberg.

Thus fortune came to him out of misfortune, and the world lay open to him once more.

The Alabaster Hand

OF all the hazards into which Casanova was led by his insatiable addiction to gallantry and his gluttony of adventure none is more extravagant than that which befell him during his visit to Madrid in 1767. It presents features of unusual interest to students of his complex psychology. To begin with, he fell in love with a hand. It is true that he assures us that it was a hand of quite exceptional beauty. Let us suppose it—as no doubt it was—long and perfectly tapering and of an alabaster whiteness. Yet it remains a hand, and nothing more.

Virilely handsome, very tall, of a spare, athletic grace of figure, and magnificent ever in his dress—seeming here in Spain the more magnificent by contrast with the sober modes of this Inquisition-ridden country—he did not look his age by a dozen years. Yet the fact remains that he was forty, that he had lived harder, perhaps, than any man of his time, that he had known adversity in many shapes, and love in many more. Therefore is it the more surprising that this hard-bitten, flamboyant adventurer of ripe experience and jaded appetites should have been inflamed—and to such absurd lengths, as you shall see—by just four white fingers and a thumb.

Not even had there been the sense of touch to quicken his infatuation. He had not so much as enjoyed the satisfaction of beholding that hand at close quarters. Between him and it the whole width of a street intervened—the Calle de la Cruz, in which he had his lodging. The hand belonged to a lady of quality—at least, so he judged from its size and texture—dwelling in the house immediately opposite; and he was permitted to see it twice daily at that distance, in the act of adjusting a green, slatted shutter of the type known as 'Venetian'.

That was all; and yet not quite all. There was, in addition, his own ardent imagination, which—working by processes akin to those of our modern naturalists, who will reconstruct you a saurian from a single tooth—constructed for that hand a body and a soul. The only difference is that whereas the scientist works to reproduce the real, the poet—and no mean poet was Casanova—labours to create the ideal. It was, we must suppose, with the ideal here created that he had fallen so madly in love.

This is, admittedly, but a clumsy endeavour to explain what otherwise must seem a lunacy. To an extent, of course, a lunacy it must remain; an obsessing madness that kept him a prisoner in his lodging, neglectful of the powerful letters of introduction he had brought, oblivious of all that he had meant to do and see in the Spanish capital.

Fearful of quitting his lodging for an hour, lest in that hour the owner of the hand might elect to give a fuller disclosure of herself, Casanova became a recluse, and, thus, an object of suspicion. For suspicions were easily aroused in Spain. The Holy Office was mistrustful of all strangers, most mistrustful of those who did not show themselves freely. And Casanova's was by now an European reputation. Many—too many—of the facts of his wild life were widely known; and best known of all, perhaps, was the fact that once, upon a charge of magic, he had fallen into the clutches of the Inquisitors of State in Venice. It behoved him to be prudent; and to be prudent was his intention. He could not guess that it was an imprudence to bury himself in his lodging, which contained of his own nothing beyond some trunks of most elegant French clothes and a box of books, chiefly the Latin and Greek authors who were his inseparable companions.

Calchas, the Spanish valet he had hired in Madrid, an impudent rogue with a rare talent for hairdressing, recommended to him by Count Aranda, began to grow uneasy on his behalf. Perfectly aware of, and secretly amused by, the true facts of the case, Calchas sought to give his master a hint. Unfortunately he was clumsy in his method.

At work one morning upon Casanova's luxuriant chestnut hair, in which as yet there was no single thread of silver to be detected, he opened fire.

'For what, I ask myself,' said he, in the detestable mixture of French and Spanish that he used with his foreign employer, 'is all this combing and curling and pomading? Each morning I dress your head as if for a levee at Court, and each day you go no further than these four walls. It is to waste my labour, Excellency.'

'You are paid for your labour, scoundrel.'

'If you bought pictures from a painter or verses from a poet merely to put them into the fire, would he account it sufficient that you paid him?'

'You are neither a poet nor a painter,' said Casanova. 'You are just a valet, probably a thief, and certainly a fool. It pleases me to have my hair well dressed. That is enough for you.'

'Ouf!' said Calchas, and turned aside to take the curling-tongs from the spirit flame. But he was irrepressible. 'And then this bewildering consideration of apparel. Yesterday it was the pink and silver; today the blue taffetas; tomorrow it will be the black and gold; and the next day some other splendours. And why? Why? I ask myself, why? To keep your chamber, as you do, a dressing-gown and a head *en papillote* would do as well. The world will be talking, Excellency.'

'So will you, which is much more immediately irritating. Get on with my hair, Calchas. It is growing late.'

'But late for what, name of Heaven! Late for what?' And then, very slyly, he added, 'Doña Dolores de la Fuente does not rise for another hour.'

Casanova's full black eyes fixed the valet, intrigued.

'And who may be Doña Dolores de la Fuente?'

'But do you really not know?' The valet stood arrested, his tongs poised above the chestnut head. 'It is the name of the lady in the palace opposite.'

There was a moment's silence. Had Calchas troubled to look in the mirror he would have seen that his master's swarthy, aquiline countenance had grown unusually forbidding. Presently Casanova spoke, very precise and coldly.

'It is only fair to warn you, Calchas, that I am a man easily provoked.'

'Oh, but that is all too evident. For that, it seems, that a mere hand suffices.'

'Ah! A hand!' said Casanova ominously.

'Had it been an ankle now——'

The impudent Calchas got no further. Casanova rose suddenly to his great height, and soundly boxed the rascal's ears. Calchas dropped the hot tongs, which in falling seared Casanova's hand. If more had been wanting to inflame the passion of this man, so violent once he was aroused, that accident supplied it. First, he took the valet by the scruff of the neck and shook him until it seemed to Calchas that his teeth were rattling in his head. Next he ran him across the room, and flung wide the door.

'Out of this, you Spanish rat! And don't let me see your face again, or I will break it into little pieces.'

He heaved him out, and sped him with a final kick. The stairs were immediate and precipitous. Calchas flung out hands to clutch the baluster; missed it, and went crashing down the flight.

Casanova stood at the stairhead to survey the damage. With a groan Calchas gathered himself up, and rose, feeling himself. He was unbroken, but very bruised and sore, and in a great rage. He stood there, in his shirtsleeves, furiously demanding his coat and his wages.

In a whirl of words, which reflected horribly, and I hope unjustly, upon the rascal's pedigree, Casanova warned him that if he returned he would do so at the peril of his life.

Calchas did not return. He stood there a moment, gibbering with that singular fertility of morphological blasphemy in which a Spaniard has no rival. Then, at length, he departed, screaming threats of vengeance, which Casanova's limited knowledge of Spanish did not permit him perfectly to understand. It was perhaps as well for Calchas.

After that, Casanova had to submit to the further annoyance of dressing his own hair, and performing unaided the remainder of his elaborate toilet. But fate had a compensation in store for him. That morning as he stood at his post at the window, intent upon the shutters across the narrow street, they opened wide at last, as if in answer to his mute and constant prayer, and he beheld the creature of his amorous dreams fully revealed for the first time—a pale and thoughtful Castilian beauty, to whom his ardent imaginings had done poor justice.

Although it was his first glimpse of her, yet it is inconceivable that she was not by now familiar with his own face and figure. Daily now, for a week or more, whilst revealing of herself no more than the white hand which had wrought the mischief, must she have been able to study him at her ease through the slats that so completely screened her. Studying him thus, she must have come to perceive his infatuation, whilst construing it as founded upon far more than was the actual case.

Arguing thus, he argued further that her self-disclosure proclaimed a measure of acceptance. That and the vision of this lovely woman, whose imagined simulacrum had for days obsessed him, ravished his senses utterly. Under the stress of his deep emotion, he carried a hand to his lips and then to his heart, and stood thus, in an attitude of ecstatic worship.

On her side, woman-like, she betrayed no consciousness of his existence. For a long moment she continued to stand revealed, but statuesque, unseeing, no trace of emotion, or even of perception, ruffling the virginal serenity of her proud pale face. Then, as abruptly as they had opened, the shutters closed again, leaving Casanova with a sense that the light had suddenly gone out. Darkness, desolation and longing encompassed his soul once more.

That is what comes of being endowed with a poetic temperament.

And now his case was become more hopeless than before. In the three or four days that followed he scarcely dared to leave his window. And yet his unremitting devotion went unrewarded until the evening of the fourth day. Then, at last, towards the hour of the Angelus, the shutters were again flung back, and again it was vouchsafed him to feast his eyes upon that vision of Castilian loveliness. And now, although there was still no sign of recognition in her wistful countenance, yet her eyes looked straight across and met his own.

He felt, he says, as if on the point of fainting from emotion. And then, with almost startled suddenness, she put forth that long white hand, and closed the shutters as abruptly as before. His consciousness, which had been all concentrated in his eyes, released thereby to diffuse itself again through his other senses, apprised him of a sound of steps beating upon the evening stillness. He looked out, and beheld a man close-wrapped in a brown cloak, his face concealed by a wide-brimmed hat, coming briskly down the street.

This man halted at a little side door of the mansion opposite, unlocked it and passed in, leaving Casanova in a passion of jealousy, through which vibrated the question whether the sudden closing of the shutters might not have been connected with this arrival.

He watched at his post all through the night—a starry, luminous summer night. And when, at last, the dawn drove him, dejected and exhausted, to his bed, the man in the brown cloak had not re-emerged.

Again it would be towards the hour of the Angelus on the following evening when next he beheld her. Paler and more wistfully appealing than ever did she appear to him now. She leaned her elbow on the sill of her window and quite openly and intently regarded him, as if returning some of the passionate longing conveyed to her by his burning glance.

Again he pressed his hands—both hands this time—upon his aching heart.

And now, at last, his wildest hopes were fanned by an unmistakable response. She smiled—vaguely, tenderly, almost questioningly, as it seemed to him. Whereupon, entirely carried away, he flung out his arms in a gesture of invocation.

To restrain him, to enjoin discretion, she put her finger to her lips. Next, leaning further forward, she held out a key and a letter, as if proffering them; then she drew back into the shadows of the room.

A practised gallant such as Casanova could not doubt her meaning for a moment. In the twinkling of an eye you behold him bareheaded in the quiet street under her window, his pulses drumming with expectancy. And almost at once the little package of key and letter thudded softly at his feet. He stooped to seize it, looked up to find the shutter already closed again, and fled back at once to his own lodging to acquaint himself with the contents of that unsigned note.

'Are you a man of gentle birth?' she wrote. 'Are you brave and discreet? Are you disposed to serve an unfortunate lady in her need? Because I believe you to be all this, I send you the key of the side-door. Come to me at midnight. I shall be waiting for you. Above all, be secret.'

You conceive his ecstasy. He pressed the faintly fragrant note to his lips, then from his window signified his acquiescence in pantomime addressed to the closed shutters. They opened wide enough to admit the passage of her white hand in token that he was understood.

Thereafter he summoned what patience he could to help him

through the time of waiting. He tells us that he spent two hours that night upon his toilet—the lack of a valet, no doubt, complicated the intricate operation—and that he brought to it all the care and selection desirable in such circumstances. Nor did he overlook the risks with which this business might be fraught; for, after all, he was no callow lad of twenty plunging recklessly to his first assignation. Yet if the bitter voice of experience suggested perils, vanity and the spirit of adventure combined to remind him that he had sought and accepted the invitation, and that he could not draw back now save at the cost of being ridiculous and contemptible in her eyes.

He compromised in the matter. And when, with pulses throbbing, he went forth on the stroke of midnight to unlock the little door, he went armed under his lover's finery.

As he stood in the complete darkness of the passage within, he caught the rustle of a gown, and instantly felt her at his side. His hand was taken in the grasp of slender little fingers whose coldness almost chilled his spirit. In silence he suffered himself to be conducted through an inner door, down a dimly lighted passage, then up a broad staircase, and finally into an ante-room, nobly proportioned and superbly furnished.

In mid-chamber, upon a walnut table, whose surface was polished to the smoothness of glass, a dozen candles burned in a massive silver branch. Their light revealed her fully to him at last, and here at close quarters he found her even lovelier than he had already deemed her.

She was deathly pale, and the great eyes that now returned his ardent gaze were pools of wistfulness ineffable. Limp and trembling, she sank into a chair, whereupon he went down on his knees before her, and with no word spoken yet between them, he bore to his fevered lips the cold hand she yielded him. And then, transported by her white beauty and the oddness of the adventure, he loosed the bridle of his tempestuous gallantry.

'Lady, I love you!' he cried. 'My heart, my life—all that I have, and am—are yours!'

She regarded him almost sadly; very faintly she smiled.

'You have never even spoken to me until this moment. And those are your first words to me! How can I believe you?'

'Put me to the test—to any test!' he cried impetuously.

'If I were to take you at your word?' said she, her smile growing in wistfulness and inscrutability.

'It is what I implore of you!'

'And if I first demand of you an oath of secrecy, an oath never to reveal what may pass here between us?'

'It is superfluous. I am a man of honour. None the less, I pledge you my word, since you demand it.'

She drew a fluttering breath.

'Be it so, then,' she said softly, and rose. 'Come with me.'

His hand tight-clasped in hers, he came up from his knees, and obediently accompanied her across the room. There she opened a door and ushered him into another chamber, in the middle of which stood a great bed, with curtains of heavy gold brocade drawn tightly about it.

This room, like the other, was lighted by a cluster of candles in a branch that stood upon a richly carved console. In addition, at the foot of the bed, there were two tall gilded candlesticks with a single taper alight in each.

By the bed she came at last to a halt, and stood mutely gazing at him.

From bewildered that he had been, a sense of dread began now to pervade him as he regarded her. For never in his life had he looked into a face that expressed so much anguish and despair.

'What ails you?' he asked her, his voice hoarse. 'You are trembling!'

'It is not from fear,' she said. 'But you? You do not tremble. You are calm and master of yourself. Look, then!' Abruptly, violently, she swept aside the heavy curtains. 'Look!'

He looked, and although he did not tremble even then, yet fear clutched his heart. For what he beheld was a man lying supine upon that splendid bed. He stepped back quickly, sucking in his breath, and his fingers instinctively sought the hilt of his hidden poniard.

Then he realized in horror why that figure continued supine and so indifferent, with eyes staring up at the canopy overhead. The man was dead.

Casanova observed that he was young and handsome, noted the

disarray of his garments, and other signs that death had come upon him sudden and violently, and, finally, the two tapers at the bed's foot, which assumed a new significance.

His horror grew. He looked at the woman, and found her watching him with glittering eyes.

'What does it mean?' he asked her fearfully.

'It means that justice has been done,' said she. 'Though I must die for it, I could not have acted differently. I loved him, and he was false.'

Casanova shuddered, and there and then completely shed the unreasoning passion with which she had inspired him. Remembering that this was Spain, where jealousy is proverbially fierce and pitiless, he would strive to judge her mercifully. But it was not for a man of his temperament to desire a closer acquaintance with one who went to such lengths in punishing infidelity.

Not that he considered himself by temperament unfaithful. Somewhere in the course of his voluminous and frank confessions he defends himself vigorously against any possible imputations of that kind. He was, he assures us, merely inconstant, and at long and convincing length he draws an interesting distinction between inconstancy and infidelity. But understanding of his academic arguments cannot be expected of such women as Dolores. And made suddenly and grimly aware of this, his passion for her turned at once to ice.

He moved away, his face almost as ghastly as that of the corpse.

'My Heaven!' he groaned. 'How horrible!'

Instantly she was beside him, clutching his arm, her siren voice plaintively beseeching.

'You are a man of honour! You promised secrecy! You swore to serve me!'

He bowed, stiff and formal.

'What do you ask of me, madame?' he demanded, ready to do, for the sake of his pledged word, the service to which there was no longer any spur of love.

'Deliver me of this,' she answered. 'Take it away. The river flows beyond the wall of my garden. Carry it thither, and so rid me of it.'

She was on her knees to him, passionately interceding. In supplication she clasped his hands and embraced his knees. Tears flowed from her lovely eyes; despair rang in her voice. And he, the gallant who had come so hot-foot to her beckoning, stood stiffly there in his magnificent purple suit, frozen with horror. At last he spoke, dramatically, tragically, as the situation demanded.

'Madame, I pledged you my word. You are perhaps asking for my life. No matter, I give it to you!'

Convulsively she wrung his hands.

'You are noble! You are great!' she cried. 'You know how to compel a woman's love.'

But the love of Doña Dolores was the last thing that Casanova desired at the moment to compel. He desired, above all, to have done with this grisly business and be gone.

'Calm yourself, madame. Every moment increases the danger of discovery. Let us make haste.'

He shook off her detaining hands, stepped to the bed, and resolutely shouldered the ghastly burden.

'Your servants?' he enquired.

'I have but two. They are faithful, and they sleep. Go cautiously, lest you awaken them.'

And then, as he advanced a step, that body across his stalwart shoulder:

'No, no!' she whispered fiercely. 'I cannot suffer it. If you are discovered thus, you are ruined!'

It was the first unselfish word she had uttered, and it awakened a response in him.

'And you, madame, are lost if this body remains here.'

With that he went forward towards the door, stepping firmly under his load, for he was strong and the dead man slim and light. Dolores followed him, lighting him with the candlebranch. Thus they went down the stairs to the door opening upon the garden. Beyond this she did not accompany him. She stood there under the lintel, perhaps awaiting his return, whilst he, staggering a little now, went through the garden, out by the gate, and down the lane that sloped to the river. He came at last to the water's edge, and shot his burden into the stream, whereafter, without further thought for Doña Dolores, he went home.

He spent the remainder of the night devoured by uneasiness, considering means of quitting Madrid at the earliest moment.

Next morning he was arrested. An alcalde, accompanied by half a dozen alguaziles, invaded his lodging whilst he was still abed. They ransacked his room and placed his effects under seal, then ordered him to dress himself and go with them.

It required all his fortitude and all his considerable histrionic talent to dissemble his abject terror. But he contrived to appear calm and composed, if pale—which might be attributed to indignation—when he haughtily demanded of the alcalde an explanation of this outrage.

The alcalde leered contemptuously out of a sallow, blue-cheeked face.

'Of course, you play the comedy of injured innocence,' said he, 'It is usual. It does not impress me.'

'It may impress you to know that I am a friend of Count Aranda, President of the Council of Castile.'

It was an overstatement, of course. He had seen the count but twice; once when he had presented his letter of introduction, and once again, later, when he had dined at his Excellency's house. And although the count—out of regard for the foreign personage who had supplied Casanova with those credentials—had received him affably and treated him with consideration, yet this hardly justified him in counting Don Miguel de Aranda among his intimates. That, however, was no reason why he should not make use of this powerful name to intimidate the alcalde. Unfortunately the alcalde declined to be intimidated.

'I have my duty to perform!' he said, snapping his lips, and that was the end of the matter.

They carried off their prisoner to the foul gaol of Buen Retiro. There they deposited him in the mephitic atmosphere of a filthy chamber tenanted by some forty prisoners of the vilest kind. The first night that he spent there was something that he remembered to the end of his days. Huddled in a corner and devoured by fleas, not daring to close his eyes lest his infamous prison-mates should rob him whilst he slept, the splendid Giacomo di Casanova contemplated at leisure the miserable predicament into which his excessive appetite for philandering had landed him. He saw himself—he, the scholar, poet, soldier, philosopher and man of the world, who had ruffled it in courts and been the intimate of princes, whose name and whose fame were known throughout Europe—miserably ending his glorious, hazardous life like a common felon at the hands of a Spanish hangman.

I spare you a more detailed picture of his alternating rage and despair in the days that followed. His wide experience and knowledge of men helped him presently to mitigate his lot, but only by a very little. By bribing a young gaoler, whose countenance he rightly conjectured to belong to a thief, he was able with the little gold upon him to procure some food and wine that at least did not nauseate his fastidious palate.

Day followed day in that unspeakable confinement, and each day brought its dread of magisterial examination. Yet ten days passed, and still the authorities made no sign. Despair took possession of him completely. It happened often, he knew, that criminals were overlooked and left to rot, forgotten in the gaols to which they had been consigned. Such a fate—to spend the remainder of his days in these horrible surroundings—would be even worse than the gallows.

And then on the morning of the eleventh day of his imprisonment, the young gaoler, whose protection he had purchased, slipped a note into his hand. Wondering, he opened it in a corner with trembling fingers under cover of his hat; then stuffing it, spread out, into the crown, he read:

My Friend,—By the time this reaches you I shall be out of Spain. You are relieved from your pledge of secrecy, and I exhort you to seek your own safety by a full and frank confession. I am afflicted by the thought of your situation. Forgive and forget your unfortunate   D.

He put on the hat with the letter still inside it, and crushed it viciously down upon his brows. His haggard, unshaven face was white, and his lips twitched.

Forgive and forget! He would do neither the one nor the other as long as he lived—which, after all, might not be very long. He made a resolve that if ever he got safely out of this predicament, his relations with the other sex would be of the utmost circumspection.

The devil, you see, was very sick indeed. Almost he yearned for the womanless peace of monastic seclusion.

Towards noon that day he stirred himself to action. He did now what he might have done before but that fear and his pledged word between them had paralysed his will. He wrote a letter to Count Aranda. It was couched in characteristically impetuous terms:

My Lord,—You cannot know that I am being assassinated in the most abominable gaol of your abominable country. In no civilized nation of the world would a man of my quality, whatever his offence, be cast among the cut-throats and pariahs that tenant this prison of Buen Retiro. I appeal to your Excellency's sentiments of humanity to order me either to be set at liberty or put to death, so as to spare me the necessity of committing suicide.   GIACOMO DI CASANOVA

That intemperate letter he consigned to his friendly gaoler, who on this occasion needed no further spur than that supplied by the superscription to see that it reached its august destination.

Within twenty-four hours the sordid prison of Buen Retiro was visited by a resplendent officer, dispatched by Count Aranda to escort thence Monsieur Casanova. An hour later, the ravages in his toilet more or less repaired, Casanova stood in the presence of the most powerful man in Spain, the ugly little fellow who dared to dispute even the power of the fathers of the Inquisition, and who by a stroke of the pen had banished the Jesuits from Castile.

Without rising from his writing-table, the great Minister looked up to greet his visitor with something between a frown and a smile.

'Monsieur Casanova,' he said, 'you have written me a very impertinent letter, in which you hardly show yourself the man of wit that you are reputed; for you should know that one seldom succeeds anywhere by impertinence.'

'I abase myself in apology, Excellency. It was written in the exasperation resulting from ten days in that horrible prison.'

The count's face cleared.

'If I mentioned it,' he said more affably, 'it was so that you may realize that my consenting to see you, notwithstanding, is a proof of the consideration in which I hold you. You were at least correct in your assumption that I had no knowledge of your position. I was beginning to wonder that you did not show yourself when I received your letter. I have since informed myself of your case, and I deplore profoundly the thing that has happened to you.'

Casanova gathered a rich harvest of hope from so much courtesy.

'Your Excellency cannot deplore it more profoundly than I do myself. I give you my word of honour that I am the helpless victim of circumstances. And I thank you more profoundly than I can say for allowing me to come before you and state my case as one man of honour to another, instead of as a felon to a magistrate. Absolved

at last from the pledge of secrecy that bound me, I am fortunately
able now to place all the facts before you without any reservation.
They are these:'

And headlong, without giving the count time to interpose a
single word, he plunged into a detailed account of the events at
the house of Doña Dolores.

When he had done Count Aranda considered him in silence for
a moment, his face utterly blank. Then he uttered a queer little
laugh.

'But this is a very extraordinary tale, Monsieur Casanova.'

Casanova bristled instantly.

'Your Excellency does not imply a doubt of any particular?'

'Oh, far from it! Very far from it, indeed. It affords us the only
logical explanation of the mystery of the disappearance of Don
Sebastian de Carbajal. Also it explains Doña Dolores de la Fuente's
sudden desire for foreign travel, a desire which she duped me into
furthering. I was simpleton enough to assume that Don Sebastian
had gone secretly abroad, and that it was her intention to follow
and join him.' He smiled wryly. 'You reveal to me, Monsieur
Casanova, that we are both of us the dupes of that unscrupulously
clever woman.'

'I *reveal* to your Excellency——' Casanova checked, and with
fallen jaw, dismay spreading on his swarthy face, he stared at the
President of the Council. Then, a gleam of dreadful light breaking
upon his dark bewilderment: 'Does your Excellency mean,' he
cried, 'that I have disclosed something that was not known?'

'That, indeed, is what you have done.'

Uninvited, crushed by the weight of his sudden despair,
Casanova sat down. In a small voice he asked:

'Will your Excellency tell me, then, in Heaven's name why I
was arrested?'

'For being in possession of forbidden books.'

The astounding answer made chaos of Casanova's already dis-
tracted mind.

'Forbidden books?' he faltered. 'I?'

The count explained briefly.

'Upon receiving your letter yesterday, I sent at once for the
alcalde. He informed me that in arresting you he had acted on
behalf of the Holy Office, upon a charge laid against you by a valet
named Calchas, whom you dismissed with violence. Your recluse

habits were already rendering you suspect, and upon proceeding to your lodging the alcalde found there corroboration of the accusation laid. He is a fool, of course, a devout man, very ardent in matters that come within the purview of the Inquisition—and in his ignorance he took your Greek Iliad, with its unknown characters, to be a work of magic. I have told him quite plainly what I think of him, and you need apprehend no further trouble on that score.'

'But on the score of this other matter?' cried Casanova in despair. 'This far graver matter in which I have so rashly betrayed my part?'

Count Aranda sighed.

'There again you have hardly shown yourself the man of wit that you are reputed.'

'I have put a rope round my neck!'

Casanova rose in his agitation. He stood, stricken and pale, the last vestige of his assurance gone.

'That,' said Count Aranda softly, 'is to pay me a poor compliment. Fortunately your statement was made as that of one man of honour to another, and not as that of an accused to a magistrate.'

'Your Excellency means?'

'Just that. It is fortunate that it was addressed to me, for you could not expect an examining magistrate to believe you as implicitly, or to take the view that your action in the matter was the only action possible in all the circumstances. The rest is a matter for the alcalde, and it is no part of my duties to assist him in his functions. I am not a policeman.'

'Your Excellency!' Casanova passed from terror to amazement. 'How can I thank you?'

'You will be careful, sir, to do nothing of the kind,' said the Minister sharply. 'Besides, I cannot altogether forgive the terms of this letter of yours. Amongst other things you speak of my country as abominable, and you imply that it is uncivilized. I cannot overlook so much. I must ask you to leave Madrid within twenty four hours, and Spain within a week. I shall inform the alcalde of this, and instruct him to see that no obstacle is placed in the way of your departure.'

This time Casanova showed himself sufficiently a man of wit to submit in thankfulness to that decree of banishment.

POST-SCRIPTUM

The episodes which have formed the basis of the stories in this series are no more than a selection, treated objectively, from the voluminous memoirs of Casanova.

We take our leave of him here as he rolls out of Madrid in the Autumn of 1767 seeking fresh adventures. He found them in plenty and of varying kind until in 1774 he is back in Venice. There for the next nine years he abides, and you imagine that he has come to an anchorage at last. But now it is his too-ready pen that brings him fresh trouble, and he treads once more the path of exile, begins life anew at the age of sixty. At last at Töplitz he makes friends with Count Waldstein, who is addicted to magic. The Count carries our Venetian off to his Castle at Dux in Bohemia, where he—who in his time has been all things—settles down peacefully as a librarian and there finally departs this life in the year 1798 at the age of seventy-three.   R.S.*

Sources

'The Risen Dead': *The Storyteller* (December 1907)

'The Bargain': *The Storyteller* (July 1908)

'The Opportunist': *Premier Magazine* (2 July 1920)

'The Plague of Ghosts': *The Storyteller* (September 1907)

'Brancaleone's Terms': *Premier Magazine* (August 1914, as 'The Sword of Islam'). Reprinted in *A Century of Sea Stories* (1934)

'The Poachers': *Premier Magazine* (December 1915)

'The Sentimentalist': *Premier Magazine* (5 December 1919)

'Duroc': *Weekly Tale-Teller* (2 October 1915)

'Kynaston's Reckoning': *Premier Magazine* (November 1914)

'The Abduction': *The Storyteller* (December 1908)

'Jack o'Lantern': *Strand Magazine* (January 1937)

'The Alibi': *Premier Magazine* (September 1914, as 'Casanova's Alibi'). Reprinted in *Turbulent Tales* (1946)

'The Augmentation of Mercury': *Grand Magazine* (March 1918)

'The Priest of Mars': *Grand Magazine* (April 1918)

'The Oracle': *Grand Magazine* (May 1918)

'Under the Leads': *Grand Magazine* (June 1918)

'The Night of Escape': *Premier Magazine* (June 1917). Reprinted in *The Historical Nights' Entertainment: Series I* (1917)

'The Rooks and the Hawk': *Grand Magazine* (July 1918)

'The Polish Duel': *Grand Magazine* (August 1918)

'The Alabaster Hand': *Premier Magazine* (15 July 1921, as 'Casanova in Madrid')